REEFDOG

REEFDOG

A NOVEL

ROBERT WINTNER

YUCCA

Yucca Publishing books may be purchased in bulk at special discounts for sales promotion, corporate gifts, fund-raising, or educational purposes. Special editions can also be created to specifications. For details, contact the Special Sales Department, Yucca Publishing, 307 West 36th Street, 11th Floor, New York, NY 10018 or yucca@skyhorsepublishing.com.

Yucca Publishing® is an imprint of Skyhorse Publishing, Inc.®, a Delaware corporation.

Visit our website at www.yuccapub.com.

10 9 8 7 6 5 4 3 2 1

Library of Congress Cataloging-in-Publication Data is available on file.

Jacket design by Laura Klynstra
Jacket photo by Fernando Lopez Arbarello

Print ISBN: 978-1-63158-105-2
Ebook ISBN: 978-1-63158-111-3

Printed in the United States of America

For Ziggy, a reefdog

Author's Note

Special thanks to the waterborne of Maui, Tahiti, Fiji, Palau, the Philippines, Indonesia, the Great Reef, the Virgins, Cuba and on around who share one reef love.

Thanks to the troops digging in to save reef critters and habitat around the world, whatever it takes.

—RW

Halfway Out to Sea

A lean and sun-browned man slithers in the shallows easily as an eel after fry, till he draws his legs under and stands, taller than the first organisms walking out of the sea but with original intent—to improve his niche, on land.

With his hair wetted to his neck, a scant loin pocket, and a scruffy beard dripping below swim-goggled eyes, he makes the amphibious transition, up and out.

An emergence from an hour or two of reef repose makes him wonder. Ankle deep, he watches two children and a dog playing naked in the waves. The girl of ten sweeps her long, black hair out of the way childishly with both hands. Composed as a tropical cameo one moment, she surges with energy the next, yelling at the boy to eat: "*Manges! C'est une tempête en mer, et tu dois manger à rester fort!*" It's a storm at sea, and you must eat to stay strong!

The boy sits on a paddleboard. She pulls it by a rope among the shallow waves. The dog barks, finally clambering aboard, where he teeters, facing the back to watch the boy.

The boy eats from a plate on his lap: baked yams, carrots, and pineapple. Little wave-tops season his lunch. The dog whines. Leihua pulls the paddleboard to waist depth and points it into the surf, then gives it a push, commanding him to eat.

Justin eats, piercing the short break, focused on the pineapple saved for last along with a piece of taro for the dog.

The man says, "Mes enfants," as a statement of being, a navigational fix on terra firma. He slogs up a sandy path, no longer buoyant. The kids and dog gravitate and follow toward the house, leaving the paddleboard high on the beach.

At the house they'll rest through the hot afternoon. They might doze. In two hours the boy and girl will tend to schoolwork while the man prepares dinner. He may process images on his computer for a while before the woman arrives from the hospital.

Meanwhile, on the way up, they pass a mound of dirt topped with smooth rocks, the topmost a marker engraved: *Skinny.* It's a final resting place, but its reluctant tenant would rather use it as a perch. She jumps to the top and wobbles off, so the man picks her up and sets her on top again. The old, feeble cat with the baby face suddenly sees him and speaks her catch-all word to the omniscient one who insists that she keep living, that she keep processing moments as she has for the last twenty-two years.

When the man and children pass, she leans forward to swat the dog on the butt but falls off trying and meows again, falling into the procession up the path.

Compared to What?

It's a shorter flight from Hawaii to Tahiti than from Hawaii to LA—only twenty minutes shorter, but the difference felt profound, as if Tahiti could be more accessible than its exotic name suggested. Though closer to Hawaii in miles, French Polynesia seemed far more distant than LA.

French Polynesia couldn't possibly have a Wal-Mart or a Sam's or a Costco, gridlock or freeways wending to "affordable" neighborhoods nestled among power pylons, transformers and oil vats from the land of Gargantua.

Could it?

Tahiti did not surge forward but rather lingered in the imagination as an outpost of Paradise.

Tension with the French seemed nominal, a minor distraction along with crumbling roads and dirty gutters—minimal development allowed things to age like whiskey. No golf courses, no rush hour, no road rage and no franchise burgers or all-you-can-eat array of American conveniences gave it a bygone feeling. Absence of stuff set a tone of simple goodness. What's that sound? It's the soft voice of the unencumbered world, where growth is still vegetative. French Polynesia still glowed, a tropical oasis isolated from a world of strip mall clutter, a world failing to keep up with a population unconstrained in its propagation and needs.

3

Where Oceania was French-flavored with an abundance of fish in aquamarine clarity, Hawaii seemed removed from tropical simplicity, building out. Greed and power had things dumbed down deeper than any time since the wagons first circled—or since Captain Cook got banged on the head at Kealakekua.

Hawaii felt more like Santa Monica than Hawaii.

That was Ravi Rockulz's assessment. He'd never been to French Polynesia, but he'd read and heard about it. He thought of it sometimes first thing in the morning, if the tourists would allow. Most often they interrupted his reverie on the way out to the dive site.

Like the tourist who stood nearby at the rail watching the bow cleave water so clear it hinted at meaning just below. The tourist spoke of his friend in LA who had a nasty rash on his arm with oozing sores to the elbow. The doctor prescribed one unguent and another to no avail until the strongest ointment in the world didn't work. Finally, the doctor broke the news: Another line of employment would be necessary because working for the circus, planting elephant suppositories up to the elbow, would keep the rash coming back. The friend in LA asked, "What? And give up showbiz?"

Ravi didn't get it at first. Hardly a dim bulb, he couldn't see why anyone would want to stick his arm up an elephant's ass just to make a living in showbiz. No joke is funny once parsed, and this joke, too, failed to rouse a chuckle. Rather, Ravi wondered how the irony underlying most humor actually comes to pass. At least he understood the point of the joke, relative to showbiz, money, and festering lesions.

He thought he understood LA, with regard to volume exchange in an urban setting. That is, pressure increases by one atmosphere for every thirty-three feet of depth below sea level. Nitrogen and oxygen remain proportionate at depth, about 80:20—but pressure at sixty-six feet is tripled, so content triples in volume too. The critical factor is that the bloodstream absorbs nitrogen much faster than it can leave, and excess nitrogen causes the bends if ambient pressure decreases too quickly. The gas tries to escape through the joints, and they twist.

4

Just so, with world population doubling again, pathogens increase proportionately. Percentages remain stable, though raw numbers rise to toxic potential. Human behavior with no ambient constraint is similar to human joints infused with nitrogen: bent.

LA looked bent, and the rest of the world was squirming.

•

Ravid (rah-VEED) Rockulz was born when Basha Rivka was thirty and beyond hope for a decent match. Still single and already elderly by community standards, a willful, anxious woman, she got by in her hometown, Haifa, and would have spent her days till that no-goodnik came along. And what happened? *Schtupi mit no chupi* is what. He left, and good riddance—but don't think this cloud was not silver-lined because it was. Mother and son became friends, seeking solace or venting frustration, as mother and son will do. When he doubted the future of the natural world, she recalled the early 1950s when she was a girl and people lived far from each other and were glad to meet. Now, ass to elbow, they defend "personal space." As a true elder, Basha Rivka shared her son's doubts on the future, and frankly she wouldn't miss this mess—after 120 years, of course.

They commiserated. She said the next generations could better cope with their needs and consequences in a world of twelve billion people minus one when God chose to call her, which could be tomorrow, or tonight, or, God forbid, in the next minute or two. But she thought she had a decent shot at 2040, given her general health, genetics, diet, and exercise. She walked every day to the market so things would be fresh, even if overpriced by the heartless *mamzerim* who had the freshest produce.

Beyond that she was an old lady who didn't need so much dark talk from her only begotten child, who was young and had his whole life ahead of him in a world surely destined to be his oyster.

"What kind of talk would you prefer, Mother?"

"You know, something else. Not the depression talk."

"Do I sound depressed?"

"Don't tell me how you sound. I have ears."

Then she asked when he planned to move to LA, where he would meet his own kind, including a girl who would give him a reason to live, and her too, with a family to remember him and his mother when they both were gone—after 120 years.

Ravi asked why he would live in LA. He asked the thin air, the blue sea, and Basha Rivka, whose answer was a wife for him, grand-children for her, and a profession that would provide for his children and his old age—and maybe hers, too, because at his current pace she wouldn't be able to relax for another sixty years.

When would old age begin? Ravi watched flights coming in steadily, each delivering hundreds of cold tourists craving the tropical balm. Traffic thickened. But no matter how overbuilt the rock became, the question persisted: Compared to what?

Any flight could bring tourists needing guidance into the depths. A dive leader makes a boat's reputation, so he could be viewed as the object of choice. Besides competent guidance, a tourist or two may also need guidance in those other depths craved by the footloose tourist women. "Yes, it's okay. Call me Ravi."

Ravi's smile reflected the skill and success that made him happy. No argument there, but Basha Rivka's concern was practical, with less blue-sky, blue-water razzmatazz and more of what a mensch must do to secure a future for his family—like wearing a suit and tie, for start-ers, and working in an office, contributing to society, getting better pay than a water boy. So the suit wouldn't be top-drawer goods at the beginning. Never mind. Quality goods will come. You'll see.

"You mean I should make more money?"

"And what's wrong with more money?"

"Nothing, Mother. So why can't you find someone to pay the best dive instructor in Hawaii more money?"

Then came the sigh and tongue clicking. But he got the point, and they both knew it, even if he didn't share his mother's motivation. Still, she was on his side, and the nudge would cease if only. . . Or it would not, though she defended him in the clutch when he quit the military on the grounds of opposing the military mentality. "I don't get it. You're one of those objectors? A fellow with a conscience?"

"No. I don't think I am. A conscientious objector doesn't want to kill anyone. I think I wouldn't mind killing someone if I had to. The population should be thinned, but I don't want to kill any *thing*—anyone who is not human. The military is so stupid. Many stupid people have many stupid meetings where they say stupid things and come up with stupid plans for stupid behaviors that kill many things. I want out. I want no part of it." Which was Ravi's explanation, to which his mother had the good sense to stay mum.

Notably, Ravi's resignation was from the Israeli military, that esteemed group held in awe and reverence, as if it were the Fertile Crescent's very own boy band. These boys lived the credo, *never again*. Consensus on the credo was unanimous: Better to die fighting than in a fake shower with fifteen grams of black soap. Oh, they knew the score. The fans raved. Basha Rivka had been proud as any soldier's mother but had suffered more than the usual angst; she was so worried, with the guns and bombs and the boys on the other side, some of them perhaps very nice boys, shooting at her son, whom they'd never even met. Once he quit the military, she could worry far less. "So. Let it be," she'd said.

Quitting wasn't simple but required a tortuous season of hearings, with accusations, character maligning, and questionable patriotism. Ravi had known he could win by accepting the foul names and not responding. He knew he was a patriot and would fight in a real conflict, killing people who hated him and came on to kill him. It would be natural. But it was tough—except in the context of gratuitous destruction called training and drills and practice for the real thing. That's what grated on his conscientious values. He feared expressing these things, lest he be deemed insane or seditious. But Ravi Rockulz could not desecrate the reefs of Eilat in war games against an imaginary enemy that in reality warranted no response. Tearing up the reef with mines, dredges, and sundry incursions would not play out for an unlikely Jewish seal, a mere boy whose knees buckled under the burden of his first tank of compressed air, who already loved the coral down to the polyps.

Basha Rivka had asked when the little polyps would love him back. He'd assured her they loved him every time he saw them. How else could he feel so happy in their company?

•

That was some years ago. Since then, he'd settled in the tropics to live in sunshine on mostly calm seas among beautiful reefs. The US Navy tested sonar in the name of national security, blasting decibels that agonized the whales, monk seals, turtles, and fish for hundreds of miles. Ravi's boat and a few others off McGregor Point one day witnessed humpback whales breaching incessantly, as if to escape. A whale breached over a small sailboat, sinking it. Navy rescue was there in an hour, though the passengers were picked up by then.

The story never appeared in the local media because the US Navy said it didn't happen, that a tourist made a mistake in thinking a whale could actually fall onto a boat—they had investigated and concluded that the event never was. So military reality claimed another day.

Besides military incursion into Hawaii, where billions in defense contracts could advance political careers, other incursion also surged.

Tourism was up, what with terrorism threatening the world and filling the airwaves of America.

Immigration to the fiftieth state also rose. More tourists asked the simple, tough questions—and gave the answers in the same awakening. LA? Compared to Hawaii? Are you kidding? So they moved to the good life from LA—or Seattle, Alameda or Portland, from Bakersfield, Boise or Butte. *Start out in St. Louie and go through Missouri. Oklahoma City is not so pretty. You'll see Amarillo and Gallup, New Mexico. Flagstaff, Arizona, don't forget Pomona, Kingston, Barmaids, yadda yadda San Jalapeño. . .* Life is not simple as a lyric, but still, it's fun to sing along. And a catchy lyric helped distract from the thickening density of bodies, cars, and pavement.

Besides using distractions to avoid sadness, it was important to see how growth was good because more people meant more money. More money meant more material comfort in the good life in Hawaii. Why not live in the biggest ocean in the world and make more money? With the Internet, fax, cellular, streaming data, a wireless world and ever-broadening bands, it could be done.

Is this a great time, or what?

But the magic was bogging down in discovery of chic, hip, cool, and the new hot thing. Spontaneous raves could erupt anytime over whales or movie stars spotted in the offing. Often nothing remained to be seen but the ruffled surface, yet people stared in hopes of another view, with disbelief that such potential in nature and celebrity could converge in one place, and that normal, working stiffs could see these things so freely. Ah, Maui. *Lucky we live*, and so forth and so on.

The place felt more like somewhere else, somewhere generic, convenient and crowded. But it felt so right to so many, stepping onto the tarmac to claim victory over the freeway, drive-by, suburban miasma back home. Many commuters knew the dream *could* come true on arrival in the tropics, where the commute could continue in better weather. Glory got real when the Matson container arrived with the car not too much later. More Californians took the plunge, indicated by more Mercedes on the road with those clever vanity plates: MAWIBNZ. Perfection emerged—a Mercedes on Maui. . . .

Could it get any better? Yes, if the top could go down. Wait! Is that a Ferrari? Oh. . . God!

Maui. . .

Ferrari.

As fantasy fulfillment ratcheted upward, the tropical magic faded. Ravi remembered his own first blush, feeling this landfall as arrival to his home. It had seemed lush and promising to a man with a reef instinct. More recent arrivals compared Maui to Orange County,

Sacramento, or anywhere USA because this gridlock/strip mall aggregate was called Maui and seemed fabulous.

Honolua Bay not so long ago was full of living coral and reef fish. A few years later, it was ninety percent dead from red dirt runoff. Construction of mega-million mansions over the gulch left only a thin strip of living coral. Ravi watched a charter boat pull in with a crowd from a Christian dental convention. The first kids jumped in and came up sputtering, "Oh, gosh! Look at this! It's unbelievable!" And so on, unbelievably, compared to Cincinnati, trending downward.

The recently landed took the degradation as collateral damage for the greater good. Burgeoning freeways with dividers replaced country roads—with a certain *je ne sais quoi* compared to the 10, the 110, the 210 and the 405. A cane field became tract housing—known locally as "track" housing—like Orange County just after the oranges went away. And genetically modified organisms in rows looked like corn but better, like a lifted face or tucked tummy, without a single worm or dark kernel. The pastoral fantasy was never so good in LA, and if more, bigger houses blocked the panorama of the biggest ocean in the world, at least they ran 6.5 to twenty million. Or twenty-two. Or twenty-nine point nine. Wow. It must be *really* perfect.

With markets so strong, prices so high, and demand bursting at the seams, this appeared to be it—the dream roll that would never end.

Ravi had landed nineteen years prior, hardly a moment on the geologic calendar that the mossback old-timers used to measure their tenure, opening every harangue on how it used to be by establishing authority on time served, "I been here twenty-seven years, and I—"

"Well, I been here thirty-three years! And I. . ."

Very few veterans could say what they'd done or contributed to help protect the natural character in those years, as if true seasoning occurred by osmosis. Years on the rock did not increase legitimacy. But time spent and soulful connection weren't always connected. Annotation was mostly anecdotal, with relevance measured in beers, shots, doobies, odd encounters, easy snatch on long odds, and so on. The verbal resume was a mix of alcohol and fun in the sun, with bawdy adventure and cocaine back in the day when an original old-timer could still take that punch.

The olden days were recalled with pride: *We used to get so. . .*

Or, one time we had this. . .

Recollection still passed for social currency in some quarters, like Lahaina, where extreme inebriation twenty or thirty-five years ago was special because boats and palm trees outnumbered cars and people. New arrivals envisioned a future when they, too, would speak knowingly, so they garnered their own rare times with all-nighters, non-stoppers, reefer madness, and ocean time. Barnacle Bills and tropical honeys deplaned from LAX, hit the tattoo parlors and emerged original, ready to share the wherefore and how-to with others seeking identity and room service. The newest crowd was younger and more chic than the last. The young'uns had a leg up on the latest look and the hot new stars of the screen, surf, or sideshow.

Nothing changed, really, except for another crowd moving in, "going native." Worse yet, besides hormonally urgent kids coming for the action, their hot-flashing elders migrated with equal fervor; Macy's went Tropicana on three floors with severely chic labels on hundred-dollar silk shirts and subtle palm tree knits. Wait a minute—make that a hundred and eighty. . . now two, two hundred. . . two, two, two. . . gimme two-fifty, two-fifty. . . okay, two and a quarter. . . Tropicana garb from the Johnny Mambo collection went fabulously with Johnny Mambo furnishings in pineapple, banana, and hula girl motif to underscore a feel for the new place and its fabulous lifestyle potential.

Parking became a problem, so lots were expanded, then elevated. So much apparent goodness brought more tourists in need of cars, till the rock had two cars for every woman, child, and man all the time. Shriveling quickly was the tropical wilderness and rural society—the old island style that defined and redeemed those days and nights of youthful indiscretion once upon a time, long, long ago, when people bonded to the place and each other.

Growth begat growth. The Chamber and the Visitors Bureau raised a cry of victory when a New York magazine staffed by New York residents called Maui "The Best Island in the World." Maybe the staff commuted from Jersey or any part of the megalithic region. Sorely missing from the "best" criteria was a measure of the magic that had spared some islands from the ratings competition—the magic of no airport with connecting flights from New York. The nebulous assessment of "the best island" was judged from that most chilling of islands, Manhattan.

The flood of people, strip malls, parking lots, and gridlock had displaced the old feeling. Making ends meet soon became a communion in itself, an unholy one. Coming up with rent money and then groceries while immersed in beauty and wonder had seemed like a trick, a good one, till resources waned and *aloha* became a useful word to compensate for what had gone away.

Ravi remembered *Pu'u Olai* not so long ago. *Pu'u* is foothill. Pu'u Olai is the shoreline cinder cone between Makena Beach and Black Sand Beach—make that between *Oneloa* (onnay-loa, or long sands) and *Oneuli* (onnay-uli, or black sands). A bump at the base of the volcano, Pu'u Olai is a steep trek for the physically fittest. The payout is the wide world pulsating with *mana*—energy and life force—from *Kahoolawe* to *Alenuihaha*, to *Molokini* and McGregor Point, spanning the glittering sea. In a beautiful balance between glory and bounty, Pu'u Olai had wild tomatoes in vast tangles on top, sweet and tart, till the top got crowded as the beach and tour boat traffic near shore got thick as the Foodland parking lot. No more wild tomatoes at the summit, with so many tourists following written directions to the secret tomato grounds that *you simply must see*. No freshwater shrimp in the aqueduct higher up *Haleakala*. No more guava or *lilikoi* to pick freely along the roadside for miles, no more *noni*, avocado, or lemon. All became for sale, as they became a topic for a few people mumbling about "not so long ago," and many more chattering, "fabulous, unreal, you simply must. . ."

REEFDOG

Kapu means forbidden—or keep out when posted on a gate; the land is private, accessible by invitation only. The guidebooks advised visitors to ignore those signs, and so they did. They'd spent so much to come so far, and look at all those other people in there, wandering around, revealing themselves as a terminal nuisance.

Kihei Road was sparsely traveled for years, except for traffic to Paradise Fruit and that first funky snorkel place. Now hundreds of refugees from a world gone to seed paid daily rent on a few square feet of concrete under a huge canvas canopy for the chance to separate tourists from a few more dollars, often for seashells taken live from Indonesian reefs and sold as Hawaiiana.

Veteran residents stopped counting time on the rock. Resigned to degradation and humanity's inhumanity to nature, many went mum. Transplants arrived decades ago, a year or two ago, six months ago, or last week, and their migration from something far less foretold what would come next. People move away from what they can't abide, only to see it again. Veterans on Maui took refuge in the soft-spoken humility that is necessary and available to island culture.

Nineteen years ago was fairly recent on the tenure totem. Time passed fast and slow, reminding Ravi how long ago the rock felt tropical, how long since development spread like spore growth, its eerie fuzz smothering the beauty and repose. The Ford dealer moved from a modest, aging showroom on Main Street in *Wailuku* to massive grounds on two acres in *Kahului* for new and used inventories that Must Move this Month! A man on the radio yelled to *Get a car! Get a truck! Get an SUV!* Those cars, trucks, and SUVs were stickered six grand or nine over MSRP, and the salesmen would nod sanguinely if a white guy offered MSRP because the sticker price was for your average Filipino, proud of the dollars that demonstrated his skill to get them.

Ravi told his salesman that the sticker-shock game could make a guy want to move to a tropical island. The salesman had asked back, "So? When you leaving?" He reminded Ravi that he, the salesman, was of Hawaiian descent, and with one more marriage on the right side of the genetic fence, his grandchildren would have "blood quantum." He agreed that the place was ruined, and he wanted those fucking airplanes to stop bringing the fucking *haole* tourists over, and Ravi could get the fuck out whenever he was fucking ready.

Haole is a Hawaiian word meaning without breath, deriving from Captain Cook shaking hands rather than touching noses in greeting—rather than sharing the essence of life, which is breath. *Ha* is breath. *Ole* means without. Haole came to connote outsider, meaning those families originating outside Hawaii, where greetings were without breath. Then it came to mean outsiders of beige complexion and not Japanese, Filipino, Chinese, Tongan, or Samoan descent. Then it was meant to denigrate Caucasians.

Well, Ravi didn't want a new Ford anyway, but he felt the sting. The exchange convinced him how nice life would be on a tropical island with no car dealers. But what could he do, stay on the run from a world outrunning its headlights? And who was he to scorn a world out of pace? Every day ended in a dead heat, with fulfillment and pessimism in a photo finish. Ravi had a thought: *Tahiti*. But a more recurring thought was his job, which he loved.

Some nights he got laid, which trumped rational thought in the short term. A young man fatigued from a day's work and hormonal depletion feels good, like a man fulfilled. Besides that, floating angst based on over-development could cloud whatever beauty was left to encounter. Should he stay angry, forfeiting happiness? He related his car salesman encounter to a Hawaiian friend who assured him that the car salesman in question immigrated to Maui via Honolulu from Rarotonga. The car salesman got fired in Honolulu. Besides that, his family descended from a genetic line that included ample Caucasian blood and other car salesmen, and the fellow's hatred would focus elsewhere if white people weren't so convenient. Aka Leialoha could calm the space around him and make hearts warm. Aka laughed, "You do da work. Nevah mind."

What work? A man of *kuleana* would see Maui evolving with soul, easing into the peaceful aftermath and small death of human penetration. Still magical, rife with flowers, mad with color and scent, termites, centipedes, red dust, and heat ripples, the place must be loved for its wrinkles, its wear and tear, its ultimate surrender to gravity. Look at this ambient femininity, this context, this immersion in beauty and nature, this life of effusion and greenery.

You want to talk about a place gang-fucked and left for dead, just look at LA. Millions called it home and had to fly back to it—had to nose under the yellow-brown cloud one more time like mites on a scab spanning the horizon. Orange groves used to be there, but time marched on, and you could value the chic bistros, swinging hot spots, dazzling cabriolets, and hard bodies of surgical precision—or not. Sanity adapted to LA, proving people all the more capable of enduring, after a fashion. Movie stars ranted against the death of nature, against children going hungry and social injustice. They could raise scads o' dough, but few things changed, as more problems came to light. People looked for someplace else. But where could they go?

How long before they think of Tahiti? How long before LA takes over French Polynesia and ruins it, too? What am I talking about? I've never been to either one.

So thoughts schooled, frenzied and faded on any given night. Anxiety and gratification hummed their yin-yang mantra of work and play, life and nature, worry and a woman. How sweet it was, as problems resolved on a roll over the pillow to the fuzzy face nearby. Then he and the cat drifted to dreamland, her little outboard purring a sweet, soft wake.

Sometimes she woke him in the night, licking his forehead or touching her nose to his. Hers was cold. If he opened his eyes, she purred again, which set the world to rights. In her little font of love, the madness shrunk from foreboding magnitude to one tiny problem in an imperfect world, a problem profoundly solved by a gentle scratching of her chinny chin chin.

He hoped that what's-her-name, the other female in the bed, was comfortable.

A Picture-Perfect Paradise

Each day began with the slate wiped clean on a bolster of caffeine and sugar, launching the conscientious dive instructor into boat prep as his mind massaged the second, third, and fourth steps of the day's work: the aloha, the stowage, the launch. The welcome aboard and getting underway were easy enough, barring no-shows, declined credit cards, stumbles, and stubbed toes, engine trouble or big wakes from boats whose captains should not have been licensed, and maybe they weren't. But even that stuff got resolved, and besides, some of the licensed guys drove like Cap'n Crunch.

Morning chores were like bubbles in the wake soon enough, with flat water, sunshine, and the best of life out front. It's hard to be dour under clear skies, in good health. Shadows could darken a day. Or a man could feel the blue sky and sea and great good luck upon him.

The format was sound, the problems obscure, till blue on blue seemed rhythmic and lovely compared to the alternative: gray suit, silver sedan, reasonable commute, airless office, benefits including health insurance and a pension to cover decrepitude. Fuck.

But even an enviable life of harmony with nature in tropical latitudes had its share of tedium, with the same predictable postures, claims and questions on depth, distance, and the desirability of each dive site. Day in, day out, the routine altered only in destination, weather, and sea conditions. Business boomed when Americans feared traveling outside the "homeland," which sounded oddly like the "fatherland." What the hell, job security looked strong. Bookings were four days out. And a hardworking, happy man could afford minor anxiety when the place still blossomed anew nearly every day.

The fleet got bigger when business boomed, and the boat launch required more tolerance. Getting underway took longer and fuel prices rose, which were not crew concerns but undermined prospects for a raise or bonus. More competition kept revenue down. So the crews competed on service and aloha to make the same pay. The first downturn would shrink the fleet to proper size. Boats with repeat business would survive the next recession, pandemic, terrorism, airline strike, mortgage crisis or any challenge to fearless spending because a Hawaii trip gets scratched quicker than a bad Starbucks habit when times get tough.

So familiarity, predictability, crowding, and tedium got worse. It's hard to be dour under blue skies, but emotional burdens gained weight. Ravi Rockulz sadly saw his island change her ways. As a marriage can outlast the love, so did he, feeling each day something less. His tropical island was going suburban, burbling to convenience, gagging chic, and LA-extravagance. The newest immigrants pushed into the gridlock with road rage, adapting successfully.

This traffic? Bad? Compared to what?

The Chamber and Visitors Bureau dismissed gridlock as a growing pain, a natural part of more money and growth, sounding foreign to those who lived for the beauty. Not quite in mid-life crisis, Ravi asked the tough questions:

Could this be the right context for the prime of life?

Did I anticipate thousands more condos, cane fields converted to tract houses, and sweeping ocean views blocked by mini-mansions probing the twenty-million range?

Can I remain happy—or revive my happiness?

Or would this malaise displace the bond between a waterman and his achingly lovely home?

For that matter, was home still lovely?

Stuck in a quandary, with each day adding to his craft, he passed too many days on feelings of inadequacy. Something was amiss. A palpable incompletion persisted. He felt tardy and not there yet but couldn't put his finger on where yet or why not. Renewing vows to beauty and perfection, he wanted to cure the uncertainty. He'd never met an itch he couldn't scratch, but this was deep.

Maybe he needed a break, a few days off with a tourist, a plush and married one looking to buff her separate vacation with no baggage. Ravi was quick and easy as carry-on, replete with excellent manners—and he loved room service, air-conditioning, and remote control. Setting aside her love, obedience, care and devotion, till death do us part, a woman could get down to the romance she craved. A sumptuous woman might reach the itch with fun and kink in a lavish hotel, with six-hundred-thread-count sheets, thick, fluffy towels to use once and throw on the floor, an ocean view, and a mini bar with cashews and chocolates on the hubby's corporate account, which would be easier on everyone, all things considered.

That worked sometimes, but usually not, because either the women had defects, rendering the experience deficient, or they had no defects and left a sensitive dive instructor alone at the dock with matching lumps in his Speedos and heart. Not that sheer frolic wasn't worth the price from time to time, but the price rose, as good female company got more elusive and lovable.

He felt like the young sailor on shore leave in Waikiki. Finally seeing the woman of his dreams, a beauty with the lift, separation, and spread of everyboy's fantasy, the sailor could hardly believe that she was real and available—that he might enter the Promised Land for mere dollars. So he asked, *How much is this going to cost me?* Understood was the whole enchilada—around the world, blow-and-go, smoke-and-fire, half-and-half, and so on—until the perfect woman smiled sweetly and asked back, *How much you got?*

What are you willing to pay? He laughed and marveled at the tonic effect of a small joke. *La petite plaisanterie;* maybe it would make the small death easier to bear. Laughing at society's foibles could keep a man sane, at least in the short term.

He still loved his island, tawdry as she'd become; surely she would save her best for him, something more than another romp in a cane-brake. Oddly for such a vagabond heart, he needed commitment. He needed love returned. He wanted to grow old together.

Among the small deaths was the spirit of aloha, its loss more noticeable to some. Ravi thought it only a toxic few lashing out, as non-resourceful people will do. But few as they were, their rancor rose with posture and noise. Many descended from plantation days as if "local" was sanctified and authorized, but it wasn't.

Racism is troubling anywhere; as a source of pride, racial origin lacks staying power. But racial claims persisted, like blood instinct as a source of intelligence in nature—not to be confused with natural smarts. Genetic claims were proven untenable long ago. The loudest claims were often incomprehensible. *Ah,* Ravi thought. *They're frustrated too.*

Some locals spoke pidgin as a first language. They resented white people making money and new residents driving prices high and the next generation away—their children—because they couldn't pay the rent. The crush was ugly, with a spurious minority claiming oppression at the hands of haoles, starting with the missionaries who took everything. *Welcome to Hawaii. Now Go Home*—this bumper sticker raced down the highway, along with *Slow Down! This Ain't the Mainland,* two sentiments claiming authority while showing volume exchange on stupidity. Pressure mounted but did not give in to hatred in most quarters.

Ravi hated the hatred, which felt contradictory, but what could he think? He knew what came of complaisance in the presence of evil. Next thing you know, liberals are laying their necks on the block to compensate for injustice of the past. Missionaries my *tuchas—I'm Jewish! We don't proselytize.*

Besides, Ravi knew people all over the world from many racial, social, economic, age, and health strata, and he judged on merit.

Natural values, love, and good manners were foremost in any culture. Maybe the Hawaii challenge was best called uninformed, not to be confused with hateful and ignorant. Still, few things got his goat like the false pride of being born and raised. Everyone was born. Everyone surviving childhood was raised. But a sanctimonious few assumed that no place else counted. But growing up local was so much less than growing up in the world. The difference began in local schools. Some matriculates put huge decals on their trucks:

Born & Raised.

Ravi wanted his own decal, custom-made:

Hatched and Fledged on four of the seven continents, deep diving four of the seven seas while engaging intimately with richly diverse cultures in their political, artistic, warrior, romantic and meditative layers. . .

Well, a message that long would require a new car with a huge back window, which might be nice but would also require giving up his current ride and identity marker signifying liberation from material gain and the burden of possessions. Ravi Rockulz was free of the rigors of undue mechanical maintenance or cosmetics that could hinder nature in her course of decomposition to dust. His vintage Tercel lost its back window and back bumper in a tribute to gravity and the miracle of massive rust in movement. The back window was good for laughs through many recollections. Little shards littered the drifts and detritus on the back seat, or on the ground where they tumbled in a sparkling wake through gaping holes in the floor.

Most males in Ravi's social set drove beaters. A beater indicated comfort in the soul. A man in a beater had beaten bourgeois creep. The first symptom of a man giving in was a new car or a car with no rust. The women loved beaters and the men who made the commitment, or lack thereof, and they matched sincerity tit for tat.

Could that be the problem? Could a devil-may-care approach to milestone events be the cause of subliminal anxiety that might be gaining momentum on the road to nowhere? Yes, it could, but no, it wasn't that.

Are you kidding? You want to call nights of wine and laughter, friendship and love a dead end? If that's the case, call me suicidal. You fucking nutcase. You. . . you Mennonite. You Taliban. Christ on a crutch, you want to take away joy and call it productive? Go peddle that poison elsewhere. Get the fuck out!

Anyone could observe that Ravi Rockulz refrained from obscenity. He left it in the bilge, favoring polite discourse every time. *Esprit de corps* made the bawdy good times all the more fun. Polite good taste, as seen in your better hotels, was a matter of choice, and it was free! Still, conversations internal were often profane, meant to discipline self and ventilate the spleen.

But it was the days of endeavor that best balanced the dark view. Could a person be more gainfully engaged than in fun, laughing aloud, or moaning to God in gratitude for what must be heaven-sent? No, he could not—until he questioned joyful pursuits as adequate compensation for a life of no security, no prospects for advancement and, in a most difficult phrase, no future. Good times rolling seemed less foreseeable than growing old. Getting high, getting laid, getting loved, getting wet was easy. Jump in. Youthful wonders are free to anyone willing to work for rent, groceries, entertainment, and no more. In California, they'd call it a lifestyle. In Hawaii, they called it life. *I submit to the court that life cannot get better than a rollicking good time, Your Honor.* Simple truth was the defense.

But it felt like a losing case, with the prosecution closing in. Hand-to-mouth existence was not a victory over wealth but was perceived as such to bolster the case. Living close to the ground had its perks— many mainland tourists envied the vibrant context as far superior to material gain and the urban commute—Ravi Rockulz lived the spirit. Many reflected on their own dull lives while flying home and through Monday morning. Just as speed and comfort counterbalance each other in most boats, so did security and adventure require a choice.

Ravi chose long ago. But something came up like a blemish on a soft complexion—troubling and hard to reckon. Was it midlife time when men panic in the DMZ between boyhood and its inevitable destination? Each day moved inexorably onward, even as the boys dragged their feet. Most men would rather lead dives than sell insurance or shoes, equities or annuities, or swing a hammer or shuffle paper in a stifling office on the thirty-third floor where the windows won't open and the ceilings have no rafters because you must wear a tie. . .

Maybe that was the rub—that a Hawaii dive instructor topped the heap and craved more, like a profession or artistic endeavor. Maybe this restlessness came from the beauty abounding, from unrequited love that needed sharing, so he and society could better appreciate it. Tourists valued his stories on the way to the reef and on the way home. He told them what to watch for, then pointed it out, then told what species and habitat meant in the scheme of reef life. He had learned and absorbed these things, and guests felt the kinship. They loved what he freely gave, and they tipped generously in return.

Maybe a bigger audience could ease the pressure. Maybe he could paint. Or something.

Well, it was a fine, pretty picture, but who could think of art and culture on such a rigorous schedule? Daily demands, with the aerobic output and relentless schlep were enough to tire a younger man. On top of that, a man in his prime wants a normal social life, which wasn't the easy pickin's that met the eye, except for when it was. But luck was fickle. Ravi did not get laid at will. No men do, except for rock stars, some professional athletes, and a few politicians. Those guys get hot and cold running leg anytime they want it, but the rockers, jocks, and pols get mostly high-mileage, skank leg with frequent-fornicator risks of frightening potential. Or mental leg that graduated from Hollywood High *Omigod!* Or they get it retail.

Tourist fare, on the other hand, included upper-echelon females of spiritual, physical, intellectual, and economic development, many of whom lusted for the simplicity of long ago. They'd worked hard to get ahead, trim down, and firm up, sacrificing desserts. They'd gone vegetarian. They exercised and lived right. Most hard-driving women suffered the same stress and compulsion their male counterparts had suffered for ages, leading to the same question, *Why do I work so hard, eat so right, and stay so trim?*

Arrival at the boat provided some of these women with an answer. They worked so hard at self-improvement so they could catch the eye of the soulful dive instructor with the outrageous body. Ravi's mystery unfolded in layers, beginning with a paradox. How could a man so thoroughly defy containment in a three-piece suit, a shirt, and a tie, yet an ounce and a half of nylon splendidly covered him?

Other layers were revealed directly. He was great at his job, in love with his workplace and committed to freedom. His water skills, rust-bucket car, beach shack, scraggly but cute cat, reef wisdom, and gentle confidence made an appealing package optimally wrapped for the short term. Revisiting the first layer—his skimpy Speedos, so snug and compelling in their underscore and highlight of the flat stomach and love missile—a woman might well gain insight to the hopeless cleavage stare she'd suffered for so long.

Maybe his exotic, happy niche was also part of the problem. His happiness had been real, with natural aptitude applied to highest and best use. But like all things seeking perfection, the path fades. Ravi was not ready to die. So what might come next for a man in his prime? What was he missing? He'd seemed to have it all. Maybe he did and would again. Could it get any better?

A steady diet of sweets had seemed like a natural value, but maybe the sweets should be set aside. Maybe it was like the movie where Nicolas Cage was a Wall Street tycoon with these knockout girlfriends, but his money and women didn't matter because life was cold and sterile. The guy didn't even have any art on his walls on account of the great leg and money rolling in. Then this black angel guy sent him back to an old date he'd stood up at the altar, and in one of those Hollywood flashbacks, showing what would have been on the other road taken, he married her. *What was her name? Don't tell me—incred-*

ible rack but much more homey than the Wall Street women with a warm smile instead of a leer. Anyway, they had two kids on the road not taken, and one was cute and smarter than Solomon, and precocious enough to make you gag. She spoke pathos and irony in every line, and the other kid was an infant who cried and shit and peed all over the place until Nicholas Cage realized how sad he'd been with only big bucks and terrific snatch in his life. . .

Nah. . .

That wasn't it. That movie was dumb. That guy had no love in his heart for the snatch or the money. *I just don't have the money.* What that guy needed was a rough cottage in the scrub on the beach and a ratty couch and a TV and some decent snacks in the fridge. Some brewskies and buds. That's all. And a few friends instead of the money-grubbing parasites that guy had all around him.

And don't get started on the lust and love confusion either—everyone in Ravi Rockulz's water world was clear that it was all love and got lusty because of it. Your very best love started with lust, and vice versa. One set up the other, and the other confirmed the one. Sure, things got melodramatic on the coconut wireless, buzzing by brunch on who was doing whom, with regrets or congrats at last. Sure, the goings and comings and secret liaisons sounded like low budget scripts. *As the Anchor Drags* was the neighborhood soap opera, and it was funny, but love happened, sometimes.

Sure, the one and only love anybody actually witnessed in Ravi was for the orange cat, Skinny, which some women on the way out called misguided, unfortunate or somehow wrong, which is what they used to say about all the cute, sensitive guys being gay. But Ravi wasn't gay, and the women criticizing his interspecies relationship didn't know about love's many forms, didn't know Skinny, not really, nor would they.

Skinny came as a tiny pup—she so behaved like a dog—sitting on the threshold, an orange fuzz ball with eyes in the center and whiskers longer than her body, till she stood up, painfully thin. She meowed for yesterday's sashimi, and a few minutes later, with her belly bulging, she found the warm spot for a nap on the feeder's chest. He called her Itchy for a few days but then sensed the long-term effects of a name on a personality—not to mention social consequences. A flea bath and brushing got the itch out, so she graduated to Skinny. She gained weight, but the name stuck in tribute to her simple needs.

She followed him around. A few feedings gave her hope, but she watched him from favorite vantage points. A cat so bereft of love may reach, as many people do, for what's been missing. She lay her head on the pillow, reaching over to rest a paw on his shoulder. She made an impression, but when he pressed for specifics on where they stood, she remained indifferent; the pillow and paw were merely convenient. As patterns became routine, she purred often. She woke him up, "Meow," because morning was only three hours ahead. She shared with no reservation and became his friend and confidant. It began with practicality and led to familiarity, with needs met. Could it be purer? He didn't know, but the thing called love returned every time to a little orange cat.

Like when Skinny was grown, and a woman came home with Ravi to engage in the romp most people find only on the Internet. Skinny watched, though her true focus was Ravi, no matter what he did. The woman bore amazing similarity to Annie Lennox on the Medusa CD but with the white hair. Call it synchronicity—the concept coined by Carl Jung and adopted by the ethereal set—or sheer dumb luck, but Ravi had that day splurged on a disc by Annie Lennox. So similar was this new woman, with her ivory crew cut and sleek body of astounding length that Ravi called her "Annie," which the woman didn't mind. Ravi loved Annie Lennox—okay, he loved her music, but who could separate the music from the woman?

So he closed his eyes as Annie Lennox poured warm honey in his ears and new Annie whispered sweet nothings. Her name was Carol or Stacy or Janet or something, but he called her Annie. Didn't mind? She loved it, wrapping herself around this sweet anonymity, as if love could never be named. This must be a win-win situation,

Ravi thought, so well could one Annie writhe while the other Annie crooned as only she could.

A fellow could bring down the eyelid movie screens, and who showed up, lithe and dykey blonde? Yeah, well, with such a lyric and score in the background, new Annie maintained the same high standards in the foreground. Just for fun, he opened his eyes on the refrain for real reality as juicy and sweet as a virtue ever was. New Annie's hair was just as spiky and the buzz cut heightened the drama. Oh, new Annie was a keeper, with her amazing posture and wondrous tits—naturals! *I'm sure of it! Wait a minute. Was Annie Lennox lesbian? Well, whatever. She's so lovable; I can swing that way too.*

Meanwhile, new Annie's beauty was only par for the course; which wasn't to say Ravi was lookist, fatist, or sexist. It was simply that new Annie was *merely* beautiful, that she lacked a certain elusive kink captured so perfectly in Annie Lennox. Who ever looked at Annie Lennox and didn't want more?

Not to worry: Things worked out with a dollop of imagination, and don't forget the fun. New Annie was a standout beauty with searing smarts, so the ride was crisp and invigorating. Quick as a whip with the sassy quip, she opened fire on any and all, but not on Ravi. He tingled at her soft touch and exquisite good taste.

So she wasn't Annie Lennox. *We'll make do.*

They could share hormones and intellect so thoroughly that a waterman could feel, in a word, inexperienced. It was new Annie putting Ravi in the catbird seat, making good fun of the whole wide world with incisive irony between bouts of sweet succor, each cycle rejuvenating its alternate in a whirlpool of bodies and minds.

The vigor new Annie brought to the table and the bed felt like an awakening. Like a cool breeze in July, she alerted the senses with chilling repartee and willingness to please. Who was this woman? Did the gods send her to taunt and tease, to show perfection that no man could ever possess? Better yet, she reigned in her rapier wit in deference to her date. Nobody wants to be ridiculed—a woman once called Ravi a macho pervert, a sex machine who wore his spray-on swim skivvies like a billboard. Who needed that?

He did no such thing. He preferred a basic nylon swimsuit, so that's what he wore. The rude woman who'd made that accusation was on the way out. So it didn't matter, and she left satisfied, like in customer service, kind of.

But new Annie was different. New Annie lived above that petty stuff, scoring at will in every category, till the toughest macho nut could feel his shell cracking. She caught him staring within minutes of her arrival and asked for his thoughts. With a blink at her extraordinary hair, so dazzling and erotic, he asked if the carpet matched the drapes. With a soft leer, she gave him the news: "This is the nineties, baby. There ain't no carpet."

Ravi laughed short—the nineties ended years ago. Were they down to hardwood? But he couldn't press the odd humor before she ditched her bikini and helped him follow suit. The farmer's market never had produce so fresh and abundant.

Love germinated a few days in, sprouting and bursting forth. It felt like love forever, even with hormonal depletion finally settling in, which took longer than usual, which indicated something else, something more, something beyond. The music was so good and the likeness so striking, he just wanted more. And so did she.

Yes, his concerns grew as his heart opened. Surely she would move to Maui; it was warm, sunny, dry and more fun than Portland. She could move in to his place, or maybe she'd find a job and they'd get a new place, maybe a rental condo with a communal barbecue pit and a swimming pool. Then again, she loved Ravi's place and said it many times, so maybe they could fix it up and make it work. Wait—she could just send for her things. Why not?

Well, she laughed again with sardonic wit, though it quivered. "The main reason why not, buddy boy, is that old hubby boy might not send them. You know, my things. Hey, grow up. Be a man. . ." And so on because it gets no better than with a married woman. Talk about no baggage: slam, bam! *This was terrific. You were terrific. Love your place. Your cat! Ah! Hey, see you next year, maybe, baby.*

Ravi wasn't finished, but she was. Sudden revelation and departure felt like a dump—via Mack truck through the front wall into the living room and onto his chest with an offload of monumental heartache. So it had been love. He'd been used, as he'd been used many times and didn't mind. Many times had sexual utility been shared, a mutual back scratch to achieve relief. But this was different. Yes, some women said they loved him—lonely women infatuated with the tropical scene, the palm trees and scented flowers, the garish colors, the cat, the beach shack and, yes, the Speedos. But the thing with Annie was no scene. It was real. Wasn't it?

Inconsolable, Ravi remained numb for weeks. The usual cavalcade was even more intrigued by the zero-body-fat guy with the incredible frontage and indifference to the luscious buffet before him. They made themselves available but could not compare to Annie. They seemed predictable, demanding, and tiresome.

But time and nature work together toward recovery, so life can endure. Ravi met Marcia from San Francisco. Marcia was smart, not streetwise and ironic like Annie, but comforting; Marcia knew things—sensed things and was there to help. Helping was her profession: clinical psychologist. Besides success and professional knowhow, Marcia had a unique worldview. She understood events and the potentials for goodness and waste. She spoke of nuance in conservation politics to hide the insidious greed therein. She sensed a disturbing contradiction in the gay agenda, yet she defended anyone's right to do anything that didn't harm anything else. What she didn't like was "disturbing." What she approved was "appropriate." The San Francisco Forty-Niners could be disturbing but were mostly appropriate. But she looked good and seemed sympathetic, with warmth and humor that made the smallest task or outing a grand opportunity for fun. Marcia's sartorial flourish seemed a tad extravagant for Ravi's social set, but he didn't mind. In fact, she seemed to be what the doctor ordered. She cured his malaise with her elegant designer sundresses, her lapis and pearls, her frilly lingerie, so exotic that it didn't exist in key dramatic areas. He loved looking at it, especially where it wasn't; it so perfectly framed her most exotic sampler. He loved removing it. Besides that, her seasoned slowness facilitated each favor with the meticulous deliberation of an older woman. Marcia was forty-five—and counting.

Marcia broke the ice with a flourish. Her enthusiasm in sexual exchange suggested years of practice in the field. Ravi used condoms religiously at the beginning of their romance but still suffered angst; she was from San Francisco. She assured him of no worries; she'd been without a man for at least seven years, longer than gestation of the dreaded disease. And she'd never been with a man who'd been with a man. How could she be so certain? She said a woman knows a few things and should be given credit. How did she know who he'd been with, and if he'd always been safe? She said she knew because she could tell and because she trusted him to tell her the truth. She sounded screwy but looked fresh as a catalog offering, so perfectly preened and buffed, with nary a dimple out of place, no creases or folds in the generous offering. Forty-five? Seven years without?

She made no sense, but with concise enunciation and eloquent syntax she could speak around an issue like it was jam on toast instead of a deadly virus. So he diddled her for a minute or two and then sought meaning with his tongue in her crotch for a few more minutes, then went ahead bareback. Hey, San Francisco. A clinical psychologist. Who better to know the odds and safe bets?

Marcia shared her vision quest. It included experiential data— her phrase—and she needed to test something for herself. Her latest dilemma was in the parental/friendship interface with her daughter. She wouldn't say her daughter's age because age should not be important. Her daughter was post-pubescent at any rate and came to Mummy, asking innocently as a young lass, "Mummy, I really liked my last three boyfriends, Darius, Martin, and Francis. They weren't really my boyfriends because I didn't want them to think I was loose, so I didn't let any of them. . . you know. They stopped calling. That's what they do. So I let Pierre do what he wants. I do what he asks. I thought it was disgusting at first. Now I'm used to it, but I still think it's weird. Ew. He says he's in love, but I don't want to go out with him anymore. Am I doing this wrong?"

The constrained response began with, *No, dear, you aren't doing anything wrong, but that doesn't mean you should. . . What I mean is, you can't. . . You can't. . .*

Ravi waited for the moral of the story. The daughter had experimented in a way the mother called unwise, though the daughter's experience in love was greater than her own. "I had sexual intercourse with a man I hardly knew and got preggers with Samantha. It was rather clinical and went nowhere, really, except for making her, meaning Samantha. But frankly, I've held back."

The bigger question: Had Mummy been doing this wrong? Frustrated and lonely as a heterosexual woman in San Francisco can be, Marcia had resisted the temptation to gobble up any straight, educated, and socially adjusted man she met. She'd met a few, but they were so predictable, pithy and urbane—and soft, like city men. She had doubts but decided to wait for the right man. And wait and wait—because her standards had meaning. She realized on seeing Ravi at work and play that he had a love affair with life, that he alone could replace Dirk. Dirk was her dildo, who she praised for selfless giving, sparing them both many evenings of solitude.

Ravi seemed perfect for the grand experiment, in which a real man would be granted the same free license only Dirk had enjoyed, to see if they could bond as one. Scratching the big itch would be easy if she could establish intimacy with another person. Is that unreasonable? No, and she was bound for glory on the highest levels of spirit and emotion. She shuddered, confiding her sense that this could be "it." She assured him that he could be so much more than the rippled dive guy in the spray-paint Speedos, and the cavalry was on the way because nobody should go through life as a sex object. Not to worry; they had their best years remaining.

Willing to bet her credentials as a clinical psychologist with twenty-three years' experience, she pegged Ravi for sensitivity. She was a woman, so Speedo-tinted glasses may have influenced her vision of his inner glow. Not to worry once more—he could unleash the love so long gone from her life.

She seemed complicated, and her psychosexual conundrum felt murky. Naturally gifted at sperm extraction, she sank quickly and woefully to love and its failures in her life. Referencing her life as a separate entity, she enumerated her life's assets and liabilities. She longed to correct her life's deficiencies. He felt her life engulf him as it had her, like a net.

On the day they parted company, she had a friend call him from San Francisco, "a mediator, if you will, to see if we might work through this." She'd left that morning, leaving him half asleep, hormonally spent, in the solace of she who understood best: *Meow*. Ravi told the friend that the work was done. "Done?" So Ravi explained that Marcia was clingy and neurotic, except in brief lapses when she praised him and God for her orgasm. "Hmm. I see."

Yet the friend persisted: Marcia needed Ravi to return her love, and she waited that very minute in her condo nearby—a short walk from where he sat—waited for the love of her life to say he would.

"Would what?"

"You know. Return her love."

"Oh. Well, maybe tell her you called me but I wasn't home."

"Oh, please."

So Ravi told the friend that he felt no love. He'd liked her at first, and liked her even more after the first sex, but he was really glad she left because she couldn't keep up, and he was a really horny guy. She called him a failure and said his life was empty. She'd asked, "How long do you think a grown man can blow bubbles with tourists?" The friend said that two lives find success as one life shared. But success for the goose was a straightjacket for the gander. Ravi told the friend that Marcia was unhappy, unstable, and unacceptable. With luck, the friend would help her work through these obstacles in finding the true love she needed.

The friend asked, "Don't you see?"

Ravi thought the friend saw very little but the view from his navel, with his head so far up his ass. But that felt unkind, possibly hostile. Ravi asked if he should move to San Francisco and become a clinical psychology intern and get laid and analyzed at will.

The friend said, "Yes! If that's what you want."

But beyond glib humor was the lesson in delusional love: Marcia would have moved in—would have phoned the daughter to pack the essentials and come on over. Don't worry—the movers can get the rest. Marcia wanted to grab this eternal love, wanted to shape him up and snap him out of his ridiculous stupor, wanted total realization of the man and his feelings. Marcia and the charter crowd asked: Who but a fool gets up at dawn to play in the ocean, smoke dope, and bag the odd tourist? Enjoying warm days with no view whatsoever to the cruel winter ahead is not a future.

Marcia ended her week in Paradise sorting stats on emasculation and reconstruction. Alas, Ravi could not cure her life but gave what he could till the weekend. By then the beach shack got crowded and insensitive. He'd wanted distance, which is not a sign of love.

Marcia's last day began and ended at first light when she twisted her head to see Skinny sitting by Ravi's pillow, purring. Ravi had been stroking her head—Marcia's—with one hand while she ate him. He scratched Skinny's chin with the other hand, generating intense satisfaction in the cat but conflict in the woman. He had naively assumed all needs met in the females nearby. With so much purring and moaning, each to her or his own, life seemed good, promising another beautiful day—till the woman stopped and spoke accusingly, "You love that cat more than you love me."

Well, fuck, duh. What was your first clue? Of course he did.

What a dumb thing to say.

But he couldn't respond. Not that it mattered; morning service was fading fast, unless he could say something equally foolish, like, *Oh, no, I love you much more than Skinny.*

Fat chance.

He tried, "No, I don't; we just know each other better."

Which was true. Marcia's initial take on Skinny had been far more challenging to the man and the cat: "Not much to look at."

Au contraire, Skinny loomed large, seven pounds of orange fluff with a baby face. Ravi had let it go, deferring to potential. But it lingered through the week to Saturday morning and *blowjobus interruptus*.

Marcia had risen, indignant as an urban professional forced to rectify the untenably inappropriate. Grabbing her things, she'd huffed to the door. Hearing no apology, no nothing from the bonehead in the sack, she'd left, her parting counsel, "Let her suck your dick."

Ravi called out, "You're crazy. She's cute as a button!" Then he asked Skinny: "Who needs three blowjobs in a night and a day?" Skinny, also stumped, commiserated in her way. Not that she, Skinny, would deny him any affection, but Marcia's suggestion wouldn't have worked, and besides, it wasn't like that between them. She was a cat, providing love, and he had the others for the other. Marcia's exit seemed inevitable, perhaps demonstrating God's plan in creating both cats and women. What a relief.

He hoped he would not hear from Marcia again. He pictured her by the phone in her condo—the friend assured Marcia's "full confidence in Ravi's integrity as a man," meaning he would call once he realized what she represented, what they had going, and the sheer, raw potential dead ahead. Except for one glitch: They had nothing. He saw it clearly, his vision confirmed by her melodramatic exit and pining, classic symptoms of manipulative people. He didn't call. He wallowed in the warm, fuzzy feel of not calling, but he set the wallow aside too; it seemed so harsh, and she was gone.

She would leave the next day anyway and could likely use the free time to regroup, reassess, fix her face, and think of home. There— there's a nicer frame for a difficult picture.

Ravi snoozed late then rose to a glorious day off with nothing to do, no dive or female company or the endless maintenance of either. He wondered what was worse, a heart-rending loss like Annie or a mental bitch who finally left. He strolled out and headed up for coffee, retail, a double latte with a pastry.

He thought of her first with warmth and hoped she might find her man, and things would be better because she'd learned what real men want and what those men will give in return. If she met a guy from San Francisco and he had a good job in town and wore a suit and made good dough and wore his feelings on his sleeve with no inkling of assertiveness, things might work out. That guy might be strolling down Union Avenue right now wondering when Ms. Right would come along—when Ms. Right would come into his life.

Marcia might approach romance more humbly with tempered expectations, and maybe she wouldn't browbeat the new guy till the second weekend. So things could work out.

Love her more than Skinny? Shut up!

Yet he could be a tad more subtle with his cat. Affection for a beast, even a cute fuzzy one, in the presence of women, should not be confusing. He and Skinny shared domestic bliss in this, their time on earth together. It was nobody's business but their own—but he would avoid spooking the guests at critical junctures. Maybe if he'd grabbed her ears—Marcia's. And he laughed.

Basha Rivka often advised: *Tzim lachen*. It should be to laugh. He couldn't very well tell his mother of this tourist woman's jealousy of a chin scratch for the cat during a blowjob, but he felt Basha Rivka would laugh too since they had their health—all three of them.

At the main road, he began to cross when a pickup with big wheels drove slowly past. The driver mumbled, "Fockeen haole suck." Ravi wanted to tell him that "fucking haole" would have done, without the "suck." But the guy had no sense of humor after spending forty grand buggering up a used truck. So he nodded and gave the right of way. The truck guy peeled into the parking lot on a roaring cloud, not quite rolling over. What a show. What a great return on investment.

Local hostility seemed isolated and rare. Ravi didn't take it personally but as a sign of the times. Maybe the signs wouldn't change.

Who knew? Once an exotic destination, Maui felt pressured, with too many humans competing for Paradise.

He crossed to the parking lot to see if he and the driver could reach an understanding. Finding the truck but not the driver was perhaps best, what with resolution so unlikely. Who had what to give? So he held communion with the truck and walked back to the coffee shop, disappointed that his shot of sugar and caffeine would be soured by a dose of vinegar. Such was the world, pressing a righteous man to balance what felt hazardous.

What else could he do? Everybody felt swept along in a tsunami of development with an undercurrent of more, more, more. Who could be more convenient to blame than each other? A few rude boys claimed dominance and something or other, even though their forebears arrived in freighters and not outrigger canoes. They also measured their substance as a matter of tenure but got no respect.

The guy could have said, *Hey, brother.* But the taunt and threat better reflected him. Things would get worse. Who got what and how much of it would further inflame, with so many haves having so much and so many others feeling the squeeze.

But was that any reason for a guy to call me a haole suck? No. His family came a hundred years ago, or two hundred, as coolie labor, in the influx of Chinese, Japanese, Filipino, and the rest, when the missionary sugar company took everything and gave little but debt in the company store. The missionaries took land from the Hawaiians and labor from the Asians. The missionaries were white.

That wasn't me, but the guy in the truck would rather be hateful than right. Let the chips fall. Is it my fault they're all blue chips in your prime beach areas? Does my place look like Santa Barbara? Do I really care if a piece of the rock was only a million dollars two years ago and now runs three million or five million, seven point nine or twelve million?

Ah, well—the sun climbed higher on another beautiful day for those who could afford it. Those who couldn't afford it wondered where to go and what to do. Or maybe they only thought they couldn't afford it. Ravi Rockulz had everything he needed, including a million-dollar view, a cat to confide in, and more recent blowjobs under his belt than a fellow needs on any given day.

Too bad the coffee place was crowded out the door with pale tourists and more tourists piling out of matching Hummers, happily exclaiming that next year they would rent the Ferrari too, just to have it for their fabulous few days, which would be way better than the Porsche. They had the Porsche last year, and it was okay, but the Ferrari along with the Hummer would really be the best package.

Hey, it was no big deal that tourists were jamming the place with flesh and talk. A guy had plenty coffee at home, along with bread for toast and a smidge of *lilikoi* jelly left. And what a great day for a walk before breakfast—except for the troubling view of the woodland by the reef down the shoreline that used to be *Maluaka* and Black Sand, being leveled for new condos at twelve to fifteen million.

A Hawaiian man stood in the road above the rubble that last week was a forest home to critters, now cleared and prepped with dynamite to blast away for underground parking for Hummers and Ferraris. The Hawaiian wore an orange vest and held a red flag. How could a Hawaiian support the destruction? Ravi said in passing, "You know, this used to be beautiful."

"Used to be," the man said.

Yeah, well, the guy in the truck was confused on which whites were which, but this sun-baked Hawaiian knew the score; it didn't even matter because the place was going down. Everyone felt the pressure of more, more, more going to less and less. What could the guy do, give up his job? Well, yes, he could. But he wouldn't.

Nobody wants to dwell on the negative, but Ravi stared out, at the end. A man lives till he dies, and he's better off any day under blue sky and water. But he couldn't help the regret; oh, man, here we go again. Here again, a man recognized a moment of change. Change should be good. Change is evidence of life. A common bumper sticker said: *All who wander are not lost.* Too bad that most wanderers *were* lost, or yet to be found, but the road still waited for a man who loved nature with a few good years remaining. Elder Brahmins or Buddhists or watermen set out with faith, only faith. Not that Ravi Rockulz was old. Not by a long shot.

Besides, nineteen years in one place did not make him a rolling stone. He'd stopped pleading his case years ago. Basha Rivka's chronic tongue clicking, wincing, and gnashing was meant to wake him up. She asked, "What is it that you do? What do I say? My son is what? He's a. . . a swimming *schlep*? What?"

"If you need to tell anybody anything, you can tell them I'm developing a career in tourism with an emphasis on ocean recreation."

"Big shot! Who knew?"

"How is that thing on your neck?" And so on, the browbeaten and the beater, till he beat her to the punch and led the fray elsewhere, to where she lived and worried.

"Hmm. Don't ask." But of course he asked in self-defense and because not asking would indict a wayward son who didn't even ask about that thing on her neck. Then he listened to what the doctor, a real *goniff*, meaning that he could steal with integrity, and *oy*, what he had her trying that week! And the other doctor was so young, so. . . dumb, but she liked him, even though he'd wanted her to try new drugs to work miracles, and we really don't believe in that sort of thing. Ravi listened to diagnosis, prescriptions, symptoms—to who was sick or recently dead, like Sadie Kornblatt, who up and quit her medications one day because she felt so bad. Forty pills, twenty each morning and evening for twenty years, she took. So many pills nobody needs like a hole in the head, so she quit one morning and that afternoon she felt better but died. "It just goes to show you."

Echoing across the ailments and mortalities a voice called out for life to begin. A swimming schlep? Of course he was more, much more, with training and experience along with the life-and-death responsibility of a dive instructor to judge conditions and decide in the clutch daily. Yes, he could be cynical an hour before dawn, in prepping and checking. Then hoisting eighteen scuba tanks aboard and into the racks with no grunts because grunting means weakness. Each guest signs in and hands his dive bag aboard, from which the regulator, octopus, buoyancy compensator, and weights are set in place, with the fins, mask, and snorkel draped over the tank, so arrival at the dive site is like catered brunch. The guests have no worries because a sharp crew makes no mistakes. Because tourists can rest assured that their weights are correctly placed for proper descent and stability; that their air is on with buoyancy compensators slightly inflated so they don't sink, sucking on a dead hose; that the tanks are full to three thousand pounds and not three hundred—Ravi Rockulz does not one detail take for granted. Playful and energetic as an otter, weaving, turning like a marine mammal who behaves for survival, he knows that vigilance in movement can avoid the unforeseen. Ravi looked, checked pressure, pocket zips, comfort level, ear clearing. . .

Are you okay?

Then he pointed out what tourists don't see on a reef. They came so far and spent so much—and spent it here; they should see an octopus in a crevice, matching color and texture with the substrate. Or a dwarf moray or garden eels or a shark on the verge or resting on a ledge. Or a manta, whale, turtle, coral bloom, flame angel, pyramid butterflies in a hundred-foot column.

Are you okay? How much air do you have left? Okay, we go out and around to the right. Okay?

Water schlep? How about water doctor? Or water lawyer? Or water accountant? How about that? Yes, the schlep occurred at sunrise and again at the end when tanks and gear went back the way they came. So? Are not a man's muscles defined by his labors? Does he carry a load with assurance, aplomb and dispatch? The short answer is yes— even if he grunts on the offload. The truth was: he was a waterman of first-caliber reputation among the fleet!

Beyond prowess, an evolving man becomes more. Ravi was also fearless in spending. He spent foolishly on friends who would go deeper than a dive plan to help him, as he would do for them. He tipped lavishly since waitpersons also needed to make ends meet. Every now and then a reasonably fresh waitress might turn her sparkle on he who spent so freely. She might assess the tip waiting in his heart. Or she might just dive in. Either/or was A-OK, but most waitresses had heard every line ever delivered by every Barnacle Bill or tourist wannabe who ever bellied up.

Indiscrete spending was an act of vengeance. Pissing it down the rat hole was a statement of life, liberty, and anarchy. Ravi's greatest demonstration of liberation from the material world began one morning at Molokini Crater, a deep dive by necessity with swells banging the back wall and turbulence down to fifty feet. At ninety feet, divers could spread their wings and fly—not a novice dive but a real crowd-pleaser. The back wall got a few jitters churning among the intermediates, mostly accountants, insurance agents, business people and the most intractable social segment, doctors. Your average intermediate had twenty or fifty dives and often compensated anxiety with good cheer. Never mind; Ravi would take care of them, beginning with a little humor to ease the tension: the wall went four hundred feet to a ledge and then down to eight hundred, making it a bottomless dive, but don't worry because the second dive would be much shallower, and topless. How they loved his *joie de vivre* in the clutch! It was just another day at the office for him—and us too, come to think of it, out here on our own in the deep blue sea.

On this particular morning, a tourist handed Ravi a severely expensive camera in an underwater housing with a huge glass bubble in front—the dome port over the lens. It wasn't for keeps but for some excellent photos of the tourist and his new wife. Did he say *excellent photos?* "Don't worry," the tourist said, pointing out a button on top. "Focus. And shutter. Get very close. Okay?"

Okay.

The shots were excellent, but the process felt mechanical till the tourist said Ravi had a gift. A moray peeked in from the right, and a curious jack cruised in from the left with a wink. "You can't hire shots like this," the tourist said, tipping the crew a hundred dollars.

Ravi dismissed the praise according to habit. Yet he savored the view for a week or two, reframing the eel and jack and newlyweds in his mind. He could have framed the eel and a coral head or the jack and hundreds of pyramid butterflies. He could have done it several ways, all perfect because he saw what others didn't. *Swimming schlep? Why must she use such degrading language? Would she be happier if I wore a suit and got fat? Yes, she would, so let it go.*

So he let it go, until another dive prep soon after. Snugging his cummerbund, clipping in his waist and chest straps, humping the rig higher onto his back and cinching his front strap D-rings, he paused. "Those are butterflies you'll see in the water column, not with wings and little antennae, but butterflyfish, as you'll see in their amazing color and grace." Oh, they loved him, plunging to the depths for the magic he so sprightly conveyed.

The next week he spent two of his three grand on a camera, housing, lens, and port—used. He could wait on the strobe, though it came the next day for another six hundred, to correct the blue-green fuzz at depth, to restore color and focus. For a week he shot tourists until the owner approved ten bucks per shot with two bucks going to the boat.

In six months Ravi Rockulz sent a portrait study of a giant moray eel to a well-known natural history magazine. With clarity and compelling detail, a personality came forth. The editor called it the best portraiture ever of the elusive, nocturnal giant moray. Ravi said, "Pshh. . . those guys and their lavish praise." He tingled for days. He'd gone after dark to the pinnacles off Black Rock near the Sheraton Hotel. Friends scolded him for diving alone. At night? Are you nuts?

But maybe a tad whacked was part of artistic fervor. Besides that, safety is best but is often forgotten. Only a fool would dive without a buddy, given a choice. But a photographer at depth will soon be alone anyway. And if his buddy is shooting too, they'll drift to different subjects. At night, twenty feet apart might as well be solitude. If a buddy isn't shooting, separation will be quicker. No buddy wants to wait on a photographer, waiting for the fish to open up and socialize, to pose in its moods. Ravi snorkeled out to the pinnacles off Black Rock that night to save his tank. He knew of night beasts who hear splashing as the sound of injury and an easy meal. So he descended on rationale; yes, he could be with a buddy. They'd drift to separate pursuits and meet on the beach, which would be no safer and could be more worrisome if either was late or came out elsewhere.

Beyond that, it was a moderate swim to the pinnacles off the point, even if the point was a bit farther out than the rock. It felt manageable with no shore break. And things began smoothly. A camera requires two hands, leaving no hand for the flashlight in the inky darkness. Not to worry, Ravi's flashlight revealed some lovely coral, a sleeping parrotfish, and a few ghastly conger eels. Then he wedged it inside his buoyancy jacket to free his hands for the camera. He worked switches by memory until the flashlight squirmed to shine up under his chin, blinding him and falling out—till he grabbed it, camera in the other hand, gaining a valuable lesson underwater, that something dropped can be retrieved with presence of mind and an easy reach. But this felt awkward, till he turned and gasped, nose to nose with a giant moray eel.

The eel wasn't so much bigger unless they went back-to-back on tiptoes. The eel would have won by a foot and a half with similar girth. Worse was the moray's presumption. Opening wide on an obtrusive display of long teeth in many rows crowding the fleshy maw, the eel assessed plausibility on swallowing the prey before him. Ravi cooperated, as it were, cringing to more palatable size.

As heart and sphincter went peripatetic in the face of death, he turned away, one hand for his light, the other on his camera and no hand for the knife strapped to his calf. What could he do with a knife anyway, stab a giant moray? He might discourage it, but bleeding could encourage others. Or an attack might trigger response in kind. Then Ravi would bleed and feel discouraged. Dousing his light to see how things might look, he stayed deep and turned the light back on.

In flight over fight, his muscles jammed into overdrive on adrenaline. He sensed survival and made a note to buy a spare light. But he slowed on realizing practicality in the sea, its nature based on need, not greed. Small fry gobble plankton. Boxfish eat small fry, and so on up the menu. Gill breathers don't kill for sport, status, or compensation for lesser attributes—or mental derangement or photo-ops. Hunger and defense drive the system. He suddenly stopped. *Some people are naturally friendly, engaging and curious. Some seem like old souls who know their way around, who comprehend compassion and a soft touch. This so-called giant hails from forebears and a social order more orderly than my own! So?*

So the flight stopped a long but short way back. Ravi turned as the giant also turned, perhaps lured by the light now shining his way. Ravi turned the light askew then shone it on himself so the giant could see: no harm intended, and a diver could not be prey without severe risk of indigestion and heartburn on so much neoprene, nylon, plastic, and steel. Giant moray snaked gracefully back to proximity as the camera rose on an emotive subject lit in dramatic overtone and nuance. . . *et voila!* Aiming one-handed, flashlight in the other, Ravi held his breath so noise and bubbles would cease. And off the point in faint glow, a tableau formed. Two tentative beings assessed the nature and intention of each other on a chance meeting in the dark.

The big galoot came on like a stalker with eye contact and intense curiosity. They scanned. One sniffed the strange, glass dome. The other made a soft clicking noise, from eyes to mottled skin to dilating nostrils, four of them, and scads of teeth defying a neat tuck into the maw, some in need of flossing. The eel opened wide to push water over the gills and purse a word, *Aaaloha.* Giant moray eased into communion as yet unseen through a lens.

"Photos by Ravi Rockulz" in *National Geographic* changed life for three days. With greatness came cash for better camera stuff with more functions a pro might need. Cash remained for celebration into the wee hours, with more cash plunked down on the waitress tray and reciprocal gratitude into the night, no cash required.

Life changed. Here was vision and purpose instead of monotony. Here was the ephemeral nature of greatness; it fades unless fed. So he stepped up. He'd cleared the outfield wall and could do it again, though he feared the eerie air of invincibility. What if he couldn't? Development requires error. What if he failed?

So he practiced humility until a great photographer said he used the same strobe as Ravi because of the focus-light setting that let it serve as a flashlight, freeing things up. "Don't you love it?" Ravi blushed. Who knew? So many buttons!

The old pro saw—"Oh, man! You held a light out to the side!" Ravi did not deny it, and greatness got boosted again.

The bad news was that he couldn't share his success with Basha Rivka. Or he chose not to; it was so premature. Maybe he held back in self-defense against her inevitable critique: *So what? You'll retire now? So now what do I tell them? You took a picture of a fish and retired, except for the swim schlep every day of your life?*

The questions could sting or itch. Best to keep it under wraps until one more magazine credit, or maybe three more.

When You Least Expect It

But futures form up with minds of their own. No matter how many photos of exquisite beauty Ravi sent off, they came back with rejection forms. He called to ask why, when his shots were clearly superior to what appeared in the magazine, *not that those shots are bad, Sir, it's just that*. . . And he got the news:

1. We're not your personal gallery.
2. You got lucky on some eel shots. Your white balance was off, and your water was a bit turbid. You warranted coverage, and we hope you enjoyed the exposure.
3. You were good to send us your photos. They are, for the most part, well done, but. . .
4. We don't build stories on photos. We commission photos to go with our stories.
   "Okay, then. Perfect! Give me a commission."
5. Have your agent make contact.
   "I don't have an agent."
6. Get one. If you're good enough for us, you're good enough to get an agent. We can't answer individual inquiries. Thank you. Good luck with your search elsewhere. Good-bye.

At least he wouldn't hear his mother's lament. But he could hear the voice within. It was no use sending his work to New York in search of

44

an agent. He proved it, soliciting fifteen agents. All said no in three stock forms:

1. You're very talented, but how would I market your skills?
2. Your skills are greatly apparent, but we're not taking new clients at this point in time.
3. You're very good to send us your pictures, but your work does not fit our current needs. Please feel free to stay in touch, and best of luck on your search elsewhere.

Low expectation helped soften the blow. It would be tough enough on iffy photos, but what could be wrong with flawless work? Oh, sure, a speck might show up on scrutiny, or maybe the New York highbrows didn't know that *larvaceans* are a pelagic tunicate and not digital noise. Nothing mattered east of the Mississippi, where all was known. So a world-class photog reeled on rejection coming quick as a lightning left jab every time he looked up.

Rejection takes a toll. Without hope, fatigue gains momentum. So a hard-working dive instructor again felt the weight of sundown. A man can relax over a beer and some bud, can ease off at last. Disappointment in the mix, however, can hinder easy transit to middle age. Not that thirty-something was middle yet. But times got heavier on tough topics, like vigor, self-esteem, and waning youth.

It got worse when an independent producer called one evening to praise Ravi's work: "Nobody has captured pelagic tunicates in a casual reef context as well as you."

At last!

Who was this guy? "I've done very well the last three years with a docudrama on three Civil War skirmishes and a scathing look at health care in the Piedmont. But never mind all that." Albert Huffman was on to reefs, in the news and dying fast. Highlighting their demise could get media play all right. "What do you have in mind?"

Ravi laughed. "I'm sitting here drinking a beer." And smoking a joint. "I don't have anything in mind. I could think of something. What do *you* have in mind?"

"I can tell you this, Ravid. . ." Albert Huffman rhymed it with "David," suggesting an animal unhinged. But Ravi let it go; better to bag big game than swat at gnats. "Danger gets their attention. This should be easy. You're out there every day, in a world of danger. We need to focus on threats. We'll ring the bell. Guaranteed. Putting the ingredients together is my specialty."

"I don't sense the ocean as threatening."

"Of course you don't. That's why you'll be the hero of this thing because you look death in the eye and go on about your business. Death is like a. . . like a water cooler or a coffeemaker to you."

"I'm afraid as the next guy. If I sense death or danger, I leave."

"You know what I mean. Take sharks. You see sharks every day."

"No. Not every day. But I see them."

"Bingo! Sharks. Death and danger. We'll open on everyone's worst nightmare, what people fear! Eaten by sharks! Perfect."

"But they're mostly whitetip reef sharks."

"How big?"

"Some get ten or twelve feet, but—"

"Perfect! Can you get close to them?"

"They're whitetips, like puppy dogs. You can put your arm around them. We had a baby out at Molokini we named Oliver. He lived on a ledge. He grew up, and he's still out there and checks us out every time. No death. No danger. He's a friend."

"He's a shark, right? He's got teeth, right? Shark teeth in rows, right? I got the working title: *Vicious Killers of the Deep*. But I'll tell you what, bubby, I think that working title should make it all the way, if you catch my drift."

"Pshh. Oliver? Vicious? He's friendly. Wait! I got it! I *was* afraid! Deathly afraid! I almost walked on water!"

"What! What is it? Better than sharks? More teeth? Bigger?"

"Shit!"

"No, what? It's okay. Tell me!"

"Shit! I'm telling you! I saw shit! It's a problem here, with so many people flushing number two, and the sewage treatment plant so small; it overflows, and they post in the newspaper that back in May you swam in shit. And the charter boats dump their shit too. I'm telling you, no tiger shark or white shark or any shark scares me more than turds. You know they can make you very sick!"

"Oh. . . Man. . ."

"What? You want danger? I'm telling you: turds! That's danger, and they're showing up in shoals. You can be out there in so much beauty, and next thing you know, you're surrounded. This is a terrific idea! Hey, *Turdfish Killers of the Deep*! Yes?"

"Look. You want to do the vicious killers thing or not?"

"Yes! Blind mullet! Turdfish killers! Of the deep!"

"God." Then came silence. Was it a religious moment, a moment of insight and gratitude? Or exasperation? Albert Huffman murmured, "I'll run it by the execs. But they won't buy it."

"Who are the execs?"

"You know. The producers."

"I thought you were the producer."

"The money guys. The guys who pitch the sponsors."

So Ravi learned the game, that rejection can be an act of mercy, can shorten the agony of New York and sponsors for danger.

The day ended on two beers, a doobie, and a downer. The buzz made more sense at a fork in the road, but the downer gave "water schlep" new meaning. Marijuana was the sledgehammer of choice in the sundown gandy dance, laying track to oblivia. But with the way station of middle age coming on, the weed amplified the wrong stuff. Maybe it was all wrong stuff, like hyping ocean threats. Albert Huffman was a pimp. *National Geographic* came on like champagne but fizzled to scuz. A talented photographer got discovered then shunned, as if art so far from Manhattan was no basis for lunch.

Ravi Rockulz could stay physically fit and ready, but he couldn't tell what for. Details seemed elusive, but the future drew nigh, and a man needed more. More than *la vie en rose?* More than tropical adventure with friends? What was the problem? Depression? Too much dope? Not enough dope? Like a sailor, downwind in following seas—he watched the barometer and horizon. Squalls come up, no problem. A squall can race across and vanish, or rush in to dump a deluge, no problem. But squall lines bunching up with the barometer dropping? That was a problem. He could reduce sail or change course. Bare poles, battened hatches, sea drogues and hove-to survival mode seemed premature. But he kept an eye to windward.

Most dive leaders gain water wisdom by thirty, leading more by presence, sensing situations. Ravi had aptitude and found a career at nineteen. How many dives ago was that? Most dive leaders don't count dives. They count income and years because age happens.

The industry was macho; hardheads got bent or failed in business. Any tourist may process nitrogen off the charts because the tables are conservative, but ignoring the tables can change a life or end it. Even the idiots knew this, so errors tended to be honest, leaving ample room for macho expression elsewhere. For example, dives got counted, then not counted. Not counting showed seasoning. Most instructors stopped counting in year two or counted to themselves. Counting was for those who hadn't accepted life at depth.

Ravi Rockulz reached six hundred dives in his second year and would break a thousand soon. No, wait: two tanks daily would be seven thirty a year if he didn't miss a day, but he would on days off. Still, in eight months, with three night dives a week, or two—he'd break a thousand by year three. That was fast. But who's counting?

A raw number indicated repetition on the drill, with six tourists daily. Ravi saw familiar faces and wondered: *Weren't you here last week, or year? Do I remember you?* Repeat customers said it was great to see him again, hoping today's dive would be as incredibly spectacular as last year's dive. *Remember? We went to. . .*

He went along: "Yes! It's wonderful to see you again." Some repeat customers laughed short. Then he glazed at the gap from then to now and the years, up in bubbles.

REEFDOG

A seasoned veteran did not count dives because it was pointless after several thousand dives. *Oh, I have thirteen thousand dives.* What? Are you nuts? Thirteen thousand? Did you count them? Would you rather dive than fuck? Will your bones turn to ash? The macho elite easily dismissed bone necrosis with a baseball cap that said: *Nitrogen Junkie!*

Ha!

Counting dives became so *faux pas* that it gave way to new expressions of expertise: *We run six, seven hundred dives a year each, so the gear has to be tough. We don't have time for breakdowns.* Get it? Six or seven hundred dives a year was the pro standard. If you wanted to stay in, stay down for five years or ten, there was your count. Twenty years? It happened, but reality took its toll. Even top dive instructors get stooped and leathery. Why would they measure exposure? They were obviously long haulers.

Besides, numbers didn't count for squat next to tall tales. Any adventure has its lore—the big one that got away or the summit unreached—so, too, deep dives daily made danger an old familiar, maybe more so. A climber failing to summit can likely climb down. A fisherman losing a big one can have another beer and two more hotdogs. Big deal. Even a sailor can tread water. But a scuba pro at depth with six strangers, mostly novices with little instinct, knows the price of error. People died—not often, but then how much of the bends, or drowning, or embolism do you need to gain attention?

Ravi could spin yarns with the best, and the boys did sit and spin over a few beers and the latest dope and a cigarette or two because nothing felt better than war stories and nicotine after breathing a couple of tanks compressed. But the yarns could turn against the teller, could tangle a reputation in dark language, like *unsafe, bent again, embolism, decompression, no safety stop, ran empty at depth, panicked on an emergency free ascent, narced at 110 feet,* and into the nightmare medley of things gone wrong. Some stories could trigger the knee-jerk—a laugh, a scoff, scorn or worry. Kill a tourist, and the details would be audited ad nauseam, till diver error was accepted.

Kill two tourists, or three, and tourists would see the shadow on the dive leader in question—or hear about it.

Cheerful but not so dumb as they seemed, the tourists were often successful suits back home. Most could sense things. A dive leader with a bad rep could wonder who knew, compensating with exemplary diligence, as if the job wasn't tough enough.

Stories of things gone wrong were not casual but shared for humor and insight. The most common foible was nitrogen narcosis, caused by nitrogen on-gassing at seventy feet or deeper. With air compressed to half its former volume, or twice its former density, at every atmosphere—every thirty-three feet—of descent, a diver at seventy feet breathes twice the nitrogen. Or is it three times? It gets tricky, and getting it wrong can bend a diver or make her sick and unstable. Narcosis is a lesser risk but still a risk. It brings on euphoria, in which the sea makes ultimate sense, answers all questions, and opens its arms seductively. In narcosis, the depths can speak with the voice of God, who can be a mermaid of perfect proportion. Ravi Rockulz warned many a six-pack—industry slang for six tourists—of narcosis. Standard procedure was to gather round on entry, treading and signaling okay, going from snorkel to regulator. The exchange continued on descent, okay on ear clearing, okay on feeling, okay, okay and okay—down to narcosis depth and deeper on the all okay. The dive plan was a twenty-five-minute drift at 110 feet along the back wall, an advanced dive, but an easy one with proper care—a favorite for drastic views: no bottom, big creatures and a current to do the work. The boat would pick them up at the end of the wall.

Except that one day the tourists were Japanese, an oddity back then when most Japanese tourists traveled in tight-knit groups of twenty or thirty. If they got in the water at all, each would put a hand on the hull, grasp the mask, look down, and come up chattering like tape recorders in reverse.

But this group was young, six fit divers doing fine to seventy feet, where one went limp. Ravi swam around to ask if he was okay, and the guy beamed, peeling off his mask and ditching his regulator to grin. Then he dropped into full speed to pursue perfection. Maybe he saw the stark difference between ultimate beauty and life in Tokyo. The guy torpedoed a hundred feet, till Ravi caught his ankle, jerked him to a stop and manhandled him into a cross-chest carry, reaching around to stick a spare regulator into the guy's mouth. The guy didn't resist or struggle but breathed hard. No wonder, as Ravi checked his depth gauge: 180 and sinking. Then it got worse: five more obedient Japanese tourists had followed to 180 feet and awaited further guidance from management.

Ravi would shrug at that point in the telling: "I called it a bounce—no decompression necessary if you touch your depth for a few seconds and then bounce back up."

It was a great story to tell because nobody died or embolized or got bent, but they could have, and he'd done the right thing. He couldn't tell the story locally anymore; they'd heard it so many times, but the tourists still loved it in the interim, between the deep dive and the shallow dive, when a body needs to hang out for an hour or so to ditch excess nitrogen. When someone asked if he ever got narced he would reply, "I got a slight case once. I saw a mermaid, but she was a little bit chunky." Not the stuff for prime time, but a boatload of tourists on reprieve from the dull commute loved to laugh. Soon came the fond farewells, the gratitude and tips.

A man in his prime is not proud of working for tips, but the gratitude felt different than, say, for a meal well served or a beer properly poured or a car efficiently retrieved from the valet lot. These tips showed respect and tribute to a dive leader who had safeguarded against so many things taught in certification training but not discussed on board because risk is far-ranging and can never be eliminated. Diving offers fun and fulfillment, and it came to pass as the tourists felt the watchful eye, keen mind, experience, and wisdom.

Still, a nagging mother would say, "It's tips. You want to call it professional fees? Go ahead. Make yourself happy."

As if a man could be wrong by making himself happy.

•

Suffice to say that every day was a full delivery of what Carl Geizen, aka Crusty Geezer, called "the package." The package opened with first impressions on hygiene and mechanical soundness and went on through the niggling details, from the gooey squish and sugar factor of the Danish to towel-dried seats to confidence conveyed. The dive team donned wetsuits and booties, rigged regulators to tanks and slid into buoyancy compensators like Degas ballerinas prepping for a show. Checking computers, fastening clips, zipping zippers, staging cameras, defogging and, oh, yeah, opening air valves and reminding guests that this will be fun.

Descent in warm, clear water to the grottos, ledges, walls, and currents revealed the magic.

Back on board, enriched for life, guests got more of the package with entertainment in the interval between dives or on the lovely cruise back. The package got fatter and sweeter with a bit of narrative at each juncture. Crusty called the anecdotal component critical and best served with some twenty-four-karat bullshit in the mix.

Crusty favored wild tales; they fit his worldview so well. With a male crowd, the crew would dummy up to prep Crusty's favorite entrée. He'd clear his throat and lob a goober to leeward—no dangles, no wipe, showing integrity and know-how with no doubts. Grumbling like an elder down from the mountain, he would venture into polite company, "You know. . . I reached a point in life where a perfect day for me is four hours of work, nice charter like this. Then I take in a round of golf. Then I go home for a blowjob."

Eyebrows rose on that note, with laughs of approval or envy, till one of the crew asked, "How's that working out for you, Crusty?"

"Oh, not too bad, really. I got a couple more weeks of yoga to get my neck stretched out, you know. But I'm getting there."

Most groups strained momentarily before cutting loose the male bonding guffaw. This too, pumped tips.

REEFDOG

Stories were neither idle nor random but tried and true; a story could be tested, once. Heavy tales were reserved for reef addicts, and even then got a long warm-up. That crowd dove two tanks daily for three days in a row, or a week, showing a commitment that would warrant service and tips of magnitude.

Ravi told his 180-bounce story for a few days till Crusty told him to shit-can the near-death experience stuff because it scared the bejesus out of the tourons. Even the heavies winced and worried. You want your passengers relaxed, Crusty said, not anxious or thinking about their lives, jobs, debts, and all the crap they came this far to get away from. You tell jokes, not how a goofy crowd nearly died.

Ravi disagreed, saying most of these people were eager to cheat death. They couldn't get that action in the office unless you counted financial death, which had zilch to do with life in the real lane. Besides that, a story about diver error makes people more alert. Ravi insisted, but he deferred to his captain, after all.

He shared another slice of the dicey side, recalling the routine off Lahaina Roads on the sunken submarine—sunk for good—with its deck at 110 feet. The sunken sub was advanced, a deep dive in anyone's book, at nearly twice the sport-diving safe limit of sixty feet. But what could you do, hang out at sixty feet in the water column? A wreck dive is often deep and advanced, with more rigorous safety measures. But people want to take it on because any dive is cake if you don't choke, and they'd heard how great it was, which it wasn't, given the effort, but every diver suffers a bit of machismo. The deck was flat, so nobody could dip twenty feet below the dive plan unless they went off the deck, which was easy to avoid, though six tourists could resist common sense on any given day.

The submarine was good for twenty-five minutes if nobody sucked a tank down in fifteen. That was if you made slack tide, about an hour window twice a day. Otherwise, it was a rip-snort current. But most days a sensible group treaded near the anchor rode, holding hands or grasping the rode, descending to sixty feet for a check and okay. The scene could get comical with six divers strung out like pennants in the current—till one let go, and the dive leader chased him down then blew half a tank getting back to the anchor rode. Even with viz at a hundred feet, it was a wing and a prayer that nobody would get any stupider than absolutely necessary.

What could a dive leader do but chase down the guy who let go? *Nothing* is the correct answer, but the chronic mishap went to dive leader failure on banging the procedural mallet. When the submarine dive went wrong too often, Crusty spliced a quick release into the anchor rode to free it from the Samson post on deck. Securing the quick release to a spare buoy, the rode went over so the boat could chase the wayward bubbles. Crusty damned his crew to hell for taxing his water wisdom, as he saved the day most days, asking what worthless piece of bilge scum would let things get so out of hand.

One day the anchor snagged on the sub deck, so Crusty went down to free it because you can't leave a fucking four-hundred-dollar anchor stuck there. He only needed a minute. That's where Ravi learned about the bounce and no safety stop required. Crusty could fix most things in a minute and rise with his slowest bubbles, or his medium bubbles, anyway. He couldn't very well hang out: "I can't babysit an anchor and keep this show going at the same time, can I?"

Ravi learned a great deal from Crusty but frankly felt better leaving the Westside for a better boat off the Southside. Crusty's chiding was mostly justified, but doubt stacked up and hindered instincts. Ravi wished the Westside crew all the best and felt free at last of chasing down tourist divers. Ravi and Crusty parted with good cheer. "Take care, brother," Ravi offered, to which Crusty grasped his hand and drew him near for a half hug with his own parting wish:

"*Aloha*, waterman."

It was the ultimate compliment, indicating matriculation to the unspoken rank bestowed by consensus or, on occasion, by the saltiest veterans. A waterman had achieved intuition and skill in seas of all depths, all weather, all conditions and circumstance, buoyant or not. Crusty's mumbled praise filled Ravi's heart and made things right, securing their time as good time, as time for making a living with nobody dying, and their friendship strong. Still, Ravi wondered when the day would come for Crusty to quick release himself from sanity and a last view of tropical blue sky.

The very worst stories got shared strictly in confidence among local divers because a story could spread like brushfire but never beyond the working crews. Some stories seemed indelible as tattoos and never went away, even if the principals left.

Like the instructor who let a guy die in *the Room*. A capable diver and journeyman photographer known for macro work showing ciliary structure *and* attitude, the instructor captured and promoted a rare scene of plankton that looked choreographed by Busby Berkeley—all legs and bodices, top hats and tails in tiers, and a grand finale fit for Neptune's ball. It was a great shot but got old on too much bragging about superior skills and expertise in species, dive table discrepancies, composition, and light, until people wondered: Why the browbeating? Tolerated, more or less, he called out any vessel or person violating his code of conduct. If a boat served carbonated drinks in the dive interval, he yelled across the water that CO_2 in the system will show up just peachy in the autopsy when some poor tourist gets bent and embolized from such a dumb fucking error. The fleet avoided him. Nobody pointed out that CO_2 is quickly absorbed and offed—or that he could stick a Coke up his ass, diet or classic.

His comeuppance seemed inevitable. He found a cave opening on an eighty-foot bottom and went in. Nobody doubted the drive or skill at hand. Sure enough, the opening proved big enough for another hundred feet at a forty-five-degree angle. Then it narrowed to a manageable bend. At that point, the depth gauge showed 130 feet from the surface. From there, the opening widened and came up at another forty-five degrees to a chamber where six divers could surface without banging each other or the lava walls—yes, surface.

By a quirk, the chamber roof was watertight, or else the chamber was fed by bubbles of some kind at a greater rate than the rate of leakage. So the divers were back to ninety feet below the surface but were actually much farther away. They could remove their masks and regulators to grin and say hello. They could tell a joke or a story. They couldn't exactly breathe the gas in the room, a mildly noxious mix of CO2 and something astringent. Lungs constricted.

Never mind. Anyone could short gasp a breath or two on a story or a punch line, notching a unique groove on the old adventure belt, on a scuba klatch in a private room at ninety feet—make that 170 feet to the real world. Machismo motivation led to a destination rich in overview and retelling; what happened when *we* were in *the Room*.

The Room became the new big thing for those seeking extreme thrills—for those needing to demonstrate an inner self as yet unshared. A few took cameras. Photos from the Room were in greater demand than spondylidae—thorny oyster shells with intricate spines and flutes in a flat, pastel finish, formerly found at thirty feet but now unfound till 180 feet because the shallower thorny oysters got plucked then set on shelves to catch dust. The shells proved something, even for the guys who got bent, fetching too deep. Some survived, till thorny oysters were associated with instability, idiocy, and danger. What a relief.

But a photo *starring me* in the Room seemed more worthwhile, pertinent proof of the adventure-lust coursing in *these* veins.

Soon those who bought admission to the Room were not allowed to take cameras because of safety hazards in the ocular incursion disparity or the peripheral dangle or the snag factor or some such. Only the misguided dive instructor could take a camera. Each diver was photographed in the room and could buy an 8×10 afterward for thirty bucks, with additional prints at varying prices. The photos were copyrighted, so non-authorized copies were strictly forbidden, as if by law. The fleet's general smirk helped balance collective embarrassment.

Another dive instructor felt the commercial pull on this rich new vein, especially with his skills as a diver and photographer. *I can do this*, Ravi thought. Nobody has rights to a dive site. Fleet consensus was dour—somebody would die, maybe somebody working his ass off right now, somebody seeking something beyond the daily grind, somebody weak on greed. Many fingers pointed at Ravi.

Scoffing at warnings, the offending instructor put an ad in a tourist magazine, claiming exclusivity to the Room. If you wanted it, you had to choose him because only he knew where it was. Only he had a perfect safety record in finding the Room. Only he could get you in and out without a worry, and he wasn't sharing. That's what the ad said. The coconut wireless had it that he threatened to sue for infringement if any other boat tried to coax the location from a tourist who'd been guided to the Room.

The Room was gladly forgotten within days of the death occurring there, within a few weeks of its unfortunate discovery.

One big risk of cave diving is silt, and no dive guide enters a cave without forewarning to kick gently sideways or in an easy flutter with fins way off the bottom. A cave often has tributary caves feeding at blind angles, so coming out can be fatally confusing without noting coordinates on the way in. Just so, an eager six-pack included a man whose past, like this cave, intertwined with tributary caverns, feeding the primary drive. He seemed compensatory, driven to achieve something or other, hungry for a leading edge. He made the first turn easily enough but had only five hundred pounds of air remaining at 130 feet. But he'd come this far, and then came the little voice that urges the inexperienced or inadequate to *go for it*, requiring him to surface to ninety, then descend again to 130 before surfacing again with a safety stop on the way. He made the Room and actually lingered for the photo op to secure his identity. Then he hurried out. Hurry stirs silt in a cave. He didn't come out—not for a few days, when two rescue divers found him hung up along a tributary just past the deep turn where he must have kicked too hard and gone awry, where a hose snagged on a rock to one side, which he may have thought was overhead, and where any number of problems could have ensued, all of which were likely incidental to running out of air at 120 feet in a narrow cave full of silt with zero viz.

•

Nobody said boo, not calling the guilty instructor a jerk or dismissing the episode with the common discount: shit happens. The instructor retired a few months later, cast permanently into the fatal column, dangerous, and worse, imprinted with murder, second degree.

Litigation on that one lasted longer than anyone cared to follow.

Far better to tell about the doctor who sucked his tank empty in sixteen minutes and grabbed his dive buddy's octopus. After hyperventilating on that, he took off for the surface, dragging his dive buddy along—a guy he met that morning—till the buddy realized they were outpacing their bubbles like a hare passing a tortoise and stopped short at sixty feet, up from 120 way too fast. The doctor, a card-carrying member of the American Medical Association, went full speed to the surface, forgetting to exhale and surely forgetting a safety stop since he was about to drown anyway, which he may as well have done. He embolized with a nasty bubble in his neck and got bent to boot, leaving him screaming bloody murder, or gurgling it anyway, writhing on the surface. Reduced to a whimper, he was flown by medevac helicopter to Honolulu at ten feet over the sea to minimize further decompression. Finally, in the hyperbaric chamber, he got pressurized back down to a hundred feet and seemed to be in less pain but died a day later anyway.

But that story was best squelched too, along with the geeks and lamebrains flopping along the back wall like clown plankton, pinwheeling, riding the bicycle, kicking heads. Realization can be tough, and the toughest yet was that this goofy shit was getting old.

Some days were better than others, but one afternoon nineteen years in, Ravi took the hand-off of empty tanks from the boat to the parking lot behind the dive shop. First came the sixty-gallon tanks for women and children, then the eighties, then, what the hell. . . 160s? But they weren't 160s, only more eighties, along with heavier bones, muscles, joints, and essential attitude, bearing down. Stooping to the burden of sheer, dead weight was a milestone. On that day, in that arduous task, he crossed the line to middle age. A moment earlier it was another working day nearly done, heading for a lazy afternoon, his to enjoy. Then would come evening recreation after a swim or some errands. Maybe he'd call a woman, though he met few women other than tourists. Tourist women felt repetitious and demanding on the glib, social side for the brief return on the other side.

But things changed on that offload. Time slurred on a moment of knowing. Repetition and strain reached critical mass. An afternoon of rest shouldn't seem so bad to a hardworking man, but reality had changed. A man slowed down. A nap in a shaded room with an oscillating fan went from seductive to necessary. A major bowel movement led to the gratification formerly reserved for sex.

On the bright side, a sentient being can assess and adapt.

Ravi Rockulz drifted into his first nap in recent memory. He was in his early thirties only a while ago. Okay, maybe mid-thirties. He woke two hours later pushing forty. Crusty used to grumble most mornings that he felt shot at and missed and shit at and hit. Ravi downed three aspirin with a caffeinated cola to ease the same feeling, then decided on dinner at a quiet cafe, to ponder options. He would list pros and cons, goals and fears. He would make a chart by which to navigate.

After a beer and *ahi poke* (PO-kee), raw tuna diced to half-inch cubes and seasoned with sesame oil, black sesame seeds, cayenne, and *ogo* (seaweed), he felt ready. So he stared at a sheet of paper with no shimmering promise. He could not plunge into 8½×11 of arid emptiness. *Who would dive here? Right out in the middle?*

How long did he sit and stare, waiting for a thought to drift into his brain, down his arm, through his pen, and onto the paper? Where to go? What to do? What to say to whom and when?

He finally wrote:

Being a dive instructor is not enough.

Beneath that, in a few minutes more, he wrote:

Hawaii. Tahiti (?) Carib (?) Indonesia (?)
Photography.

He waited. He finished his poke. He waited, doubting that insight would come, until it came: Okay, go ahead and decompose. Waiting didn't help, so he ordered another round. And with it, the future arrived casually, out of the blue and into his heart, random as the first amino acid on a chance encounter with electrons—three women. Like any women can appear, these women seemed unfathomable. Such is man's weakness for the trick of nature.

Ravi did not visit tourist honkytonks—too loud, too weird, too tediously posed with half-drunk youth claiming identity by virtue of a six-hour flight and a few beers. Throw in some sunburn and call it experience. Those places felt alien, and though a cynical outlook can be tough, reality has standards.

He'd heard last week that a bar in Kihei was "crawling with leg." It seemed creepy and got worse: The light fixtures were dried blow-fish, the same creatures swimming yonder who might have known a certain waterman and approached in greeting. No, not the same because. . . Never mind. The grimy pub bought the blowfish from Asia, but the drift was the same. The place was vile, willfully ignorant of the reef neighborhood and blind to everything but a postcard pose. Ravi ate at home; it was so much better and cost much less. And who would go looking for leg when it schooled up on the home reef? Still some nights needed a change of pace.

Yet he felt like a tourist with no local knowledge, or maybe fatigue had trumped instinct. But no. . . Two of these women were very good-looking and doable in a blink. Who wouldn't jump at the chance? The third woman felt different, a cameo classic and a cool drink of water for a tired soul. Did he look too old? She had to be younger but seemed indifferent to his petty concerns.

Minna Somayan, a *hapa Kanaka Maoli* (meaning *half pure Hawaiian*—her phrase, spoken blissfully) explained that she was of pure descent on one side and a cross of Filipino and Chinese forebears on the other. High cheekbones offset her Polynesian lips and almond eyes. Pearly whites with no cane holes or yellowing highlighted her skin—golden brown as heart *koa*. But features came second. First came grace in a lead from the hips, the eyes, and fingers. Oozing like lava, compelling as *hula*, she could take a man down, yet she mercifully flowed around him. In Hawaiian terms, she combined humanity and nature; her embodiment of the elements was a consensus of components. She smiled on the trim, fit fellow alone with his little beer, his little dish of poke, his little chopsticks, and his pen writing his little list, probably mapping out a good life for himself.

Ravi Rockulz understood current, surge, and undertow and how these forces relate to the power of women; no matter how strong or skilled a waterman may be, he can only stay calm, ride it out, and survive if he's lucky and smart. Great loss may come otherwise if he challenges a force of nature. He knew as well the profound scope of peripheral vision, what a waterman and women sense in the company of predators. Hard and hungry stares do not go unseen. Ravi knew the game, often picking his beauty *du jour* and ignoring her. With practiced indifference, he might reel her in by sundown. A beauty not gazed upon wants to know why. So he looked away.

The trio headed for a table close by. Passing Ravi, the first two women whispered. With her eyes on him, the third woman smiled like a long-lost friend, a friend in need, not a family friend and certainly not a sister. She stopped. "Aloha." She stated what would survive them, what would transcend what came between them, whether a brief greeting or love as durable as time.

Keeping with tradition, Ravi said: "Aloha." He matched her smile and met her eyes, casting indifference to the wind.

She offered both hands at once familiar yet formal, cordial yet symbolic. Grasping hands was spontaneous, warm and natural, a first connection. What a woman. He stood, taking her hands in a reunion of sorts, like intimates meeting after time apart, after returning from the waters of forgetfulness to a reef remembered. "I'm Minna."

Dumb as a fence post where a nightingale just landed, he said, "I know." But he couldn't have known. Could he?

She laughed. "What's your name?"

Ravi. "Ravi. I'm Ravi."

"Ravi? Is that French?"

No, it's not French. It's Israeli. "People think I am French because of my accent. But it's. . . Israeli."

"Oh, wow! That's so cool. I mean, Israel."

"Thank you."

"You're not a tourist."

"No. I am a dive instructor."

"Oh, wow. I love that. I mean I love the water. I'd love to learn how to dive and what not. I know I can." He squinted; how did she know? "I mean I've been around the water my whole life. I can, you know, free dive and what not."

Free dive and what not? She sounded like a valley girl gone native, which is better than stupid but not by much. But then how stupid did he sound when he asked like a college boy at a frat party, "What's your last name? Do you have a job?" Kicking himself for spewing questions so early in the game, he shut up. Not to worry. She didn't think him stupid, just dumbstruck on her beauty and appeal.

"Somayan," she murmured, squeezing his hands, infusing her magic. "I work in a shop. For tourists. I got this *pareo* there." She did a pirouette and tropical curtsey. "Don't you love it?"

"I do. It suits you. What's the name of the shop?" Yes, another question felt stupid, but so far, so fast held no alternative. He wanted to tighten the drag and put her in the boat, and he shuddered at the thought of gaffing.

She smiled more sweetly, assessing him for potential hazard or savoring the moment before murmuring again, "Edith's Beach Treasures." He knew the place. "I work tomorrow. Eight to five."

"Okay."

"That's not what I want to do for my life and what not. I'm in school to be a nurse. I work at the hospital too, as a volunteer. But only twenty hours because of my paying job and, you know, other stuff." Ravi stared at a different kind of woman. She could only give selflessly for half a normal workweek, on top of a regular job and school. She stood apart from the standard waitress or shop clerk or tourist woman and seared his reverie with, "Good-bye, Ravi."

"Good-bye, Minna."

"*A hui hou.*"

"*A hui hou.*" Till we talk again.

She turned away and turned back. "What language do you speak? I mean, you know. Israeli?"

"I speak English."

"Yes," she giggled. "You know what I mean."

"Hebrew is my mother tongue."

"How do you say good-bye in Hebrew?"

He shrugged, "*Shalom.*"

"That's amazing," she said. "It's like aloha."

"Yes, it is."

"That's so cool. I mean, you're not haole."

"I am Caucasian."

She drifted. "You know what I mean. I'm born and raised."

"I love that."

She beamed on cue. "See you."

He sat down aching for another three beers but too dazed to remember how to get one within meters of a woman who had altered *Life as He Knew It.*

Sizzling like a scorched sapling, he found the wherewithal to uproot for a transplanting elsewhere rather than risk a flame out here. Besides, he could get a twelve-pack on the way home for twice the price of a single beer here, which was like two for one and then ten for free, or some such. But even twelve wouldn't douse this fire. Ha!

So he went home and lay down after a tiring day and exhausting evening. He slept like a rock or a very tired Rockulz till five, waking to a cat's tongue on his nose a half hour early. He pondered the future, Minna Somayan, diving, photography, and Minna Somayan till Skinny insisted on eats right now.

She was everything and then some, transcending physical with spiritual—and she held up under scrutiny. Hardly thirty hours from their first meeting she whispered, "We could wait." He shrugged. Wait on what? He could not have her any more than a person could own land. Stewardship might work; they would care for each other according to needs. But waiting wouldn't matter. Besides, they were naked in bed.

They didn't wait until they had to. They craved beer, wine, and liquor to buffer the need after so long apart. The alcohol calmed things to workable levels so they could proceed directly to where they left off in the sweet by-and-by, reconnecting desire to fulfillment at the far end of a long time apart. Some buds made things misty—or foggy—never mind; immersed in beauty or dreamtime, they went deep. They resurfaced and dove again, going macro, seeking detail, until Skinny jumped off the bed like a jaywalker dodging traffic.

This was narcosis, in which the seasoned diver and novice lover ditched his mask and regulator to see more clearly and breathe between the water, to inhale his loved one.

Then came more, to depths where no human could survive. Appetite reduced every experience prior as nothing, as a series of strolls down empty streets. But then love never did make sense.

At one time a two-pack-a-day man because nicotine can take the edge off so much vigor and seething energy, Ravi had quit years ago because smoking can kill you and makes you stink till then. But she lit up and offered, and he took it, inhaling the small death, a reasonable price to pay for this taste of perfection, in which every qualm is incidental to the timeless aftermath. She told him she knew it from the moment she saw him.

He figured most women had the power to know whatever they want from whomever they want, but he agreed, "Yes." He told her he saw her too as different, as a presence, so warm and commanding that he could hardly avoid the whirlpool.

She smiled sanguinely. "Yes. My presence is regal, but I don't say that from vanity. My family was *ali'i,* but we don't talk about that. You see these Hawaiians claiming cultural rights they never had in the first place because what they claim like fishing grounds and netting privileges and what not were *kapu* to them. They would have been killed for those things in the day. We don't talk about it because we lost so much and whatever anybody gets back is a good thing."

They smoked.

Ravi got up for a beer for him, more wine for her. She called, "Do you think I'm stupid?"

Only when you say what not—

"Why would you ask such a thing? Why would you be stupid?"

"Because we were more than *ali'i*. We were regal. That's why I can say that about my presence—for generations my family was held in awe. Nobody could look upon us. People bowed their heads, or they died. But we don't talk about that time either. Some people will kill you today for talking about those things and those times. But I think you felt it—I mean my presence."

"What things don't they talk about?"

"Inbreeding for one thing. We did that. We like to think it's all played out. It was five or six generations ago, mostly. The royal families did it. That's why we lost because our monarchs were mentally retarded. You can't say that. I can't say that."

"I never heard they were mentally retarded."

"You won't. Maybe they weren't."

"But you worry about it?"

"Sometimes. Sometimes I think I sound stupid. But then I realize most people sound stupid sometimes. So maybe I'm only normal. Besides, I have so many other bloodlines. I think we might have had some, you know, ditzies on *da kine* side."

He laughed. "That's not a very nice way to put it."

"I told you. I don't talk like that to anybody else. Only you. I think we'll be together a long time."

You do? He didn't need to speak, with his eyes asking and her eyes confirming, till he blinked. "The missionaries were compelling. They conquered many places besides Hawaii, where monarchs didn't interbreed."

"Maybe. It doesn't matter now. I just don't want to sound stupid." She turned to him. "Promise you'll tell me if I ever sound stupid."

"Don't say what not."

She sat up. "God! What is it with you men? Not five minutes after you get what you want, you're telling me what not to do!"

"No. I didn't mean it that way. You asked me to. . ."

But she was only pulling his leg, laughing and showing him the true meaning of promiscuity in the tropics and what not. Immersed in her simple solution to the mysteries of the universe, he wondered how such a being could ever think herself retarded.

Could This Be It?

Of course, Minna Somayan was a milestone for any man and could pick that man at will, but she'd picked him—a working stiff wondering what and when, and then winning the Love Lotto. Life would never be the same. How could it? She brought spirit back to life with love. She came on from ten paces out, aromatic as *pikake, plumeria,* tuberose, or gardenia. Her feast for sore eyes was a *luau* on wheels, and what wheels they were: toes to ankles to calves, thighs and up. At the summit he jumped for joy and a bit more altitude.

The future became incidental overnight. He felt intrusive on sexual felicitation, on appetite and need hitherto unknown, but communion was mutual and natural at sundown and ten, midnight, four, and first light because love, like time, is constant—right after breakfast, home for lunch, and mere minutes after quitting time. This is crazy!

Yet from anarchy came reason. Each had a past. Ravi knew a nice tourist woman whose name escaped him for the moment. She was it, he'd thought, his one and only, don't stop, and so on and so forth. Better sense prevailed because she wasn't it. She was gone.

Then came Marcia from San Francisco, who taught that great blowjobs could show fervent love—or need. Marcia compensated for what she lacked, but a sated man gave back the difficult truth. So smart and successful but alas, she insulted the cat and had to go.

The real article, on the other hand, kept on coming. When one whimpered, the other followed. Between rounds they slept like the dead, like lost souls, fatigued from the rigors of catching up. Snoring like bears, splayed, drooling, pillow-wrinkled, they woke to see each other as the graceless lumps of flesh souls are born into and then wear out, and they laughed and mounted up for another awakening.

But such rigor cannot endure, not with hope of growing old together, which was the road unspoken. Ravi sighed, dreaming or awake—it didn't matter—recalling Crusty Geizen yelling that he, Ravi, was a bumbling idiot who could fuck up a wet dream. Ravi had nearly cried but now laughed; maybe this was it, and he was pulling it off and never wanted to wake up. This was what became of him, what he would be. Marriage had seemed unnecessary for the two decades since discovering women. The adventures were enough; thank you and *adieu*. Except for what's-her-name with the spiky white hair.

Boy, good thing she split.

Marriage still seemed unnecessary, a socially contrived ceremony to secure commitment. Marriage was a device invented by the female faction to enhance long odds on what might last. Women historically wanted security from aging and gravity, from loss of the nubile magic. So be it. Here was love immortal that needed no such contrivance. Here was a woman Ravi would not want to lose. Pure and simple. And if life could be easier on a bourgeois formality, then let it be. It still wasn't necessary, but he flat didn't care.

It happened in a blink after a rousing exchange triggered by her absence. She'd worked the swing shift at the hospital after a half day at the shop and afternoon classes. She came home to announce a promotion, one with no raise or benefits or what not. But the new title recognized her skill and service: Volunteer Coordinator. She wasn't sure, with the paper pushing and less time on the ward where she could make her biggest contribution, but she'd give it a try because it could lead to administrative bonuses once she got her nursing degree.

Ravi surged, his woman's beauty was dynamic. She was a key player, like him. He disrobed her to make his contribution, which she called a benefit after all. They browsed the pornography section, and soon it was time to relax. But Ravi searched his CD pile for something to capture the moment: Annie Lennox. He didn't miss Annie and couldn't remember her real name. Maybe she'd be back. Maybe not. Who cared? Annie and Minna together?

He glanced back. She watched him.

"You want to marry me?" He whispered it in hoarse uncertainty, as old life drained out of him to make room for something new. Nearly tearful together, they shared another summit, this time calmly as she came to the embrace. They cried and laughed; getting married seemed so much easier than another fuck. Let life begin.

Their love was their relief.

She sang the song all day, not waiting in vain for his love—sang as she made arrangements with the Justice of the Peace for a ceremony at the cottage, "tomorrow?" Skinny would witness, but the State required a human.

So Ravi called his mentor with a "Mayday. Mayday." The lovebirds laughed, but Crusty didn't think it one bit funny to call mayday if you weren't really going down.

"Crusty. Cut me some slack. I want you for my best man."

"You want me?" Crusty canceled his whale watch and put his four passengers on other boats and showed up in a three-piece suit and a mermaid tie.

"Was that your bar mitzvah suit?"

"Yeah. If that means fourth marriage and shit-faced." On a lazy shuffle, he stepped to the line, ready to witness. It happened quick.

The magistrate stepped up with a bible and a red ribbon place-marker that looked unfamiliar. So Ravi said, "Can I see that?" And so he saw the words would bind him forever to his true love in Jesus' name. "Oh!"

"What?"

"This says 'Jesus.' I'm Jewish."

"Good news: Jesus was Jewish. He was the king of the Jews."

Ravi wanted to brain the guy or tell him to get out, but he said, "Are you a civil servant?"

"Yes, I am."

"And this is a civil ceremony?"

"I pick my own ceremonies."

"Good. You pick your ceremonies, and I'll pick mine."

"Pardon me," Minna said. "We want non-denominational." She asked Ravi, "Is it okay if he mentions a higher spirit?"

"Sure. A high spirit is okay." Ravi wondered if she was alcoholic but didn't ask, fearing she might be. That was a load of wine she soaked up—but it was a load of fucking too, so. . . Never mind. She said she was Buddhist and hoped the magistrate understood.

"A higher spirit is okay," the magistrate replied, "but the son of God is not okay?"

"I don't want that," Ravi said. "I won't have that. Will you go along, or not?"

The magistrate stared until Minna touched him. "I'm Hawaiian. We might do this again with a *kahuna*. We won't have Jesus there, either." She stopped smiling. "Jesus would want us happy."

So the magistrate disclaimed responsibility if the ceremony did not stand for leaving Jesus out of it.

Ravi said, "No Jesus. Okay?"

"Jesus is God," the magistrate said.

The signal seemed insistent; this was wrong. A non-Christian groom should get a licensed captain on a boat. That would be cake, with Crusty there, but his boat was over on the west side, and the channel would make everyone pukey, especially Skinny—he laughed.

Let it go.

The magistrate shrugged, "It's your funeral—I mean, wedding."

"What a jerk," Ravi laughed. The magistrate laughed too, so Ravi told him, "Your humor is offensive and not funny. You insult people because they don't believe as you do." The magistrate shrugged again, like a good Christian or something.

Ravi wanted to shake him up but held back—but this *would* affect the tip. *Oh, I know about tips and what a smartass gets at the end of a trip. Asshole.*

"Shall we?"

In minutes it was done, cast in stone and on paper. Minna served *musubi* with pork. Ravi let it slide—she didn't know, and he didn't care, but he felt the presence of those who would care.

Let it go.

He poured champagne.

He tried a summer roll, or was it a spring roll? He could never remember which was fried and which was soft. These were soft, with raw vegetables rolled in rice paper, which wasn't fried but refreshing, till Minna said, "Oh, no. Sprouts."

Crusty glanced up as Ravi asked, "What?"

"Oh, nothing." She blushed.

"What?"

"Look. Alfalfa sprouts inside."

"So what?"

"Nothing. My girlfriend told me they taste disgusting."

"What are you talking about?"

"It's nothing. She said when a woman performs, you know, on a man, it's supposed to taste like alfalfa sprouts."

Crusty's eyebrows rose on that swell. Ravi said he didn't know that and wondered what girlfriend. Never mind. He checked his spring roll for viscosity and tossed it into the hedge. The phase called getting-to-know-you takes months or years, not hours, even at warp speed. Surprises would spring out of nowhere like jack-in-the-box for a long time. He nearly asked if it was true but let go again. Mongoose would find the spring roll and join the celebration.

Mongoose has to eat too; time to move on with life and what not.

Skinny got a shrimp, a scallop, and a squid stacked like in a fafa restaurant that gets ninety dollars for the same entrée. Crusty finished his bubbly and a few more, taking the edge off one thing and another, easing into the lovely afternoon. The magistrate took his leave. Crusty finished the bottle and cried; he was so happy for the lovebirds and for friendship for all time. He fell asleep on a chaise in the shade.

Wedded bliss began on contentment, transcending hunger, thirst, and desire. Propping pillows on the headboard, Ravi lay back with his beloved in his arms. They watched the minutes slide by. They dozed as if peace and quiet were consummation.

They woke near nightfall when Crusty cleared his throat at the foot of the bed. With fond farewells they wished each other long life and a safe drive home. Crusty shuffled out to his car, far from fluidity, high and dry, not yet aground but an apparently old man.

Back in bed, they stared again, perhaps seeking details on the future ahead. Skinny leapt from the dresser to the chair to the nightstand and onto her place by Ravi's pillow. She wanted another entrée. Or maybe she was jealous of the exchange between those who had found the moment.

A week into matrimony, Minna said she would be away for a few days, not to worry. He thought the better part of honor and obedience was to let it be. That worked so far, but a husband should know. So she explained that things happened so fast; she needed to visit her family to ease them into it. "You didn't tell them?" She had not—but he knew that, or would have known, had he thought about her family. He didn't because it felt like a full house already.

"We eloped. You can't tell your family you're going to elope. Once you tell them, you have to invite them. Don't you know, silly?"

She had a point, and he'd been spared the *mishpocha,* or rather the *ohana,* who'd still be hanging out, sucking down the Coors Light and chopping up a few chickens and rabbits for another round of *hekka* in the carport, had they known.

Okay, so go. Then come back.

Okay, and she was gone. Relief and depression rotated. Unmitigated happiness round the clock needed a reprieve. Depression came naturally too because he did love her. He'd loved his old life, and then it changed. It was a joke on board when Ravi forgot to latch the safety cable closing the gangway when the last passenger came aboard. Harmless comments drifted down the deck about Ravi needing to lighten his load, or wanting to lose a few overboard. Nobody laughed or said boo when he left a tank valve closed, putting a diver in with an empty buoyancy compensator, so she sank, sucking on a dead reg.

He snatched her back up from four feet down—okay, six feet, no big deal. Did she honestly think that kicking and screaming *underwater* would improve her prospects? Did she think he'd let her drown? What was that? I'll tell you what: Not the first shred of faith is what.

Is that the same as faithless? No. It's not.

Every diver has a certification card legally allowing her to dive with compressed air. The card indicates successful completion of training. The training began and ended with, *Think and act. Don't react.* She had three quick release clips to remove her buoyancy compensator and lead weights in two seconds flat. Short of thinking and applying her training, she had her legs and adrenaline to kick back up to the surface. So it was on her if the power and adrenaline got covered in mush, and she flat fucking forgot her quick release. Come on, three clicks and out. And up. . .

He could be partly blamed but not wholly. How could anyone think that a charter dive would relieve them of fundamental responsibility in safeguarding her own life? She hadn't even checked her air valve.

Fortunately, more pressing demands minimized Ravi's muttering, and other mutters made it a rare day of no tips. Who cared? Tomorrow would be another boatload—plenty more tourists where these came from, enough for a few more days, weeks, months, and years as necessary. Tomorrow's tourists might have the wits to dive as trained.

Solitude should relax and regenerate a love-bent man. But the old routine closed in. *I need a few days to explain things to my family.* What? That she'd married a white guy? Worse yet, she'd married one from a cult that eats Christian babies for Passover. But they might like that. Who knew? Still, she'd left, and that was wrong. Then he remembered that he was married and in love.

And what about his family? He would face a gauntlet on his marriage to a *shiksa*—an oriental shiksa. Basha Rivka would fire from all directions, beginning with the children not yet born to Ravi and what's-her-name—what would they be? How would they know, and so on to emotional fatigue, to the most pressing question: *So when, tell me, do I get my grandchildren?*

The next day wasn't so bad, till Ravi stared off at meaning as the boat came up askew on the trailer. Somebody yelled, so he backed it down for straightening. Anxieties revolved around Minna. Minna smiling. Minna sleeping. Minna chatting. Minna listening. Minna riding on top. Minna whimpering, oh, oh, oh.

Ravi smiled again, hoisting empty tanks.

She scolded him on the overbearing needs of men, and he stifled the obvious questions. Questions would surface eventually, and he would get to know his wife. Two weeks already felt like long ago. She could touch her lips and then his, easing a pang with a fingertip. With his second beer in hand and more in the fridge, he faced an empty afternoon. It felt unnatural to keep thinking about her, and surely he would think of something else, by and by.

"Meow."

"Yes, I'll think about you. I always do, but you know it's not like that with you and me. I mean, you're Skinny. I mean. . ." *I mean, this is nuts. What's-her-name was right—I'm reasoning with a cat; it's out of touch. Not every cat is as reasonable as you, Skinny. But still.*

Scanning key scenes was like a movie about two young people everyone wants to fuck or watch them fuck—the plot was thin but the action compelling. Minna was a fantasy applied and easy to recall. He pondered gifted directing and new angles.

He reflected on love and depths unknown. He'd been blessed, living high as the rock stars, pro jocks, and politicians. Dive instructors were forgotten far inland, but dive leaders alone could showcase their wares so the women could shop, as women like to do. The difference between watermen and rock stars, athletes, or politicians was that women on vacation weren't pale or raggedy with nipple rings and cootch tattoos, clawing their way backstage. Tourist women didn't need a speech or drugs or the dark. They took care, building careers and raising children, looking good in the light of day, with a fancy for something sinful but harmless.

Where better than three thousand miles away, or six? Who better to bang than the bronze man with the rippled stomach and bulging Speedos? They saw his gift as he explained the rules for not dying on the dive ahead. He moved among people and equipment, his leadership fat-free and easy.

Was that a facecloth rolled up in those Speedos, or was he happy to be here? And what a view it would be, over the ripples to those gray-green eyes. Oh, and those eyebrows, framed by those sandy, sun-bleached curls and the cute little hook in the nose.

Women observed. Some offered, subtly or abruptly, eyeballing or leaning in to press the urgency. "Are you free later?"

He often said no, he was not free later, with the assurance that, "I am not a womaner." Oh, they understood, but he finally got corrected.

"That's womanizer."

"Womanizer?"

"Yes. You mean you're not a womanizer. I love that. I love that you turned me down. Let me tell you what I had in mind. . ."

So from time to time he gave in. The cruder crew stood no chance because they couldn't stop eating and drinking, but they coached—as long as they could distinguish strategy from disrespect. Even so, he came away from nature's bounty feeling relieved but used. These encounters highlighted the shortfall of a service career; who ever heard of a banquet in fast-food format? Some dive instructors worked the buffet, snatching dishes and avoiding the encumbrance of a sit-down. Like all crew, Ravi loved the sinful richness.

But regrets in love earned the nickname "Avid Ravi." He could not disguise the mourning after, so Avid Ravi stuck like a nickname can, harmless but poignantly profiling his vulnerability. Newly arrived women took heed, inferring that Ravi was avidly loving, which he could be. But they often left him bereft. Intimacy felt intimate, after all, and didn't happen so often. Then it went away. Ms. Right had yet to stick around, so the seven-day cycle often began anew, as if hope or something sprung eternal.

But Ravi Rockulz spent most evenings alone with a photography book or new equipment or software or working his images. He might watch a movie or hit a bar for a beer or two. His solitary demeanor appealed to those who took note, like Minna Somayan. They engaged early and often in the spawning ritual, but that was different because just for fun never had a chance against love everlasting. So why did he worry?

Women had stolen his heart before, but this one would be back— best to stay busy on a new learning curve called digital. Technology made his artistry more accessible—no more film expense or hesitation on shots. Now he could freely compose.

The hot and cold social flow and tedious repetition were done. No more morning wake up to see a woman sleeping sweetly and him thinking *yes, pussy is great to have nearby. Should I make breakfast?*

Now was better, but he woke alone. What was she doing? She felt like a puzzle part in a big picture, a wide angle with fisheye distortion. Her scent and smile seemed karmic and eternal, yet her absence distorted the balance. If this was love, he hated and loved it. How could anyone be so bound to another and enjoy it? *And why me?*

Why not? She had her pick. He wasn't bad looking and his manners were better than most, so maybe that was it. But he felt something more, something mysterious. They met by chance. She took the initiative, and maybe that was the odd component—anything he said would have sounded like a line. So he said nothing and sounded like a genius.

So why am I worrying?

It's because she didn't say where her family lives or how long she'll be gone or why on earth she didn't take me along—me, the husband in this marriage. This isn't insecurity because I'm not. And it isn't jealousy because I don't suffer from that.

Or at least he never had. Most tourist women had boyfriends at home, or husbands or children. A few had grown children, and some had grandchildren. They went home by the weekend, leaving the dive guy behind—or they took him along vicariously, for recall in the perfect tropical fantasy. Nobody got jealous.

He counted several maids and waitresses among his friends. Here too he'd remained free of jealousy. But this was love. He wanted to know everything about her. He wanted to know her past with men and boys, maybe not down to macro because it wasn't jealousy but curiosity. Surely she'd had boyfriends, and the pleasures she'd shown him were learned before. You don't get those skills out of nowhere.

Images of her with another had its doubt and pain, but it wasn't jealousy. He avoided that rancorous emotion through reason and practicality. So what? Given her poise, would not another man, or men, of her choosing also reflect character development? *I think he would. Or they would. Or did.* Curiosity showed concern for her welfare. That was all it was. Did another hard-driver fail in the gentle touch? That seemed unlikely, but he did not fear some dingdong going pneumatic on his one and only because it didn't happen.

Hey, let it go.

Yeah, fine, but this didn't add up. Marriage was more than a vacation fling, and Ravi sensed the downside. Family complexity and former boyfriends could be tough. Anyone ever married dealt with transition. It takes a while and begins with sharing. But just as a sailor won't whistle or hope for wind, so a man should avoid knowing everything.

Why?

Because he might find out.

No

Minna Somayan returned four days later, knocking on the door soon after his shower and a beer at the end of work. *Who would knock at her own front door?* The answer was Minna, filling the room and his heart with joy on a sweet touching of lips. "Hi, you."

He melted. Four hands floated like butterflies in a garden, in which buttons are flowers. They cross-pollinated, opening, discarding, breathing steadily as a healthy young woman and a dive instructor can do in a daunting situation. Naked, he laid her on the bed, at the gates of kingdom come.

Moving slower than an old boyfriend ever could, he feasted his eyes and senses. She watched with equal fervor. He resisted his own volition, savoring the moment. He twitched, prolonging the sweet agony till tides could wait no more. In a moment, the world would be his. Why would a man so wealthy need to rush?

So he gazed, not meaning to ask where she'd been. He meant to bemoan his days and nights without her, the distraction of it and, oh, his tarnished image on board because of errors—but it came out wrong. "Where were you?" It sounded like jealousy.

"Oh, God! You're not jealous?"

"No. I don't get jealous."

"What? You don't get jealous?"

"I told you: I don't get jealous." He shrugged to prove it. The delay in physical contact got strained but felt necessary. He stared up. "I've never been jealous. That's a good thing, don't you think?"

"Yeah. It's the greatest. . ." She sat up to slump on the edge of the bed. In a monotone she said she'd been home. That was it. She'd been at her parents' place, explaining things. They wished the newlyweds well and hoped for a long and prosperous life.

The End.

Except that a man so seasoned at depth doesn't need to see a thing to feel its presence in the periphery. He sat up too. She said she also used the time to recover from an episode of. . . well, female things, if he must know, things of a personal nature.

If he must know? Oh, how little he knew. Why would she leave for her period, if that's what it was? He stood up. He looked out the window and back at her snatch, as if for clues. He looked down at the old ramrod, so rudely left alone for so many days.

And, he might as well know, she made good use of her time by getting rid of the asshole responsible for. . . a major part of her problems. Or tried to get rid of him at any rate, though the incredible jerk had this sick notion that she was his property till he was good and goddamn ready to let her go, and anybody who tried to take what was his would be in for a bumpy ride on a very rough road.

Getting rid of the asshole?

She laughed, "What a jerk. You would not believe this guy. He can't even talk. He says, 'You like die?' Like I'd hang with that low-life forever. Like it doesn't even matter that I'm married now. Hell-oh-oh. . ." She smiled in the cute, pixie persona of happier times but failed on a quiver.

Frankly embarrassed that the woman of his dreams touched his thumper in the same sentence of disclosing a former thumper, Ravi shivered in a sudden chill. Goose bumps rose like samurai from the underbrush, as she cried out, "Look at you, with the chicken skin!" She laughed again, a small, forced laugh to salvage the difficult moment, playfully prodding the other little samurai.

"He's. . . what? Your boyfriend?"

"Was. Fourteen years. But it's over. It was a mistake. Hey. I'm twenty-six years old. Okay? This guy, he takes advantage when I'm only twelve. Yeah, I went along. I was mature for my age. But fourteen years? Enough already. One time, I fuck him. One. It wasn't so good. The other times were terrible. It doesn't work with him. He thinks he owns me. He too rough is why. I get out because I want something else. That's why. I want you."

"You mean he didn't know about me, so you had to go home to tell him we're married?"

"Yeah, that's what I mean. I tell him every time. I mean, not married every time. You the only one so far, married and all. Still every time he get all huff and puff, want to blow away whodaguy."

"Whodaguy?"

"Yeah. This time, you da guy. Hey. No worries. He been saying that for years."

"You didn't tell me you had a boyfriend."

"I don't. I told you. I used to. You never have one girlfriend?"

"Why are you talking differently?"

"Pshh. Because. I been around that guy. That's why—hey. You been taking steroids?" She addressed the thick-necked, muscle-bound bully in her hand, which she coddled and coaxed toward testimony one more time in the face of rigorous cross-examination.

"So what? He wants to. . . make trouble?"

"He won't do nothing. He's my cousin, Darryl. My uncle would kill him. My mother too. I always look up to him in school and what not, but I got so sick of him. He's crazy. I been done with him since high school. Eight years already. Besides, we married already!"

"He wants to shoot me?"

"All talk. Listen. You the one. You different, Ravi. I love you. I want you to be strong. Look at you. Look how strong you are."

She'd spoken Standard English, with a subject and verb for each sentence. She'd displayed proper grammar, syntax, diction, and enunciation. Yet she receded to pidgin security. Pidgin is jumbled slang with marginal meaning. Pidgin communicated on *da kine*. Ravi asked, "Can you please stop talking like that?"

She laughed, "Ah dunno."

He went mum, remembering that marriage is forever. She saw and tried to take them back to lovely times, as if the physical could preclude the regretful. But it could not. What had seemed heaven sent got reduced to wrinkled foreheads. He asked. "You tell him every time?" Skinny complained from the dresser, as if to remind. *It's not like I didn't tell you.* Yet she too sympathized for the fools before her.

Ravi shook his head and lost the loving feeling.

"No you didn't." He meant that Skinny had said no such thing, that sweetness and light had fooled them both. The strange woman between them moaned, so the pathos between them could give in to the old pleasures. She peered up, but the kaleidoscope refracted the scene to broken glass and nothing more.

So a mover and a shaker in the charter community pondered his afternoon agenda and how to send this date down the road. She'd stayed longer than most. That's what a pretty face can do. Maybe he could begin that evening, charting a future. Who was that guy, who'd felt eternal bonding in a world turning perfectly at last?

Married? Fuck.

So the world turned back from light and magic to mundane reality. Shadows stretched over the garden, where nothing took root. No more butterflies and gentle pollination. No more mystery and metaphor, where buttons were flowers. A tiptoe through the tulips was just another jizz fest—a great one at that, though a bit heavy on sentiment. The guys laughed that women were all the same once upside down. Ravi had thought different, especially this one.

Then love ended, like life. The woman looked up with a swollen smile to watch his Pyrrhic victory, to see the difference between sweet agony and agonizing loss, and she moaned again.

That was some pent-up mustard. But what did she expect, and why on God's blue earth would she tell the ex-boyfriend about a marriage?

Would she tell the ex everything, as if the ex didn't know? So he asked again, "Why did you do that?"

Glancing at the window, she asked, "You can make more, can't you?" She underscored her familiarity with manly function, not that Ravi Rockulz would begrudge a beautiful woman her frolicking past. But this was different. This woman was his. . .

Yes, many sexual helpers were married or had boyfriends. This was different, with spirit and intimacy—not like that nutcase Marcia who swore she'd keep sucking him off till they were eighty—or ninety! Because she loved him sooo much. This wasn't like that! Minna had a reason to tell her Cousin Darryl about her husband. Maybe telling the cousin was revenge. Some women need to hurt the macho men who "own" them.

Or maybe she wanted to egg him on.

Some women need to win the macho game. Whatever; the beautiful wave collapsed on a strange woman he did not know.

"Oh, God!" she said when a rattle-bucket truck roared up and screeched to a halt. Ravi peaked out at the goofy truck four feet off the ground on mongo tires, with two big trannies, sixteen shocks and a fortune in silly hardware chromed or painted red or yellow. Springs, shafts, gizmos, padlocks, exhaust trumpets, U-joints, and the works. Jumping to the ground, a swarthy man with a Fu Manchu, a potbelly, and a handgun, looked around for signs of life.

"You little cunt! I'll kill every bone in your body!" He fired a round in the air.

She whispered, "Sh. He's so stupid. He'll never find us. What's he going to do, knock on the door?"

Ravi whispered back, "Why are you whispering then?"

She giggled. "Sh. God. You think you're jealous. He's insane."

It was fun, but it wasn't. "At least I'm not haole."

"Hey. You know what? I wouldn't go out to tell him that. Okay? Aw, shit! Look! No wonder he get so mad. His windows all webbed."

Besides that, the irate ex then bellowed like a sad animal, "Our son needs you!"

My Hero, I Mean, You Know?

Wait a minute.

"Webbed" was slang for glass that's been fractured by a hard object. Webbing had displaced keying as de rigueur in minor vandalism. Breaking a window or windshield seemed just as hateful as trashing a paint job and more practical. Most cruisers could take a key down either side to no noticeable effect. Who cared? She still run.

But go broke da windows. For starters, the glass dribbles out in little pieces. Besides that, if a thief breaks in, and you get robbed, that goes to *shit happens*. No big deal. But webbing means you did somebody wrong. A webbed window means revenge.

Minna Somayan's cousin Darryl couldn't be certain if the guy who went webbing his windows was the dude on the bicycle whose ear he barely tickled with the side mirror, or was it that *skinny haole suck wen try fuck his woman*? Hey, that bicycle guy was just for fun, and hey, the mirror missed, not even one little tickle. It was the haole suck, he knew it because of seeing the guy walk to the place where Minna guys like go for coffee and stuff and then mumbling so the guy can hear him, *You fockeen haole suck.* Then he go inside for find the bitch and set her straight but she not there yet, and then he go back out not ten minutes later, get all webbed already.

Ravi remembered Darryl too and his truck and reaching the windows with his back scratcher, which wasn't a back scratcher but a billy club.

83

Danny Blackwell gave him the billy when he quit sport fishing. Danny wasn't even thirty and could name the boat he wanted to work on because he knew the currents, tides, shoal water, lures, baits, combos, seasonal changes, what birds worked what fish and what birds lied, hooking, gaffing and boating a fish, any fish. It ended one morning at five. Danny didn't give notice but took his billy club and faded like a big one into the depths or what was left of the night. He didn't want the billy club but didn't want it clubbing the snot out of another fish, either.

Farther down the dock, he told Ravi that he had a dream starting around midnight, with this big blue marlin swimming up alongside eye to eye and not saying anything but cruising for hours. It had to be the marlin he'd killed the day before—not a record, but a big sumbitch, six-fifty, seven hundred pounds. The deck ran red. "This fat fucker'd been shooting orders all morning, like I was his boy. That's okay. You know it's the fat fuckers tip good cause you took their shit. Anyway, this marlin came on playful, batting the bait, teasing us, like it was time for water polo, not fishing. The fat guy missed three times, so I took the rod and set the hook for him. He reeled for a minute and turned purple, so I got the fish to the boat. Took an hour or so, and the fish didn't look too good, not ashy gray like they get but not much gold or green or blue left. But some, so he might have made it if the sharks weren't around. Didn't see any, but you don't know. So I was ready for the measure and release happy horseshit they go through, and the guy yells, 'Put him in the boat!' I stood there looking at him, but it's his nickel, and he wanted a murder one, so the fish came on board with my regular expertise, quick and safe, nobody stabbed with the bill or crushed underneath. Usually I can take a fish out with a few good shots."

Danny hefted the billy club.

"But this fish didn't want to go. And the fat fucker starts yelling where to hit him, and not so hard because he wants it to last so he can take more pictures. I killed the fish quick. I wish I'd killed that fat bastard. I wouldn't feel so bad today, I can promise you that."

Danny Blackwell frowned like a child on the verge of tears, shaking his head and blurting. "It ain't even tired. It's what I seen about that fish and that fat fucker. Man, that fish was my brother, and that fat fucker. . . that fat fucker. . ."

"The fish seemed more worthy of living than the angler. I believe he had a better life," Ravi said.

"Yeah, man. That's it. I'm done. I don't want to. . . I won't. . ."

"Hey, Danny." Ravi took the billy club. "You did great, man. That fish didn't die for nothing. Think of the great fish out there that your fish saved by showing you what was up."

Danny Blackwell tried to see this greatness but could not, just as Ravi could not see why he got the billy club. Danny calmed down and said: "You're from Israel. You'll know what to do with it." Ravi nearly made a joke about clubbing Jew baits, but he held back; the moment seemed so adequately resolved. So Danny added, "Whack some assholes with it."

Ravi laughed, "The world's got way too many assholes for me to make a dent."

Danny liked that. "Hey, man, you'll know what to do."

Ravi heard it before: Send in the Israelis. They know what to do. He didn't respond because he knew what to do—learned what to do in military training from age fourteen in the Sayeret Matkal. A boy or man is scared shitless, dropping from a chopper forty feet over the Red Sea a few miles from Eilat. After so many times, fear becomes a petty anxiety. Training missions were good for that.

Training taught him that reason rules the survivor's mind. Emotion kills. A military stealth diver learns practicality—nothing personal, just business. Every mission needs a method. Adding emotion was like smoking near a fuel tank, not a behavior of the naturally selected. Nobody gets revenge.

Danny Blackwell quit fishing five or six years ago, and the back scratcher proved handy for webbing. Why would a guy carry the back scratcher to coffee and Danish? Ravi wondered on his way out and picked up the back scratcher because having a thing on hand often precludes a need. And he felt ready to out-asshole the best of them. Hey, it was a game, harmless and playful and maybe useful. It scratched an itch now and then. So he looked both ways before crossing, then whacked a starburst. It felt like a little bang in his universe, and he felt better than usual and knew why.

Or maybe he was wrong—willful and vindictive, caught in an undertow. But some guys need webbing so they have to hang out the window so everyone knows of their bad behavior. Ravi stood up to it, not as a reaction but for truth. Okay, maybe a little bit reaction, but nobody was perfect. Like when a guy came out for a dive and pegged Ravi's accent. "Israel!" Ravi nodded. The guy said, "I got nothing against the Jews. It's the Zionists I hate." Ravi stepped up with his back scratcher, and the guy ducked and screeched, "Crazy fucker!"

"I think you have a problem. All Jews are Zionists."

"No, they're not. You think the Jews in Damascus are Zionists?"

"Is this your mask?"

"Yes." The guy peeked out for his next lesson in politics.

Ravi tossed it over. "You see? You think that mask has value. I just proved that it doesn't. Don't worry. I'll get it for you."

So the guy couldn't dive and got a refund. Ravi paid it because the guy couldn't dive from a Zionist boat anyway. The guy said he didn't need any charity from a you-know-what. Ravi stepped up again, this time with a fist and question, "No, what?" But everyone aboard stopped the detonation.

The mask, a Sea Hares Deluxe with fancy icons favored by divers who go rarely and want to look good, was lost. Cruising at eighteen knots left a huge area to search. Ravi won, kind of, pointing out that the mask was a toy, not quality goods. Besides that: *The guy was a Jew-hating son of a whore. So what? I should apologize? I should pave the way for this hate-mongering bigot? I will not.*

Ravi got probation, termination pending, for three days, to calm the customer, who called the Department of Commerce and Consumer Affairs—groan. Who cared? The hiatus allowed for composure rejuvenation on a man worn thin from hard work and personal issues. With many errands complete, he returned to work, no hard feelings. The boss reminded him that the tourist went away, but the issue might not go away. Ravi said, "So what? I'll call the ACLU or the Anti-Defamation League. Or B'nai B'rith, or Hadassah. . . Might not go away? Fuck, man. Wake up and smell the *halvah*." Then he walked away because it's a free country, where anyone could kiss his *tuchus* if they insisted.

But Ravi's fuse had always been short, and it glowed. His own mother—she who would lay down her life for her only begotten child—admonished long ago: "Nobody gets revenge. That is not what we do. Revenge is not justice."

She had a point: a Jew is not a Christian to turn the other cheek, but if taking a punch or two can lead to peace, then why not? But some people don't like a punch. Or two. Especially from punk idiots. Better to tap their windows to slow them down in their hateful ways. Squint through this, you inbred midget.

Ravi laughed because satisfaction is a terrible thing to waste. Besides, he would grow out of this foolishness and mellow out. In the meantime, a youthful prank didn't hurt anyone.

Well, he wasn't as young as he used to be and the fun seemed less lovable than it once did. And his fuse felt longer. Sometimes he waited for days to get revenge—make that parity among assholes, which often requires patience, just like love.

•

Epiphany in series can be overwhelming, like glimpsing the face of God then turning abruptly to Satan's grim puss. In staggering succession, answers came to a hapless waterman who could not remember the questions. In ghastly perspective, he grasped the window shade and the tortuous nature of paradox. Like the smartest fool on earth, he saw that love is willful—and uninformed. The squat fellow waved a gun in the air. The object of marital devotion squatted between them for a peek at her cousin Darryl, armed and dangerous—and comical. Cuz Darryl looked like the spawn of Yosemite Sam and Cheetah the chimp. What a joke, but looking funny was not humorous. Ravi longed to rejoin the laughing.

"What a fool," Minna said, grinning up at her husband, as if the moment would be remembered for fun. Ravi gazed in disbelief and pity—in pathos and best wishes for her future. "He goes to all these hearings and what not, where people want to stop this and that and what not, like gill nets and aquarium collecting and everything. Darryl guys go out all the time. He can make six hundred dollars in four hours, so he goes to these meetings where these pussy haoles cry and moan, and he threatens to shoot them, and they shut up." She giggled at the notion of educated white people afraid of her cousin Darryl. She watched out the window.

Then came the crux, full circle from only last week when Ravi got struck by love lightning. The next bolt turned the frieze to ash. Objects held form, even the fleshy one of his dreams, who chattered on, as if unaware that she would soon crumble. But she knew. How could she not know? How could she be blind to love departed? Odd looking as her former boyfriend, she grinned. He winced at her smudged lipstick. "You look like Monica Lewinsky."

She felt her jaw and laughed. "She's somebody, you know."

"What is it that I know?"

"I mean, like the president. How awesome is that? I mean, yeah, it was gross, but now she's a household word. She can do anything. Jenny Craig, political whatchamacallit, analysis and what not."

"You want to do that?"

"I just think it would be awesome to have people listening to what you say and. . . I don't know. I was too young then. But maybe."

La vie en rose faded to gray. He was a modern man, free of jealousy. And so he would be because this woman, Minna, was so thoroughly. . .soiled.

The fellow outside would not step up and knock on the door, but he'd rocked Ravi's world. Images rolled on other needs at play, as the little guy blasted away, chipping a fascia, taking out a window, yelling, "I know you, muddafucka." Cuz Darryl paused to reload.

Actually, the ruffled boyfriend did not know Ravi Rockulz. Maybe he meant *I know who you are*, or *I know what you did*, but not *I know you*. Not that it mattered. Nothing mattered, not even two men jilted on their notions of love or jealous pangs ricocheting like stray bullets.

As a realistic man, Ravi knew where experience came from, and it wasn't the tooth fairy. Cousin Darryl appeared to be swinish and psychotic, and not just some of the time. Darryl combined the worst traits imaginable in a true love's ex. Then again, the poor fellow was equally pained. How likely was he to get another date? Then again, wild imagery stung like a branding iron.

Of marginal consolation was the old world waiting, without the turmoil. Soon he could reclaim a demanding but satisfying schedule, good work, good friends and good times. Time heals, and that would be the key. In a few weeks or months, a stable man could stabilize, leaving so much flotsam in his wake. An appetite would return in a day or two, or five, anyway. In the meantime, falling free of emotion already felt better. So what was the catch? For one thing, no more heavenly Minna—not that she was still heavenly; she only looked that way, and memories would linger. She tricked him—him, the willing fool. She told him nothing till they were married, then she swamped him on one wave, a breaker out of nowhere. She played him for all he was worth, which wasn't much on the material side, but as a beacon of light, he shone somewhere.

Hey, who was kidding whom? What difference did it make? He could never see her again as he'd seen her before—no makeup and mussed hair was nothing compared to this. Sinking in quicksand, he reached for vines that snapped like false happiness every time. A fool rushing in doesn't take the time to learn because he's a fool. So the images broke with pain and loss no matter what angle the camera took. Love could fool, and a fool is most easily fooled.

At least Ravi Rockulz would never feel so certain again—good thing, maybe it would be the big benefit of this whole nasty affair.

Let's face it: women are no different than us, with the sexual drive and pornographic needs, except for the aftermath when they want to have babies and convenience instead of fun, as life goes to seed.

Worse yet was the certainty of never getting laid again, not really laid by a woman he cared for. How could he care after this? The angry fellow outside muttered epithets and whose bitch was whose. He shuffled off to leave before the cops came. Then again, that would be rational, so maybe he was only tired. At any rate, Darryl climbed back up and left, leaving no doubt that the havoc had only begun and that he would win her back with his unique attributes.

He'd get no challenge here. Ravi slumped onto the couch and stared at the walls, still as an empty bucket. Skinny jumped from the dresser to the chair and over to the sofa to sit and stare and then walked onto his lap and purred because the crazies were beginning to end. He said, "I want to be alone and what not. Okay?"

"Yeah, sure." She stepped clear of the shambles like a witness at the scene of a tornado. This burg was leveled.

Already out the door, she stopped when he called: "Minna." She waited, bracing for the executioner to speak the finality between them. "You have a child?"

She turned back. "No. A miscarry. Darryl still. . . I told you, nothing. He's a *lolo* head. It was you."

He didn't belabor but rather wondered how the pristine situation between her legs could be so picture-perfect after so much. . . traffic. He nearly asked how that could be, but no. Her magical snatch was another trick of nature, to which he slowly nodded comprehension.

Then, like an injured songbird with a broken warble, she struggled for the old magic. As if digging out from a sordid mess, in which a little tune and clever lyric would ease the tears in her eyes, she sang on stifled sobs, "Your love was my relief. . ." She smiled sadly, turned away and left again.

•

REEFDOG

The days following would have been good for work, to forget. But images buzzed like mosquitoes till he swatted them away. The crew traded glances over the pitiful remains. A woman who worked the deck of another boat came over to Ravi's the following week to help. He said no, but she tried anyway. Alas, she could not help and, in fact, heard Ravi sob as he rolled away.

Then the practical world made more difficult demands. Ravi got word from the captain, "We got audited."

"We?"

First mate Randy said, "Not you. You're illegal. That's why you get cash. They don't know you exist. You can't get audited."

How did Randy know Ravi was illegal? Maybe he meant off the books, but he said illegal was the reason why the payroll came in cash. But Ravi was no longer illegal since he got married. But then. . . "The boat got audited. And Steve."

Steve was the owner. Steve was despondent. Steve spoke from the gloom, explaining the State's demand for unpaid taxes, even though the taxes had been paid. The State wanted more taxes, ninety-eight thousand dollars more because Steve had called himself a consultant on his tax return, so he owed four percent on his income, even though he'd paid four percent on the boat's revenue. The State was willing to put a lien on the boat, which would ease the debt on paper but make the State a partner—a partner pressing for liquidation to clear the debt.

Hawaii has had more state employees per capita than any other state in the United States since it became a state. Steve said the state needed money to make payroll. "Look. You guys keep working the boat. I'll be busy with this for a while. Anybody comes around, just grunt. You don't know shit. Ravi, I can give you two weeks—unless the state guys come around."

Ravi chewed on two weeks. Did Steve mean two weeks, as in notice? Steve shrugged. "I been paying you cash. That's illegal. You got married, so now you can come on the payroll, but I got to let you

go for a while. Maybe two months—but maybe six. We have to see."
Steve didn't expect Ravi to hang out with no job for six months, legal
or otherwise. Ravi had been counseled on annulment, but that could
annul his legality too. Who knew? His counselors were boat crew, not
lawyers, but a few had been to jail.

He also shrugged, a man in a bind, resigned to another round of
adaptation. The passengers arrived for the adventure of a lifetime on
a beautiful fucking morning with plenty good cheer and big aloha.

Hey!

Ravi could not deliver a wonderful time. Events played back in
sickening detail. The handful of days since a casual evening to plan
his future swirled in a vortex of broken hearts, delusion, and failure.
He'd held up admirably till things got cloudy, and the adventure of a
lifetime went dry—no anecdotes, jokes, repartee, site review, nothing
but booties, wetsuit, BC, reg, mask, fins, snorkel, weights. Oh, and
tanks, with the air turned on and the pressure checked.

Got that?

Yes?

Okay?

Okay.

On arrival at the dive site, he said, "Okay, stay close by me. Watch
my signals. If I ask if you're okay, you say yes, okay." He made a circle
with forefinger and thumb: okay. "Or no, not okay." He shook his
head and drew a slice across his throat. "Or eh, maybe." He held a
hand out flat and tipped it side to side. The tourists laughed, though
nothing was funny; "eh, maybe" was a legitimate answer underwater,
meaning things might not be okay. They knew this, or should have
known this. They were certified. So why were they laughing? Never
mind. As he spoke, he tallied two weeks, twelve more days of pay
added to his savings before he would need to. . .

To what?

To walk across the desert on a horse with no name is what. Another
thousand dollars should clear. He wouldn't need any groceries. He
could eat the canned stuff. Pick avocados and papayas.

REEFDOG

Then he jumped in. The tourists followed. Everybody signaled okay, and down they went, perhaps relieved that underwater a dive leader wouldn't seem so morose because the mask hid his face, and his bubbles could fill with happier thoughts. So they cruised the coral heads and boulders, through the nifty arches and along the walls, each tourist stopping to check things more closely, one or two kicking somebody's head. Ravi kept an eye on a tourist who profiled likely to suck his tank dry. Profiling was based on body language, body fat, and water comfort. Like rock, paper, scissors, any component could cancel another. A wiry, nervous man with no experience and apparent fear would suck a tank dry in forty minutes, or fifteen, depending on warmth and movement, while a plump woman with experience and comfort could go ninety minutes on the same tank.

It was hardly rocket science. So he spotted the guy who'd go empty first, a wiry guy flailing and kicking, a guy named Ray who tipped his hand side to side. As Ravi reached to check Ray's air, Ray reached for Ravi's spare regulator—a panic move that every dive leader knows to counter. Ravi did not react, but let Ray take it.

Except that Ray still had a thousand pounds in his tank and moved Ravi's spare regulator in and out of his mouth in a suggestive fashion. Ray offered Ravi his own regulator, but Ravi declined—on a bad day of a bad week in a bad phase of life. Ravi gripped his octopus, bracing a palm against Ray, and yanking it from Ray's mouth, pushing off and tossing Ray's regulator back at him. It felt like one more exit in a series of departures from gentle understanding. Ray wasn't the first man or woman tourist to suggest intimacy with Ravi, but the timing and place were unfortunate. Ray seemed to have had the air punched out of him, as he gave in to melodrama on an emergency free ascent, surfacing with threats of litigation for. . . assault! "You saw it, didn't you?"

So the morning adventure became another round of foolishness. Another tourist on board told Ray to shush—to no avail till the follow-up: "I'm a lawyer and a material witness. Anything you say can and will be used against you."

The ride back went from glum to glummer. Partly cloudy skies bunched up in scud and a squall line and a weather tantrum drew nigh. Moist and rhythmic went to wet and bumpy on mutterings of spurious good cheer.

Good thing we went early.

Yeah, good thing.

Yeah.

Glad we're not headed out now.

Hmm. Yeah.

They huddled and shivered. The dive leader smiled forlornly, his heartache fitting into a world of gale winds and showers.

Then came farewells, "See you next year. Gee, it was great." A scowl implied threats of legal wind and showers, followed by no tips and offloading twenty tanks. Comfort came cold, on faith that life's milestones can be for the best and nearly always show up in hard times. Like a critter in winter finding a few breadcrumbs, Ravi nibbled on faith, muttering yes, all for the best and tomorrow. Well, next week at any rate. Or next month. Or year.

Steve advised after the tanks were humped and pumped that today would be Ravi's last because, because. . .

Never mind, Mr. Steve. Finality was expected and understood. You can't punch the customers, even if they deserve it.

Glum was the balance.

That his car wouldn't start seemed consistent with life's new message, whatever it meant. Long a source of fond association—Ravi and his beater—his Toyota Tercel nearing its fourth decade showed more rust and webbing than not. Massively non-existent on the inside from saltwater dripping off scuba gear, it was hailed for excellence in ventilation and drainage capacity—and its superior view of the road between your feet, no matter where you sat. If the seats had too much *cacka* for your lily-white bottom, *no problemo*: Just peel off the towels for a wash and lay them back down on the springs. Ravi's beater was iconic to an era, *the Time of Ravi*, when fun, adventure, random love, and transport on the lowest possible budget equalled happiness. Then it ended, as if scripted by chance.

So Ravi at the wheel went nowhere, a driver of stillness in the aftermath of the wheezing death throes of the vehicle of choice.

Hail Atlantis! It's a fockeen car! A material object gone the way of all else, proving that we win again!

Or something.

Seeking meaning or coherence as feebly as his tired car tried to start, he too sighed and wheezed, as if he and the car had thrown off the yoke together, cogs missing their niche, metal clanging, teeth chipping, springs chirping, stuff breaking up to the last belch and dying breath as the spirit left the body. Metal, rubber, flesh; all slumped to eternity. Sitting still in his still, dead car, he wondered and waited to see what would die next. Perhaps his own frail pulse would cease, making him part of the pile, ready for the scrap yard. He felt comfortable with that, and relieved because some days must be endured, and tomorrow would be a brand-new start—and the shit stacking up relentlessly could be sorted with fresh energy. Oh, boy.

Numbness filled the afternoon, and a terribly long day felt like days in passing. The awful series of events had been a collision—make that a pileup, into the aftershock. . . shock, shock, clanging like the trashcan lid they put over Tom the cat's head and banged it with a sledgehammer because Tom was the cat, and people love the underdog, who was Jerry, the mouse. But that was a cartoon and over in minutes.

Fuck.

Bleak and foreboding, at least the events of the last few days felt fixed—beyond control of the players, especially the main guy, absolving him more or less from responsibility, relieving him for that matter from the clutches of assessment and decision. Be reasonable—what else could a stand-up man, a *mensch* among tourists, do in these situations? Cave in to tourist whim? No. Not now or ever.

The heavy wind and squalls whipping and slashing on the home stretch had felt fucking perfect, like the denouement in a tragedy with an overture composed by a German, taking the man down to remnants: breath, tactile sensation of salt, sweat and weight, and of course, the ultimate burden—pride, not in sinful measure but in fortitude, in asserting what was right, drawing the line on the wrong.

I win. It doesn't feel so good. If death is the ultimate depression, this must be the threshold.

Mates and friends passed by Ravi in his beater. They passed on foot or rolling out of the gravel parking area, slowing for their friend sitting dumbfounded in his piece o' junk car. They mumbled, *See you.*

Or, *A hui hou.*

Or, *Later, man.*

Hey, it's beer thirty!

Pau hana, brudda. Time for suck 'em up.

Ravi!

He looked beat, without resources, without hope, solitary and done. Maybe later that evening those friends truly concerned and not too buzzed up would stop around at Ravi's place for solace and to review the options. And remember the great good times they'd had.

Twenty minutes of catatonia seemed to do it, maybe providing adequate rest for the bunched muscles that clamored to move lest they stiffen with the wreckage. It was time to hobble home. So he got out, pausing with gratitude for the hunk of junk and the great good times they'd had. He set a hand on the roof to feel the energy. He got none. Hey, what do you expect? It's a car. But still, it's hard to think so many miles and such good fun could not be felt by the vehicle of his youth, what was left of it.

He began the struggle of peeling off his wetsuit for a change into his shorts but fell short once the shoulders and arms were wrenched free. The reserves felt tapped out, and the wind, gray sky, and fatigue chilled him anyway. So he looped the sleeves around his waist and wore the damn thing, stuffing his street clothes into a net bag for the long walk home, or rather the long walk back to the crummy little hovel that would give shelter till the end of the month, next week.

REEFDOG

Passing the Kiawekapu General Store, he recalled his plan to save money on groceries as an exit strategy. That seemed like a long time ago, and he headed in for two beers—the liter bottles that stay cold long enough to drink them if you hurry—and some cat food. Fumbling with his net bag, digging for a pocket in his balled-up shorts to find the money, he stopped when Gene, the big woman behind the counter, said, "Hey. Forget it, Sugar. I got this one."

He looked up, more curious than grateful. Then came the flood of comprehension—of gratitude and regret. She knew. The word was out. The coconut wireless had buzzed with the speed of light. All the words were out. Ravi Rockulz was out of here.

Which felt like perfect timing, but then timing was also the biggest challenge. Gene gave such a small gift on such a hard day that no sooner did Ravi smile halfway and try to say thank you then he cried. He turned to cover his face, to get past his weakness, as she walked around and pulled him to her massive bosom, assuring him that we all have tough days, and he had more friends than he could ever imagine. "Don't think about anything. You'll know what to do tomorrow. Just drink these and take the day off. Take the night off, anyway. Take it easy, Honey. Take a break."

Just as a knotted muscle can let go by the touch of a caring hand, so can simple guidance be a godsend, a loosening agent to reveal what can be known. Relieved by the outflow of pent-up emotion, Ravi walked out and down the sidewalk fifty yards, where he stuffed the can of cat food into his net bag and sat on the curb to drink the first beer. He must have been having fun; the sun was so much lower than usual at this point of his journey home. He pondered destinations briefly, what waited where, what he would leave behind, where he would go. . . and opened the second beer. It went down quicker than a second beer usually does, but the day called for stronger dosage of available antidotes.

He looked up to a twinkling star and looked left and right to affirm its firstness in the evening sky. He could make no wish because of the futility of wishing. But he watched it, as it seemed to ask, *What are you staring at?* He had no answer but felt refuge in its singular twinkle, hardly a wish come true, but a reasonable destination for a wayward soul stuck in life. Soon came a few more twinklers, till any more refuge would have brought on the nausea.

So he stood slowly, carefully, too late to avoid the stiffening, too full of beer to walk farther than the nearest hedge, which would be okay that late in the day with so little light because it would have to be because a man can't very well walk home with a two-liter piss sloshing around inside. So he squirmed to peel his wetsuit down below his pee-pee and to make sure he didn't dribble on it. He could have pissed in it and rinsed in the shower down the beach walk where the tourists rinsed. Except that pissing in your wetsuit smells like piss and marks you as a tourist. Besides, a two-liter piss once begun is harder to stop than a mountain stream, which this piss was, except for the missing mountain.

Recovery can gain momentum on basic relief. No matter what was happening in the world, it was a better place after a major piss. The day still seemed endless in its onslaught, but that was mostly the onslaught of bad events replaying. He'd endured the worst and had only a few more hours till sleep. Then he could start over, in faith.

In the act of rearranging his essential self back into his Speedos and pulling his wetsuit back up to waist level from where it had slipped down to his knees, Ravi knew that the pickup truck passing slowly behind him was local—and way undersized, on way oversized tires, in a compensatory display, way overplayed and entirely tedious.

Then he knew it was slowing and would stop, just as he knew who was inside.

Of course he reacted to the duct tape covering his mouth, but only with nominal resistance to so many hands. Jarred, confused and fatigued, he gave in to what nature had in store because he had nothing else to give and because it wouldn't make a difference, no matter what he gave. So the rough boys who seemed like Cousin Darryl's other cousins muscled Ravi to submission, binding his knees with more duct tape and so on around his ankles. They taped his wrists behind his back and finally heaved him into the truck bed, where he landed like dead weight, no bounce.

Ravi searched for the first star, to wish belatedly for a little cyanide ampoule to crush between his molars for an express ride to the sweetest sleep a man could have. But the truck bounced so badly he couldn't focus on any single star. The giant piss had been just in the nick of time. That was lucky, or not, possibly depriving the best thanks to show these abductors. But then Darryl's cousins wouldn't notice a pissy smell.

What smell?

Oh. The truck.

What, you?

Born & Raised assured from the rear window that no matter what, it didn't mean shit if you weren't born or raised. But he was, but never mind because the miserable ride was brief as the backtrack route to the boat launch. The place was empty at dusk, except for a little aluminum boat with a single outboard idling at the dock and another cousin standing by, waiting officiously for the unsavory task at hand. With the truck backed down to the last inches of traction, all four cousins dragged Ravi from the bed to the dock, where he got propped near the boat. He noted no kicker motor in case of primary motor failure and no anchor to hook the bottom in case of power failure on a lee shore or strong current in shoal water. And no deck or scuppers—this little sardine can could sink on the first wave over the rail. Then again, practical safeguards are incidental to superior seamen.

Besides, no safeguards or practicalities would matter to the fucking haole on board, with the scene shaping up as one more spot on the evening news, taking a minute for the who and the what, with the when and where as yet to be determined. On a nudge, Ravi toppled the last four feet of the boarding process, also noting on his way to one more impact that this little bucket was *Opala* brand, notorious for bad behavior in heavy seas and for its singular flotation mechanism: hollow seat wells. In front of the biggest hollow seat in the center was a plug for easy drainage once the little boat was back on the trailer.

Ravi's head banged the same center seat athwart the little boat, so he passed out, not quite with the same relief of the cyanide ampoule of his recent wish on the little star he could no longer find, but it was a reprieve in any event.

He came to when they were underway. Rolling onto his back on roly-poly waves he wiggled into place. The little drain plug jabbed his back, inches from the figurative jabbing of the last few hours—never mind because the drain plug was also in his hands. Nobody minded when he sat up to see because what he saw made no difference: McGregor Point to starboard, Makena to port with Molokini just forward of that. Kahoolawe loomed ahead, Lanai a faint shape to starboard, so it didn't take an ace navigator to know the plan. They were bound for the aggregation buoy, around which aggregated the complete ocean food chain. Algae and plankton clung to the buoy and to the chains and netting. Little crustaceans and fry made a home there, and so on to the top of the hierarchy. Tigers and oceanic white tips would feed as soon as not. So he lay back down, grasping the drain plug, twisting to test for movement, assured that his escorts craved a satisfaction more complex than brother shark ever did.

The cousins spoke of the old etiquette, by which a hated enemy was sunk with a black rock so family and friends searching wouldn't see the body. A respected enemy was sunk with a white rock, so the corpse could be more easily spotted. The other three cousins laughed at the brutal simplicity of the code and sighed for its honest brutality. Darryl called them stupid, telling them to look over and count the rocks. "Foa hunned feet already. Fockeen *lolo* heads. Fock."

Darryl had a point, and with wind and seas mounting, the other cousins had other concerns. The five-mile rule delineated the proper distance from shore for bad people to go over the side. They agreed to forget the white-rock/black-rock rule this far out, and the five-mile rule seemed equally moot. They didn't call it moot but reached consensus on the key question: "Da fuck?" Why go the full five in these conditions? Hey, three and a half already. Four miles was way da fuck out—no more land already down in the trough, between crests. Four miles would do it, or even three. With anxiety showing and practicality gaining momentum, they claimed their right to be scared shitless in a little boat out so far in the dark. They agreed on *da kine*, four miles, but Darryl steered and restated the full five miles. Nobody else could make the call, on account of *da kine*.

Ravi had wondered how he might face imminence, not as grist for the masculinity mill but as part of his job. Dive leaders must respect the hazards of a daily adventure, must think and act and repeat as necessary to the bitter end. A dive leader lives in the risky suburbs of tourist instability at depth.

Complacency never happened in stealth commando action with explosives and mortal enemies, but leading tourists was a walk in the basil—and that was the hazard. Nobody knew what calmness he would find at death's table. Posing questions at this difficult juncture, he wondered: *Why would I cry over the gift of beer but stay tearless in the face of death? How could love come to this? Could these guys be so stupid?* Images drifted in and got shooed away, like flies on wounded carrion. Should he taunt Darryl on sexual perversion with Minna? Darryl was a brush fire in need of water, not gasoline, but developments warranted drastic measures. At any rate, another strategy was firmly in hand—one that would take the final play to extreme satisfaction. That made sense, with odds so low.

A wave broke, its lip sloshing water on board, alarming the seafaring cousins. Two sawed-off Clorox bottles floated among them, so they bailed. Darryl said, "Cross sea. No worry. No scared. Hey, you." He nudged Ravi. "You scared?"

Yes, Ravi was scared, but a man with sea time and a few thousand dives knows the game is on till the last bubbles rise. A blunt-tipped dive knife snugged his ankle inside his booty, hidden because some tourists wore calf-wrap dive daggers, as if to kill Jaws VI. A dive leader with a knife only encouraged their folly. Pointed knives could stab flesh or a hose, so he hid his stubby knife until pulling it to cut fishing line from reefs or himself free of invisible net fragments.

But a knife at his ankle was worthless with his hands behind his back. So another idea emerged on a ray of hope that maybe, just maybe: "Darryl," he croaked.

Darryl would not answer the man who had caused such pain.

"Darryl, I want you to know that. . . in private times, Minna spoke your name. She called me Darryl. I asked, 'Who is Darryl?' She said, 'Darryl is a man I love. I mean, used to love.' Darryl, she's young. We meant no harm. If you. . ."

Wait, wait, wait. Do you really think this half-baked psychopath will see the light and turn back? Will ease up on a haole suck, coming in here and taking everything? No, you don't. So don't blow this chance to survive, maybe not for long but for long enough.

"Can I. . . have a cigarette?"

Darryl called cousin Kevin by name, but Kevin shrugged, *da kine* all wet. With the wind and waves, they never get one lit. Never mind. Ravi didn't smoke and bumpy seas are best for cutting back. Still, it was a test, showing mercy in small doses.

"One last wish." Nobody turned. "Can I scratch my nuts? Please? I've had this wetsuit on all day. I'm getting a boil. Please."

That was ridiculous in a little tin boat on boiling seas, with all hands bailing, steering, or hanging on. Itchy nuts? Go fish. . .

And a big moon peeked over Haleakala, lighting the froth. In a minute, Darryl hove to and put the engine in neutral, so the little boat turned sideways and another load of water sloshed aboard. The engine sputtered and died.

Sliding down the face of the next swell, Darryl gained steerage using the outboard as a rudder, pulling the starter rope to no avail. Winded, he kept the stern to the swell, cursing the motor like it was another thieving haole. He pulled and pulled for nary a sputter. Fuck it; let the execution begin—better to ditch ballast to work da kine.

The cousins pulled Ravi to his knees. How could he resist? By grasping the drain plug—that's how. So they jerked him free, and nobody noticed the easy flow in. Ravi gripped the plug. Darryl handed a knife forward. A cousin cut the tape from Ravi's mouth. "No need scratch your nuts, haole. They stop itching pretty soon. You like sing one star tangle banner? Have at. I no like you sink wit *da kine* air hole tape up. Make you float too soon. I like you stay sink." Darryl nodded again. They lifted Ravi's ankles, yelling to keep from going *kapa kai* and *maki*—from turning over and going dead. With knees grinding and belly banging the rail, Ravi Rockulz was over and into Kealaikahiki Channel. He'd never felt quite so old.

But this was no time for reflection. He sorely wanted to call out a friendly suggestion that the born and raised among them could take turns sticking their dicks in the drain hole. Maybe they'd figure that one on their own. Meanwhile, a waterman could dead man's float, face down, turning up to breathe as necessary, easing the drain plug into a working grasp and hoping the metal tab was sharp enough to cut the tape on his wrists. He couldn't feel his wrists and didn't want to feel them, and he laughed at the paradox facing a depressed survivalist. He'd hold off for now on cutting his wrists because bleeding to death would take far longer than *Mano* and that gang if they got wind of the hoedown at the aggregation buoy. But a feeding frenzy was a source of fear, so he set it aside and followed directions as written in the manual.

Drifting beyond recapture or hoping they would try it, he breathed. The cousins watched, enjoying sweet revenge at last. Then the tape on his wrists was cut. Should he toss the drain plug at them? No, a pissing contest at that point could have no winner. So he reached into a breaststroke and pulled away as the engine sputtered on another indictment: "Fockeen suck! Stole a drain plug!"

How strange life seemed, awash in a rowdy sea at night, smiling at revenge, evenly served. Was this sweet? The engine died again. The odds on two beaters dying the same day were actually good because beaters die every day, and one of these was doused with seawater. So he retrieved his knife and cut the tape from his knees and ankles to begin the next struggle, pulling the top of his wetsuit back onto his arms and zipping the front.

Another passing image crawled up his spine to snuggle with his brain, the one where George Orwell wanted to know his prisoner's greatest fear. It was rats, so a cage door got pressed onto the man's face, and the rat got him—it was scary and unfair to rats. Ravi Rockulz could set fear aside on the technical level if he had to surface swim at night. But he knew who worked this beat and what would trigger a feeding. The big signal was fear itself, a unique frequency in water, like a tiny dinner gong. He couldn't stop the fear, but few people were better trained or prepared for these dire straits.

What? What was that sound? *Oh, Mister Big Shot, better trained!* The rueful chorus—Basha Rivka and Skinny—*kvetched* and mewed on cue. Who but a fool would count himself better off than most, up shit creek with superior treading skills? But it should be to laugh, and he would look back and laugh, God willing—

What?

Did you say God?

Okay, like the man said, it was down to practicality. *Control your breathing and the fear will dissipate.* But breathing could also ring the chuck wagon triangle; injured fish breathe at the surface, calling out for nature's mercy. Or his breathing could sound like a baby whale or a monk seal. So he kept his breathing quiet, striving for a smooth, uninjured stroke—not a crawl but a breaststroke, easy, with minimal splashing and a nice rhythm. Oh, hell, the current would carry him out anyway, so what difference could it make?

Fear surged every minute or two, as it would in the strongest of watermen, till it subsided again to manageable level.

There.

Fear filled in between heartbeats till it seemed steady, like part of normal. But how can a body sustain such emotion? It can't because the baseline shifts, and by the wonders of adaptation, it is normal.

Until fear spiked at a surface layer of brown foam demarcating two different currents. One side of the foam line was quicker, the seas higher, as the wind bucked the tide. A tide rip was the fishermen's action zone, where the food chain worked from the bottom up, with little critters trapped in the swirl and bigger critters feeding, up to apex, drawn to the diverse menu with the convenience of a buffet.

Thoughts and images swirled and thrashed. Ravi clung to the surest flotsam in the ink-dark sea, the twin visage of his mother and cat. Both chided: *Look at you! After all I've given.* After all her love and patience, he was still bull-headed like his father, that bum. What a waste for a boy with so much advantage, and for what, a little piece of *babka?* Go figure.

He hoped Basha Rivka could meet Skinny and wondered if they would. No. It was too many miles, and Skinny was a cat, so she couldn't leave Hawaii without mortal risk in quarantine on her return, and Basha Rivka was a *kvetch. You want me to what? Travel halfway around the world to meet a vacocta cat?* He could feel the shame and waste of it all, could see the other one, the cat, staring at the immutable truth on her silent meow. He wanted to tell them what a rich and creamy babka it was but kept his mouth shut so one could prattle while the other watched from the dresser as he pulled through two miles, which wasn't too far, really, unless it was part of a four-mile swim. Because any waterman worth his salt can pull through two miles before his arms weigh a hundred pounds and he can't feel his legs. Then he slows down because the last two miles are worse.

So it was near first light, two miles out that Ravi Rockulz gave up. A survivor cannot choose to quit but loses control of arms and legs— fails to find another stroke. Reduced again to a dead man's float, he looked sideways to lift the blowhole clear for another breath. A shark would hit a dead body sooner than a live one, and with the last half gram of energy, he focused on his limp body as a distance swimmer. He had no oomph to laugh at this great joke on himself.

But with strength ebbing to zero, a man resigned can spike on adrenaline, can rise an inch to the better view. Only a hundred yards away an outrigger canoe came on to the harmony of five old men chanting in Hawaiian and a sixth old man in the stern.

Ia wa'a nui
Ia wa'a kioloa

Ia wa'a peleleu
A lele mamala
A manu a uka
A manu a kai...

Six old men? It was the Old Guys Canoe Club. Not that the Old Guys was their real name, but they were old: fifty-five, fifty-eight, sixty years already, some of those guys. Uncle Walter Kanakaokelani and Keahou Lehuamoku had a pact that each would paddle as long as the other. Kimokeo Kapahulehua used to be Bully when he was in your face and stomping your feet, before he found his *kumu*, Kimokeo Manewanewa, who taught him to be Hawaiian with a Hawaiian name and said, "Take my name. Don't mess it up. Don't get it dirty. Represent." The charter crews called them Old Guys because *Elemakule Mea Hoe Wa'a* was hard to remember, and charter crews are simple by nature. The Old Guys garnered respect, descendants of the original watermen.

They paddled more mornings than not, sometimes taking to sea for Niihau or Papahānaumokuākea hundreds of miles out. An open canoe demonstrated what Hawaiians did and yet could do. On their return, they picked up the pace to show what they could do. It wasn't macho but manly because they worked together and loved the sea.

And here they were, moving too slowly on such a unified stroke—but a second glance told why: the little tin boat and its forlorn cousins came into view, bailing, in tow, riding low.

The Old Guys could connect a few dots, so finding four boys in a tin tub with a failed engine and no anchor—and no fishing gear and no drain plug—was suspect. The Old Guys looked annoyed because the Molokai Channel was no sleigh ride. They'd crossed at night for easier wind and waves, only to ride the roller coaster Pailolo Channel and work on around, past Lahaina, Olowalu, Ukumehame, McGregor Point and into Maalaea Bay pounded like poi, only to find a boatload of bad boys adrift. They'd paddled a zigzag course to find Ravi, to save him from drowning while saving the bad boys from murder one.

Whatever the reason, the morning emerged more mercifully than yesterday. Ravi waved an arm and squealed, "Hoy! Hooyee! Hoy!"

The outrigger veered, till the helmsman told Ravi to duck under the *ama*. That was easy, but he could not lift himself aboard. Not to worry; he wasn't coming aboard—not aboard the canoe, anyway. He would go in the little tin boat, home to the land of aloha. So all the boys and men sat adrift, listening to Uncle Walter indict wrong behaviors and enumerate the reconciliation required of these lands and waters.

"Our *kuleana* to care for the sea is no different than our care for ourselves. Our *kuleana* to our ancestors and our descendants goes seven generations back and seven ahead. We can have no *kuleana* without *kokua*, with responsibility we must have cooperation. We share as we share fish or bread, like Jesus guys, though we did it first. You guys. Shame. Shame. Do you hear what I say?

"My *hanai* daughter is a *hula kumu*. She is mainland born. I am her *kumu*, and my family is hers. She came to me troubled. She heard bad things from people who may have been Hawaiian or some-thing else. Mean-spirited things. They hurt her. They went against my teaching because I had not completed her lessons. So I taught her that Hawaiians have a great sense of justice, besides righteous-ness and love of the land. These values take care of everything. If you are not Hawaiian, you can live Hawaiian. You must trust in the care of things and don't get angry and *huhu* and swear at people. It's not Hawaiian nature to do that. By your actions, you know aloha. Giving way to anger brings resentment to your blood, and that is not Hawaiian. A true Hawaiian will avoid confrontation. You see locals complaining because they are proud of being born here. They're often not Hawaiian, but we know what's been lost. We have faith in justice. You will hear a Hawaiian only by listening. . ."

He spoke in English and Hawaiian as the old guy crew shifted in their seats, cooling off but staying mum because of crimes recalled, like when he, Uncle Walter, got picked up with Keahou Lehuamoku. Keahou sat one seat up, as he'd done since the day he got saved with

Walter from another drowning and murder one. The details mattered for naught but to remind of responsibilities to place and people.

"You. Bring him up. Take care. Show him what you know, so he won't call the police, as he should but maybe won't. Because if he doesn't call the police, then you won't be in prison for years. Unless you find another way to get in. Okay?"

So Ravi Rockulz came aboard the little tin boat for the second time, hauled in like a ghost net, as a lifeless lump with spent flesh trapped in the mesh. Three cousins attempted aloha by virtue of no threats, no epithets, no hints of violence and no talk of bitterness or blame. Darryl hung his head through Uncle Walter's talk, as Ravi came aboard. He spoke when the tow party got underway again, with strong young men sitting, as the Old Guys paddled. Dishonor rose with the sun, with sky and sea bearing witness—as the lead boat found its rhythm and pulled, as it had across Molokai and Pailolo Channels at night. The boat in tow seemed derelict in spirit.

Couldn't even kill one fockeen haole. Looking feebly up, Darryl asked: "When you. . . make *da kine* with my girl, she say my name?"

Overruling this criminal's spurious thoughts, Ravi dredged up a salt-hoarse voice that grated like a rusty hinge. "No. I made that up. That was a tough. . . situation, you about to kill me for fucking Minna. We fucked. . . what? Fourteen days, once an hour, hour and a half. But then when you wake up and want to fuck again, it takes so long to blow your chum, and then once you fucked, you know, six, eight times in a day, then you got to fuck and fuck to get the hot sauce out. . . Two weeks, six or eight fucks in a day is— what—a hundred twenty fucks or so before I knew you existed. She didn't tell me. She was blowing me when you drove up in that circus wagon. Wiping her chin when you got there. You know?" The cousins looked worried. But not Darryl. Seasoned veteran of the pissing contest to the death, Darryl smiled. Ravi said, "Hey. This good, eh? Talking. Listening."

Darryl nodded, agreeing at last. "Let me tell you what I know." And softly he spoke, as the grimace moved awkwardly to the face of paler complexion.

So the shoreline came on as Darryl twisted the dagger. Squeamish reaction could not be contained, so Darryl honed on sordid details. "I knew you was lying when you say about my name. She no care who, she get one Portagee sausage go *fump, fump, fump*. She no care, she love one cornhole cozzin." Darryl's narrative raised a few eyebrows until the cousins pondered personal prospects for cornholecopia. Speculation ended when Darryl asked, "Ey. You like die?" The cousins looked down because no, they no like die.

Darryl's skill in a shore break was another point of pride, keeping the stern to the breakers till the bow thudded and surged another eight feet on the next wave to high and dry. All got out and slouched for the road but Ravi, who crawled out and up, not like a first critter evolving from the sea but as a waterman surviving attempted murder. Tourists passing on their fabulous sunrise strolls said hello. Rising at last, he gazed up. The early birds murmured, "Did you see him get in?" These long-distance swimmers were truly remarkable, another wondrous part of Paradise. A woman said, "Lucky we live Maui."

Ravi looked drunk, completing the task begun fifteen hours before, staggering home on a heavy shuffle.

He drank from the hose but had no strength to pull off his wetsuit. So he cut it off, cutting this bond of servitude, though it might have saved his life. The net bag with his shorts and cat food sat on the steps. Gee, it was great to have friends.

Walking inside to the little red beacon flashing on his answering machine he pressed play on his way to the drawer for the can opener. Small voices told of tomorrow's charter and low pressure with a system moving in and high pressure from a tourist woman who wanted to get a drink or something to eat or something. Then came: "Hey. Dis Steve Shirokiya wit da Immigration Natchazation Service. You no need one lawyer. Okay? Call me back. Okay? Plan to come

right down. Okay? Oh! Bring your green card. We get one problem."
Hammers fell in sequence, banging numbness to oblivion.

Never mind. He opened the cat food to quell the demand, as if
she didn't know where he'd been or how it compared to a glob of cat
food. In the hot shower, he shuddered and cried again but stopped.
He dried, oiled his body, and lay down. He got up, made coffee, had
a can of sardines with crackers and gave one to the cat. She chewed it
halfway and left it, underscoring the indifference of love and nature.

Laying back down, he dozed deep and woke to a knock at the door.
Two people stared at each other as if to ask, *What are you doing here?*
Each held papers.

A court server served a subpoena from Hundred-Grand Kreeger,
the ambulance chaser from hell, famous across Hawaii for suing the
state over any accident on any beach or charter boat, citing negli-
gence, claiming damages of 1.5 to 5.1 but mostly settling for a hundred grand. The insurance companies settled because defense would
cost a hundred grand. On this subpoena the plaintiff's name below
HG Kreeger's read: Darryl Ito, seeking damages of one point five
million, demanding proof of legal entry on charges of civil rights
violations on attempted murder by stealing a drain plug on the high
seas, and on to discovery and deposition and on and on.

The server left. As Ravi drifted back in, the once true love followed, saying that a love like theirs didn't happen so often. "Once or
twice every few years is all, and, I mean, if you could give us another
chance, I can show you love like you never had." She stumbled over
salacious potential on her way to innocence.

He laughed short, more of a snort over one thing or another, till
she slapped his back. He waved her off. "What did you bring?"

"Oh, this." She unfolded a newspaper to a story of plastic garbage
smothering a swath of ocean. "I thought you'd like to see it. You're
such an enviro and what not."

The paper said: *A plastic soup of waste floating in the Pacific Ocean
is growing at an alarming rate in an area bigger than the continental
United States, scientists said. It's a hundred million tons of free-floating*

plastic adrift between Japan and California, an island of plastic garbage that you could almost walk on.

A lawsuit for one point five and a dying ocean could darken a day but felt like chaff in the breeze. Among those annoying flecks he saw what he hadn't seen before. *You're such an enviro and what not. . .*

Challenges aligned to reveal their lesson: failure to see bears consequence. A randy young man opted for a romp in the canebrake instead of a rightful path. He'd seen the way but held back. Now the trailhead opened. "It's time to move. Someplace not so crowded or pressured. Someplace still tropical." He looked up. "You know?"

She didn't know. "It's strange, how you feel about people. You're so good at what you do, and you like some of them, once you know them. But you hate them as a group. They disappoint me, too, and I love you. I haven't figured that out, but I think I'll be here forever, probably down at the hospital in the worst of it."

Inanimate as a fence post where lovely songbirds perched, she no longer beckoned. He needed time to sort and forgive—and to step away from blaming her or himself. Because dying many times through a night makes a new man in the morning, more or less. He looked out at her car. "Can you take me to the airport?"

Yes, she'd take him to the airport or anywhere and accept whatever he chose. He was her hero—oh, she'd admired him already for the usual heroics and his great skill with people in the water. She knew why so many sought him again, whatever boat he worked, one year to the next, and why women came to him, even if that part made her self-conscious, compared to those others. But the big thing was, "You swam the aggregation buoy! Fuck, man! Darryl guys are good with their little boats and what not, always showing off, taking stupid chances. They don't know what you know. They don't want you getting any of this." She meant fish or *puhehe*, not one little speck o' da kine because it's theirs, only theirs. They'd see it die first, and you too. "But you! You swam the aggregation buoy. You know how. You know what it means out there. Ocean spirits feel you. *Ikaika*, man. You it. And I know you. I feel proud of you.

Maybe I cannot be yours, but I love you like the ocean loves you, and for the rest too."

He wished she'd said *for the rest too and what not*, but a strong man forges ahead, no regrets. "Someday I'll know what got me in. For now, I think about what got me out there." Tears welled in her sparkly, almond eyes. "Come back in three hours. I'll call for a flight."

Yes, she'd be back in three, and meanwhile, she would just, you know, hang out. She hesitated as if for a look, a nod, or a touch.

A kiss? Then she left.

•

And so our story begins.

Cut! Cut! Cut!

But not quite yet because no matter how twisted, a yarn can take another kink. The world spins in disarray. Life is daunting till chaos finds a pattern and perversity seems part of the weave.

A tourism professional won't ask, "Are you fucking kidding me?" But the question disgorged in a calamitous cavalcade when an Israeli passport proved not viable for entry to French Polynesia without a special visa—never mind that one's US visa expired years ago. The French were not opposed to Israel, as the French government representative assured the Hawaiian Airlines service rep at Kahului Airport, with Mr. Rockulz listening on speakerphone, "But! An Israeli cannot enter French Polynesia without the special visa."

Why not?

"It is not possible! But! You may obtain the special entry visa to French Polynesia at some Israeli consulates, though you may obtain it most easily in Tel Aviv. If that is not good for you, you may obtain it almost as easily in Los Angeles. Or in San Francisco if you prefer. It won't take more than forty-five minutes."

The good news was that the Papeete flight would not depart until tomorrow night. "So you have time." Beyond that, the Hawaiian Airlines service rep frankly had people waiting in line, people with flights reserved and paid, people more entitled to service than this rude. . . *what evah.* "So? Whatchou want? LA? San Francisco? What?"

"Why did I get a reservation for tonight if the flight is not till tomorrow night?"

"Show me your reservation."

"I made it on the phone."

"Next, please."

"Wait a minute. How can I fly to San Francisco or LA and make it back in time for tomorrow's flight?"

"I have no way of knowing that." But the service rep did know the remaining option: deportation back to Israel, charged in advance. If the passenger didn't have the fare, no problem, he could go to jail, which is not a bad place for the destitute. Ravi hoped to avoid further referral to Immigration Naturalization, who would surely expedite a solution. Avoiding INS seemed hopeless with an expired US visa, but he'd only have to explain to the immigration guys that he was done being illegal and had, in fact, landed—a married man entitled to the pursuit of happiness, life, and stuff.

Then again, that tack could land him back in localville, with the picket fence, the pit bull, and big-wheel truck. Escape from America seemed best for all parties, but he did want to avoid the pesky deportation process, with all those forms and phone calls likely to take the staff past four, what with required clearances from the FBI, CIA, Homeland Security, and so many new departments mandated to keep America free. He did not want to return to the Middle East, and he could buy a ticket due south. So maybe they could ignore the visa violation and help the alien onto a flight to French Polynesia.

Ravid Rockulz qualified for immediate removal from US soil despite his affinity for Hawaii reefs and for his service to society, his photography, artistry, and lovable traits—which should qualify him for a ration of aloha, if you don't mind. Maybe marriage would count for much. Where was the wife, anyway? Or the marriage certificate? Was this trip of a commercial nature? And whereas the destination country requires a return ticket, in this case the country of departure requires it strictly one way. INS knew the tricks of strangers marrying illegals for a few grand then thumbing their noses at a bureaucracy that busted its chops to keep America free. Worse yet, a marital audit could reveal the shallow brevity leading to matrimony. Was the marriage a sleight of hand meant to slip an alien in? Or was this love?

Married in two weeks?

Ravi and Minna's marriage paled next to the magnitude of their love. Does that sound convincing? But it's fact: Ravi and Minna gave in to social contrivance in a spirit of cooperation. They had done the right thing in a context of non-stop kinky sex. They did not rush to the altar. The marriage was not to make Ravi legal. It was for love. Since then, things changed.

In one more week?

Yeah, well, it's like the bumper sticker says: *Shit happens.*

He found out she'd dilated indiscriminately for weirdoes. She took refuge in pidgin with prideful ignorance in her semi-retarded delivery to claim a spurious identity: local. What could a citizen of the world do, stay married? The INS should send *her* back. She was like the alien who jumped out of that guy's rib cage. Why would he stay married to her?

He wasn't too sure how to untie the matrimonial knot. But they have ways, annulment or no-contest. A lawyer would know—a good Tahiti lawyer. Besides, what do these *lolo* bureaucrats care about my marriage? *They don't. Sundown and payday—they care about that.*

So with discretion as the better part of practicality, Ravi took control. "Hey! I just remembered. I'll be right back." And he walked away from the ticket counter, a free man on the move.

Minna could not compensate the damage but seemed intent on trying. So he shuffled out to the curb where three security guys blew whistles and yelled to move. She got out to open the trunk, but he called, "Wait!" Wait because he couldn't get a ticket without a special visa—without a trip to Israel, LA or San Fran at six hours each way plus airfare, cab fare, hotel, and meals, plus the vagaries of a foreign consulate in California and unbearable fatigue. He'd look like a world-class schlepper at every security shakedown.

"I might have a way," she said, as he pondered rushing the last hundred yards onto the airplane.

"Almost noon already. Tomorrow is Saturday. What can you do?"

"I can call my auntie today, and maybe you can go tomorrow."

The day was hot but coldly practical. Minna's Auntie Velma had not spent the last thirty years running a federal judge's office fa notting. Velma had also been classmates with Kevin Kaneshiro, with whom she shared a career path and a joke that the judicial and legislative branches would always communicate on their watch. Besides that, Kevin was Velma's fifth cousin. Auntie Velma and Kevin Kaneshiro had another cousin Kiki Hironage who worked as receptionist at an Asian consulate in Honolulu. Kiki was *mahu*, a friendly fellow whose occasional boyfriend was U.S. liaison at the same Asian country's consulate in San Francisco, next door to the Israeli consulate, where another gay fellow. . . Five phone calls can move the world in an hour on proper connections.

In this case, *ohana* Somayan needed removal from the fractious folly of its n'er do well nubility, Minna of the woeful judgment. She what? She marry one haole, and now he get all itchy for leave already? Well, whatchou going do?

Auntie Velma could also help with annulment if the ex could come up with a permanent address where documents could be sent.

Who said things couldn't happen for the best? By early evening, Ravi and Minna shared a new satisfaction. She'd secured his exit. They rode back to the south side. He got out and leaned back in. "Your mother doesn't seem to hate me. Not like Aunt Velma."

"She is nice. My mother."

"What did she say on the way out?"

Minna shrugged. "'Cute *da kine*.'"

"Thank you," he said. "I owe you one."

"*Nada mucho*," she replied. "You don't owe me."

Maybe not, but still. "How come your aunt and cousins got names like Kaneshiro and Hironage?"

"Poi dogs. Velma's parents and grands worked the cane fields. Now everyone cousins and in-laws."

"Sounds painful."

"She's okay. She just doesn't want to hear it from you."

"Your family pulling strings to make it happen. Impressive."

"You should see what George Bush's family did."

The laughter felt spontaneous but faded fast. Would she pick him up tomorrow at one thirty? She would. "I'll call when I get my seat assignment. Then I'm kosher, I mean legal. . ."

"I know what kosher is."

"Oh, yeah? What is kosher?"

"It's like, you know, da kine."

He laughed again and stepped back to wave as she drove away. Inside, the scene of his life was an empty set. He went back out and up the beach to buy sardines and crackers and a bottle of water. Back inside, he lit a candle and sat on the floor to eat lower on the food chain. Back out for a quart of beer, he returned for the last time and slept to the wee hours before heading back up the beach in moonlight to Gene's house. Gene and Skinny would be sleeping unless Skinny ran off, feeling abandoned after giving her love that was supposed to be returned forever. How do you explain life to a cat?

Stars beckoned again as a better place to be, till he stopped to feel the place—his place. He wasn't leaving the tropics. He was only changing latitudes. He would only change a pattern gone bad. Things were working out. He would wait on Gene's porch for daylight, to tell Skinny again of life's changes. . .

But the little orange cat waited, front paws tucked in moonbeams. She called, "Meow!" So he held her to weigh his greatest loss: pure love. What the hell was Gene doing, letting her out on her first night, in a new neighborhood with unknown hazards? But he shuddered with relief; no dog, no collar hooked on a fence, no nothing. Skinny purred: This is what we've come to.

"I know. I thought I'd hang out. Why not?"

He sat against the wall and she curled onto his lap, where they drifted into slumber the few hours till dawn. At the edge of the lot he set her down for a leak and joined in. They watched each other and the breaking day, knowing it was different. She cried, so he picked her up and walked back to Gene's porch, where Gene waited with coffee and two dishes, one with water and another for shrimp, which Ravi called extravagant till Gene assured him the shrimp was too old to sell, but Skinny loved it, and it was cheap next to psychiatric care.

"Who needs psychiatric care?"

She lit a smoke and gave him the look. "You need coffee?"

"Yeah." They sipped. "Why did you let her out?"

"She got out. I couldn't find her. Where was she? On the porch?" He nodded. "She knows. She's fine. Don't worry. She's eating."

"Yeah. Shrimp."

He peeled his shirt and arranged it in a corner, where Skinny curled again, and Gene pulled him in for a hug. "Take care of yourself. I got Skinny." She went in to get ready for work. Ravi watched his cat another minute then left quietly, except for the heaving sobs.

He packed and called for a seat assignment. The airline agent reviewed the file and confirmed the unusual visa status, not allowing continuing stay in the US, but he was free to exit on special provision of the Federal District Court of. . . "Federal Court?"

That was none of an agent's business, and if you want to go ahead and assign a seat, then everything will be okay. Okay?

The exchange felt locally vetted and secure.

Minna came early. He was ready. On the way he asked that she check on Skinny—alone, please—and see that Gene stays okay with the situation. A question lingered in the air: Why? She gave him a card with her mailing address for news of arrival and whatever he might want to report and what not. Neither one mentioned his mailing address or what it would enable on the man-and-wife situation.

At the airport, she honked and waved at friends, remarking how much fun Leila used to be when she was drinking. "Twenty-five and no more for her already." She called it terrible, pulling to the curb in a better mood, again praising his water wisdom. He sensed another wisdom, displacing the difficulty. They should say goodbye like friends who had taken care of each other and not mention the promise they'd shared before witnesses and the state.

It went okay, hoisting bags, finding his itinerary and passport, down to the easy farewell. He feared an embrace and a wrong message but couldn't just walk away. Teetering between wrong messages, he got stuck, till she came in to whisper love forever. So he gave in, though he longed to forget. He said, "Thank you," and her sad smile quivered.

He turned without looking back. "I don't mind," she called. "Don't forget."

He raised a hand to affirm his knowing or in farewell or maybe wishing her peace.

·

Okay, once more, from the top, with feeling:

·

And so our story begins. . .

We Will Begin Regular Boarding in Just a Few Brief Minutes

Modern times present a sensory overload thick as white noise in a fog. The electron melee numbs a modern person who must insulate the self from the onslaught. That person might seem "out of it," as reclusive intervals allow deeper access to a singular place of meaning, to sort valuables from junk in a crazy, mixed-up world.

Reflection commonly occurs at the gate, between check-in and boarding. Ravi Rockulz wonders with faint jocularity if the airlines hire psychiatrists to enhance the travel experience so the adventurous, uprooted, disenfranchised, and homeless might take inventory of their hurried, empty lives.

Let's see: This item used to be happy, so I'll lean it into a corner with these other tidbits I once thought were good. While this, that and those other items are sad, very sad, so I'll stack those on the middle shelf, next to the huge shelf already sagging with tragedies.

Ha. Ha, ha.

Very funny. Why am I not laughing?

Ravi Rockulz would have called anyone crazy—or in need of a scratch on the head—for suggesting that he would abandon Skinny. Well, not abandon. Not really. Gene loves kitties; she said so and has three of her own, and it's the same neighborhood, so she'll know where to look if Skinny goes home. Or what used to be home. It's still home in many senses. And a fellow can always duck back in for his cat, once he gets settled in his new home, in Tahiti. Maybe. Maybe they have a special three-day visa for pet rescue. Or a half-day visa to salvage the last vestige of love in life. Maybe an in-and-out Skinny visa? A fifteen-minute quickie on account of she only weighs seven pounds? Who knows? Maybe Hawaii will get easier on the tidal wave of construction and the forced march to convenience. Maybe Aunt Velma will agree to something or other, and the old place will be up for rent again, and he and Minna can be friends with some personal friction now and then for understanding. Why not?

But speculation on the old neighborhood and salt-o'-the-sea soulful living one more time is a symptom of happiness going away. Old neighborhoods do not shape up again. Wishful thinking is a last gasp, especially with former happiness front and center on life's lazy Susan. You can watch it go round, but you can't reach it any more than bringing money home from a dream. They fade away, the moments, the wish, the happiness, the life. For that matter, what's the diff between a moment and a memory? Each is illusory, giving way to new moments and memories in the making, until they too. . .

Fuck that. You're so full of shit. Happiness in the moment is fun. It feels good unless you're a nincompoop schmendrick who needs to call it illusory—a bump on a log who never cut loose and let go headlong for no tomorrow, for a million moments in a row, like from jumping off a perfectly good boat down to a hundred and forty feet, where reality can't get any more real. That is, with tanks and daylight and magic, not tied up in duct tape at night.

Fuck that, too. Let it go.

Except that letting go might be the new buzz phrase for modern people processing the overload. Except that cliché is often grounded in reason and necessity. Like now when a man of fortitude can let go with alacrity—except for Skinny. She'll likely leave the body in this life before he does, and that's a consolation—a difficult scenario made worse by departure. But enough of that. All people and cats must take the journey sooner or later, always alone.

Enough.

Put your mind elsewhere. See the future as an oasis, beyond the shimmering heat, forming up and solidifying.

Hey, I told you to ditch that illusion noise. Horizons are good because life can be dynamic, and mobility can balance the view with cross-cultural experience, not to mention the interconnectedness most integral to the yadda yadda, hitherto and forever more. Outer-connectedness? That's good but can't very well be integral. Outegral?

Let's face it: Until the last hundred and fifty years, a trip over fifteen miles took a whole day. That was on land, and a seafarer could cover what, a hundred or two hundred in a day? That doesn't count here because life on board in the olden days was a commitment of no return, for a year or two anyway.

Now a traveler can span half the globe in a day, ostensibly adding years to normal life span in time saved. Besides that, jet travel adds scope to life, with access to exotic places formerly reserved for intrepid or wealthy adventurers.

Except that time saved is not time earned. Frequent flyers actually get less return on effort than their ancestors, who seemed happier on fewer miles and no amazing free gifts. They lived free till the end—free of surrogate adventurers in oppressive density chattering tediously about physical contact with places never understood, never lived but merely visited on brief reprieve from personal ruts. Like now, in the gridlock of vacationers at a gate, suburbanites, pedestrian masses yearning to be free, sighing in wonder at the fabulous sights and sounds they will soon own by virtue of physical presence. I was there. I did that. Count me in for six days of it before returning to the job—or the position—where promotion and a decent market share mean more of the best of everything.

Then comes supplemental acquisition, a third car or an extra TV. You can't beat the newer, bigger screens with hi-def, hi-tech. New wall-to-wall carpet a few years ahead of schedule might be nice, along with new appliances or a nip and tuck. Like that couple on the far side of sixty: Her cereal bowl tits and his drum-tight neck make them right for a zombie thriller from Hollywood. How much better could things get for people like that? Well, they're headed to Tahiti for starters, or finishers. Who cares? They're not hurting anything. Unless he's an industrial asshole hell-bent on killing nature for personal gain, like the billion-dollar developer on the Westside who lives in Europe but insists on fouling reefs in the name of livelihood—for the people, don't you know? Still, the tits and neck are enough to make you wonder where we'd be without growth.

"Mark my words," says the disheveled man in the seat beside Ravi. "One day soon, this will be the Executive Club."

"What?"

"The Executive Club. You know what that is, don't you? You pay a few hundred bucks a year, and they treat you like a human being, like they used to do for free—like washing your windshield and checking your oil. You're old enough to remember that. You look old enough— no offense, but you been run hard, huh? Anyway, now you pay extra. A few hundred and they *give* you cold soda, air conditioning, pay phones, and magazines."

Ravi nods, hoping the man won't go berserk, though events of recent days and nights have fairly inured him to hazard. The gate area is choked with more bodies than seats, with people squeezed in, sitting on the floor, mulling, lingering around the counter, where they are reminded to stay in front if they're in line and somewhere else if they're not. We must follow these rules for security.

To keep America free?

Nobody listens because no place else is available. Still, reminders defer to rules—more rules for more people doing wrong things. But what can they do? They could stand on their heads or lie down, but that wouldn't free much space. They could vanish into thin air. . .

"You see what's happened? That building shields the sun on half the gate area, but the rest gets direct sunlight. You think you're hot? You're sweating? You think it's beading up between your eyes and rolling down your nose and your neck and ribs? Me too. But I got news for you: We're in the—pardon me—fucking shade. Ten degrees hotter over there. We got the good seats. I'm telling you: this'll be the Executive Fucking Club." Ravi swelters but feels grateful for marginal shade. Wiping his forehead, he ignores the fellow next door.

But no—"Okay, we feel it. They feel it. You watch. Next thing: They'll see what we see. It starts small—up-charge on Executive Seating. That's shade. You got what, two hundred seats on this side? They'll start at five bucks. That sells out; they'll test the market on ten or twenty. What the hell—you spent hundreds on the ticket, so why not start cool? Not cool, but not so hot. Get it? I'm in business. Tourism. That's business. That extra twenty bucks adds up to what, say, two grand on a full flight? And most flights are full. That's pure gravy. Two grand could make the difference between profit and loss on some flights. You'll see. People crowded tighter than a gnat's asshole in the not-so-fucking shade. Make that cool, soothing shade. Or you sit with the poor grunts sweating bullets on folding chairs, no foam, in the sun. Sweating. What they do best. You wait."

Ravi waits all right, avoiding the nutty guy nearby, even as the disturbed man tremors on aftershock: "Shade, my ass. You can't say it's cooler, but it's not in the sun. It's like calling an open flame cooler than a blowtorch, but death by fire is still hot."

Overhead TV keeps the area up-to-date on the war for democracy. Then comes news of accidents, tragedies, corporate criminals, and insulation from due process. Children balance the news, coping with disease, starving or excelling at sports or studies.

"They call this air-conditioning," the troubled traveler bemoans. "Except that there's no fucking air, and it's not conditioned." He has a point, but a bray does not soften the truth. Does he think nobody knows without his saying so?

Can, anyone quell the blubbering? Maybe a brief response would calm this guy. "You know. . ." Ravi wades in. "This airport used to be small. It had those stairs on wheels, and you walked across the black-top. This used to be a peaceful place."

"Yeah. Used to be. You should have seen it before *you* got here."

Was that a presumptive you, or did the man mean nineteen years ago? Who cares? He's a bigmouth—even to a tourism professional with solid haole blood quantum.

Ha!

No matter where he's from, an idiot can make a tough scene worse. Ravi Rockulz is emissary to evolved persons of the world as they visit the tropics. The problem is that nothing stops a diarrhea mouth but insolence—possibly a threat of greater magnitude. But conflict won't likely salvage a situation, and frankly. . .

"Good afternoon, ladies and gentlemen. . ." The voice advises that regular boarding will begin in a few brief minutes. . . A minute is sixty seconds, not more or less, though they can seem longer, down to heartbeats. "Those who need more time or with small children."

"Yeah, a few brief minutes," the smoldering fellow says. "Like ten or twenty. Like we're not already a shitload of brief minutes late."

"You know," Ravi wants to ease one man's burden on everyone, to explain the difference between discomfort and horror, but he stops. He stares. . . Is that a bird of prey swooping in? Are those wings, or pectoral fins? And the teeth. . .

"Yeah, I know. And you're about to find out."

Prey can die on a gulp or require killing prior to eating. Prey can suffer heart failure. Prey can squirm. A predator won't pause for a brief minute before the jugular. Time stops in nature's transition. Lightning quick or eternally slow, brief minutes can stretch for matting and framing until normal cadence resumes. A minute can be far from brief.

So the night passed. Heartbeats, flutters and the crowd below gave consolation in acclimation. Fearful minutes can shift a baseline until fear is the new normal. Which isn't fearless if you're still scared shitless. But death becomes familiar: *Oh, death. How's it hanging?*

"Scared shitless" is a figure of speech but feels literal on gut tremor and regret. You can't go back, so you pull for the lights to the southeast where fine folk savor aperitifs this minute, until a burbling stomach grasps a woeful scene: woofing *Jorge's Chili on the Fly.* He wishes he hadn't, not yesterday or any day, or was that earlier today? *Jorge's Chili,* convenient and filling, bubbled lightly on its little gas stove. But Jorge giveth and Jorge taketh away. Heavy cayenne did not balance hygiene, as Jorge added beans, burger, and water as the vat went shallow, as it pumped a head of steam to *Jorge's Cannonball Express* screaming round the mountain with the station coming on. . .

Good thing, no date tonight. . .

A gob of saltwater down the hatch melts the brakes. . . but wait! A waterman knows, squirming to free the shoulders to peel the sleeves and pull the torso, so the train won't crash into the station.

Then he'll sprint because sharks love shit.

Then again, a sprint could ring the dinner gong. Then again, drifting may be worse because predators prefer the easy meal, adrift with no movement. So a bone-tired waterman is yet again between a shit and a sweat. But time and tide, chili and saltwater wait on no man. Unable to peel a shoulder without sinking, he vows to buy a new wetsuit with that stretchy material, if only he can. . . But he can't. So he sinks while peeling the neoprene off his shoulders. It's only four feet or six, what else can he do, spew in his wetsuit and draw the toothsome gang to chow? What former sins could warrant such balance? He laughs and cries at the karmic correction upon him and begins the surprisingly easy process of drowning. Only then does the old familiar welcome him home, as the shoulder dislocates and he's free on a shot, make that a double. Pain is another punch line.

Peeling to below his butt, he floats like a dead man. Another swallow of seawater wrenches the gut with a presence, neither threatening nor loving but compelling. With fear at Mach IX, he sputters: *Yea, though I swim through the valley of the shadow of death, I will fear no evil because they're nature's creatures in their task. I won't rise from under a tree to the green shimmer. I'll shimmer in blue until my guide also weakens and—unnggmmph. . .*

He seeks grace, parting ways from a former self. The burbles persist. Pressure rebuilds, and he remembers a tale first told long ago, about a guy with a stutter who couldn't get a date because he got stuck on: "Wwoo. . . woouulld yyou. . ."

The guy finally met a woman who presented well but twitched like spit on a skiddle, especially when she got excited. They dated, and it felt like love, so they wed. She wore white and got excited, wedding night and all. So his pals tied her to the bed and rigged the ropes with slipknots and led the ends to the next room, for privacy. Then the guy with the stutter told her, "I luuuu. . . luuu. . . lluuvvv. . ."

"Come on," she said.

So he got her clothes off—what a dish—and eased aboard, and it still felt like love, straining at the braces, so the guy yells, "Okay! Cccc. . . cccuu. . . cccuuuuut her loose!"

What a laugh. Ravi drifts, wishing the guys could see his perfect delivery. But open mike night is brief. Nature hones on stink. So a man swims quickly from a shit slick, trailing his wetsuit till he smells nothing more to lose. Feeling good as dead, blinded by salt and darkness, he feels the approach and squints for a dorsal fin—but a shark seen is never so frightening as the one unseen. . .

There! He anticipates the bump and hit. He drifts. . .

•

"Please have your passport open. You must have your passport open along with your boarding pass."

"Now you're fucked," ventures the slovenly fool, who likely judges by accent that Ravi is Israeli and not French. "It's the whole wide world, and then the Jews. Am I right?"

The derelict got it right, so the intrepid Jew smiles and so does Skinny, who slides over for Basha Rivka, glum at her misbegotten son fleeing the Land of Bondage. He will fly to Tahiti *in spite* of ignoring the special visa when it was easy in *Yisroel.* He'd refused because he refuses her, his only mother, but she still knows best. He reasoned that Hawaii is not Tahiti, and he would not chase a wrong visa because a man draws the line. *But look: married to a shiksa! And not a generally goyisha shiksa either, but a real shiksa chilarium! Now tell me again, what are the children supposed to be?*

The goat bleats as Mano hovers in the murk. So what?

"We will proceed at this time with boarding Zone Two."

"Two, schmoo. They ought to proceed with the Twilight Zone. You remember the Twilight Zone?"

A man of sultry nights and mosquitoes in his ear ignores the buzz. He rolls to Minna, who drove him to the airport twice, with devotion, who would have driven him home in the parking lot, as if. . .

As if what?

As if she's very horny is what. What the woman from San Francisco called "bonkers horny," an ugly phrase perhaps suited to Minna Somayan. Not a bad girl, except for her unscratchable itch—the same itch that made her perfect not so long ago. She had baggage and worse. How could a woman open herself to a beer-bellied macho idiot? Hateful to boot, with his beady eyes, swarthy face, faint moustache, and chin stubble. His grubby hands.

Oh, that side are not her people but interlopers by marriage. They claim originality in postures of machismo—and she could only love me. What is that? *You did what with that guy?*

Nothing! She revised her story with happiness and light: *No! Not like I did with you! What difference does it make? He made me do it. You didn't. Did you like it? Do you think I'm good? Did you think that was my first time? Did you think, gee, she's a natural, first time and all? No. You thought: Oh, God. Because you think only of yourself. You were the one, and I'll tell you something else: I loved how you felt. That should make you happy, but it doesn't because you have to bang your stupid question: Compared to what feeling? Do you have a problem imagining a man who isn't you? Would you feel better if it were a little white guy with tan lines on his ankles?*

No! Ravi doesn't care. He can't say it because she won't understand. It was not other guys—it was Darryl. Not that any other guy would be okay; just that Darryl is disgusting. Romance? With Darryl? Like with kissing and everything?

REEFDOG

I'll tell you something else. I never got intimate with Darryl. . .

You never got intimate with him? You just told me you did. Now you say you didn't. What, he didn't want to get intimate?

Oh, no. He wanted it. They all want it. I wouldn't do it. I couldn't—not any more than you could do it. It was. . . ugly. Never.

But you just said. . .

So the replay obsesses on sharing and denying and the distinction between flesh and love—till the bedraggled man says: "Listen: The difference won't go away. She's practical; you're irrational, down to your passion for reefs and a cat and women you hate to lose. She knows you but can't defend casual sex, so you distrust her." Ravi senses insight and fate, whimsical and unavoidable.

Life will be easy down south, away from a love mugging and casual bad judgment. The stranger says, "You look like a *shmata* from the washtub. Did your mother not teach you to look like a *mensch*? Don't worry; you fit in. But look at you. Would a little effort be so much to ask? Do you care what people think?"

Patting the wrinkles on his shirt, Ravi feels less reasonable than last week. What he wouldn't give for a quiet seat somewhere else, but it's a terminally crowded world, so he turns away.

Tell me: Would your mind rest easier on a man in a tweed suit? Or stripes with a vest? Or seersucker, so to speak? No, it would be no easier—that's what you're blind to. But a woman's experience is the same as anyone's. Men are stronger but weaker. Self-abuse is not necessary but compulsive.

But what did she expect, hearts and flowers? A night of humiliating fear and attempted murder at the hands of her inbred cousins should lead to what? Lime on the corpse is what, down to nitrogen, potassium and the other. Calcium? No, the other, not calcium. Never mind. It's none of your business anyway. *I'm not sure why I'm even talking to you. So shut up. Bug off. Okay?*

"Whatever you say, brother. I don't know why it came up. We're at the airport, Tahiti coming on. Let it go, wouldja? What the fuck?"

Yeah. Whatever.

Except for the stink. He survived. He crawled from the sea and up through the Valley of the Shadow of Bureaucracy, which begs the question: Integrity has what in common with detainment/deportation? Neither is adrift at night. Get it? *Deportation, shmeportation; I'm outa here. José, can you see?* He nods off and jerks awake, laughing at love's delusion and the road not taken. Let's peek around the bend to twenty years married and forty pounds gained, with drinking and denial—or maybe just drinking and kids, four or six because they couldn't stop. Her smile twists on a litany of demand and regret.

The future could have recalled the fork again and again, each time wishing on every star in the firmament, first or fallen, that the fork had done its job. And so it has.

"Thank you." He's headed out. She lacked depth; he was over his head. How else could it play except to play out, as fleshy passion will? But something lingers, a vestige of fear. Or is it love?

Aka Leialoha called it spirit and said it could displace fear with the other. Fear shows lack of faith—you're on the menu. One man's angel of death is another man's spirit guide. Sharks feel comfort. They smell fear. Prey is afraid. Love is a phantom. Like Mano, it must move all the time.

Why? It doesn't feel like love, leaving home with some camera gear, a laptop, and clothes in two duffels with some dive gear. Nobody travels with tanks. Or weights.

I got my weights because they're expensive and my cross to bear, though we don't use that phrase because of the burden—too bad for Yushke and us. And him a Jew, too. . . Some sandwiches and sardines. Some crackers. Why not? You drop forty clams on a few snacks. Money falling off for hotels and meals. No job. . . No cat. She must wonder who will scratch her neck just so.

Mano shimmies past and comes around, like Skinny in her way. "So be it," he says.

"Be what?" asks the hobo.

Minna is home, commiserating with her nosy in-laws and judging him—*him*, who has forgotten more about their near shore than they'll ever know. She likely ponders tonight, heading out with the girls to get loaded for relief and to see if something new and slick might come along. She'd do anything for him.

Thanks, really, you've done enough.

Is Mano smiling? Or is it indigestion or impatience?

Ravi sings like Bob Dylan to those nearby: When you got nothing you got nothing to lose. . . Is he worthless? Is she perfect? She eats and belches, laughs at the wrong time and speaks poorly. Yet he exceeds her. Does he love her? Is a new car less worrisome on a first ding?

Or am I only tired? Should I not stay and let us season in our love? She's sleek as a mermaid, and I want to. . .

"We're now ready for boarding all zones."

"About fucking time," the grumbler grumbles.

"I'm not going," Ravi replies.

"What? Not going? You're here. You'll get nailed on the ticket!"

"I already got nailed. I don't got to go. I got a beauty in love with me, and I didn't look back. I hate this shit." He grunts, hoisting his bags. "I'm not going." He turns to the wino to say so long because the easy way out is the way back in—he can hole up at her place, so to speak, till INS gets it straight: A married man can join the struggle to keep America free. They'll lose interest by their first coffee break, and things should cool off elsewhere too. Any man can get another job—are you kidding? A reefdog of renown, on a boat, in Hawaii?

Announcing his decision to thin air, he turns to face Mano. She yawns, like it might be time for snacks and nappy poo. Except that a shark has yet to visit a boarding gate, and the obtrusive fellow butts in with advice. "You can't go back. Not now. Not ever. Face facts. Get a life. Get some balls, man."

"I hope I never get like you," Ravi mumbles, shuffling forward with the line, boarding at last. He'll make distance from that guy. *What's it any of his business? Why can't I turn back?*

He inches along, timorously wondering: What's the chance of him sitting next to me? Given the odds on recent events, a grumbler one seat over may be a five to one. . . But the grumbler is gone, defying the space-time continuum, not to mention the thought-speech inter-face or the eccentricity-insanity high wire. He inventories faculties, brain synthesis, and fundamentality, facing a challenge that any dive might come upon, but. . . *I will not react, even as eyeballs roll back. I will think and act. I will breathe slow, deep and steady. I will surface slowly as my slowest bubbles. I'll hang out, fifteen feet, three minutes. . . No, ten minutes. . . No. Three is plenty.*

Stabilized at a socially acceptable level, he scans to see who's watch-ing the loony-tune in blithe functionality. He restates his position and context, hoping he doesn't look like a mumbler. He wishes a nice day all around and wonders if it's technically over. The day. And it's night.

Where is that nutty guy? Did he occur? Time can disappear in a gulp. . . so he scans systems once again because a man so jolted can suffer a figment or two and may press the boundaries of appropriate-ness in his attempt to function and/or reboot. He often scorns com-mon values as seen on TV but needs to sort fantasy from real. . . ity. He thinks, perhaps, that the voice was his, so he asks the lady behind him if. . . there was a. . . you know. . . a man, an unkempt fellow who looked—he chuckles in good humor—who looked hosed down and dried out. "Like we say in the boat business—like he was shot at and missed and shit at and hit. . . Did you see him? Here?"

A whimper escapes through the woman's compressed lips. Ravi shakes his head, and she does too. But it couldn't have been him. He doesn't talk like that. He laughs again to sustain goodwill, but the woman steps around and marches to the gate. Not to worry—he's too happy to be that other guy, but where did that guy go? And why do so many eyebrows bunch up on a holiday traveler headed south? Well, this is no weekend outing, and he might look a tad unhinged, so he strolls into the approach tunnel, squinting for stability in the eddies that indicate movement of a large being just below the surface.

Oceania

Arrival at the Papeete airport is after ten, closer to eleven—way past ferry service, and a man shuffling into a hotel with two duffels gets a rack rate of a hundred and fifty dollars for the few hours of night remaining, for a crummy little bed and a toilet.

Or he can shuffle three blocks to a grassy area for more frugal digs on a bench at more popular prices. Arranging his nest, he walks off to squat and laugh again, this time at two dumps under the stars in short order—till the waves mount, and he topples against the tree alongside. He stays buoyant; never mind the uncouth character of getting by.

But Your Honor, a dog did that. Big dog. Woof.

Thanking his lucky stars for life's continuing function, he sacrifices a handkerchief to the greater cause and is uplifted, a homeless man in a park in a foreign country farther from friends than a man would care to be. He feels irrationally happy, like Skinny, who pushes sand or dirt over her business, then chases in circles or jumps for a leaf. He picks a star and wishes Skinny upon it so they may beam up and down together. He is neither homeless nor friendless because of Skinny and years of aloha and old friends and other reasons best sorted tomorrow. So he nestles in, laughing one more time at the customs agent who asked the nature of this visit. He shrugged at the open camera case and shrugs again on a park bench. "I'm a professional photographer. You have beauty here in need of immortality."

French humor may be questionable, but *esprit de corps* is immutable. *Et voilà, Monsieur*: he's in. He sleeps.

In the morning, he spends a fraction of the evening's savings on French pastry and a double latte and is still a hundred forty-four clams ahead of the game. It's a short walk to the ferry for the next island over, a few miles out, but the ferry should not go *huli* or have cousins for crew. It'll be like the morning run, underway that very minute. French Poly is due south with a dash of east, in the same time zone but long ago, and Ravi Rockulz feels a brand-new day.

For starters, the southern hemisphere has a fraction the landmass of the northern. Human population is also fractional below the line, which shrinks the cockles on a misanthropic heart. He feels giddy at prospects for new friends of differing fins and feathers, so to beak—*I mean speak. Ha!* With so much ocean and so little land, a man can meet others of his ilk, instead of avoiding eye contact.

Moorea draws nigh on lush greenery, unlike Papeete, an urban center on a rock called Tahiti. At least it's only the twenty-first century and not the twenty-second or twenty-fourth.

Never mind. Nine miles will be the moat to the tropical castle.

A spring tide lifts all hearts—but wait. What if?

The ferry plies into the channel between the breakers to either side, as life turns to the flip side. Arrival anxiety is a nice cup of tea compared to sea monsters, engorgement and. . .

"Fuck." He shudders in the lessons learned, on fear and faith.

This is homecoming. Crosscurrent and undertow are everywhere. So what? It's time to grow some moss under the tropical canopy, time for hot blood to cool down. Pushing forty is not pushing fifty or sixty and should be wiser than pushing twenty. So he tingles on the approach, as a million fronds wave in the breeze. Who knows?

He asks the bus driver at the ferry dock for a cheap hotel. "Monsieur, it is only cheap if you are rich. Are you rich?"

"No. I'm not rich. But I. . ."

"Taverua."

"Okay, take me there, *si'l vous plaît*."

134

The ride is good, hot and ponderous in a place that makes sense. Tired and sweaty by mid-morning, he feels landed in a dream of what happened to Ravi Rockulz back in the day when once upon a time a man arrived on a tropical island. . .

Regret and hope seek balance. Oceania in a dewy, green tint and heat-rippled haze feels receptive. Into a happily ever after, a child of misfortune and man of the world become one. Tropical beauty with very few human people is vaguely recalled in Hawaii. The home stretch feels off kilter, unhinged, and disconnected, heating up on re-entry. Soon this jungle and sea will feed the hunger and quench the thirst. The monkish might call this view a delusion of desire, as they obsess on itchy garments, celibacy, silence, saltines, and water in a lust of their own. Is this so different?

I, waterman, am here.

A man who makes his living underwater, who packs his worldly belongings in two bags and flies on short notice to an island below the equator on a vague ideal is not your average commuter. He knows that a blessed life is better than a stifled one. But what if it isn't—but damn, this looks right. And a mid-life migration is liberation from attachment. What could go wrong, with nothing more to lose? Or is that a loser's rationale? Or the sophistry of the spirited failure?

Ravi Rockulz may be one more salty dog seeking snug harbor, but he is by no means average. Farther afield than most, he seeks a tropical paradise not yet gone to seed. Most men choose the grind with a woman of mental, sexual and cooking competence, defaulting on a weak laugh to what we must put up with—as men.

A few keep horizons in view, curious to see beyond the compromise—but most settle for less because security rides a unicorn. Ravi Rockulz went nineteen years on a razzle-dazzle romp and steady work with no tomorrow. Women saw the fire in his eyes and wanted to camp beside it, to roast a few weenies and tell stories, to drink and dance and fuck till Sunday. Some of them loved it. . .

Then he fell onto the bamboo stakes. . .

Stop that—

He never had the money or inclination to pledge rent, groceries, clothing, medical, and a nest egg for the children. He avoided average life with stunning success—then failed on a snatch distraction because they're not all the same, upside down.

A guy makes mistakes; it's okay—even constructive if the guy comes out smarter. Am I up and out, or what?

This is not sophistry. Like they say in Vegas: *If you don't play, you can't win.* Life is a casino, and you can lose, too. But a betting man enjoys the roll because everyone craps in the end. A bachelor with no friends, no job, or home is not a loser. He's down on his luck, is all, but this feels right—no more tropical props; this is real. Is that so hard to fathom? Palm trees should be more than commercial landscaping and reefs need fish more than aquarium hobbyists do. Hawaii excels in fantasy for sale and regret. Commerce trumps culture, and money rules. Decimation and growth are made to glisten in magazines and fetch top dollar. Or lower dollar in group sales. Scenic vistas and terrific cleavage prove value either way, and the money rolls in on jobs, affordability, and growth.

French Polynesia is merely hot, with so much less and so much more. Growth is green; vines creep amid species not going extinct, no landscaping required. Bird chatter and insect hum blend as the bus door shuts on a man delivered to the country road of his dreams. The smoke recedes, and so begins the now here. He listens in a meditation of minutes or years and walks up the drive. Gears shift and fade.

They call it Hawaii fifty years ago, though the road from the ferry dock was foul with excavation, heavy equipment, and reef destruction. A woman one seat up pointed at the clubhouse, restaurant, and golf course under construction, the first in French Poly after years of struggle, till the yen prevailed. Japanese engineers with clipboards checked for perfection, preserving their honor and nothing but, avoiding personal failure and self-destruction. Ah, well, fifty years might be time to get through this life of madness.

The house up the drive is asleep, though a child ambles out with a key, pointing to the bungalow at the top, advising that he come down later to sign and pay. "*Après midi*," she says and runs back inside. The top bungalow is plywood nailed to studs with big screen windows, all slumped in stillness that seeps into senses. Thick air collects in droplets and rolls from forehead to chin. It drips or runs to the neck and on down the chest till the shirt sticks, and so do the pants. Fronds rub. Bugs pop knuckles. Birds chirp. Waves break across the road. A ceiling fan groans. He drifts for an hour and wakes up wet, not so tired.

He shuffles down to pay and takes comfort at sixty dollars a night. The beach house ran three bucks less, but that was with income. The bungalows across the road on the bay run a hundred sixty per night, but a room is only a place to sleep. So brief celebration is in order, in the rustic dining area across the road, over the water.

As a newcomer arrived from the future, he has bad news of what's on the way. *Aloha* and *ia orana* settle like a lei, and he wants to shout it out, that a spirit dies when supply falls short of demand. Magic fades below the range of human perception, and then it's too late. They don't seem concerned, and the news feels urgent. This just in:

Humanity will overrun here too. The airwaves will promote jobs and God for the common good, as cells divide—as aberrant growth spawns gridlock, and silence goes extinct under the din of boosters making sure we do this right. Eye contact will be avoided, and nature will be for postcards. Security will trump freedom in the name of the children as other species go away.

"But they're not my children," mumbles the man at the rail near the pier. A couple one table over look away. Ravi turns his swim goggles like a rosary and wonders how fucked up he might be, feeling them for salvation. "I mean the children they're always saying to do things for. They're not mine."

They eat their omelets with rectitude.

So he gazes over Cook's Bay and below the surface for better company. The pier runs over the reef, out thirty yards to where the bottom falls away. The Taverua caretaker ambles out, tossing bread chunks to either side. Fish churn thick as humanity at rush hour but with simpler needs, with no cars and no rage. Who would not smile at such color and joy? A squall rushes in with a quick shower, as the caretaker rips two more baguettes, as his pets rise to brunch.

The squall passes just as fast. The rainbow is briefly incandescent then vanishes in the sheen, and the world is right. The husk cracks, germinating at last. Three hundred thousand residents and two hundred thousand tourists annually in French Polynesia seem far easier to take than Hawaii's two million residents and seven million tourists. But anyplace can go away, especially a place like this, not yet discovered and exploited for maximum return on investment.

"I did love America." Ravi mumbles. "But it changed."

The honeymooners leave as the tide rises. Will Ravi Rockulz be happy here? It's a question of process. Will Ravi Rockulz find success as a marine photographer? That's desire again, and the bigger question goes to shelter from the storm. A tropical wilderness can take a body down to nitrogen, potassium, and phosphorous, in the comfort of his own home—that's it: phosphorous, the basis of bioluminescence, enhancing dissolution with the glimmer of lost souls. Now there's a success.

Could I gasp my last with no sirens, no insurance caveats or regrets? I nearly did, didn't I? I think I'll get the pictures. I think these images may open eyes and hearts to the fishy world, which may not end with ours. Is the reef healthy? Is it dead, and the fish come in for bread? Does the drop go deep? Why do I see no snorkelers? Why are dive boats running to the outer reef if this reef is any good? Is the coral intact or broken by the common crowd? Is it tangled in monofilament or net remnants? Is it brown? Is it choked with algae with no herbivores—all gone to aquariums? Or silt?

Ravi remembers Henry Hollings' mother lode on electrical contracting when Henry made more in a year than in the ten years combined, before the boom. Henry stopped diving—no time, too tired. He came out again when he won a bid on three hundred new homes—overbid by three times value with no other bids. But the homes were on his old wandering grounds, and Henry quit, walked away on a sad, twitchy grin.

REEFDOG

But recollection of man's inhumanity to himself stops on submersion. Questions resolve, and the prognosis is good. The reef is clean, no siltation or brown algae; fish numbers and species diversity seem extreme. Butterflyfish, damsels, and angels approach to see who in God's blue ocean is here. Soon their tiny hearts warm, and they peer. *Ravi? Is that you? We heard you were coming.* So the new guy arrives again. He frames shots with his fingers and feels the love, clicking portraits for the gallery in his heart.

The ocean is my shepherd, I shall not want. . .

A smile leaks seawater and the taste of home. Free diving at the drop, he rises slowly among emperor and regal angels, blue damsels, turquoise chromis, all the little fins aflutter till—wait!

Flame angels!

Just there—a mated pair, peeking out and darting to other cover, demure as a deb, brazen as a beau, and more virtuous than either. Red-orange bodies and black bars are their glory and their doom. Flame angels were the heartthrob of Hawaii's reefs but went to glass tanks in America and Asia.

Gone.

No more—but not here. *I don't think here.* Could it be here, too, that another collective death occurs? Not with so many baby fish on hand. *Hello, my friends.* With healthy coral heads, no trash or damage or monofilament, our place feels secure. People won't come if it's not convenient, so we can live the life, naturally connected.

These shores are lined with human habitat—with cesspits long past their useful lives. But the numbers are low and growth is slow. A man should not take on the worries of the world, so he looks up with invocation. "Lovely. A beautiful day. The first of many." The moment balances an interminable night.

French Polynesia was liberated for the Godly pursuits of food, fine wine, art, and sex. That's different from the Super Bowl, *We're number one*, March Madness, NASCAR, Halliburton, the religious right, obesity, Coke, box office returns, and war for oil. An outpost in the limitless sea may stay that way for a while, remote as the seventh moon of Uranus, culturally speaking.

So faith is bolstered on seeing friends. Hope is no longer a pipe dream but a reality forming up. Crossing the road to his cheap digs, he slows to wonder: How can he keep a roof over his head and buy groceries? At his bungalow, he finds a hose for a poor man's shower. And the cold truth is that having no money on the one hand and wanting to make art on the other are a source of worry. Who can live on inner light? Inside he sits. He breathes with the rustling fronds. He isn't the first man at a loss. His poor old gray-haired mother knows that he won't be a lawyer or a doctor—or an accountant or movie star or anything to wear on her sleeve. Not that her sleeve is his goal, but she counts for something and doesn't even know where to find him. She may be worrying this very minute. Why wouldn't she?

His new French home will sting him for forty bucks on a call home. A cheese sandwich for nine dollars? The French tropics will require attention and diligence. Still, it'll be forty bucks well spent, on a call wisely reserved for post-arrival, to report a safe flight and rich prospects. Things are working out for the best. If he'd called sooner, he'd only have to call again anyway. Near sundown, in the same time zone as Hawaii, he's back at Taverua.

"Hello? Who could be calling at this hour?"

"It's me."

"Me? Me who?"

"Hello, Mother."

"So tell me what is wrong?"

Why must something be wrong? Why must she energize the negative? Why can't she assume good news? Why does she believe that nothing happens for the best? But this exchange wore itself out long ago. He won't belabor and accepts the badinage as the lesser of two burdens because she is Mother.

"Nothing is wrong. Things are going right. I've been thinking about moving for a long time now. . ."

"Where are you?"

"I'm in Tahiti."

"Oy, *Gott.* Tahiti."

"I love it."

"You love it. You love Hawaii!"

"Yes, I do. Can I have only one love?"

"How did you get in? They won't let you in because you wouldn't get the visa like I begged you. I begged, but you wouldn't."

"Don't ask."

"You won't listen. You're a rolling stone. . ."

"Yes. No moss. But I still don't want some. This place is so beautiful; it's unbelievable. The corals and fishes—I saw flame angels right in front of the hotel."

"Oh, you're staying at a fancy hotel, making friends with little fishes. Tell me why I should worry?"

"You should worry because that's what you do best. But try to worry about something else. I've never felt better about a decision."

"And what did you decide to do in Tahiti? Make more with the bubbles business?"

The question of the bubbles business looms on the intrapersonal plane. The correct answer will take a while longer, but a response is required, and so it spurts: "Take pictures. It's my calling."

"It's your calling. Who's listening? You're going to take pictures of fish and then what? Trade them for your dinner?"

"Yes. You do understand. And to think that, all this time, I thought you saw me as a failure. I was wrong."

"Never a failure! A waste, maybe, but not a failure. Never a failure. I want you to come home and be a *mensch.*"

"Mommy, dearest. In case you haven't noticed, I am a *mensch.* My pictures of fish are highly regarded. I'll sell them in New York, just like I did last time. Maybe even to the same people. . ."

"Maybe, schmaybe. I remember what they said, those same people. Maybe parakeets will fly out my *tuchas* too."

"Are you getting feathers down there?"

She laughs. Finally.

Tzim lachen; it should be to laugh because that and love will survive us. So the long distance shortens with the best they have to share, rendering all well on the immortal plane that will survive them. Things get better when he gives her the Taverua phone number, but please, she should call only for emergency since a call will cost him about a hundred dollars, besides the terrible expense at her end.

"A hundred dollars?"

"It's a hotel on the water in Tahiti. They got overhead."

"So what do you need with such a fancy hotel?"

"I don't. I stay much cheaper across the street. They know me here and will come get me for emergency calls. That's *emergency*. Okay?"

"Everything should be good. Are you making friends?"

"I just got here, but already if I have any more social demands I won't be able to get to my work."

"Oh, pardon me. Your work."

He lets the silence congeal so disrespect can be recognized, so it can leave its damage at both ends of the line since she too factors money per minute. And for what, so Ma Bell can get rich on deficiencies they don't deserve?

"When will you call me?"

"I'm calling you right now, as we speak. This is a call that we're on. We're in the moment, which is a great achievement, you know. I'll call you again when I have more news. Okay? Now I have to go."

"Okay, go to your next important moment. Be well."

"Yes. And you."

He feels better when the call is done and he's back in his bungalow. He knew she couldn't hear him a few nights ago, but she would have heard what became of her son and spent her days in those bleak hours prior to sinking. Still, he'd called her by name, so maybe she saved him, a psychokinetic force to reckon. She has the psycho part down and can drive strong men to irrational behavior. She can be a world-class pill, a neurotic of notable perseverance. Add her strident instincts for motherhood, and she might control things from afar. God knows she's tried for years.

REEFDOG

Then again, some mothers lose their cubs. Mothering skills range from casual to fierce. Maybe some can conjure against the odds, against reality. . . But the depth and darkness, the troughs and crests, the visions of imminent. . .

So the sweat rolls into rivulets that converge to streams and rivers flowing to a shallow estuary that rises on night squalls pushing inland from a troubled sea. Waves break over the rustling fronds, and the moon rises. A man hangs on, sinking into middle age in violent resolution. Which is only the force of nature displacing the foolishness of youth.

Who knows? Maybe the next part will be easy.

A Night on the Town

Daydreams are better, not so violent, and they fade with the afternoon to dusk and twilight. He wanders in the eaves, in pleasant deprivation and thoughts. Basha Rivka Rockulz did not marry Zviki Rahnoose but got a son. "Meeting that bum was the best day of my life." She sang a little ditty to make her whimsical disclosure: "First comes the son, then comes marriage. . . Who cares? You got your health!" A son was all he had given her before he left, before Ravi could walk. He walked back to Lebanon for a piece of hashish or a whore and a nice cup of mint tea. Good riddance. So what should she do, let her only son struggle with the name of a stranger? The father called himself Lebanese but wasn't—nor was he Syrian, Iraqi, Iranian, or Saudi. Thank God and praise Allah too. He claimed Armenian but could have been Jordanian, Omanian, or a Buckeye. Who knew?

And the initial attraction? "What got the romance underway?"

"You talk like a crazy man." Was Old Dad crazy too? And a leg man? But really, a fellow would rather not think of Mother that way.

At peak physical condition, give or take, lying down, he feels strong as ever, more or less, with some road wisdom in the mix. He's a man of notable skill with a handsome face, in the prime of life. The optimal view grants the benefits of a few doubts. But what should a man think, that it's all downhill from here?

No, he should look up. Life begins at forty, two years off—okay, a year and a half—and livelihood should be resolved by then. A man should have rent and groceries dicked at forty—are you kidding? He should hit forty in stride, with the dough rolling in, so he can focus on his work. He's not an ivy leaguer and has no birthright or family ties or social connections or collegiate associations. He came up the old-fashioned way, on his wits—not too sharp in the recent past unless fate played a hand. Never mind. Wits fare better than a silver spoon any day. A year and a half should be plenty of time.

The future begins with definition of self and the mark he'll make—no, scratch that. No marks. No footprints. Only nature's sweet embrace will linger on a path chosen long ago. He hasn't ignored his calling; he merely failed to see it. Now he sees the work ahead, though a look back looks good too. He misses Skinny one minute to the next, and he *could* go back and forget this little chaos. He could be home in time for Sunday's charter, or Monday's for sure, legal—what can they do, the local *mishpocha*? He's one of them. *By law!*

But no. He cannot go back any more than a wish upon a star can deliver comfort. Life goes forward. The past is written, unavailable for reshaping, except to the right-wing media, remembering what never was. Otherwise, life is present tense, and he must grasp the moment just so, not too firmly, not too light.

Only a handful of people in New York were too stupid or jaded to see the beauty in his shots, not to mention technical excellence. Plenty more where they came from. No shortage there of suits filling space, killing time, fantasizing the vagabond life in Tahiti. The true artist pursues his work, no matter who says what in New York. The true artist is often unpaid, with amateur virtue intact to the end, like Vincent. Only the work survives. By forty, a man is no longer imagined but has become who he'll be—who he is. He's a man of means or spirit, a common man who takes pictures of fish on his way.

The eaves reveal merit and downside. He may work in obscurity, manually for money, but he'll work artistically for life. It doesn't matter. What could he be on a vibrant reef, famous?

Which brings him back to the place and fish tumbling like colored shards in a mirrored tube, but beautiful symmetry in the eaves is not guaranteed in the world. What would he do, given a choice? How about a tropical island as yet unblemished, with a job and reefs? *I'll take it!* Already he hears people complain of too few tourists, too little spending. But whining is human nature. In America they whine when gas goes up twelve cents a gallon, like God killed their firstborn. Three dollars a gallon or six; who cares? Let 'em skateboard.

Or scoot—he'll get a scooter and ride the perimeter road to new reefs. He'll go to bed early, eat and drink at home and head over to Papeete to be away. Then what? Bad question is what, leading to nowhere but the first step. A person reborn to prospects might stumble, but the path remains clear. He will not resist. He's a dive instructor: reefdog for hire. He's older than many instructors and more seasoned. On the inevitable question he'll chuckle: *I don't know, seven hundred dives a year. Twelve years. Fifteen. What's that, times seven? Maybe ten thousand dives. So? I'm learning.*

He'll also learn local currents, drops, surges, wildlife, and weather. Not speaking French is more perfect still since nobody speaks underwater. He has his gear and can borrow tanks. And his camera and lenses will show extra value, recording what is going away as it could be saved. That's why he's here, meaning here on earth. The shutter may open on something great, given the man behind the camera.

So he feels good, better than a man so challenged should feel. The feeling seems natural, but who would waste time wondering why he feels good? Tomorrow he'll begin. The French know about life and mystical import on wine, cheese, and a baguette. Hold the pâté for now. And the place may be spared the onslaught for another lifetime or two. Inevitable loss seems as sad as mothers losing cubs, but he'll be dead by then. What a relief.

How's that for feeling good? So he comes down from the eaves to dress and walk into the world. At the road, he turns left—no, right—on his way to dinner, something French, as rich and extravagant as the future. Descending into the atmosphere of a more manageable dream, he feels his heat shield cooling, rattling less, his glide pattern smoothing toward touchdown, a water landing of course.

REEFDOG

Early moonrise feels lucky, as the white bulb lights the grassy shoulder. Traffic is sparse, and two miles feel productive and illusory. But enough of doubting; he comes to a resort hotel that looks good in moonlight and beyond his needs. Perfect. What's the alternative, saving ten bucks by walking back to eat across the road? Ten bucks is half a tip on any given day, and the days will come again.

The seafood and French buffet cannot be justified. So he pays the forty dollars, hearing Mother encourage it. What the hell, a man who gets married, swims from the aggregation buoy at night, moves to French Polynesia in a handful of days, and plans his future on an afternoon shouldn't blink at forty clams. Or cocktails at seven bucks each, so he has three in the bar since the buffet won't open for another twenty minutes because the French eat late and three drinks absolve all doubt. They flow, the first on a shudder, the second with a twist, the third with a bow wake on mirror-flat seas. . .

Then it's time to eat, which all living creatures must do—but to survive as he has done and then to eat as the French do is another match made in. . . not heaven because he would not repeat the experience any sooner than he'd stare at the face of God, but he has seen something awful and divine, so the match could have been made in the heavenly realm, on Neptune's choreography.

He makes a mental note to come back tomorrow for a word with management on swordfish and its mercury toxins, black tumors and the awful by-catch of turtles, birds, and marine mammals killed wantonly on swordfish long lines, as if anybody should suffer one more minute in blissful ignorance of the murderous carnage or the black, slimy poison excised in the kitchen before cooking the swordfish. Tonight he'll simply pass on the swordfish, scrunching his nose and wagging his head at the woman behind him, so she might catch on and pass the word. He makes another mental note to learn the French word for *tumors* and the words for *by-catch, leatherback turtles, marine mammals, seabirds,* and *crying fucking shame.*

He laughs and so does the lady behind him.

He forks a steak—a tough, cheap cut, so he chews a piece slow as a minute in the pitch-dark depths. . .

Stop!

Everything else is perfect: fillets, scallops, shrimps, salads, spinach, and broccoli and these little pastry shells with delicious things inside and Caesar salad, fruit salad, pasta salad, and tabbouleh. Sliced cukes in yogurt with dill, sliced tomatoes with olive oil and garlic, cheeses, baguettes, and—sadly but also scrumptious—lobster tails and crab. Three trips seem in order, or five, with an evening to span, so he settles in to dine like a Buddhist with a most honored guest, his newly minted self.

But wait! Never sentimental, he bows his head to a private God who can be called for personal favors if the begging is sufficiently strident and the need sufficiently needy. Oh, the Holy, Holy, Holy One was frequently paged, questionable existence notwithstanding. Ravi gives thanks to the ether and feels the moments, this sequence no different than the other, even if he'd drifted the wrong way and could still be treading, and this is merely. . .

Stop!

He shudders and exhales to join the rising steam. He inhales the perfect scents of sweet and sour and gives thanks to the plants and animals who made this meal possible. He lapses to the fear of all living things just prior to passing. Or would that moment have already passed to awe and wonder?

He eats.

Never have taste buds stood so tall in tribute to sheer, shameless flavor. He can only nod at the waitperson's suggestion of the hotel special wine for the evening, continuing his immersion into the extreme opposite of recent encounters. . .

But enough! Let it go.

And he lets go of letting go as well because bad things fade at the same pace as good things, the same pace as life itself, as the first sip of Bourgogne Burgundy Blanc displaces all things with goose bumps on taste buds. Anything more on the happy side of life would make a grown man cry. But he won't cry. He laughs aloud as onto the pool deck serving as a stage walk six dazzling women and, not to burden a random encounter, a lead woman whose shape, face, and essence trigger a feeding frenzy of insatiable eyes that don't exactly bug, but then they do. This fantasy seems foolish to say the least, not to mention irrational—or insane—scoping a woman at this juncture. What's the chance of repetition in romance? Slim to none because nothing is the same. The mirror universe is merely an idea. Yes, he was out to dinner when he met what's-her-name. So what? This isn't out to dinner like that. This is way the hell out to dinner, like this.

He laughs aloud but stops when she drops her rhythm for a personal scan, for a nipple slip, loose ties, open zippers, and the safety checks triggered by your casual tourist pervert laughing for no reason. On a misstep she blushes in staggering beauty, and he laughs again at the maddening wonder of random events. He shakes his head to show that he's not laughing at her but at life's crazy turns. He'd thought Minna—that was her name—was beautiful, with the legs, hips, ass, tits, face, grace, and the rest. But he was wrong; she was harsh, with the liquor, dope, slutty sex, and greaseballs. Who knew?

And who minded the slutty sex at the receiving end? Nobody is who—nobody who matters anyway. The trashy stuff could not factor on first sight of Minna Somayan, though the baggage was hard to ignore on the way in from the aggregation buoy. At night.

But this beauty is different, below the line and pure Polynesian—maybe that's the crux—not in the Polynesian but the purity. After all, Tahiti and Tonga, Samoa and the Philippines, Fiji and the Cooks are hardly a hand span on the globe. How different can beauty be? Minna looked pure, so who can tell if this beauty has cooties too?

But she's likely free of the pop culture pollution smothering Hawaii because the watery realm called Oceania was buffered against missionaries. Missionary *modus operandi* was to convert the chief or king so the flock would follow. But it didn't work so well down here, where island nations confederated, and a converted king came to Jesus alone. Over a century later, the southern hemisphere is free

of big sugar, price supports or massive ownership by sugar/mission-
ary families. The spirit remains free of resource allocation, and so are
bitterness and regret in shorter supply. Maybe that's the difference in
one beauty and another.

From first pee-pee in his diapers to the final pissing his pants, a
man will err and go on. He'll bear no shame, and a lesson recently
learned will not be soon forgotten. This feels different, with luxuriant color on a cleaner canvas. This dazzling dancer doesn't seem like
a mental case, but Basha Rivka would call her just that, with the
coconut shells on her bazoombas and her *pupik* jiggling like Jell-O.
Yes, and mothers are often right—and wrong. That's why children
leave the nest, to make their own mistakes and get smarter, having
an adventure or two, like this one, with its jiggling pupik and garlic
mashed potatoes with tarragon and lobster tits, *I mean bits.* . . and hip
gyrations to make a young man smile, and, *I think, olive oil? Yes—ah!
So good, with a hint of. . . what is it? Dill? Yes, dill!* Till a mouthful
and eyeful are nearly too much—don't speak, but ogling with a full
mouth is okay, as every doubt sinks to inky depths.

At night.

So Ravi savors flavors, swaying like a cobra in synch with his
charmer. And why not? Why wouldn't a man in his prime ogle a
nubile woman in her paean to fertility?

She is Vahineura, but family and friends call her Cosima. She dances
for love—of music and movement, which is better than money. It's a
pittance at any rate and could hardly match the art of the thing. She
touches the nerve by which Ravi feels his future in art, with no return
but the purest love in the world.

Her day job is manual and pays another pittance. She answers
tourist questions on things they may buy, like hand-carved vase holders, *pareos* with Gauguin prints, black pearls, calendars with naked
women and men of splendid beauty, sundresses, T-shirts, guide
books, and stuff. Ravi looks glum, and she asks why. He shrugs forlornly, and she says, "But I also dance."

Her gossamer touch makes him tense because he's sensitive. He wants to remember this scene rather than recall it. He says a *chachka* shop for tourists means that it's begun, the noising up and dumbing down, the effusion and clutter. Signs, pamphlets, barkers, and con men will spread like fungus on the common sense of life till hideaways are no longer hidden, names of reefs and fishes, histories, and legends, people and myths get boiled down to babel and stocked on a thousand racks so tourists can disgorge the wonders you simply must see. The overstock will go to the dump to make room for next week's load.

Where lush vegetation teems in virtually visible growth, front-enders and closers in boiler rooms will gouge thousands with great good cheer. *Do you want vacations? Do you need vacations?*

"You are so right!" the young dancer agrees, covering her mouth with her fingers, then touching his arm again. "But you are wrong. I would never let that happen here. You talk like a man who's been to war. It's not like that here. Business is very slow. The shop only exists for hotel guests. I don't think it makes money. How could it? It's so slow. And it's only souvenirs. You know that word?"

"Yes. Everyone knows that word."

"Oh. I didn't know. It's French."

"It's universal."

"What is chachka?"

"Trinkets. Unnecessary stuff."

"What's wrong with a little thing to remember your holiday by?"

"What do you mean, you won't let it happen?"

"I wouldn't. Why would I?"

"What could you do to stop it?"

"I have powers." She falters. "Maybe you'll see." Maybe he sees. Maybe regal notions are common in tropical climates, among the girls who wanna have fun. Let her cast a spell of love or something or other. Any bear would stick his nose in this honey pot. But circumstance will come later, past laughter and chiding, on the way to losing and finding himself again—after what he's been through.

The last long swim altered his outlook, but what a prize. That is, Vahineura's troubled relationship with reality includes her pledge to any man who swims Cook's Bay after sunset and swims back before sunrise; he will earn the cherries. What else can a young woman of paltry means offer? She is a queen in need of a king. Or something.

She will share her fantasy in monotone, revealing her delusion that the rightful king will claim his crown. The offer is long-standing—since she reached the age of consent, if not reason. "You'll have sex with any man who has the balls to make the swim? You know balls? *Les oeufs profonds?*"

"*Tu es drôle, mon pauvre Ravi.* Who ever heard of profound eggs?"

"I thought you liked me."

"Oh, but I do."

"But you want me to swim that bay at night?"

"No! Not you!"

Will he get the cherries without the swim? Or is he not in the running? He doesn't ask because logic seems incidental. She's luscious and warm, aloof yet accessible and oddly disconnected—look who's talking. Never mind; she's not like the other one, not even close, unless you count the quirks and bold moves where least expected—and the character malfunctions revealed on a long swim.

At night.

Which should make an impression, but Ravi the rockhead has a fatal appetite for tender leg. But can all women be mental? Probably not all, only the ones he meets. He takes cold comfort in consistency but feels bona fide stupid. A healthy appetite is not wrong and can provide happiness for others, and a young dancer's fantasy may be a curse, and he could end it by claiming the prize—like the guy who cut through the sticker bushes to kiss Sleeping Beauty. The winner won't be much older than Ravi. Two elderly fellows tried and failed already.

I'm not old. I can swim that bay on my back. Besides, she had to be relieved when those old guys drowned. Neither was wealthy. At least I got potential. Well, I got no flab.

But why would anyone drown in that pond? It's a mile, maybe—unless drowning was easier to tell than disappearing with no trace. But pondering the pond will also come later. Sooner, on a day pleasantly resolved, Vahineura approaches. "You are laughing at us. Why are you laughing? What do you see that's funny?"

Eating his third pass, Ravi puts a forefinger in the air, clears a swallow and shakes his head. "I am not laughing at you. I am laughing at. . . life. At my life and the. . . I don't want to give the wrong impression, but I. . . I laugh at the turns my life has taken in the last few days. Please, forgive. . ."

"What impression is the right impression?"

"You're a beautiful dancer. I'm sorry if you thought I. . ."

"You looked, and you laughed."

"With delight."

She smiles because he said the right thing; so few men do. "When the show is over, we invite our guests for pictures. Perhaps you would like a picture to send home."

She pegged him as a tourist. That's okay, and he says yes, a picture would show his mother he's having fun.

"Did you bring your camera?"

"Yes, but it's for diving, for underwater pictures. It can take regular pictures too, but I don't have it here. It's too big."

"All right. You can use our camera. See that woman there?"

Fate paints a picture on simple strokes. Yes, he sees that woman, the dancing troupe's matron, more middle in age than he is but well preserved, tawny with a slight cushion but firm and obviously formerly svelte, like Aunt Hadi, who was not Mother's sister but a friend. Hadi let Ravi watch if he pretended to sleep and only peeked through eye slits when she played with herself. Here she is again, still affable and affectionate.

"She is Hereata. You will love her. It's only Polaroid, a thousand francs, about twelve dollars. You're here for pictures underwater?"

"Yes. I am here for that."

"Good. I am Vahineura."

"Ravi."

"I don't mind if you laugh at us. I only wanted to know why."

"Laughter sprang from my heart, which is different than laughing at you. You see?"

"I see. I see you later. *Comme ça?*"

"Yes. I mean, *oui.*"

She drifts back to the stage. His appetite is gone, or at least changed. Besides, hardly a spare cubic centimeter remains in the old bread-basket. Pubic centimeter? That's disgusting, but men in emotional turmoil can display incorrigible behavior, often as pussy hounds. Or is that unbearable? Either way. Speaking of sweets, some pineapple upside down would align nicely. She smiles at him, connecting dots, feeding potential.

So things round out on a lesson: Get out and mix it up or stare at the walls. It seems so clear until a meatball rolls from the buffet in loud jams drooping below the knees because the waistband is below the butt crack. This guy could have a load in his crotch with nobody the wiser. He offsets with gold nuggets—a watchband and matching rings and earrings and a beefy nugget necklace demonstrate success in the Russian mafia. Maybe he sells timeshare on the Caspian Sea to former Commies who like vacations, want vacations, need vacations.

Russian is the profile, but what else do you have with a bald head, pudgy hands, lumpy shoulders, thickness overall, and a borscht accent? He swills what is clearly not water and watches like Nikita Khrushchev on steroids at the General Assembly, ready to pound his shoe on a table. Fleshy folds bunch between the head and the neck. He takes a stance, arms folded, legs apart. On his left butt pocket is *USA* above an American flag. Below the flag: *We're #1!* The other pocket is a dive flag—diagonal white stripe on a red field—making him one more macho idiot with a scuba certification card to prove it.

The diphthong/glottal mix sounds Slavic or Curd or maybe Slobbovian. He's drunk, keeping his little world safe for bad taste. His date is heavily rouged and confused. She goes along, apparently hired. The scene is ugly but avoidable—till he blocks Ravi's view.

REEFDOG

Let it go, Ravi murmurs and does, through the photo op. Then he steps up to the meatball's video camera with a smile. He no speaka too gooda de Française but says, "Vous êtes trop gros pour une fenêtre mais très parfaite pour une porte, n'est-ce pas?"

The thick man rises, as the matron steps between them like a referee. She instructs, "Arrêtez, Monsieur." But the glove is thrown and calls for a response. So the two men glare till the thick one lunges past the matron, who hooks his ankle. Ravi sidesteps to make room for the sprawl, which would be all she wrote, ending the spat with manageable loss of face. But the drunk is up to his knees on another go, so the matron plants her toes in his ribs. "Ne pas ici, Monsieur! Not in my show. Not in front of my guests. Go home now." She hovers, discouraging a third lunge, and three bouncers in triple XL lead him out. He looks back, his brow set on revenge.

What is it about me?

She turns, "What is it about you?"

"Thank you, but I didn't start that. He stood in my way when. . ."

"Yes. I saw him. Here." She hands him a card with a two-digit number. The Polaroid ran out of film, so she went to point 'n shoot for quick and easy prints, but he'll have to wait until she can finish with the guests. Each gets an embrace and a Polaroid. He stands by, watching his special dancer blush and blink on her way out.

The crowd thins and cleanup begins. He decides to come back later for his photo because he needs a walk home on lifts and headers to sort the days and details on a freshening breeze. Seas are figurative, unlike those of the recent conundrum. This turmoil is part of a pattern, and it must change. Why does a man attract trouble at every turn? A blustery night may clarify the why and wherefore of things. Why couldn't he close his eyes and let a meatball take his meatball video and roll away to his meatball room where he could slip into his meatball hooker and his meatball dream?

"I am Hereata," the matron says.

"Yes. I know. I mean, the dancer. . ." He indicates the exit.

"You mean Vahineura."

"Yes. She told me your name."

"I saw that, too. I'm sure she told you more than my name, and I must advise you. . ." But she stops short of advice. Flexing her supple self in subtle provocation, she suggests the unavoidable, that grace is merely typical to a fulsome woman in a clingy dress, heels, lipstick, and womanly wherewithal. Body language is a harmless amusement, really, a cultural ornament to please the eye. "Come. We make a print for you. So you can send it home, and they will see you having fun."

He follows through the lobby to an office, where she squats to rummage for the power button or look for a pencil she dropped last week. Who knows? Her dress rides up, and she swears that God invented computers for revenge on sinners, and if this *merde* hotel weren't so cheap, it would get one of those printers where you just stick the thing in, *et voilà!* But no. . .

"I can come back tomorrow, please. It's not a problem."

"Your family should see you having fun, so they don't worry. Or your friends. That way you avoid a bigger problem."

"How do you know my family will worry? Or my friends? Why do you think I'll have a problem?"

"Maybe I guessed and got lucky. Whose family doesn't worry? What friends don't want to hear from you?"

"Still, I can come back. Better in the daytime."

She stands up. "Okay. I think you're right. What's your name?"

"Ravid."

"Rabid?"

"No. Ravid, with a *v.* And it doesn't rhyme with rabid. It's rah-veed. Veed! But call me Ravi. Okay?"

"Okay. Ravi," she shrugs. "Where you from?"

"I came here from Hawaii."

"I don't think you were born in Hawaii."

"I was born in Morocco, but I'm from Haifa."

"You're an Arab?"

"I'm Israeli. It's a long story from long ago."

"But you came yesterday from Hawaii?"

"Yes. How do you know it was yesterday?"

"Maybe I guessed and got lucky. It's Sunday. You look new. I don't know. You look familiar. I think I know you."

"We've never met. I would remember."

"I don't mean that we met." She proceeds to more earthly tasks.

How else might she know him? He'll sort that as well on the blustery walk home. "What else do you know?"

"Young. Confused. Handsome. Lonely."

"Are you psychic? You are correct, but I was so hungry and had such a good meal, and I was having fun. I thought the. . . uncertainty didn't show, at least for a little while."

"I'm more logical than psychic. I see what there is to see. You looked hungry all right."

"And you?"

Such a question prompts eye contact and feminine flex in an expressive woman. "What about me?"

"What about you? What are you? What do you feel?"

"What do you see?"

An equally open-ended question prompts caution in a man of seasoning who senses a door opening. He can't quite see inside but she seems friendly, and she's connected to tourism in a high-end hotel. What a person to know. So he looks and says, "Good looking. About my age. Generous, brave. . ."

"You think I'm brave because of that scene? You don't know tourism. Besides, it's not brave if you're not afraid. I had backup. That man was drunk. What could he do?"

"Sorry. I thought you were brave. Not every woman could kick a guy in the ribs. And I do know tourism. I'm a dive instructor."

An eyebrow rises. "Come. I'll buy a drink. I want to hear. You can help me wind down. You know how it is on the late shift."

Another drink seems unnecessary, and he begs off; he's too tired and his belly is too full. She suggests a cognac as *digestif*. He nods because a drink with a mature woman in tourism may bode well. "Okay, you can buy a drink if I can buy one too."

Soon they relax at the bar, free of life questions, staring at their drinks. The silence could be awkward for people who just met, but it's not. "They say silence is golden, but it can be a wall between people who have nothing to share or have trouble in their hearts. But when it passes easily, it means we're compatible. Do you feel it? I think I'll know you for a long time." She turns to him.

He smiles and says yes, a friend would be good. Her angular cheeks, Polynesian lips, dark skin, and compelling cleavage heave gently, and she blinks like a beacon on good anchorage. . . He laughs short; would that be sandy bottom or loose slag over hardpan?

"What?"

"Nothing."

"Not nothing. You laugh. Tell me what."

He watches his drink and says, "It's different here. Less of some things. More of others. I think I like it."

"Hmm. It's more French here. Not so Christian, like Hawaii."

"Yes. . . Why did you warn me? Or start to warn me."

"I didn't warn you. You practically picked a fight with that man."

"Not about that. About the dancer—what's her name?"

"Oh, Cosima—Vahineura. She's a nut, that's why. She already got two guys dead and broke a bunch more hearts. And for what? A nut."

"Why warn me?"

"Because you're a man. I think you been through enough."

"What do you think I've been through?" He swallows half his cognac. "Now you're guessing."

"Maybe. But I know what a tired man looks like. I told you: You look confused and tired. A man your age shouldn't look so tired. Life tired. I don't know what you been through, but I think it was tough. Physical tough, mental and emotional. Yes? No?"

"How old am I?"

She squints in scrutiny. "Thirty-eight, going on fifty-two."

He slides a hand over his hip pocket to feel his wallet. Well, she guessed and got lucky. So he looks a bit tired. "How old are you?"

"Younger than you. Only forty-eight."

He laughs, downs his drink and signals the bartender, knowing the trick the sauce can play and loving the sauce for its trick. "Are you psychic?"

"I think so. I see that I weigh less than you do, too."

He scans, thinking their weights close enough for a wrestling match. He would suggest two out of three falls but holds back. "Do you see reason? Direction?"

"Sometimes. But I told you: What I see is more logic than psychic. Did you forget? You can see for yourself. My visions are ordinary, not extraordinary. What's strange about seeing things as they are?" She shakes her head. "I'll let you know when I see something." They watch their drinks, comfort settling between them until she relents. "Okay. I see water. The ocean."

"So? We're surrounded."

"At night."

He moans.

"That's all for now. It isn't happy. I see this because you're showing me, and you're telling me as well. It's not psychic. That's why I warn you about Cosima. I don't like to say things about a person who may be nice inside where it counts, especially one of my dancers, not my best dancer, but she's learning, not so clumsy as she was. You're a man, and I know what happens, and I saw what happened when she spoke to you." So she tells of Vahineura—Cosima—and the curse/fantasy that a man will swim over and back between sunset and sunrise to claim her.

He won't ask about depth, current, sea creatures, and shoals but holds his cognac to the candle. "Is water ever happy?"

"Of course it is. You of all people should know that."

"I should. But I think it's not sad or happy. It's only. . . efficient."

"Efficient does not mean it's unhappy. Don't be foolish. No man should get so tired, especially a man your age, who may recover."

Or he may not, yet he warms to her common sense—her optimism feels informed. The bar closes. Her small house is in a field below a piton, a short walk up. She's nice and smart and also on edge—a far edge—but her manner and presence make her flat-out doable at closing time. So he asks the tough question: Would he pick the same tomato in daylight, sober? *Stop. Take your petty needs home in the dark and let a friendship be.* "I'm staying in a bungalow by Taverua."

"That's two miles down!"

"Yes. On a beautiful night for a walk."

"With squalls? No moon? I think a tired man is a dangerous man."

Slouching into a downpour does not seem so invigorating as a while ago, but he's seen worse. He follows her out, *comme ci, comme ça,* happily adrift on dry land. The rain starts at the top step and pours by the bottom. "Come! My house is near." He faces foul weather or perhaps another failure.

"I don't think so."

"You can stay at my house. No funny business. Do you hear?"

"Yes, I hear." Maybe it's best. But how could it be—but she takes his hand to lead the way, downwind. "You're so sad and drunk. *Venez! Vite!*" So they head up the road in the dark on a rocky shoulder in the rain and traffic. She chatters over life since before the road got paved, when it was dusty or a mud bog, but paved will kill you quicker. She's walked it for years, often in worse conditions.

Yes, he's familiar with the changing world. At least the side road is still dirt. She grasps his waist and points a flashlight, like he's convalescent, headed to the infirmary. Dim light and dancing shadows favor a seasoned woman. On the porch she steps out of her slippers and regrets the dark, but who knew she'd drag the cat home? She laughs and turns on the light, and he sees boots, size twelve. "Effective, don't you think? A woman learns these things."

Inside is brighter. It's a roof over four walls with a kitchen table and chairs and a couch that unfolds to a bed. She points out back at the *salle de bain,* telling him to pee-pee from the porch to the left on his way out, not to the right—*sur la gauche, pas à la droite*—where her garden is trying to grow. He would ask if she also makes pee-pee from the edge but knows that she does, "but only in bad weather," she says, frittering over no rest for the weary, wet clothing, and catching her death, even in Paradise, where such things still happen.

She disrobes casually as an anecdote, peeling the clingy dress to reveal the truth of the situation, so the parties of the first and second part can dispense with speculation. It's normal, after all. Wet clothing must come off. She says the place sleeps very well, and they'll walk back up in the morning for his picture, so his family can see him having fun. She plucks a towel from the wall to dry herself. She'll walk back up anyway for work, so it's no trouble. Tossing him the towel she crawls under, keeping to her half. He watches like a statue but follows here too, turning to hide the awkward truth of his relationship with the world at large. Burdened by youth and feeling better than in recent days, he crawls alongside, keeping to his half, hoping to avoid obtrusive behavior. Silence is again natural and eases the strain. He reviews the meatball, the buffet, the long walk back to his bungalow, until she rubs his arm. "Go ahead. Tell me."

Her touch is warm, her hands soft. He would rather close his eyes to feel it, but he'd fall asleep. So he sighs, opening the book of fate. It begins on the restlessness common to spirited people everywhere. He was out to sort things out when a beautiful woman walked up and. . . turned life into heaven. . . and hell. The ex-boyfriend came around shooting, and he got deported, after the boyfriend kidnapped and tied him and put him in a little boat and went way out and threw him overboard at night, and he swam in. . . four or five miles. . . at night.

He breathes like a distance swimmer, gushing forth to this angel of understanding that he's only human, that every life is beset, but he's had a run that is wrong. Buried in the rubble of what had been a lovely life of days, he felt death as a presence to test or kill him. He survived but lost his will and frankly felt so indifferent, now that. . .

Survival was a delusion—a void, without happiness, without hope, with overwhelming loss and regret on every rise—proving that he did play out, but he's still alive, like a mouse in the paws of a cat. The eating is inevitable. Mice know that. He feels his soul going away, lost. "That guy tonight—that was good. That's how I used to be, you know, which makes me think I might recover, as you said. But. . ."

But he's not the man who got put over at the aggregation buoy. How could he be, with death beating in his heart for so long? He's lived apart ever since, a spirit divided, watching from outside, failing. No more house and home, no job or friends. "And my cat, Skinny, who I love, and she loves me too. She knows me, and we have this routine we still carry on, and it's painful. I miss her so badly."

He sobs, bringing the tale to Tahiti, where he can't tell down from up, which feels like vertigo, which is why she saw fatigue and confusion, as a woman of logical perception will do. He rolls her way. She sobs for his loss but cannot absolve it. They caress. "Come. You need a friend. You are not a mouse. You will eat the cat."

He would rather not think of Skinny in that way, but friendship is so long gone and seems to restore him. Following her lead yet again, he sips the aperitif; call it *liqueur de frangipani avec citron*. Make that lime. Where did that come from? Wait. It's frangipani and nitrous oxide. Or maybe it's just the oldest remedy of all. . .

"What is nitrous oxide?" she whispers.

"Juth one hit an' it doethn't even mather. . ."

"Mmm. . ." She seems to comprehend. "How did you know?"

"How thith I dow wha?"

"Mmm. . . I wanted your lips. . . there."

"Lucky gueth. . ." Yes, and a hard-worked waterman eases into snug harbor. It feels like love; so profound is the comfort. She is not like Minna Somayan in any way but gives like an angel on a day of displacement, in and out go the good and the bad. Easing him over and rolling on top she towers like a giant in the land of little people and lopes to the peak in long strides, laughing or crying, he can't tell which, though she too seems restored. He catches up, and she cries, as some women do. "Thank you, Here. . . uh. . . Herea. . ."

"Hereata."

"Hereata. Thank you. I won't forget you."

"Forget me?" She sniffles and wipes her nose. "You just met me. How can you forget me already, after what I have shown you? Me. You never met anybody like me."

"No, I haven't. You're right. I only. . ."

"Sh. . . I know." She snuggles, easing him in to home sweet home. She finds his lips for a goodnight kiss, their first.

Where the Sky Meets the Sea

Ravi dreams of a scraggly little cat who shows her age in a puffy face nose to nose. "Meow!" She demands snacks and affection in the wee hours, but affection alone will do for a while if administered just so, softly stroking her chin. Pressing his finger, she marks. Today is her birthday. *She's only nine and mine all mine.*

So at two he whispers, "Happy birthday, dear Skinny," and he laughs; she's so cute, with such a sense of humor. He wills his birthday wish and wishes her beside him. She purrs, affirming her presence. Or is that the fuller lass nearby? Maybe the skinny one uses the other as a medium for the message. Why not? "Meow," she arouses him, but who cares? It's a mode of expression most available to healthy men. It's not sexual, and it's nobody's business but their own. He loves his cat, and if that's not okay, you can *chob'm'n tuchas. Or kiss my ass if you'd rather.* She has none of the attributes he seeks in sexual liaison. He gets a boner when he scratches her chin. The End. So what?

Besides, here comes another lovely dream of Hereata, not even turning his way but leading the way once more to a perfect docking. This too is love. Warm and dry makes special dispensation to the warm and wet. Most species relish the exchange, but human people seem most driven. What is about humanity, with its penchants for killing and fucking and sport? Analysis is brief, soft, and scented. Lightning bolt tattoos cross her shoulder blades in dim light. He reaches around, and they mate like turtles on the surface, and it's not so bad. . . to be human. . .

They part and drift, back to lovely sleep until four and again at six when sunbeams peer into the window on another rise. Facing this way or that doesn't matter, as a new day solidifies on logical conclusion. Frequency may reflect the strife and turmoil of recent days. Does a man go to seed near the end? Is love so strange, a skewed pleasure meant to compensate for life? How long can a waterman swim against a current? Then again, it doesn't seem so bad with such a. . . such a. . .

What was that?

Footsteps in size twelve muddle poignant questions on life and its rare blessing. A few days up, Ravi will learn that he did not suffer *interruptus* but *reservatus*, in which tab A remains in slot B but becomes noodle C, slithering ignominiously to oblivion. *In flagrante* triggers several scenarios, including Ravi's jump out of bed and into his pants, grabbing his shirt on the fly. Or he could hide under the covers or crawl under the bed or into the wardrobe or continue flying out the back door or the window if the window opens. It must, or out the front door. *Oh, hello. Beautiful morning.*

Potentials resolve in mere moments after Moeava counts flip-flops on his porch. But who is to say this man is her husband? He could be a brother or cousin or lodger. Or gardener. She has a garden. Then he's inside, much bigger than his shoes suggested, big in the head, the neck, the arms, shoulders, belly, butt, thighs, and calves. Polynesian girth is genetic and from poi because taro is a complex carbohydrate, key to survival in many tropical climes. The life/death interface is still fragile, as the big man stares at the people in bed—presumably his bed, one of the people likely his wife who opens boldly. "Eighteen years I care for him, and to this day I care, but for what, so he can act the fool and try to kill himself?"

To whom does she speak? To the big man? In the third person?

"Care for me still?"

"Nothing happened. This boy will tell you. I could not bear to see him ruin what we had. But he still tries."

"What we had?"

"We had a home. Each other, till you threw everything away. We live in Paradise, for you a fool's paradise."

"You don't know where I was."

"Trying to swim across Cook's Bay to claim your nasty prize is where you was. Postponing again because you scared is where you was. Doubting delivery of the little biddy hen is where you was."

"Was not."

"Was! You know it. I know it. This boy knows it. So don't deny it. You are caught red-handed. Be a man, not afraid like you was all night!"

It's not *hutzpa* but *chutzpah*, with a guttural *cchh*. It's both Hebrew and Yiddish but converts to any language or culture among those who have it. Hereata has it. With classic chutzpah, she is naked in bed with a non-spouse, engaging in sexual copulation at the moment of apprehension. It's a textbook setup. Guilt is real, just as the sky is blue and sunrise is in the morning. Chutzpah begins with counter accusation that the intruder is the culprit who becomes guiltier on momentum. If still enjoined, the practitioner may verge on extreme chutzpah, applying pressure. Fear can be part of chutzpah, in the extreme.

Moeava hangs his head. "I was not afraid."

The successful practitioner allows no slack: "Oh, you were afraid. Or you would not be here. You would be drip-drying on your way to the chicken coop." She laughs. "He likes the scrawny parts."

"I was not afraid. It was windy. And choppy. I was smart."

"It's windy and choppy every time you try. Why that?"

Ravi backs from the lair as the big man turns to go. Then he's gone, his footfall fading down the dirt road. She rolls over with a laugh, "Did you see that?" She reaches for her playmate, but all is lost.

"No. No more. Please, for God's sake."

"Because of that? He's like a son. I raised him. Did. No more. He gave this up. This! So he could risk his life for one little fick with that nutty *putain*. Do I need a man like that around here? A man who insults me? A man who throws my wisdom out the window? A man with less regard for his most important person than for one little rooster spit because that is all he would get. Then he would get the no, no, no, I have a headache, no more, not now, *si'l-te-plaît*. No. Now come here!"

"No, please. You raised him like a son, but you must see his point of view: this is painful for him."

"Who knows more about love? You? I don't think so. A son never got more love than Moeava. I mean love, you crazy man. You're all alike. You think of one thing only. Now come here."

"No."

Her solicitous smile is a tad grotesque in first light. Defiantly radiant, she beams with the dawn, though her new day is already long in the tooth. Yawning like a hippo, she shows moderate dental care and great spirit—and appetite. She laughs, so sleepy and horny all at once, first thing. Can you imagine? She moves in, as if the night had only begun, but he's played out, out to the porch and off to the left, dazed and doubtful on a new day that looked so promising only last night.

She waits her turn, then hikes it for a squat, aiming expertly as ever a woman could. He turns politely away. She fills a basin with fresh water to splash here and there and brush her teeth, calling out that he's welcome to share. Back inside she slips into her dress and visits the mirror for a few strokes of the brush and lipstick, and she's ready again—still willing for a morning go, after all.

But they move to the front porch and onto the road of life, kindred souls getting by, and he laughs at the way of things. Suddenly aware that her dress is inside out, she tells him nothing here is funny.

"You said your friend was after. . . one little fick?"

"I did not. I said Moeava is after it. He's not my friend. You got it wrong. What he's after is a tiny sliver of the cake you had last night."

"Why would she give herself only once?"

"I'm not an attorney. You'll have to ask her. But do you really think you'd be happy eating the neck and the feet once you had the breasts and thighs? Do you really think she could satisfy like I can?"

Ravi gazes on her primal force. "No. I don't think she could provide the same as you."

"Then tell me why you ask, not one hour after giving it up for the fourth time in one night? Four times! Almost five. Why?"

Ravi doesn't know why, but he'll know soon. "I can swim that bay."

She stops. "Yes. I think you can. Over and back in the dark. But you won't. Why would you?" Cars pass, but few people stare at the odd couple because the place is French. People have sexual relations and heated discussion by the road. It's only natural. He hopes a potential employer won't see him, but such concern is residual baggage from a culture of constraint, where nosy people take note and gossip.

On a new tack, she wraps her loving arm around him. "God is my witness. I will fuck you four more times in one night when you swim the bay and back. Not before. Don't worry if you think you can't, not the swim but the other. I have ways, as you well know."

"Hey. I was joking. I have no need to swim that bay anytime."

"You don't want to fuck me four times?"

"I don't want to swim the bay."

She steps ahead on the steep shoulder. "We shall see."

The hotel steps look cracked, chipped and stained, leading up to a fading edifice in need of paint, new siding and general sprucing. She takes his hand in a set piece, in daylight, showing off her catch as any angler would. He doesn't feel caught, but he squirms. He doesn't want the photo from last night; he wants his room across from Taverua.

"Come." She opens the office, starts the printer, plugs in the camera and waits. Fidgeting with a loose thread, she remembers. "My God. I'm inside out." Giggling like a schoolgirl, she crosses her arms to grab the hem and lift the dress overhead for another revelation in the light of day. Tummy in, chest out, she titters, "I think you make me crazy."

Another go might be good at some point, and it's only been an hour. He steps to the lobby window to block onlookers, but nobody looks. They're French. They see a woman, dressed or not. They see a man unshaved, hair mussed. He is tolerated and he smiles. "Coffee?"

"*Mais oui.* Almost." She hits a key and the photo slides out. It shows a tired man beside a dancer with coconuts on her chest. "Put that on my list. She needs salad bowls instead of coconuts. Ha!"

At a table in the corner, she says breakfast is a perk. "Food and Beverage is not even here, but our friendship is strong." How far back do they go? But this is not jealousy because he's free of that, always has been. She scurries to the buffet for pastries and coffee. "They love me here." She engorges a pastry. "Mmm! *C'est très bien!*" The faces of a new friend are many. She pushes crumbs into the hopper.

"Hereata."

"Mmm! You got it right! You know my name!"

"Of course I know your name. Do you know my name?"

"Mmm. . . *Mais oui. Tu t'appelles* Raaaa Veed!"

"Okay. Call me Ravi."

"Okay."

"Hereata. Does the hotel have a dive boat?"

"We have a boat. Yes. You want a job. I know."

"Yes. I want a job. That's what I do. I take tourists diving."

"Yes. I know the dive manager. He is also the captain. You met him very briefly, but he will remember."

"I did? Last night?"

"No. Not last night. This morning. Moeava is the manager. And the captain. It's his boat."

The Danish are soft and cloyingly sweet. She says Moeava's boat is bigger and faster than any boat around, with the best reputation and a full manifest every day from the best hotels, whose guests tip the best. She takes his hands. "It will be the best boat for you."

"But he's your husband!"

"My husband? C'est mon fils. He is my son."

"Your son? But he's. . ."

"What? Believe me, no son wants to see his mother do what I did for you, but he wasn't made to watch, and besides, every son wants his mother relaxed, so she can be nice to the people around her. You did that for me. And for him. So you should get a job on his boat, after all."

Random events seem inevitably linked. Another cup brightens the moment, and the pastry tastes good again. "Does he need somebody?"

"*Mais oui!* Of course we need somebody! I just told you. It's been difficult with that strange female taunting him with her little parsley patch. It's not my place to tell him, but I can't help it. I'm his mother. I worry. Who needs to swim a bay at night?" The short answer is nobody unless a bay at night is the only route to the sparse parsley of his dreams. Moeava could be nineteen or thirty or thirty-five. He looks older from some angles, which would make Hereata thirteen when he was born. "Come. Finish. I have a cot in my office."

Ravi sees her meaning, till she reaches over to ruffle his hair. "Hey. I'm joking too. You rest. Till later. Tonight. Maybe I'll get off early, but don't worry if I can't. We'll get an early start anyway so you can get your rest. You are tired, and my needs are simple—I have a job and a place to live, unlike you. I need only love, which isn't always simple, but it can be. I think you may be *l'homme gentil* to make it so. You will see. We understand simplicity. I am not French. I am Tahitian, but influence is everywhere. You know?"

"I can imagine." At least this situation should not be life threatening. She ruffles his hair again. It's annoying, till she moves deftly into scalp massage. In a minute she says it's time to visit Moeava at the dock, and he follows to the future of her making. Her son? The best boat around? It feels awkward and untrue, a fantasy that cannot last. The morning goes gray with clouds from the north, and he laughs; the bay is so flat.

"Tell me what is funny."

Swim this bay? I could drift this bay. "Nothing is funny. I laugh at how things go."

"Yes. It will go." She squeezes his hand at the walkway by the over-water bungalows. "Eight hundred dollars per night. Plus a hundred dollars for meals. Plus tax." He'll not soon move in those circles and doesn't want to, preferring basics and a reef. "We can stay here." She squeezes again for the fun times ahead and murmurs, "You are not dead, and this is no dream. This is Paradise, what you came to. . ."

From the lavish digs they cross a vacant lot to a dock with a shack at the end. The boat sits opposite where Moeava sorts lines, shackles, bumpers, and anchors. She stops on another squeeze and leans in. "*Nous sommes ici. Bonne chance, mon amour.*"

"You're not going to introduce me?"

"No. You are a man. He is a man. You make your introduction. He will hear you. He will see. No need for Mommy. No more."

"Unless he wants to swim the bay for parsley."

"I know what is best."

Moeava watches the lovers up the dock. She takes her leave without a kiss, leaving Ravi alone, yet again with nothing to lose. Anyone with sea time knows that if the best boat doesn't work out, another best boat will need help. No sweat, except for the beads forming in the usual places. It's last night's liquor and fitful sleep and the strange bed and a woman of indeterminate age and effusive needs.

Do I smell like B.O. and pussy? I'm not ready. Ah, well. . .

He wipes his forehead and smooths his hair. He'd rather shower and change, and a dump wouldn't be bad. But the door opens now. It won't be his first job interview on the fly. Confidence is second nature for seasoned dive crew. That's the stuff. Besides, many Frenchies stink and don't brush. So? "Hello. Bonjour." He speaks from a few steps out.

"Hello." Moeava is ponderously soft-spoken, a grazer. He coils a line with no twists. A waterman can coil in the dark, but he's coiling a bow line when the stern isn't even tied off. But he remembers Ravi, the guy who bagged Mom last night. Moeava is big and casts a bigger shadow. He's hardly twenty-five. Certainly not forty.

"Your mother is a character." Moeava recoils. "A lovely woman," Ravi leads the way through pleasantries to the clearing just yonder where mutual benefits await a dive boat and a dive instructor.

"Do you love her?"

Acutely familiar with sudden challenge, he pauses to think and act, not react. "We just. . . I mean, I think she. . . She's. . . certainly. . ."

"She's not my mother."

"Oh. . . I thought she said. . ." Maybe he's adopted, or she raised him as a *hanai* parent, a common practice in tropical latitudes. *At least we're past the brambles. Now we move gently; don't force it.*

"She tells people she's my mother. But she's not. She wants you to think she's younger." Moeava drops the coils to begin again.

"You can't blame her for taking credit. It's not easy raising a son."

"I told you, I'm not her son. She's my nana—my grandmother. I'm her grandson. It's different."

"Ah. . . Yes. . ."

"What is it that you want?"

"I want a job." Moeava looks puzzled. "I'm a dive instructor."

"You have no job?"

"No. I arrived yesterday. I want to work."

"I think you work fast, no?"

Ravi shrugs off the pussy he scored on night one from the potential employer's grandmother. Best focus on the task at hand: "Fast, slow; it doesn't matter. Sometimes you go fast—like now, with squalls pressing in." He looks up to the clouds as if Moeava doesn't see them. "They're closing slow, so you won't notice. They don't want to look hungry. They'll move out or pounce. What can you do?" He feels good, showing his stuff, yet he doubts this lump will see much.

Moeava breathes through his mouth, over a heavy lip, and looks dim. "What I got to do?"

Ravi shrugs. "You got a boatload of divers, you want them in the water, so the cash register can sing. Cha-ching cha-ching." Moeava gets it: the money song. "Blue sky, flat seas, some big tippers, you go slow. The important thing, fast or slow, is safety with attention to detail. You want to make money fast without losing more money faster."

The big head nods. "I think you have experience in this area. I saw you, with your attention to detail. I wish my nana well, but you are her concern. My concern is for what is mine. Cosima is mine. Mine to have. Not for you. Do you see this as you see what serves you?"

So the *meshugana putain* with the little parsley patch blocks a livelihood. The big man can shove his boat up his ass, or Ravi can give peace a chance. "I'm not interested in what you think is yours. I want a job on a boat. Is your operation sound?"

"You're too old for her."

"You're too fat for her."

Moeava steps up. "I am not fat. Not too fat."

"Then why don't you swim the bay?"

"I will swim the bay."

"I'll help you."

"I don't want your help. I don't need your help."

"I'll still help you. I'll give you a week to swim the bay. I won't even try. If you can't swim in a week, I'll do it—backstroke. Okay?"

"What is it that you want?"

"A job."

Moeava hangs his head. "You can't help me swim. I have to swim."

"Why haven't you done it?"

"I will do it."

"You haven't done it because you can't because you're not a good swimmer. Or you're afraid. That's what your. . . nana said. I heard it."

"I am not afraid!" Moeava yells at his fear and the fellow before him. He grasps the bow line like he knows what to do.

"Tell me, Moi. . . Moiv. . ."

"Moeava."

"Tell me, Moeava: Who lives in this bay?"

Moeava feels the crux of the situation. "Fish."

"Shark?"

Moeava nods.

"Big shark?"

The nod gains gravity.

"Tiger?"

Moeava pumps again.

"Mano is my guide."

"Mano?"

"Shark."

"Ah. *Ma'o*."

"Yeah, her."

"What you mean, guide?"

"Ma'o is scary. But. . . don't worry. . ."

"You no worry." Moeava looks worried.

"I worry, Moeava, when I have no faith. That's the hard part. You get scared, and Ma'o smells you. You no scared, Ma'o leave you be."

The clouds pile on. "You no scared?"

"I was. I used it up. Not too long ago. Mano—Ma'o—was there. You must not doubt, or you'll do it wrong again."

"If you was scared, why he no get you?"

"I don't know. But you run shark dives. You make money on Ma'o. Ma'o takes care of you. Why should you be scared?"

"Blacktip on shark dive. I no scared."

"It's the same spirit." Moeava's face skews to the clouds. Ravi doubts that esoteric banter on fear and parsley will help job prospects. But cats' feet scurry, and a water witch rises on the bay, whipping froth like an eggbeater a thousand feet tall, coming this way.

In the melee Moeava yells in French or Tahitian that needs no translation. The boat bucks on sudden gusts and pulls the line between his hands. He should have tied to a cleat ten minutes ago, before the rocky banks on either side became a threat. Ravi fends off the stern to soften impact, as Moeava loses the line. The bow swings free. The stern rounds again, and a wave breaks on board to swamp the deck. So Ravi jumps aboard, sloshes to the console and turns the key. "Aargh!"

With deck, batteries, and ankles submerged, the complete circuit sends twelve volts up both legs. Moeava yells to stand on the seat, and the engine starts. Heavy torque dips the stern to near sinking but moves the boat. The waterspout collapses. Clouds cleave. The sun slides through every fissure, and Cook's Bay lies down flat.

The job application ends with Ravi at the helm in a victory lap to drain the deck through the scuppers. Coming around lighter, he throttles down twenty yards out, finds neutral, jumps to the bow for the line and eases on in to kiss the bumpers, toss the line and tie off the stern with a half hitch. Moeava ties off too and lumbers in for a hug but slumps when a dorsal slices the surface. At about ten inches, the fin suggests a young adult in the seven-foot range. "*Là-bas*. Your friend." The fish lolls in a lazy circle.

"This is contact. *Aumakua*, brother. On the day of our reckoning."

"You want to swim with that guy?" They see it's only the dorsal tip above the surface.

"Bigger than I thought. Maybe fifteen feet to the tip of the tail."

Moeava steps back. "Three, four times every week he comes by."

The shark rolls to show her bottom. "I've never had it this close. Look at her skin. She's perfect."

"Why you say 'she?'"

"No nuts. A male tiger that big would have nuts to his knees. Hey. Tell me you don't feel it."

"Oh. I feel him."

"Hey, this shark isn't as scary as imagining her and not seeing her."

"Yeah. This not scary. We standing on a dock. Hey, your own self. Why you no swim with your good friend?"

Ravi laughs. "I think we will."

"You crazy."

"I heard that before."

"Why you wait?"

"I hope she likes me, but I want to be sure. You know how it is with a female. If I'm wrong, I won't get the job." The big shark cruises south. "See her rocking. She's not hungry. She's enjoying life. Everyone should. You believe that, don't you?"

Moeava seems sanguine at last. "Okay. You get one job."

"Thank you. You mean dive leader?"

"Yeah. And you be captain too."

"But I thought. . ."

"No. I just learning. You show me what to do."

"Hereata said this is the best boat around."

"Ah, *oui*. What can she say? She is my mother in all things."

So they agree to begin tomorrow if the hotel books passengers. Today, Ravi can get his gear and have time to rest after long travels and longer vigils on the island of his dreams. If the hotel—Hereata— finds no divers on such short notice, they'll practice because those who would run together want to see the other's comfort and air consumption.

Moeava must know how to run a boat. But then why. . . But squalls are rare. But any waterdog knows that shit happens, or he hasn't been wet for too long. Will he know what to do with Ravi below on a six-pack in a squall or a current or both? If Ravi brings them up in big seas, and they're invisible in the troughs. . .

Well, fuck it. This was your idea.

But why would a guy get a boat and a prime spot with a dock and a shack if he doesn't know squat? Niggling questions and gnats buzz under the ceiling fan. Ravi dozes on a dream of workaday worry. Won't it be great in a year or two, looking back on these tiny *maninis* in the bigger picture?

Workaday, and then Tomorrow

Hermit crab is a messy eater—good for anemone riding on top, who snags debris and provides camouflage and may attract small fish. Hermit/anemone friendship is based on mutual benefit.

Moray and jack cruise in joint venture to find a burrow and stake out the entrance and exit. Prey exits from one or the other, and chance will balance the catch.

Surgeonfish pluck algae from turtle's back, as turtle gets cleaned and soothed by the gentle touch.

Cleaner shrimps snack blithely in moray's maw on tidbits, and moray gets a dental cleaning.

Ravi and Moeava share means and know-how. Tolerant and flexible, they give and take with tact and difficulty. A new operation needs time to get the word out. And a free day will ease the veteran back into routine. A trial dive seems best because Moeava is likable, which counts for nothing or worse at depth, where things can change. The morning schedule further defers to need, with Hereata at the dock first thing, wrapped in a *pareo* to accentuate her best and soften the other. She is no contender in Cosima's league but can still throw the knockout punch on lips and nipples, fluffed and highlighted. With six for tomorrow, the boys are optimistic, kind of. Moeava is a certified diver, but so are a million nimrods flashing C cards, kicking heads, blowing off tanks in a few minutes, grabbing octopuses, or glomming some narcosis and going deep.

Moeava might be sound and should be trainable. They head out to a pass, but anchorage and tide are hard to read. Ravi follows the chart plotter to fifty feet, to keep things simple. In mild current on sandy bottom, they set the hook and go over. They check the anchor, signal okay and meander into the current. It picks up, bringing groupers and lemon sharks with a few Galapagos sharks in the mix. A few more sharks fade in and out of visibility. When the current gains to a knot, they work another hundred yards then drift back, until Ravi clears his mask and spews blood. It could be congestion from bad diet or liquor, but then comes the headache.

Rising slow as he dares, he skips the safety stop because it was hardly sixty feet, and time may be short. At the surface, a hock and a snuk gush with bloody snot. He feels it coming and rolls onto his back to avoid drowning, as delirium takes over—as he flops intermittently to face up and now down.

A test has been failed, as other tests arise. Moeava can't move too well or cross-chest carry another diver in gear or tow Ravi by the scruff and make progress against the current. He could ditch the gear but fears the loss. He squeezes Ravi into place, as if to prevent the rollover. Ravi gurgles, so he heads for the boat. Finally, awkwardly aboard, he ditches his rig, cranks the engine, shags the anchor and motors over to drag Ravi onto the swim step. Ravi convulses and pukes blood.

Moeava blows blood too, and carbon monoxide is the easy call. Ravi moans on the ride back—he cannot work with anyone so dangerously dim. Moeava ties off as he's learned to do, as Ravi shuffles to the compressor. It's not so old and chugs along, pumping tanks to three grand. Welded exhaust extensions get the smoke twenty feet from the fresh-air intake to avoid monoxide poisoning, but somebody wrapped each weld with resin. It slumps, thick on the bottom, thin on top, crazed from sunlight, letting pinhole jets of exhaust into the mix near the compressor. He glares. Moeava sees. "Shit happens. You know that. From what I hear, you're an expert."

REEFDOG

Like siblings they swat and insult through the basics of clean air compression, no carbon monoxide allowed. Details of ultimate consequence are reviewed as welds are cut and ground clean, re-welded and covered with fiberglass roving, matt, and more roving, with epoxy in three light coats between layers, then duct-taped against sunlight. On groans, curses, and admonitions, the lesson sinks in as their lovely life together takes another step.

•

Moeava cops to the mistake. Shit does happen, but it shouldn't always happen. He pledges care and picks up the slack on prep, driving, docking, anchoring, fueling, servicing, and cleaning the boat. He sees the potential and need at hand. He does not own the boat but would like to. He leases from an old friend of his nana. Ravi can't trust his work without review: engine oil, hull plugs, the outdrive leg, lines, knots, thimbles, shackles, seizing, anchor, spare anchor—the minutiae a dive leader depends on.

Ravi is clear on Hereata's recruitment campaign. He doesn't mind. Tit for tat is fair play. In the catbird seat all along, he got a job made to order, or it could be, and the money should pick up. The two-tank fare times six, times three hundred would be great, and it's a full boat the next day.

Distraction continues with the meatball and bad intention. Hereata struts alongside, trussed again to advantage for the good of mankind, with the heels, the lift and spread a man can admire. Bound for glory, she virtually demands that we all just get along. "You will have a wonderful dive experience."

Moeava steps up to grab the thick fellow's dive bag. "Get on. We go already."

Ravi stows and begins the briefing. Moeava translates on depth, bottom time, buddies, hand signs, what might be seen or expected. Long ago regarded for local knowledge, no casualties and the seal of approval from the Crusty one, this drill is perfunctory and French. He skips the details and for laughs eats a banana and drops the peel, pretending not to see it, so he can step on it and barely avoid breaking his neck because the French love slapstick. But a man picks up the peel and flings it overboard, and they laugh like hyenas. This might take a while. Ravi plays it straight, looking overboard for his banana peel. They watch.

Then it's off to the pass. He only dove the first half, but snaggletooth lemons should come in for a sniff; hammerheads will cruise around the corner, and Galapagos may dart in on a dare.

The current is stronger on the surface and sweeps to another current, heading out. Currents this strong can't be resisted, except by fools. Tourists assume that the crew knows conditions, so they wonder why he's taking so long, like he's stumped or worried. "Spring tide. Everybody comfortable with current?" Moeava puts it in neutral and translates. Ravi tells him: "No anchor, drift and watch the bubbles. Sixty feet. Fifty minutes, and we come up with the boat right there. Okay?" He watches Moeava till the big man turns away. Donning more like a cat burglar than a Degas dancer, he sits on the rail. "Backflip. Okay?"

Moeava helps with fins, air valves, and regulators; it's like checking for mittens, lunch money, and nametags but worse. Ravi emphasized the back roll into the water all at once so they can stay together. They stare until Moeava says three words, and they nod. Once in the water—*dans l'eau*—they will descend quickly. Holding his mask and reg in place, he rolls back. They follow with a few kicks to heads and regroup at the stern, where they share the okay sign and descend. Ravi eases into the drift, signaling to follow close. He can't hear the engine, and the current is gaining. He can't slow down and can only hope Moeava will keep up. Above all, he stays calm.

The little troupe speeds along, with nobody hanging onto a passing rock or trying to go back. A hammerhead cruises past, which counts for a highlight only a few minutes in. They wend along the bottom from sixty feet to seventy, going outside the dive plan but in less current. Eighty feet on a sixty-foot plan is iffy and ninety is what Crusty would call fucking with the phantom. But ninety gets them under the current, and a gang of mantas approach in single file. A female leads twelve males in the manta love chain. They swoop within inches, securing all fares on drama. Tips should also peg the meter, and word-of-mouth will add value in the birth of a reputation. *Should I tell them about my perfect day, with four hours of work and a round of golf?*

Less secure is the rest of the dive, off plan, improv, and maybe out to sea. Fifteen feet for three minutes might be a dicey safety stop, given goofballs, meatballs, and current. Local knowledge would be valuable, if he knew someone who had it because Moeava is local without the knowledge. *Let's take this one step at a time.*

He signals slow ascent and at thirty feet sees the anchor coming down at a slant because Moeava is feeding the rode slowly over while steering and peering over the side. Give the boy some credit. The anchor hangs behind the boat at fifteen feet. Or is he trolling? The divers gather as instructed, but air expansion in six buoyancy compensators ascending from ninety feet to fifteen hurries the rise because every diver dumps on the way up, unless he doesn't. A waterman wishes he'd gone into sales or construction or anything. He won't get bent if he can stay down. Something feels, wrong, or is that just part of a pattern?

He scurries among them, seeking dump strings. But each releases a trickle, and they rise—until he sees the meatball grin or wince, hard to tell. The fleshy man is pressing his inflator in short bursts to offset each dump and keep the group ascending until the dive leader cures the problem. A meatball might tussle on a pool-deck stage, but underwater he's flotsam.

Ravi pulls his knife. The meatball throws his arms up in defense. Ravi would puncture the BC to secure the safety stop. The lost BC can be charged to the meatball's credit card. Maybe. Or maybe Ravi Rockulz will be looking for a decent boat in Cucamonga or Timbuktu, where crews snigger over a load of tourii, bent and drowned, ascending from ninety feet on a sixty-foot plan and lost at sea, where some may still be, in parts or globs of lumpy shark shit. The blade flashes. A BC can be stitched over a new bladder—who cares? But the meatball kicks away and shoots to the surface. The group settles back to fifteen feet, hugging the anchor.

Soon all are on board, murmuring over the shark and mantas and the safety stop that wasn't so safe. Most keep an eye on the thick fellow who mopes and the lean fellow who sits beside him and speaks. "That was great. Wasn't it?" Moeava translates. Most mumble agreement. Ravi tells them what happened. "We got out of our plan. That's never good. But look—" Reaching for his gauge, he points out maximum depth, ninety-three feet because a challenge will come down to facts and witnesses. "Our dive plan was to sixty-five feet, but we got in a current with manta rays. Ninety-three feet for twenty-four minutes calls for a safety stop at fifteen feet. Three minutes would do, but we stayed five—all but one of us. So we're within safe limits, and I anticipate no problems. But we take precaution. Okay?"

He waits for the translation then turns to the thickset man. "I will report you to the police for terroristic endangerment of every person here. Good luck with that. You're at risk for decompression sickness. Are you stiff or sore yet?" The big brow bunches. "You'll know soon enough. Remember, no exertion. No beating off in the shower. Okay?" The bigger man is subdued with concern.

A woman leans in. "Can I walk on the beach?"

Ravi shrugs. "You should know. You may have nitrogen in your system. Stimulation can be tricky. How much stimulation? You tell me. Maybe you can stay calm. If your blood pressure goes up on too much nitrogen. . ." He shrugs and pouts. "*Capiche?*" He moves to the helm. Moeava regards him with a glance and steps aside, relieved that there's more than one fuckup in this outfit. The second dive is shallow, brief and boring, ending their first day at the office.

At the dock farewells are again perfunctory with forced humor; and no, the frogs don't tip. Ah, well, the crew laughs at any rate when the meatball lumbers up, pausing to lean on the handrail, mumbling Slovakian. Moeava says, "That guy. Do you think he will bend?"

"He could. Fifty-fifty." Ravi turns with a game question: "Would you like to find out?"

So they put the boat to rights, hose off and drive twelve miles around to the hotel facing the channel near the *motus*. Over a few beers in the bar, they review the depth and godforsaken current that somebody local should have known. Moeava recalls what went right, and they determine sites for tomorrow.

Three beers in, the heavily rouged woman from a few nights ago slides in at the bar. Ravi gets a receptive smile for his stare, so he signals the bartender. She orders "the usual," which looks like the working girl's toddy: top-drawer vodka, make that a double, straight up. It may be prearranged, with the bartender serving water with a kickback, but who cares?

She agrees to perform as requested for fifty thousand francs, or five hundred dollars. Okay, three hundred—okay, one fifty because Moeava is too big for a discount; come on. But this is for Oybek, her recent date. She relents on a pledge of more work in the future.

At the sundries shop nearby, Ravi buys two bottles of sparkling wine, *La Vie en Chartreuse*, bottled in Cambodia, and a small container of cobra liniment because stimulants trigger the bends. Charisse will visit Oybek, get the bubbly into him and do him up like no tomorrow—"Like a bronco buster, baby. Can you do that?"

"I am professional. You don't know what I can do."

"Good. He's depressed. We want to snap him out of it."

"I don't finks he is depressed. I finks he is. . . malade."

"Tonight is our special surprise. After the hoochie-coochie get him into the shower and rub this stuff all over. Make him a pussy cat."

"Oui, mais ze pussy cat c'est moi, Monsieur."

"Yes. But he broke up with his girlfriend—didn't he tell you? Such a martyr. She looks like you." Charisse is confused, till Ravi assures. "This is what he loves. He's a wonderful fellow."

She rolls her eyes. "I finks one hundred fifty will not—"

"Okay, two hundred. But, when you get him in the shower and get him rubbed all over, then give him the. . ." Ravi jams tongue to cheek, pursing his mouth on the imaginary shaft, in hand. Charisse needs no charade. Nobody doubts her skill, but Ravi stipulates a hundred now and the rest later. And it's off to see the wizard. It's only a prank, and it's good to act out.

Oybek is difficult at the door, not in the mood and not hospitable, but Charisse coos that she can't stop thinking about him and his grandeur. He demurs in Slavic slur. She eases in.

Ravi and Moeava lean on a tree near the louvered window in back. Ravi whispers that she's either offering the freebie or a discount.

Moeava laughs. He hadn't thought of that but thinks he too would maximize profit if he could sell pussy. "Why not? I would fuck every night if I could get paid. Why not make more?" As a boat whore, he can only charge once. They stifle their giggles, bonding as men, and Moeava pulls a joint from his pocket. He lights up and inhales a third of it before offering. "You like marijuana?"

"I believe I do." Corks pop inside and soon begin the grunts and groans and yes, don't stop, yes, there. . . *La petite mort* is silent, till Charisse wants a shower. He grumbles to go, let him rest. She smears hot sauce on him, and he moans. She titters. She finks she can get him up for another go, over here. Bring the bubbly.

Very stoned, Ravi wonders aloud if they have wasted their money on a menace to society. Moeava shakes his head. "Not my money."

"Maybe it'll be a good lesson for a reactionary prick."

"Yes. May be. He is a prick."

"Not him. Me. It should teach me to lay off the revenge and spend my money more wisely, like on pussy and liquor for me."

"And me." They laugh again, until the lament. They peek in as Charisse leaves half dressed, carrying the rest of her things.

Moeava turns to go. "Wait."

Ravi ducks between bungalows and around to the open door. The big man on the sofa doesn't quite convulse but quivers on the verge. Steam pours out the shower. Moeava steps up. Ravi says, "Medium case. I've seen worse. I think he won't die. Unless he's got other problems. Hard to say. Muscle guys show it worse. Come on."

"Should we call somebody?"

"I don't think so."

Oybek mutters what could be gibberish or the Ukrainian national anthem. Then he yelps. They roll the hulk to his side, so his face is into the sofa to muffle the sound. They turn off the shower and head out to Moeava's small truck. On the road, Ravi suggests another beer. Moeava says, "You really something. You get that guy. For good. Now you want more beer."

"That guy got himself."

"I like that. I like how you do that. You all American."

"No. I'm not American. I never was. I like what it stands for. What it stood for."

Moeava slaps the wheel and says he wants to be more American, like Ravi; it was so fucking perfect. *C'est fucking parfait!*

"It's not great. It's a personal problem. It's never been great."

"Whatever you say." They ride in silence, till Moeava slaps the wheel again. "Man!"

"I wish we hadn't done that." It's bad enough behaving like a psychopath, let alone teaching someone else. Regret sinks in for a few more miles.

•

"You know what I think?" Moeava is reflective.

"No. *Je ne sais pas quoi tu penses.*"

"Pas quoi; ce que. Je ne sais pas ce que *tu penses."*

"Mais oui. I don't know what you think. But I wonder."

"I think you got no regret. I think you say regret, so nobody think you crazy. Nobody but me think anything anyway. *Je pense que tu es mal, et tant pis.* I think you crazy no matter what. That guy got the bends is crazy too. Everybody *un peu mal,* but he much worse crazy. *Il est trop mal. Il est mal, froid.* I think deep down, *dans ton coeur,* you want to hurt that guy. You need to hurt that guy. Maybe kill that guy. You say, *il est mort, peut-être; tant pis.* I think you would not be so good at hurting him if you did not want to hurt him. It was good. Man. It was very good."

"And why do you think I need to hurt people?"

"I don't know. But I think I find out pretty soon."

"I think I need help. And pretty soon you will too."

"I think you help yourself. Don't worry. We don't need no stinking regret. Ha! Hey. You see that one, with the guys all farting?"

•

Moeava is a contradiction, an oaf on the one hand, insightful on the other—as if the one is a ruse, a clever pretext to highlight the other. Maybe he's stupid like a fox. Lingering doubt compels Ravi to double-check most of his work, especially where life and limb are at risk. Other doubt lingers on personal assessment: Ravi is a known commodity at home, but he's far from home. So what has he become? What's become of him? What still wells up inside? Home can be anywhere with friends and a family forming up, and maybe this is it. Or maybe he's doomed to repetition. He thinks himself a regular guy who swung at a curve ball—make that a meatball out of nowhere in a screwy world calling for screwy response. That's all. Yet Moeava's correction hits with realization that he is superior at revenge.

•

Supple as a walrus at depth, Moeava flounders on the surface and lumbers up the dock. But he opens up to guidance. "Look." Ravi coils a line slowly, dismissing the figure eight, to avoid tangling on a rapid payout. "Lay it flat. No tangle. It looks better, and you won't trip on it. Look. . ." He throws a half hitch, a braking half wrap and a trucker's hitch for securing with no slack. Finally comes the bowline that won't tighten under load, advising his boss to practice till it's mindless, till the hands can tie it without the brain.

Ravi swims alongside and dumps the big man's BC by half to settle him a few inches deeper. Moeava strives for coordination. On the bottom, he can move the anchor and twenty-four feet of chain easier than two smaller men, moving ground tackle away from coral to sand, preserving livelihood.

When the big shark stays gone, Moeava swears she came twice in the week before Ravi arrived. Ravi takes it as a compliment and says a tiger shark will stay near a food source till it's gone—or will come around with a message. Does Moeava feel it, the kinship? Moeava laughs. "*Je ne sais pas, mais. . . je sais qu'il n'est pas Ma'o.*"

"*Pourquoi pas?*"

"Because. She scare shit from me."

Ravi nods. "Me too, but. . .that's the test. If your spirit guide is the Easter Bunny, you're a pussy. You get money under your pillow for teeth falling out of your head. Is that what you want?"

"That would be *la petite sourie. Et oui.*"

"Same difference. It's warm and fuzzy, great for kids, but not for men. With no test, you get no faith."

Moeava ruminates. "Why must I be afraid? I like Easter Bunny."

"Easter Bunny is a rabbit. He hides colored eggs."

"What is the problem? I was happy. I want to take Easter Bunny for a boat ride. Not Ma'o. Fuckeen' haoles. Always tryin' change things around, with fear and guilt. . . Hey. No offense."

"None taken. I'm not haole; I'm Jewish. And this isn't my idea."

"Pshh. . ."

"You scoff. It wasn't the Jews who came to steal resources or convert people to the correct religion."

Moeava stoops with a grunt to open the cooler. "Jews did something wrong. You know this. Everybody pissed off at them."

"Not everybody. Only those in need of a scapegoat."

"I don't know. I think it has to do with the money. You know how everybody talk about getting Jewed."

"Are you getting Jewed?"

"Hmm. . . I don't think so. But I don't know. Am I?"

"I don't think so too. But don't worry; you can't help yourself from offending me. So I take no offense. Haoles. Jews. It makes no difference who you blame for your troubles, as long as it's not yourself. Right?"

Moeava chews this bone and finally agrees. "I think you are right. It is the others who are to blame." His final dive of the day is under the ice and colas to the bottom for the Hinano six-pack sunk there hours ago. Done with glad-handing, clearing and rinsing, sorting and stowing, he pops two and offers one. "It is good that you see this. I can say many things to offend you. But you will understand."

They drain two-thirds on a synchronized glug and sigh in harmony. "I understand," Ravi says, ending the ceremony on a baritone belch. Moeava ups the ante on a scale and two chords. They laugh like men, bonded stronger still. So friendship forms on the stone-ax simplicity of their forebears.

Moeava woofs fried bananas and farts out loud. Ravi calls him disgusting and dribbles *poisson cru* on his T-shirt. Moeava says, "You eat like an animal."

"I am an animal." They agree, drink beer, and tell jokes. It's easy, until Cosima comes lolling, casual as Ma'o but more posed, possibly angling. She's an eye-popper but not a bonding event; Moeava laid claim; Ravi acquiesced. But it won't settle. Ravi has a woman, a zesty wench with zero inhibition. Yet he salivates at the dish nearby. Who but a fool would risk everything and hurt a friend? Not that a dive job is everything, but it's all he has. And for what? Some parsley? Let's face it: parsley is best in butter, oozing, bitter and chewy, a perfect garnish for baby red potatoes or life. He ignores Cosima in a sheer blouse for the good of his friendship with Moeava and for fun. Moeava grew up with topless women but squints like an astronomer at a little man on the moon. Ravi works on, cleaning regulators.

She approaches her admirer, scratching an itch on a breast. "Have you been swimming lately?" She turns to Ravi, "Not you. You don't have to swim. Just him because he can't."

Ravi won't look. "Why is that? Do you want him to drown?"

She thinks it over. "He can drown in water, or I can drown in blubber. He has a better chance. No?"

"So what? I get a freebie?" She giggles. "I thought it was a magic spell, and you are the prize. If you give it away with no swim, the big winner only gets second. Not so good."

She hurries off like a waterspout but more huffy. Stuck on a shrinking view, Moeava concedes, "Second prize. Not good."

"Wouldn't be bad. She's plenty prize to go around. Besides, she's crazy. You don't want to be number one if she's crazy."

Moeava wants to be nothing but number one, so he fetches another beer. "You girlfriend or wife, whatever she is, got used up by a. . . *malade* before you met her. You don't mind? Why you here?" He lumbers off to avoid the friction. Ravi tinkers with a reg. Did Hereata tell him everything? Does he doubt that Ravi could pluck and eat this little peach in a blink with no regret? *Loyalty goes so far, Mssr Moe. You pay an honest wage for honest work. I throw a lifetime of experience into the bargain. At my age with my know-how, Mssr Moe, which is mechanical and nautical and social and touristic too. I throw in some loyalty, no extra charge. But we have reached a point. You can't swim the bay, night or day, so why worry? Why taunt me?*

Except that it wasn't a taunt. It was self-defense. Ravi would not regret eating Moeava's peach, but he'd hate the sticky aftermath. Still, it's easy to ponder the skittish woman. He blows out the reg, screws the case back on, shags another beer, and sits. Day is done, not a bad day and not so different from the old days, except for missing the old crowd and options forming up. But slow times are part of transition, settling in, getting connected, enjoying less as a means to more. He's not looking at death or dead ends, and a sixty-watt bulb is enough to read by. Or he can walk up the road in the dark. Or have some sardines and head over to Taverua for another beer and perhaps a recent divorcée in reasonably good shape. Or he could sit right where he is, into the night and following day, waiting for the future to begin. He recalls a similar funk, in his beater Tercel. That was worse, with the girlfriend, make that wife, and her crazy woes. That funk led to scar tissue. This one is nothing. Things are working out, shaping up.

He perks to a scent and sees boys under the tree by the picnic table, laughing and smoking like a small factory. He moves slower than only a few years ago—maybe twelve years or fourteen. But he's spry enough for a hit or two to pad his cell. The boys are game, passing to the new guy—the old guy—who steps into the circle of universal language. Soft as cashmere, time slows. . .

He drifts back to securing things and looks up to where he wouldn't look before. She's back to tell him there's no show tonight so she'll work in the gift shop. She removes her blouse and skirt to change into her *pareo* for work—and to steal his better sense. She says her job is menial and pays a pittance.

He shares his hope to build the dive business with Moeava and engage his camera soon. They trade details on identity and goals, like urban professionals in a chic bistro, clearing the way to sex, to uplift a day or an hour. But this is tropical and remote. She repeats her special dispensation that he need not swim the bay because she knows he can. He's very stoned and can't tell what comes next. He'd like to duck in for quick sexual relations and pretend it never happened, which seems easy. But he reminds her that giving herself without the swim would undermine the spell. She says he would not be excused but would make the swim later.

"How about now?"

"It's not dark." He laughs again, as if laughing at her, and so he is. She's so serious and nutty, and a quickie seems like a terrible hurry on such a feast, and he feels the crosshairs on him, as if he learned nothing. Moeava is no whacko cousin. He's a harmless *blala* who may be a brother in need. But the devilish rack is ready to poke him in the eye. . .

"I didn't mean right now for the swim."

"Oh! No, I have to work! I told you. After that, okay. I get off ten thirty. All finish by eleven. Okay?" She takes his silence for affirmation and drifts. Time winds back to forty beats per minute. Or is that the clop, clop, clop of high heels from the opposite direction? The step adjusts to avoid cracks like dissonance in a Monk tune, and she rounds the corner with a practiced leer. She steps up and takes his hand. "Come with me. Smoking that stuff will make you stupid. I want to feed you. Then I want to show you something." So he sighs and goes, glancing at Moeava watching out the window. How long has he been there? Moeava nods, so maybe it's not to worry.

She leads the way to a new lair of lavish comfort. This is not the future foreseen. He will soon learn that she's fifty-three, not so old, considering a grandson of twenty-six. But age is incidental on the way to seeing what she has to show, which is a honeymoon bungalow over a former reef that was cleared for construction then dragged back in hopes of recovery, to amuse discriminating travelers. It's painful to imagine but feels like a dream with a viewing window in the floor and a light on the little fishes, so cute.

Hereata's inflamed gum won't give her a minute's peace till she removes an incisor and bridge and sets it in a glass by the bed. The top third of her hair is also removed to a lampshade on the escritoire. Her nail clippers hack a stubborn overhang, big toe, left side, as she moans with satisfaction. Then it's time for the entrée: himself. But all that stuff is *manini,* in another pattern that's not bad because a man will choose sex and room service over sardines and a bush bird any day. Are you kidding? He could be dead tomorrow. Or someday.

Fifteen years his elder and past her prime doesn't matter; she's so generous with a bevy of moves and a mini-fridge. She easily trumps a book and a long shot. Better to jump to princedom than to grovel in the pond. Better to slip into fancy bedding with a hostess of means than swim a bay in the dark. This is not the thrilling adventure of a new woman or a game second go. It's a routine. She rides like seasoned crew, rolling delectably to the ocean swell. . .

From the aftermath and sleep, he wakens to see the clock: 10:30. 10:31. 10:32. He watches the minutes and knows that sexual relations with Cosima will be better in a day or two when they're fresh. And he sighs, free of the silly pursuit. But he can excuse himself for something or other—not beer because it's in the mini-fridge with the snacks. He could go for a walk—that's it, a walk. Then he'll be back.

Yet she grasps a leg and another leg and oozes over, plying the back muscles to the neck and shoulders as she turns him for the pin and puts him back to sleep at 10:42.

The sun rises on a nameless man with no coordinates in luxuriant comfort floating anonymously. He remembers: it's a top-drawer bungalow, thanks to what's-her-name, Here. . . Hera. . . the unusual woman who gets him up at will, which seems odd for one so elderly. How does she do that? Eyes open on cue as the hostess with the mostest looks up with a weary grin. That's how. Reality jams into overdrive. Mascara runny as erosion rivulets, a missing tooth, and service orientation make it memorable. Ah, Paradise. This is what happened. It could be worse. Coffee and Danish served at the front door are excellent. So he showers, eats, and bids adieu on a kiss and gratitude for another full boat. He'll take it easy tonight at his place and see her bye 'n bye, maybe tomorrow.

She caresses his cheek. "You are right. Tonight is Thursday. Buffet dance. All you can eat. Very late. But you are wrong. Tomorrow I leave. You will not see me."

"Where are you going?"

"Away." She turns away. "I'm going away." That means he'll have time to find a place to live, with a kitchen. "You won't see me."

"I heard you. You're going to Papeete?"

"Yes."

"And then you'll come back?"

"I haven't decided."

"What are your choices?"

"It's not up to me." Oh, no—what he must not ask is whom, in fact, *it* is up to. Her charms are so rich around dusk, only to murk at dawn. "I said it's not up to me."

"Yes. I heard. What are the choices of whomever it is up to?" Well done, asking the obvious question yet avoiding the trap.

"I suppose one choice is to have me stay away. I suppose the other choice is to have me come back and see what I have to show then."

This too is a skillful parry. To avoid the mortal repartee, he says, "Very good. I'll see you when you get back."

"Yes?"

"Why not?"

"What do you mean, 'why not?' You're so ungracious, after all that I show you. I can tell you as well: the over-water bungalow is rare and will not happen often. We will be at my house. You can move in at that time."

"It's too small."

"No. It's just right. Moeava will be living at the dive shop."

"He can't stay at the dive shop."

"It was his idea."

"I won't be the reason he moves out of his own house."

"It's time. He's twenty-six already."

"He told me twenty-nine."

"He lies. He needs psychiatric help, but it would cost more than the lies. Who cares how old anybody is anyway?"

"You make a good point. But I'm not ready to move into your place, even if he wants to move out. I want my own place. I just got here. I need to get my life in order first."

"Qu'est-ce que c'est premier? Qu'est-ce que c'est vie? Is this not the life? A very good life, I might add. A life many people all over the world would envy. Tahiti. Me." She sits up, chest out.

"You sound like my mother."

"She must be a smart woman."

"Yes. She's neurotic too. Always insisting."

"We want what's best for you."

"Many people do. But I'm not so dumb as I let on. Trust me on this—we'll get along, but not every day and night. I appreciate what you have to show, and I want to keep that appreciation fresh."

"I think you want to chase girls."

"Maybe. Who knows? You seem confident in your hospitality."

"I am. It's true. You would be foolish to give this up. You might think me old and fat or uncouth, any of those things men think once they get rid of their stuff—oh, they think they can do without for an hour or two. Then it's honey, baby, where are you? Am I right?"

"Yes, you are right. And so am I. We understand our love."

She perks. "Don't say that."

"You're right. I shouldn't say that."

"Unless you mean it."

"Okay. I'll be more careful."

"Come here."

"No. I have to go. We'll fuck again on Saturday if we don't get a better offer."

"I hate that word."

"It's better than love, *n'est-ce pas?*"

"Fool."

"Toujours, ma cherie."

The Future Thrust Upon Us

Hereata's benefits and demands are compelling and consequential. *Coming home* feels familiar and secure when it occurs as a duet. Comfort displaces challenge when the world steps back, and a man can relax. She'll be sixty in a few years, which may account for her focus. He can't blame her or meet her need. For now, a man and a woman provide for each other, accepting the terms of peace because she'd rather have some sugar instead of none.

He'll find a place of his own to avoid moving out later. How would she feel at sixty, with a man of forty-five? Never mind. The bungalow near Taverua is not a home. Better to find a place now for stability and to keep things fresh.

So after the morning charter and with no divers booked for tomorrow, time opens up. And so does fortune when a wayward reefdog meets another dog—an underdog who works Taverua. Bungalow to restaurant, this tail wagger seeks goo-goo talk and hand-outs. He might get a shout or a shoe, but what's a dog to do? Ravi shouted twice to stop him from following after sharing a Danish, but give a dog a break. Expressive and quick, the pup seems a mix of black lab and something smaller. A terrier with a stepladder? By this time Ravi knows the manager/owner, who calls out, "Hey! Do you want that dog?"

"I can't have a dog. I have no place to live. But if I did. . ."

"Okay. I thought maybe. . . I'll call for the pickup. He begs my guests. We can't have it."

"But he's so cute. Look at him. Just a little dog."

The dog wags and jumps all the way up to lick Ravi's chin.

"A dog needs a home. He can't stay here."

"What will happen when they pick him up?"

The manager/owner shrugs. "What will happen is what happens in these things. Believe me, my friend, we have no shortage of dogs."

"Could you keep him as a mascot if he had his inoculations, and he gets neutered? I will have that done. Your guests love him. A dog is good for business. Most of them miss their own dogs. If that little dog lives here, they'll take pictures of him. He'll be on the Internet. He could get more hits than Lindsay Lohan on a DUI."

"What is a Lindsay Lohan?"

Ravi smiles, affirmed in this new place. But the manager is too busy for sentiment, "We can't have him here. I have too much to do. You may ask at the humane place if they need another dog, but look around. They don't. Nobody does."

The dog heels, pressing his face to Ravi's knee, as only a smart dog would do. A tourist says she's going past the animal clinic, and they sometimes find homes for dogs, and she can give them a lift. The dog jumps in, sensing home at last; never mind that it has no walls, furniture, dishes, yard, or anything but the bond. Never mind that home is a car; it's where the heart is, and a dog's heart is with the pack, at that moment defined. Obvious to the dog is that life starts now. They ride in back. "What's his name?"

Ravi thinks briefly. "Little Dog. I call him Little Dog."

"Little Dog? Not much of a name. But cute."

"It fits." Little Dog tongue-lashes his new pal. Ravi wipes his face, scoffing but pulling the dog close.

Two women at the humane place do not need another dog, not with a dozen dogs out back in eight kennels, four dogs coming in and many more in need of shelter. One woman is a volunteer who speaks only French. The other is speaks spotty English and French slow enough to follow. She knows a woman whose uncle is looking for a dog for his farm on Huahine.

"They don't have dogs on Huahine?"

"I don't know."

"How do you know Uncle won't. . . eat the dog?"

"We don't think that will happen. People really don't do that here."

We don't finks zat weel happen. . .

"They really don't? Does that mean they sometimes do?"

"He probably wants a dog to bark if someone comes onto the place. We cannot know more than that."

"Will Uncle get him inoculated?"

"Yes, the dog will be inoculated and neutered in the near future."

Little Dog tries another lick. "Can I have a minute to think?"

"Of course you can."

"Um. . . I'm looking for a place to live. Is there a paper that would list places for rent?"

"You may do better driving around. Most people with a place to rent will post a sign."

"I don't have a car, but maybe I can use my friend's truck."

"Look." Behind her is a bulletin board with notices in French. One says, *À Louer, ici* for a room with good light and ventilation, *une salle de bain et une cuisine* for three hundred XFP per day, or three dollars and twenty-five cents US.

"Do you know where this is?"

She puffs her lower lip. "*Regardez là. Ici.* You are here."

"Do you take dogs?"

More annoyed than amused, she says, "Mais oui!"

And in that brief moment, roommates find a place. Ravi suspects esoteric powers at play in his home search. How else could he be so lucky so fast? She interrupts with news that Little Dog will be liberated soon. Did she smirk? A three-button reveal on her snowy white chest shows two low moguls where bunnies perch. The chilled landscape blends with the smug certainty above, in stark contrast to Hereata's hearth fire. But the landlady seems curiously committed to others, so Ravi seeks reason. "I know it's different for dogs, but he trusts me, and I have a hard time. . . And he'll be with me if we could forget the. . . you know?"

"*Monsieur*, I do not know. Can you ask in a different way?"

Ravi scissors two fingers. "Fixed. The dog. I have a hard time."

"*Monsieur*, it is no different with dogs and humans. They should be, as you say, fixed—*tous les hommes*. Are you seeing how many dogs suffer? Be happy that your dog has a home. And he will not lose sleep over that same little flesh that cost you so many nights. We can schedule you for Tuesday. Okay?"

Little Dog leans in, happy to be discussed. How did she know? "You mean schedule the dog."

"That is all we can do for now."

With tentative cheer, he asks her to call a taxi, please. Hereata glows next to her anemic rectitude and will be back tomorrow to represent the womanly wing of the feminine party: *Oui! Oui! N'arrêtes-pas!* He smiles in anticipation, but Monique tells him to walk back for his things because a taxi could take an hour, and it's only four miles, and he can stick his thumb up and maybe get a ride. "Don't worry, the dog can stay here."

"I thought you were going to say to stick my thumb up my ass."

"*Vous n'êtes pas drôle, Monsieur.*"

"No. I'm misunderstood. It happens, as you must know. *Vous n'êtes pas drôle non plus.*"

"We're very busy now. Okay?"

It's more than okay; it's a home and roommate before lunch. She's humorless. So what? So he says *merci, bon*, and walks out, no need to one-up: he feels so good. Little Dog is also pleased to head out on the next adventure. Ravi picks him up to share the plan and carry him back in. Monique takes the handoff to a kennel behind her. Little Dog howls on Ravi's second exit. So he goes back in to see if a tail is caught in the door and says maybe he'll walk with the dog and explain the ground rules. Monique huffs, handing the dog back on a leash. "I finks he is explain to you already."

REEFDOG

They soon come to a quaint place serving lunch in a family *fare* with folding tables and chairs on gravel under a thatched roof supported by log pillars. Camp stoves and serving bins smoke and steam, and a dog on a leash is welcome. Ravi is surprised when the dog sits and waits but doesn't beg. With soft jaws he lips morsels into the choppers. "Where did you learn this?"

Packing and checking out are quick, and the four miles back is faster when a flatbed truck pulls over.

The new room is small, not so primitive as the *fare* at lunch or fundamental like Vincent's room but similar to both. Twelve by fourteen is room to spread out. The counter on one side has a hot plate and sink near a small fridge. An electrical converter facilitates American plugs by eliminating one pole, changing 220 to 110 by using the ground as a neutral, *I think*. Turning on the laptop is tense, *mais voila!* Artistic endeavor will have the benefit of software.

A small market five minutes up sells beer, bread, cheese, sardines, crackers, mustard, eggs, lettuce, and *legumes*. Dinner is steamed and spritzed with olive oil and a bit of pepper, green or red, and perhaps some salt—*et un peu de poivre, vert ou rouge, et peut-être du sel*. And sliced onion—*oignon*—and a head of *chou-fleur*. It's not so bad for a newcomer. The bigger market is back down past Taverua, and the trip occurs weekly in Monique's car. Ravi and Little Dog ride shotgun and keep their yaps shut.

•

And so our story ends, insofar as any story will. Even passing from the flesh is often no more than a milestone. A narrative will meander on retelling as drama ferments. Ravi Rockulz's life in a new land transits happily ever after on a routine of artistic pursuit.

Nothing is entirely smooth, however, starting with Little Dog's separation anxiety when parted from his one and only. He shrieks but stops when Ravi returns. Returning right now supports bad behavior, even as the bond grows stronger. Setting Little Dog on his lap he explains that he must leave for work, to dive with tourists and little fishes for money for dog food and crackers, and he'll be back later. Pointing to himself and saying his name, he then points to a paper cup and jumps off with his fingers to dive down and. . .

Little dog watches the silly charade and barks when Ravi sucks his cheeks in and purses his lips like a fish, then he lunges for a tongue-lashing. Ravi takes it and tells him to stay. Stay and be good. And be quiet in the room or hang out in the yard with the other dogs. Little Dog barks again and heads out to the yard.

Other problems come and go like sunrise, sunset. Hereata tolerates the dog, pondering the mystery of love. She spends more time in the mirror as if to meet the challenge.

Day in, day out find rhythm. Warmth, color, and scent abound in people, a dog, flowers, forest, and reef. Hereata waiting and cold beer give succor to a tired man. Her kindness restores him. It's not romance but comfort, like marriage, and it's good, giving a time and purpose to the season—a season of compromise on the spirit of youth but with profound healing effects. She lets other freedoms ring. Little Dog likes to watch but falls asleep, the scene is so predictable and *bourgeois*. So what? *Fuck buddies* is a crude phrase best avoided, but they are friends who dine and fuck. Which isn't to call things bad or good but some of each, like life. So who needs to call anything?

Submersion, on the other hand, is a passion reborn with a mistress who loves Ravi Rockulz all the more. Purpose, pictures, and life gain focus. Income relieves pressure, and days feel tropical in the traditional sense. Honing on what he loves, he comes home at last.

A man can bog down in lofty imagery. Better to dive with no expectation but a reef view. With repetition comes insight, and style takes form. Like a backhand, a syntactical pattern, the opening slice of an appendectomy, a riff at four beats to the measure or seeing fish, he learns that top shots and back shots are boring. You dove on some fish and scared a few. So what? Face shots emerge in phase one, till he realizes that mug shots are too skinny. . .

What is she doing now, this minute?

REEFDOG

•

A man settles in. All who wander are not lost, except in brief, difficult moments. He finds a postcard showing a naked woman with a pretty face, huge melons, a flat stomach, small waist and luscious hips. He stares and laughs. "She doesn't exist."

The clerk assures that she does, but she lives in Brazil, not Tahiti. Rubbing a red bump on his face, he says Tahiti women don't look like this. Ravi wonders if Brazil has decent reefs and laughs again at the foibles of men. Minna, Cosima, and Hereata look great. Ah, well; and so he writes on the message side:

Ia Orana Skinny,
How are you? I am doing fine. I found a nice place to live. You can
write to me at Le Chien de Bonne Chance, BP 1121, Maharepa,
Moorea, Polynésie Française.
Please let me know how you are doing at Gene's. Okay?
Yours,
Ravi

He's hardly had time to ask about an attorney or a divorce or annulment, but he will. Won't that be a relief? Meanwhile, she can forward his mail or legal documents. And he wants news of Skinny.

Okay, where was I? Too skinny, even for a wafer thin fish seeking camouflage on minimal profile. Nature is dynamic, but the wafer thin view misses the flourish, even with two eyes straddling a snout and pectoral fins fluttering like petticoats. A better shot would flirt with the viewer—would show color and pattern as part of the movement. But a side shot with a mug shot would be clinical.

Breakthrough is simple but tough. Many fish approach and peer into the lens. The face shot seems obvious, but few divers get the shot. Ravi gets it but sees that the money does not come before the turn or after; it comes during. In turning, the fish bends its body, changing direction. The pose is not head-on and not a right angle but oblique, a forty-five-degree curve showing one or both eyes and the snout, along with pecs, shape, and coloration—and a certain contact. Dorsal flair is a bonus, with translucent membrane spanning erect spines. It becomes a signature shot, with drama and flourish.

The lateral line along each flank parallels the dorsal contour and is the hub of neuro-sense in a fish. Dorsal spines rise with emotion, and that's the shot he wants. Some fish are shy, others gregarious, defensive, amorous, curious, hungry or hambones seeking discovery. Ravi captures essence, panache, and charm. He secures them for art. With luck, two subspecies pose in the same frame or a matched pair or a symbiotic duo. He follows a puffer and coronet for so many days they become a trio. He doubts his contribution to more efficient survival till his teammates scoot to his far side when a grouper comes on strong.

The next phase is vision, the elusive mode of framing a shot that he used long ago on a jack and a moray over a tourist's shoulders. Great composition can't be called up. It's a gift. So he waits. He sings into his regulator the tune about the mountain that was, before it wasn't, and then it was. He tries not to get it. He lets it come, but it doesn't, so he strives to stop striving, which is a laugh with no laughing. Finally, with repetitive failure, the bell rings, and he laughs out loud. Wasting so many shots isn't the waste it used to be. Come on: it's digital. No film to buy or processing to pay. How can he know what to do without mastering what not to do? Less is more at the base of a non-mountain, as art oozes through the birth canal. *Pardon my mixed images of fetal mountain and failure reborn, but I think we have lift off!*

So comes the second verse, in which the butterfly emerges. . .

Shots of Moorish idols head-on, as well as frontal-at-forty-five curvature, show clarity and drama, highlighting Bette Davis eyes, exquisite lashes, and the pout. He senses the rabbit hole in which down is up in a mental maze to confuse a weaker mind. And he searches harder to find the way. Focused on idle idols or cheeky wrasses, he leaves tourists on their own. They complain and don't tip.

He shrugs. They don't tip anyway, and people led by the hand will never figure anything for themselves. But tourists not led will get lost.

He wants to be a good dive leader but lapses again on Moorish idols, a tiny infant too small to curve with a blunt snout, a dorsal stub, and baby-face. It hovers in the curvature of an adult idol casting motherly suspicion, one eyebrow raised. . .

Oh, yes!

Do Moorish idols birth live or deposit eggs? Do idle idol fry get mothered or drift as plankton? What are the odds of a tiny idol posing with Mom? Could it be? Is the adult female? But the greatest question is: Who cares? Just look!

The grail is not at the end of the journey but the beginning! Here is destiny and calling for Ravi Rockulz, marine photographer—here is the family portrait for the ages: Mrs. Idol and her son, for posterity, for matting and framing and spotlighting in any gallery.

Yes, Mother, this is what I do, what I was meant to do, what you can tell anyone who needs to know.

And in case anyone else needs to know what's none of their business, the fact is: Ravi Rockulz may be among the top reef artists in the world—the whole wide world, that is. So allocating two thousand dollars for a printer with eight ink cartridges for extraordinary color in 17xwhatever is only natural. It's not lavish or foolish but necessary. The expenditure postpones a rebreather. But a rebreather runs much more, and the work needs printing. A rebreather will allow depths to two fifty or three hundred, but the vision phase is shallow, twenty feet, where sunbeams dance. The rebreather will make no bubbles or noise, so fish will approach with no fear. The rebreather will come for its rightful phase: big ocean animals.

Meanwhile, the printer sits on a table, covered against dust, salt air and dog fur with a blanket and a plastic tarp and a damp-chaser below, except when making magic of a fish or two, getting it right and righter still. Little Dog plays in the yard with others less fortunate than himself as the gallery fills.

Moorish Mama and Baby Idol is a hit. Then comes a reef shrimp series. Banded coral shrimp are common as sand fleas, hardly of interest, until Ravi shares harsh truth on aquarium trade extraction and what happened in Hawaii. Like American buffalo, Carolina parakeet, Hawaiian Monk seal, hawksbill turtle and giant Pacific leatherback turtle, all gone or going away. . .

Stop.

Reef shrimp still ply Moorea reefs, cleaning and grooming as they did in Hawaii before dying in transit or amusing their keepers briefly before dying in glass tanks. Banded shrimp look like candy cane for an inch or two and two more inches of skinny pincers. Scarlet cleaners are golden with a scarlet stripe down the back and two white stripes to either side. Candy canes feed at night while scarlet cleaners feed in the day, and he goes for both.

The best foresight is often based on hindsight. He shoots shrimp from every angle, as if they're going away. They raise claws in greeting, tip their hats or stroke chin whiskers in microscopic intimacy. He splurged on the flat port because the dome would fit any wide-angle lens. But the hundred five millimeter macro requires a flat port and was only eight hundred—each, for the lens and flat port—and art calls for whatever it takes, not a budget.

Besides, each tiny spike shows tinier barbs and hairs in immaculate detail, as the shrimp visage goes from mechanical wonder to otherworldly. The miniature universe emotes fear, appetite and comfort. Portraiture suits the shrimp clan, too.

So Ravi the family photographer pursues the more adventurous crustaceans to their place of work. These shrimp clean, not floors but gills and teeth—long, pointy teeth slanted back for ripping and tearing, often filling a predator gob opened wide so the little dental tech can get in deep, to pluck stubborn snags.

Dive leaders often find cleaner shrimps, hold the regulator aside and open wide for the photo op. A shrimp or two may enter the mouth hole to clean with less fervor on Spam and eggs but also to secure great good cheer and a tip. Ravi frowns on false contact; it's not natural and not art, according to the Ravi Rockulz rules to create by. But he allows a shrimp to taste a morsel between thumb and forefinger, then ride to the nearest eel and walk on in. Many eels open wide to get their choppers cleaned. The show is compelling, with spectacular teeth of ghastly potential. Dragon eels are mottled orange with droopy nostrils and snaggle teeth, where tiny shrimp work with immunity. Violent potential could suggest *Vicious Killers of the Deep*, until a teleconverter gets close on the dazzling shrimp cleaning the icy stalactites. Intrusive proximity is another mystery: why do eels tolerate a lens within two inches? Just so, the shutter clicks.

Ravi favors a gaping whitemouth, its needle teeth and snow-white maw perfectly framing the banded shrimp, who reaches up for a nibble and down for a nosh in a stretch that blends the whites of the eel's mouth and the shrimp's bands, contrasting both with the shrimp's other bands. And we have a winner! Lens vignetting and chromatic aberration can be artistic too.

Monique ponders gill-breathers, realizing critters she's never considered, seeing her tenant beyond machismo to artistry. She says her little animal hospital qualifies as a non-profit on several American websites offering software for the cause at a fraction of retail. So an aspiring artist gets the Photoshop ensemble for a hundred fifty dollars instead of eighteen hundred and soars to the summit of rendering.

Working and saving every franc for the next purchase—make that investment, in art and life—Ravi soon feels seascape, which can be tricky since particulates can haze what appears to be clear. Never mind; this too is an act of faith. The new lens is a wildlife special number that would be available as an off-brand clone at significant savings to those of limited resources and commitment, but a purist seeking perfection will wait till he has fifteen hundred dollars for the best optics in the world and another few hundred for port extensions and gear rings to support it. One day is all it takes, and then the next, till it's done. Monique suggests Tiputa Pass at Rangiroa for a departure from up-close and personal to big fish on the move. They cruise the pass in November.

November already? God, time flies. Well, it's not for two months yet, leaving time enough to make the money. Ravi reads of hammerheads in extra-large to huge, cruising in great schools with no known motivation—unknown by humans, that is. The sharks know something, or feel it. Then come the rays, eagle rays in the hundreds and thousands with a few stingrays in lovely integration with the hammerheads and a few jacks and barracuda. It's a flotilla of sea power a human navy could envy, except that the fishy armada has no destructive potential as a means to victory, to stabilize the region and secure a nation's future. Don't get a rowdy man started.

The atoll barely rises above sea level on a nine-mile stretch of perimeter and seems saved from development by prospects for flooding and perfect for a diver/artist enamored of natural anarchy, but he doesn't know the area. Monique has fantasized the show in Rangiroa for years but will never see it because she can't dive. It is impossible, with so much to know and tend to. Ravi shows his own pout because she can know and tend to and have this fantasy because good things should come to one who helps so many. But she won't try because it's impossible, and she's too young to drown. He promises to keep her from drowning. She juts a lip and trembles, seeing the possible.

Paler and thinner at the water's edge—her blue vein network constricts under goose bumps crowding her translucent skin. A small wetsuit is baggy—and he says she has room in there to entertain. She's in no mood for jokes, so he says he'll get her a child's wetsuit for the next dive, to keep her warmer. She says it won't be necessary, a different wetsuit or a second dive.

Hereata watches from higher up, remarking later on the poor girl's stick figure and breakability. Hardly generous, Hereata remains calm because Monique is no threat, not even with the giant moray lurking in her man's skivvies. Monique shows up clothed and drops into local custom, changing on the spot. Hereata's smile is meant to remind him of his bounty, but he can see for himself that muskmelons are bigger than kumquats. And he loves Monique's determination.

She does all right. Her uncertainty goes away as she sinks and breathes—underwater. She holds her own with someone to hold onto. So he gives her the book and says they'll dive a few more times to get through the skills, and then he'll test her on the book. She declines; it is impossible. The passes are different.

That may well be, but she should continue till impossibility is proven. So she warms up on a few more dives and a better wetsuit and eases into prospects for the pass at Rangiroa. He emphasizes the tricky nature and hazard of currents, and that any drift dive can challenge a beginner if she fights it or panics. She'll have her own private guide to stay near, but out of his shots.

Stoic by nature and short-tempered in a world that abuses its dogs and cats, Monique is joyful. An adventure with wild animals makes her giddy. She hugs him, pledging to pay her way and translate and find dirt-cheap digs with her friends at Rangiroa. And so they go, bonding in a new way for both, which is not to say sexless since he consents on request. Clinical but heartfelt, she says it's been years since she was with a man. She doesn't miss it but wants to see. Has she not seen the giant moray of the Speedo depths? Ravi says he's very fond of her and flattered, of course, but. . .

She asks for this personal favor on the ninety-minute flight to Rangiroa. Neither taking his hand nor seeking eye contact, she coldly asks for closure on a tired subject. She has no itch to scratch and feels indifferent, and so she turns to him and says, "It is okay if you wants to say no. Oh, please, believe. . ." She touches him. "It is terrible. An imposition that I would hate if you would ask it of me. It is not fair, but if you would. Or would not is okay."

Why would she risk her integrity and sense of self to be with a man? She assures that neither he nor his *merguez* have any bearing on her integrity, and she doesn't want to be with a man—not the whole man. She only wants to feel the sausage in her *vagin*, to be sure. She doesn't think she's missing anything but would hate to find out later that all the fuss is actually warranted.

"But you've done it before. You know how it feels."

"I told you. It was years ago. He was a mean boy. Too rough, too fast. Besides, we change, may be." And Ravi is not any man.

In humility he awaits praise. It comes faintly, as she calls him emotionless, except for the love of his dog and fish. She admires his focus and feels him suitable.

"Because I'm loveless?"

"*Au contraire!*"

"What if you like it?"

She shrugs. "Then we will do it again—I mean we *can* do it again if you like it too. But it won't happen again."

"Why should it happen at all, with severe doubts?" She juts a lip. He says the sausage isn't so fat. She agrees; she sees bigger anytime, at the butcher—*tout à l'heure, à la charcuterie. . .* He doubts it unless she means bratwurst, but the French don't eat bratwurst. He doesn't mind; she's so good to the animals. She deserves a helping hand. Or a helping bratwurst. Will the little Colonel ten-hut for Monique? He feels confident, not so much in the chain of command but in the colonel's singular drive. She's too thin but has hips and loves the fuzzy species, so it should go well. Who knows?

He doesn't know after a minute of it. She glares as if trespassed, and so she is. "Wait!" She leans him aside and rolls on top but shakes her head. He comforts her by pulling her near to press her cool, dry lips to his. Bad idea—she shudders. But on a slight fibrillation, her eyes squeeze shut, and she endures. She waves him on with both hands. His eyes close so Cosima can take over, and it's over. She apologizes for exploiting his weakness but didn't think he'd mind.

"It's not weakness. It's friendship. And love. And I don't mind."

She puffs a lip and stands up, all done, over and out. "I like you but not it. It is not fair that men can achieve climax with anybody."

"I thought you did."

"Please."

But she did, which counts for something, but he's not sure what. Awkwardness lingers to early evening and dinner at another *fare*, where she reaches across to take his hand and ask that he please keep their secret because Hereata is a friend she wouldn't hurt for the world. She checks out the waitress.

"Can you achieve climax with any woman?"

"Of course not. We're different. It has to be right."

They let it sink under two great wines and avoid eye contact. He further eases the strain with logistics and objectives for the morning dive, deep and in a swift current.

She follows well, holding on when she can, hovering nearby when he moves to catch an angle. She checks her gauges when he does—until they level and drift. She watches him, signals okay and gains comfort among vast shoals of muscular fish who seem indifferent to the marine mammals among them. The odd one with the camera squirms for angles in a three-knot current then rolls like a seal to silhouette the traffic overhead against the shimmer a hundred feet up. He captures the pass and passing minions in sweeping displays of a food chain moving in meditation. The flow of life is a set piece, a reprieve from life and death, in grace. This is not the lion lying with the lamb but shark cruising with ray. Without hunger or fear or the drive to spawn, predators become pilgrims at the shrine of being. Framing the flow in unique perspective is a signature approach of marine photographer Ravi Rockulz. Have you heard of him?

Realization of self merges at last with artistic potential. Scene splicing is a technique—or a trick—but a rare panorama moves past, slow enough for three frames on the fly. So he fires three in a row a dozen times at the great herds lolling and swaying from near to far.

Hammerhead fills the near frame, her head and eye spanning the foreground, curiously indifferent. Eagle rays circle, nose to tail, in a smaller wheel of life. A cog of life?

Monique whimpers over raw files on his laptop and again over finished prints at home. On another faint fibrillation, she congratulates his success; one day she will say she knew him when he had nothing but was already a great artist. Like a nun drawn to Holy Spirit, she is French and drawn to Art. He reminds her that the trip was her idea, and success is hers to share. She demurs; she only tagged along. She hugs him for his soft strength, enduring one thing and another. Little Dog barks.

In the next few days come family portraits—back to macro—of harlequin shrimp, haughty and mugging for the lens.

Long-nose seahorse male spews seahorse babies from his pouch. They squirm like larvae and roll and tumble in perfect miniature to current, surge and hunger. A more orderly trio of brown-banded pipefish relax on a rock two feet deep, blending with dappled refraction, stretching their necks left and right.

Clarity, color, and surprises come daily among Neptune's minions. Subject and composition vary, but the trend is drama and clarity, angular insight and incandescent emotion as a function of repetition and luck. What else can it be?

It's the hours and hours and then some. It's love, what the jazz crowd calls attitude—what Desmond brought to Brubeck or Getz to samba. Take blowfish in the fourteen-inch range. Similar to porcupine boxfish in Hawaii and likely related, the Tahiti cousin has shorter quills and darker coloration and is also shy enough to blush. He'll pick a reef and make a home, shooing for cover on any approach, like he does on seeing Ravi ten yards out and ducking out of sight. Snorkeling with his camera and no strobes on a mild current makes for liberation and a pleasant change of pace on available light—sunlight, softly radiant and perfectly metered. Ravi hovers, countering the current with a gentle side kick, camera raised and ready, allowing the distance to close slowly, till little puffer peaks out to see if the coast is clear, *et voilà*!

Behold the face of innocence, eyes wide, mouth open. Classic youth in startled amazement is like a Norman Rockwell child but with a fish as the child in a candid expression of social order.

Emperor angel turns to foreshorten his flank, where black, turquoise and ivory swirl in a vortex, with the head in deep shadow, except for the fire-orange voltage arcing from the eyes.

Triggerfish poses in sunbeams that suffuse his chartreuse fin webbing and turquoise piping, spines erect, with inner glow.

Trumpetfish freezes, pre-pounce, while tiny speck waves goodbye. Fluorescence can be explained as bioluminescence in predator and prey, emotionally triggered—or shining with eternal light. Mercy takes mysterious forms. Flexible and godlike, trumpet rolls his orbital eyes up and down the long snout, presumptuous as a seasoned winner. Lemon yellow and flecked with tiny diamonds, he shimmers in Sol's morning light—except that it's too deep for sunlight, and strobes would burn the key players, even with the aperture squinting at F22. So what? So he thinks outside the net is what.

Who could imagine turning off strobes to preserve chromatic light? Low light could blur the image on prolonged exposure. So he goes manual, bracing the camera against a rock and hoping trumpetfish stays still to avoid detection by the marine mammal gently clicking his shutter.

Eternal Interim is a still life that moves. Ravi pretends to be busy, watching friends watch the picture and turn to new angles, as a faint fibrillation of his own makes him tremble. Soon the little room fleshes out, wall-to-wall and wainscot to ceiling. The photos represent victory over the odds and a challenge for more. Where to go from here? When does more become enough? Worse yet: *What the hell am I supposed to do with all these fish pictures? Who wants to see them but my lesbian landlady, my aging girlfriend, and my dog?*

Extreme macro goes to the nose hairs on a coral polyp, as wide angle captures seascape across the Society Islands, the Australes, and Marquesas, where big pelagics cruise. Then it's back to the Tuamotu lagoons as yet untrammeled by teeming tourist refuse yearning to be free. Makemo, Ranoga, and Anaa offer direct flights, cheap digs, and peace on Earth. Questions of when and what are simply set aside. The best path is forward. If an audience gathers, Neptune's treasure trove will enrich a hungry world—will slow the pace of life as they know it when they see like the fishes do.

Or they won't. No artist can know, especially these days, with the world as callous, greedy, and self-centered as ever in time, unless it was always this bad but had no media. Monique consoles on art history; great artists are generally unknown prior to death. Recognition is best at the end, with the body rotting and the body of work complete. Meanwhile, without notoriety, an artist is free of nuisance. Ravi is not consoled; he would appreciate an audience. What artist wouldn't? In any event, Opus Rockulz will support the cause sooner or later, maybe. He begins anew with Maupiti. He'll go alone. Why not? Solitude is often the crucible for contact.

But Monique pleads: Why not? He doesn't know why not, even as she pledges silence, translation, local know-how and no demands. *On y va.*

They get a ride from the airport to a lagoon and wade across to Motu Auira. It's only three feet deep, so they shuffle to disturb rays rather than step on them—most are hidden under a layer of sand, but they lift off and scurry at the slightest provocation. Halfway across he asks her to hold the bags while he rifles for his mask, snorkel, and camera. Why can't they settle on the *motu* first? Then he can come back. He says she sounds like a wife and slips into his gear to seek a ray or two at eye level.

With signature evocation, light and focus come perfection at wading depth. Then they wade on across and make camp. On a plateau of technical excellence, he ponders his approach to more perfect perfection. Monique relaxes with her music box, some marijuana, and a small cooler. Following her lead in life as it relates to art, he joins in servicing a few pleasure centers in a luxuriant setting. Why not? Not ten minutes in, he has a stunning stingray series in the can. It's time for a break, for intellectual and French liberation, naked on all levels, secure in friendship and tropical wilderness. Success is grand and abundant on many levels.

Monique oils up and splays to the sun. Ravi thinks she's foolish, and for what, no tan line? He prefers a playful demarcation on the special reserves. She drifts, lifting her knees to ease her lower back. Framing and composing her crotch as if for artistic study, he hopes the right woman will find her. He didn't mind the little experiment, awkward and unnecessary as it was. Like a gemmologist examining facets and luster, he affirms consistency of form, even on one so thin. Are her lips getting sunburned?

Unstretched by childbirth or traffic, she's pert and fresh as an *hors d'oeuvre*, a small sampling to whet the appetite—but then what? He salutes is what because she deserves more than a quick experiment. Given the sultry setting, the bud, and cold beer, he thinks better data may be available.

She opens her eyes and says he looks like a husband, stoned, drinking beer and listening to music. And chronic.

"This music is seductive." She stares back. He feels tantric, but her knees close. Her ankles cross.

She chides, "You are staring."

"I'm trying an idea. Do you realize that making art is the least destructive of human behaviors?"

"Art can be self-destructive. It is not life. It is a drug."

"I love it, maybe too much. I sometimes feel like the only person alive to it. I want to stay down there sometimes."

She sits up. "That is not good."

"Does it make sense?"

"No. I hope it makes no sense to you too. I finks you need a break, I finks zis feeling is not good for you and is not good for your art."

"You like my art."

"Maybe your depression is good for your art. Maybe you are a genius who will swim down one day and never come back, and ze world will love your commitment. But be careful." She eases back down. "You can be famous at last but cannot enjoy it."

"You think that's what I want? You think I'm depressed?"

"Of course you want it. And you are depressed. How could it be otherwise? What artist wants less? Why do you think fame is bad? I think not. You have none. Welcome to art." *What artist want less? Why you finks fame is bad? I finks not. . .*

"You're right. I do care, but so many fools are famous in America. I think for me it would be different. My art is substantial, not just a downbeat on some tits and ass. You know?"

"Yes, and it is not just foolish in America. Any place wis newspaper and TV will have famous fools. But a few great artist are famous too. Don't forget. I finks you will be. You might not have to drown yourself to get it."

Her French view is sound. He appreciates her insight and speaks to her crotch as the knees re-splay, and her eyes close. "Monique. . ."

"No, *merci*."

"As a favor, between friends."

"No. Maybe anozzer time. No today."

"A better day will not come along."

"I would for you, as a favor. It mean so much to you. I finks it mean too much for you." She sits up. "I finks you convince yourself that you want to have me, but you don't convince me. You merely want. You want every woman you see—most of them. You are not bad. It's what men do. I wiss you will learn of romance as you have learn of art. It is not. . . ficky fick."

"You don't think I love you?"

"I finks you do. But it is not romance."

"You don't want romance."

"But I do. *Merci*. Listen to me. I have an idea. I won't tell it you, but I finks I will like to try a different man. If I don't like him too, zen I will let you do it."

"We're here. Now."

"Yes. We are here. Now I will relax. Okay?"

"Monique?"

"*Oui?*"

"I finks I am lesbian."

At last she laughs. Then she sleeps.

Could he wake her gently with his tongue to show romance? He wonders when he'll stop being so clever. With her little moguls melted to slush, he achieves growth in shrinkage. Sex is good but will one day cease. His tongue will wake nobody then, so romance must take other forms, starting now. He loves Hereata but he doesn't. He doesn't want fame but he does. One day they will separate but they won't. He smokes more dope and drinks more beer and goes deep.

REEFDOG

In the evening they cook and talk by a fire. They sleep under the stars till first light.

They go home Sunday at noon.

He sits and thinks, too late for morning, too early for a nap. He searches natural histories of reefs and species in French Polynesia, to see what other phenomena these reefs and passes might host.

Rapture of the deep occurs at seventy feet or below. It steals common sense. A diver wants down for more of the perfection available there. It must have a different name at sea level. He's not stoned or depressed; he merely imagines great depth, moving out. Like an addict, he wants greater dosage. Or maybe he's a whiner in French Polynesia, living his dream and calling it inadequate and rigorous. Artistic purity means no money and he feels at a loss, past the restlessness of youth and still grasping—or gasping like a fish on a dock, seeing water so near but unattainable.

But wait a minute: I feel good.

Minna Redux

The big four-oh can pass quietly if a man is careful. Ravi thinks life can begin at forty just as well without the folderol. Who needs it?

But Moeava needs the serial number, the certifying dive shop number, and other numbers from Ravi's certification to complete the insurance form. Moeava sees the milestone birthday coming up and takes note and makes plans, inviting people to the surprise fortieth birthday party for his good friend Ravi—that's right, forty.

He invites Cosima, in case she doesn't know of Ravi's old age. She treats him better these days, maybe appreciating his dedication. He asks for special favors as Ravi coached, promising to make the swim right after. But such favors are impossible. They would break the rules, making the prize meaningless. He says meaning will not be lost, and soon he will die.

She laughs. Only a fool would expect a reward for doing nothing or failing. Yet she keeps hope alive. Has he lost weight? He'll make the swim soon, she says; she knows it. Meanwhile, he invites his nana to the birthday soirée, so she begins the forced march toward optimal advantage in feminine presentation.

With Ravi gone in the truck, Moeava visits Monique, who stares in grim resolve. So he makes haste, inviting her to Ravi's surprise fortieth. She says yes, of course, and tells of a call to Le Chien de Bonne Chance Animal Hospital. A woman asked for Ravi, so Monique said he's only there some nights. She got the woman's number in case Ravi needs it or the woman doesn't call back.

Moeava calls the number and says, "Ia orana, Madam." He answers questions about himself and Ravi. She says it's two years since she and Ravi spoke, and she has news, not to worry. Moeava says yes, he knows the party to whom he is speaking.

She needs to know if Ravi wants his cat because the old beach houses where he lived and Gene still lives will be torn down for a hundred fifty new places in stucco with tile roofs in the four to fifteen million range. Gene is moving to a condo that doesn't allow cats. Whatever Ravi wants to do is okay because Minna can keep the cat, but she thought she should call.

Moeava says yes, Ravi will want his cat. "He talks about her, you know. Very strange."

"I know."

"You send cat?"

"I will if that's what he wants. Or I might find somebody to bring her, for money. The flight is every week, and I should find somebody sooner or later."

"You bring the cat. We will have *une grande fête* to celebrate his old age. Forty. Terrible."

"I don't think that would be a good idea."

"You might be correct. He talk about you too." Rattling on the line is probably a long distance malfunction. "Oh, he talk about you good. He say you very beautiful and perfect in beginning."

"He says that, beautiful and perfect?"

"That is his meanings. I think he want to see you more with the cat on your arm. Besides, how he will feel if anything happen to the cat?"

"Yes, but only one flight a week from Honolulu. I can't stay a week."

"One week not so long. You like this place. Three weeks from Sunday. Okay?"

"I have no place to stay."

"You stay in his room. You and him and the cat. And the dog."

217

"He has a dog?"

"Yes. Little Dog. You all get along. You not fight like cats and dogs. Ha! The dog only want to smell the cat from behind."

"She likes that, but I won't surprise him. Not for a week."

"You must. It is why you call, no?"

"No. I don't know. But I won't surprise him."

"But we all surprise him. Listen—if everything does not work out so good, you stay *chez grand-mère*—at house of my nana."

Chez grand-mère? How bad could that be?

"Maybe. I have to make some calls. But I don't know."

•

So it is that Minna arranges for Skinny's move to Moorea, re-engaging the political wing of *ohana* Somayan. French Polynesia's quarantine on domestic dogs and cats would surely oppress any feline with four months in a hot, dusty kennel and at her age, eleven already. But the Tahiti quarantine is waived for those countries without rabies, like New Zealand and a few others, but not the United States, except for one state, which is not a sovereign republic in the mid-Pacific but could be.

Of greater import is that annulment can proceed at last, contingent on all signatories present. Some phone calls, a promise, small talk, and official processing *et voilà!*

Skinny doesn't like any aspect of moving, beginning with the cat carrier with its waterproof floor and soft towel that bunches at one end. She howls till Minna lets her out. What else can she do? Skinny doesn't run down the aisle but nestles on Minna's chest, watching clouds out the window. They look familiar, though strangely near. Is this kitty heaven? She closes her eyes and purrs.

Why did Minna lie to her family about signatory stipulations and annulment when he's not even met with a lawyer? She doesn't think he's met with a lawyer. He would have made contact. And why did she agree to a stupid surprise party instead of a simple phone call to see how things stand? He probably has a tight-ass girlfriend anyway who's heard all about the crazy wife—make that ex-wife for all practical purposes. At any rate they can get things started. It's got to happen sooner or later. And she'd just as soon get Skinny moved on a personal delivery. It's great to get away, and Skinny is a good travel companion. He'll be grateful and not so mean, and that alone is a good excuse to go along with the surprise. So? Who cares? Still, a week is a long time to spend alone in an exotic place.

Minna and Skinny touch down in Papeete late Saturday. Moeava offered a pickup in his boat at the ferry terminal in town, but Minna opted to sleep over and take the ferry because a small boat would make Skinny sick and be a real kick in the ass after everything else. Besides, hanging out till Sunday will preserve the surprise—what fun. Besides, she may get back on board the ferry after handing off the cat. "I might not stay."

"*Pourquoi* no?"

"*Pourquoi* do you think? Does he have a girlfriend? Do I really want to hang out near that for a week?"

"He has many friends, but he is like a monk with the diving and the pictures. I think he want to see you."

On the cab ride from the airport into town, she assesses a week of it. She doubts too much embarrassment or humiliation; he seemed so soft when he left. Yeah, soft in the head, but who can blame him? Fucking Darryl. *What was I thinking? But don't start again.* Serves that *lolo* right, ending up with Eunice—three hundred pounds of toothless *tita*, and for what? One little ten-pound baby? *And to think. . .*

Has Ravi had time to sort things out and be himself again? Could he turn down the full meal deal? No way. But he did and might again. *What am I doing? Oh, yeah. Annulment.* We'll definitely see to that.

Or might love return to her and her. . . what? Her man? Her husband? She wishes she'd brought Skinny on a quiet weekday instead of this stupid surprise party weekend. How annoying. But there's only one flight per week. Oh, yeah.

The other guests share her annoyance, and so does Ravi because every surprise party victim finds out. Nobody enjoys the ride because it's stupid, everybody pretending they don't know about the birthday because they don't care because the victim is nobody, really. It's meant to show how they really feel: surprise!

For he's a jolly good fellow. . .

Ravi found out when Hereata shook the phone bill in his face, asking how he could spend forty dollars on a phone call—a phone call! And to whom, might I ask—*et à qui je demande*—was you calling, anyway? But it wasn't him who made the call, so he couldn't very well know whom anybody was calling, as if she didn't know. Ask Moeava.

So she asks and finds out and grows despondent, holing up *dans la salle de bain*, moving from the mirror to the toilet to see and to think, to strategize a plan as it might relate to a woman's needs, a real woman with plenty left to give, if only a man could be man enough to stand and receive. With practicality as her co-pilot, she invites a guest of her own, an admirer of proven zeal, whose many ovations may warrant a response, even if his phone calls get tangled in Slavic knots. But if it's love, or could be, the truth will out. At least Oybek's intentions are clear—or apparent.

On the eve of this fortieth birthday, Ravi reflects on the start of his fifth decade. So what? More importantly, it's a night for image enhancement, so he escapes to software, where an hour or three can vanish in no time. He hasn't asked Moeava about the call to Hawaii because he recognized the number and thinks it was a call returned. How else would Moeava get the number? He thinks Moeava has done something stupid, but he won't ask if Minna is on her way. He fears bad news, and the idea will not settle. He'll soon see Minna or not. Either way, the next forty years will start clean, starting tomorrow with a lawyer. There: it feels good to resolve what's waited too long. They both deserve it and are far enough removed to see it through. He sets thoughts of Skinny aside, till tomorrow.

The day shapes up for resolution, with an annoying gathering later in the afternoon. It's not so bad, with a fat manifest and the vigor to lead the dive of a lifetime—or point them in the right direction while he experiments on telephoto with intentional noise. Telephoto?

Underwater? He comes closer than ever to a troupe of garden eels swaying like ballerinas and might be getting the perfect shot for yet another breakthrough. He would rather hit the software for more perfection after the dive. He'd rather be alone and mostly content. But a man has to do what he'd rather not do, so he hoses down and cleans up and with a poker face strolls to the front office with a grin. Monique does not yell *surprise!* She's not there. The place is empty. He misread the clues—what a relief. How much better the afternoon and evening will be in solitude with what he loves. It's fun to get it right, given raw images so close to the mark already. And here they are, downloading in a choreography by Neptune himself. One frame to the next, garden eels arch and shimmy, moving to the music they share.

It's a beautiful and eerie thought—good thing since eerie beauty is the point of technical obsession. A technocrat is not an artist, but technical excellence is a basis, really, when you. . .

"Surprise!"

Interruption is the artist's nemesis. And through the door to commemorate his birth, a promenade sallies forth. It's Monique and Cosima with Moeava in tow. Hereata follows Minna, who chats with Oybek Navbahor, who could have croaked but obviously didn't since here he is. But he must be *très* pissed; his pig eyes slant inward, squinty and mean, yet he seems serene and. . . Sociable? What's wrong with this picture? Hereata might be open-minded with Monique because she can't be jealous of a big-hearted, scrawny woman so kind to animals, after all. . . But Minna is a challenge of a different stripe. Just as summer heat and winter cold can't be fully recalled in their opposite seasons, so has Minna's beauty lapsed in the memory of her chosen one. He sees her fulsome self and feels her fill the room and remembers yet again. Sure, she's faking through the awkward moments, yet she brings the old allure—the mystique that won't go away. He wasn't alone in love, though he alone was blinded.

He flashes back. Minna and Hereata chat like girlfriends, avoiding the difficulty between them. Hereata leans on Oybek playfully but cannot hide her apprehension. She should win by rights, and Minna seems to agree. But memory defaults to an air of renewal. It's another first encounter with repercussion coming on. What can he do? Options pass before his eyes till the old aloha comes out. They approach warily yet according to custom. Joining hands, they embrace with a kiss on the cheek and faint breath exchanged. He says she looks well. She says he's staying fit, too, for an older man.

And they know it's over—that two people forfeit their chance of revival on the first utterance of suburban nicety with a dash of canned humor. Hereata shifts to the other foot. Forcibly happy for the reunion she urges old friends to drink and eat. Did Minna tell Hereata of annulment, and that puts Hereata at ease? Or is Hereata. . . with Oybek? He's a strange one, though closer to her age. They met when she escorted him to the boat on that eventful morning after the night of. . .

"*Oy!*" All roads converge at the summit—or the canyon. "*Nyet.* Oy. Bek. Bek. Oy-bek. Zank you so big for save life of me when I die from conwulsion and you roll me so I breathe. You, I owe." He bows as if in a head butt to the chest but then stops to gaze at the monitor, where garden eels pose in *plié et pirouette*, in synch with random fluidity as yet unimagined. "Achh! Is this you?"

"No. It is not me. It is a photograph of garden eels. I took it this morning, but it's not corrected."

Oybek straightens and sneers, "Have you more?"

Ravi matches with a smirk, raising a palm like the pope to indicate the rest of the gallery and his world.

•

So our story ends again, insofar as stories ever end, even when the characters die, as they do that very moment, never again returning to life as they knew it.

Oybek is urban by choice. Where Ravi feels comfort among sea beasts, Oybek also swims among predators. That is, Oybek looks piggish and mean, and may sometimes be, but only by necessity of his calling. His natural self is open, more or less, and strives for more and gains traction, tooth and nail or by whatever means necessary.

Growing up short on looks and money but long on adventurous spirit in *Karakalpakstan*, young Oybek explored shipwrecks in the desert, what had been Lake Aral in Moynaq. He found happiness in solitude, away from the other children who teased and taunted the ugly little boy with hurtful names. Oybek did not allow the hurt within. He looked cruel and threatening even then, as nature made him and as a mode of self-defense. What could he do?

He would be an ocean explorer one day. But epilepsy and a rare condition beefed him up with fleshy folds. Slogging onward as a young man must, he began the first dive magazine in Uzbekistan with photos from divers around the world. He copied the photos from other magazines till he claimed to have the best dive magazine in the region. The three divers in the region asked, "Compared to what?"

Oybek wandered tropical latitudes making friends where he could, including women who could provide what he wanted.

When the Internet emerged, Oybek's magazine pioneered reef photography combined with photos of those women. *Reef Art Magazine Online* went global a year prior to litigation for artistic theft. But the reef shots were great, in the meantime, and so were the women. The name soon became *Refart Magazine*, with fart jokes to boost readership. The jokes were great too, like the one about the divers who had beans just before. . .

Oybek moved to LA, where marine photographers competed, just like everyone else, for a break, which goes to show what the right address can do for credibility in art. And now you know the rest of story, so far. Oybek Navbahor is the publisher of *Modern Reef Magazine*. "Please. My card." He calls the photos on these walls superb, world class, fantastic, worth a fortune, just say the word and then you watch, the best he's ever seen, not so much technically because everybody gets that these days, but in another way. . . a way that is. . . what you might call. . .

"Artistic."

"Yah! Artistic!"

Oybek wants exclusive rights. Ravi is flattered in a cold wash of confusion and fear. Like a factory in Novotroitsk, Oybek blows smoke up the whole world's ass. So a tinge of buyer's remorse and a double dose of embarrassment and humility accompany the courier delivering the message so craved. Well, Ravi Rockulz never wanted fame; he wanted a rightful audience, like any artist would. But fame precedes recognition in a mixed up media world. And so the kliegs blaze as solitude, anonymity, and youth are banished from the kingdom. Oybek finds his stride.

He insists that Ravi move to LA, now, before his prime is over. Forty already! Because life in LA is the greatest, and living there is necessary if you want to make it as an artist. Besides that, LA is amazing, with smart people and women. Ravi must live in LA to turn his wonderful artistry into money. Who knows how much? A few million, anyway. That's annual—did you think it otherwise? Why stick around in a place like that if you only make it once? That's with proper management. It's not like you can get off the plane and see the cashier for your check. Oh, it's work, but so lovely.

Oybek is a seasoned C-list technician who knows the score, starting with the value of a million bucks, which ain't what it was; come on.

Ravi can't believe; the guy is so smarmy, so strange and smutty. But he can't stop hoping. He's heard the rant on money and power—it comes to zero every time, *finito, rien, caput*! Only a bona fide loser wears his power on his sleeve. Yet Hereata's slow motion nod says something else, like she checked this guy out. How could that be?

Well, she has an ear for his thick talk and translates when nobody else can. His pig eyes smile on her, and so do Ravi's. He may never sample her wares again, but he's off the hook, and maybe he will. In the meantime, she won't wear out like a bar of soap. Will she?

Minna sees. Minna knows. Minna stores for later use as necessary.

So the party begins with misunderstanding buried like a hatchet so new understanding can blossom like sunflowers; they laugh at what has happened and what's to come. Yes, Oybek appears to be threatening, but it's only the shape of his face and what those muscles do. He also winces in the mirror, but it's the threat of no threat and honestly facilitates success in the entertainment industry. He still feels terrible for pushing the wrong button on his BC inflator and putting those people at risk. He felt worse spoiling the gift sent to his room, but the epilepsy was in remission for many years, so he was surprised at the symptoms and the surprise gift—and here he is relating his two surprises at a surprise party!

With great good cheer comes Cosima's *poisson cru et ahi tartare*. Moeava promotes beer and good things to eat and rolls marijuana, so the festive air is unavoidable. Except for two former loves, who take time outside to catch up and confirm their status. Ravi is content. He says Monique thinks he might be cracking up, but his mental disturbance is focused on art, what he wanted all along. The path is beautiful and revealing, and he thinks the direction correct.

Minna got her nursing degree. She quit the gift shop and volunteers at the hospital and will soon become full-time staff and got recommended for intensive care. She loves the recognition of her intensive skills and may take the job. It pays more but not so much—surely not enough to make a career. Besides that, the ICU guys are really crazy; it's so much life and death on a bunch of TV monitors with lights and bells like Vegas, and it's all night and all the time and what not, and you can hardly blame them for being crazy because they don't call it intense for nothing. The craziness actually balances the crazy scene.

But something about that floor, with the need and the rush, pulls her in for now. And the service—you would not believe how lame the hospital is, leaving the patients completely out of the process, leaving the ICU staff to console and counsel, though they're not supposed to because of the liability, but sometimes you have to offer a comforting word or go crazier. So, yes, she might do it for a while. For the experience. You know?

He knows, sensing emotion in the depths. This highly regarded birthday on which life will begin begins with pride for what she does, who she is—or rather who she has become. In conveying his pride for her, he chokes up. He can't tell why. On a new tack to clear the airwaves, he assesses medical services here in Paradise. Or would that be here in the moment? The airwaves won't clear.

Why is she here?

So he defaults to predictable charm, telling her he's proud of her and happy to see her and this and that, and they too stick like a bone in his maw.

She gets him off the hook saying Skinny took to international travel like a veteran, napping on her chest or staring at clouds and what not.

"Skinny?"

She thought he knew. It's only natural that Skinny sleeps it off. But he doesn't know because it's a surprise. She leads him to the front office where Skinny sits in a kennel, nose to nose with Little Dog. Little Dog whines.

Skinny hisses.

"Little Dog." He points to the far corner. Little Dog retreats. He pulls Skinny from the kennel and holds her eye to eye. "Skinny." She meows, demanding an explanation, after the things he said and so many sweet nothings. He slumps with regret for what feels like the neglect of a loved one. With his face next to hers, he breathes her scent. She purrs. He cries; it comes so easily and he's not sure why, but of course he knows why.

Minna hugs them both, but the sobs build to a tumult, too much for Skinny who wiggles to get back into the kennel. So the two former loves entwine and take cover till the bad part goes away. Minna's bedside manner is not what it was. Well, maybe later on that issue. For now, they struggle for absolution on more seasoned ministrations.

But the difference between them runs too deep for absolution in a minute of surface skills. Her speech is still clipped, too fast with many clichés—never mind. It's her touch that has changed, tapping into comfort, easing the discord, letting go of guilt, loss, and pain in a process of sorting and release. She talks about the old neighborhood. "What a scene. Man, that Gene. She refused to move from her beach house, even though she was only renting and couldn't stall forever because they brought in the court guys, but she needed more time to find a condo that would allow a cat. Because she promised, and she really loves you. I'm not sure why, but she thinks you're the greatest guy who ever got roughed up on South Maui. She loves Skinny, too. Man, you think you're all broke up and feeling *huhu*; you should have seen Gene carry on. And poor Skinny—she didn't know whether to be happy or sad. She traveled like a pro. I think she's happy now. I don't know how you do it."

He laughs. He touches her face. He sees what happened to her and to him. It should be back on. Why not?

She doubts it. How could it be? We don't need another knock-down drag-out of the rough stuff or the bumpy aftermath. It was bad enough one time. Neither one rushes into legal needs, but that doesn't mean it's a romance revived. So it's a push, on the fence, teetering this way and that, and that's where it sits by tacit agreement, as if avoidance of tough issues is what they lacked all along. Of course any modern counselor would diagnose repressive denial, and that might solve their problem in the short term but can never be the basis of a successful relationship, much less a marriage.

But these two veterans of the headlong rush don't need a counselor to know that they can't salvage a life together with a few hours of footsies. So they set life aside. They seem to accept the outcome, one way or another, which a different counselor might diagnose as advanced behavior, allowing an issue to resolve on time and manners, by distracting themselves from potential pain with more productive behavior, in this case setting Skinny up with water and a piece of *poisson cru* rinsed and cut into bits. And another. Because the best remedy for most ailments is giving to a greater cause, and Skinny is the perfect greatness—so small, so expressive, so fuzzy, demanding, and cute.

They watch her eat.

Ravi arranges a shirt as a nest in her kennel. She curls up and watches them back. He puts a hand on her head and she meows, then purrs. Then she sleeps. Holding hands again like kids sharing an adventure, they let go and return to the party. The gathering has gained momentum, loosening up from initial stupidity and stiffness, becoming animated and interesting.

What harm in holding hands? Or resting an arm on a shoulder or around a waist? Or brushing fingertips or the other's skin? No harm at all, and it adds dimension to the soirée, challenging the audience to observe obliquely and murmur discreetly. So the narrative plays out to an audience enrapt, straining and waiting to see which ending the players will choose.

An equally compelling subplot is Moeava, a professional diver sharing life and times with two women who listen attentively while watching each other. Cosima and Monique must be acquainted but behave as if just introduced. They scan each other while touching the man between them, fondly or vicariously; who knows? The giant diver regales them with know-how, close calls, and exotic encounters, his sheer size the perfect protection some women crave. Don't they? Curiosity demands discretion here too, though conjecture is rampant. Who will go home with whom, and who will be on top?

Ravi stares from within his own sphere of doubt and wonder till he sees Hereata happily, spuriously engaged. She also sees and knows, her sad smile an epitaph to what might have been—or what used to be. The strange new guy is on her like a shadow, like he knows her from experience. So Ravi steps up to put an arm around her and tell Oybek she is among the wonderful people of the world. Oybek's agreement is hard to watch; he assures that he is well aware, fully informed, absolutely apprised, sated, glutted, and yadda, yadda, licking his chops like a giant lizard over some delicious ducklings. Oybek is not your average friendly fellow. Ravi wasn't so wrong to draw the line, but a dash of self-redemption is in order and feels redemptive one more time. Will they become friends? Who knows? Stranger things have happened. In showbiz.

Oybek apologizes again for any bad impression. Ravi says, "No. I am the one to apologize. My anger makes me a fool. I can't bark and lunge at every stranger."

"I am happy to hear you say this," Oybek says—*I love you say and honor you this.*

"But you *were* an asshole. That night at the buffet. You were wrong."

"Yes," Oybek laughs. "Asshole me. All the time but especially drink. Not good. Please forgive. But, please, I not asshole in dive. Only bad diver, me. But you, you good man. Thank you for save me."

•

A rich and happy life has many endings, and even the last one may lead to another beginning. The final curtain may fall on one act and rise on Act One. Emigrate? Immigrate? Who knows where things go or come? Being or not can get problematic with no flesh and love unless it also endures in a form as yet unimagined. That stuff can go either way—plenty time to worry later. For now, anybody can be happy once he's logged enough heartbreak. Ravi Rockulz feels blessed, or maybe he feels that a blessing is near, as his pages turn to what comes next.

The new chapter begins only three hours hence when the guests are gone, each farewell an effusion of best wishes and love. Hereata whispers, "You never told me she was so beautiful."

Well, of course he did, but rather than correct her, he says, "You are so beautiful." She blushes, and all is well, or might be better later. Oybek bows, shakes hands with his host, wishes him the very happiest of birthdays and leaves with his paramour.

With the place secure, doors and windows shut, Skinny is allowed to wander the room, read the scents and take note. Little Dog is allowed in with strict instruction to lie down and stay. Stay. You stay.

The former loves disrobe like locals getting ready for sleep. They pause at the bed. Then comes what neither can remember from the past: the soft kiss. He wants to assure her that this is going nowhere but shouldn't matter, really—no, not that it shouldn't matter, but it shouldn't hurt anyone, considering what they. . . But he finds the better part of explanation again in silence and in fear of blowing the brief moment. She wants to say that they may give of themselves with no commitment but also fears that any words could discourage him, that he may abandon hope. So they sway on the precipice.

They recline. A few more tears fall for what's been lost, the inevitable impasse and the chance for peace. Who knows?

Night falls on shipwreck survivors washed up on a distant shore, hugging the warmth between them. With a whimper in the wee hours, she asks if he's in love with Hereata.

"She took care of me, and I love her for it, yes."

"That's not what I asked."

"I am not in love with Hereata."

She says he might not believe her, and that's his choice, and she's learned these last two years that she must respect his choice. But she never loved Darryl and she never did those things. "I know what he told you, but it's not true."

"What?"

Never, ever—and, in fact, she only allowed *da kine* once, back when she was nearly fourteen and didn't know notting—I mean, anything. She wants Ravi to hear this—whether he believes it or not because she knows how his mind works, or used to work, and how little things that shouldn't bother him build up inside, and then they do bother him. And she doesn't want that, so she needs to stop the pain before it starts. Because it hurt her too—hurt like crazy because he had the soft touch of a pneumatic jackhammer, *I mean Darryl did,* and besides that, he was gross and ugly.

She didn't want to do it.

He forced her and thought she loved it because she never called the cops. "And that's the truth. I swear it. I had to tell you. I know you think I'm evil, but I'm not. I don't want to sound like a victim, but Darryl is nothing. He did a mean and ugly thing. It's like when you step in dog poo, you know? You wipe it off, but it still stinks for a while. But it goes away. I mean you don't throw your shoes away. You know?"

Ravi wonders what could possibly possess a woman—a wife—to describe another man in gross terms to her husband.

Minna knows what all men think they must hear in order to let a thing go—even as they glom onto the sordid detail they think will stop their minds from churning.

Ravi takes a brief moment to sort the images and gets hung up on a tough one: "What is the *da kine* you only allowed once?"

"Oohh no—not like that. Not that. Only coochy *kine*."

Which moves things along to what must be easier, which is the lingering scent on her shoes. He sighs. "One time? And he get all strung out for life?"

"Hey. Some guys, you know. They cannot let go, ever."

No. They can't. *Lucky I'm not one of them. I mean, I can live with that, for now, even if Darryl is thinking of Minna and his one go this very minute so hard he's squeezing tears from the corners.*

He rolls to the side so she can see his forgiveness in refracted moonlight—even as stray pangs interrupt this program. But they melt away too, as all will in the watery bye 'n bye.

She sees. She smiles back, wondering if he bought it, hoping that he did and that they might finally have peace, whatever their legal status. Is that too much to ask?

No, it's not too much, though life presents regular tests to all seekers, so they may apply what they've learned. On the one hand, they'll see if attraction survives—not on firm bodies or lusty potential but in the light shining between them. On the other hand, they must keep a few things buried, events and regrets that will undermine spiritual growth, until those things have time to decompose and fade away, as some things should.

The first opportunity for ending and beginning comes in the morning on learning that Moeava blocked the day off, no trip. With intuition and foresight, he anticipated a hangover but did not likely foresee his windfall of women. On the surface, it looks impulsive as a fling, inebriate and fun, a casual *ménage*, with derring-do, surprises, demands, and good cheer among newfound friends. Except that sunrise finds the trio waking but unwilling to untangle the fondness stumbled into.

Realizing his role as a practical functionary in the drama playing out, Moeava grows worldly wise, evolved since yesterday when he was merely big and lonely. He offers no detail or flourish, not the first hint or tease, nothing but an affirmation of great good luck to have two girlfriends who like each other. On second thought, he corrects himself: Monique has both a girlfriend and boyfriend who get along and may someday like each other.

"But you already liked Cosima. Since before we met—long before, I would think."

That may be, but the one-way affection of yesterday is as removed from last night as flat water from pitching seas. Cosima lacks experience and initiative. Monique provides all of the above. Cosima does what Monique says. Monique likes to watch, and Cosima likes her watching. Neither cares if Moeava watches, so he watches for a while, but nobody minds if he takes a little snooze while they play together. They wake him up, sooner or later.

Wait a minute. She didn't lack initiative with me. But he accepts again and again as necessary, though some scenes shimmer for a long time. Never mind. Monique is oldest and wisest and best suited to lead the way, to manage needs and gratification, and let's face it: friends bonding in love are better than one man's satisfaction. What a relief. What a show. *N'est-ce pas?*

Moeava will not belabor complexities of dominance, submission, or reciprocation other than Monique's first rule of respect: that nobody requires anybody else to swim the bay, night or day.

•

The morning stretches to casual brunch and a spontaneous outing to Taverua reef, which is different than an old life resumed.

Minna has a week and then another. Their schedules merge. Growing affection is balanced by Hereata's lingering regret and adaptation.

Oybek is gregarious, magnanimous, unctuous, and tedious on heightened self-esteem. He calls Hereata the love of his life. She demurs. He speaks of greatness and showbiz. Loser tourists have blown smoke up Ravi's ass for years, flaunting their wares far from home. Talk of wealth, name-dropping, and personal questions mark the common commuter in quiet desperation. The smoke billows from LA too, but LA is where success waits around the corner, any corner anytime. Could you be part of my new project? Fuckinay, baby, you might know Spielberg. I do. Do you?

Granting the benefit of all doubts, Ravi does not think Oybek a loser, even as Oybek talks about a decent advance, nothing too big, say twenty grand, which will be peanuts next to what they'll soon do, but it should get the lovebirds by for a couple of weeks. Oybek reviews immediate needs for their migration to LA.

Ravi laughs.

Minna smiles at his laughter.

Oybek softens the situation with his own bedside manner; they won't need to stay in LA forever, though many artists do, for the wonderful social life, the artistic and intellectual stimulation. Duration can be decided later, though a few years will be necessary to get things going.

Ravi feels foolish asking the obvious question: "If it's that easy to make millions, what are you doing here?"

"I discover you! I make millions, yes, with a property—you! Without a property, I make nothing!"

Ravi is made to feel more foolish when the fleshy fellow explains the obvious, that an underwater photographer living in LA will take far more photos underwater. That sounds typically deluded and maybe stupid, and he feels more foolish still, conversing with last year's foe, who this year blows smoke up his ass. Make that smog. Or was that the year before last already? At the foolish summit is the ridiculous subject of LA itself and the pros and cons of living there as a prerequisite to artistic success. LA feels like a joke or a curse or a laughable, pitiful reality.

Oybek says that Ravi's reef artistry will span the globe from French Polynesia to the Andaman Sea before it dies, to the Maldives and Truk—ooh and the Red Sea. "You have been there?"

"I am from there."

"Iloji yo'q! I knew it!"

Oh, man. This guy is strange.

The day before returning to LA, Oybek hands Ravi a check for twenty thousand dollars. Ravi holds it gingerly, asking about a contract or some assurance that this is not a debt.

Oybek laughs too loud and says not to worry because he knows the difference between an advance and a debt. He promises a contract soon that will satisfy all parties and secure a prosperous future. If you don't like it, don't sign it! In the meantime, spend the money. Enjoy.

And don't worry; the money will be made back because Ravi has been officially recognized for genius, which is what Oybek does for a living. Do you understand this? Could a seasoned professional be so wrong? Yes, he could be, but he's not been wrong yet, and some of his picks were far less certain than this one.

"Look this!" Oybek beams, pointing at an octopus peeking electrically over a boulder.

Well, yes, the octopus shot is remarkable, so Ravi accepts ovations of greatness. Who knows? Maybe success can be guaranteed. Twenty grand is more than Ravi ever made in one day or had at one time. He can't yet retire, but he doesn't want to. So he rests easy and ponders the future. Such is the power of a solid C-list operator.

The next month passes in reverie, what younger lovers envisioned only two years ago. Ravi dives and shoots in the mornings. Minna helps at the animal hospital. She notifies her family and the other hospital that she'll remain on extended leave, and that the annulment is off. She won't spell it out but leaves it to them. Better they figure it out than hear the bad news.

She visits a medical care facility to see about a job and hits the language barrier. So she begins French lessons and attempts the new language in her daily life. She thinks she can get it until Ravi makes the official announcement: they will depart Tahiti soon, to live together as a married couple—in LA, to gain a solid footing in marine photographic art, but only for a year.

Or two.

Or maybe not because it may all vaporize and so many things do with regard to fortune and art, except that the move gains momentum and feels like it's on, even as the smoke billows up their ass and tickles. They giggle, happily sharing a wisp or two, and then giggle more when Ravi says he's had so much smoke up his tuchas that he can't even fart without coughing.

Oybek's revenge would be huge, if that's what this is. But Oybek is a self-made man—in show biz, which is also known for smoke and hugeness. So? Jump on!

Why practice French if the show is moving to LA?

Don't worry; you can practice anything you want in LA.

Does a Mother's Opinion Count for Nothing?

Well, yes.

And no. Of course Basha Rivka's two cents is worth every penny because she is the mother after all, and let's face it: you only have one mother, and if you don't factor her views and assessments on the big picture, then her wisdom and experience are wasted.

Wasted! Your choice.

Yet in the practical sense, what difference can it make at this juncture? On the bright side, Basha Rivka is pleased; Los Angeles is a cultural hub, where a young man can be with his own kind at last, even if a proper wife is temporarily beyond reach.

Okay, so he married a sh. . . a lovely girl who just so happens to be go. . . not Jewish. If she makes babies and is good to Ravi, then they should both live and be well. Besides, once she sees the light, she may convert, for the children's sake.

"But tell me something, Ravi. Aval tagid li, hi be-herayon?"

"No, Mother. She is not pregnant."

"Why not?"

"Should I put her on the line?"

"I'm asking you."

"Maybe she's a virgin."

"I wouldn't be surprised. Yes I would. Tell me when."

"When what?"

"When I can come to LA to visit my grandchildren."

"It will be at least nine months from now."

"God willing."

"At least."

"From your lips."

"We'll begin right away. Make your reservation."

"I knew you would make me happy. Someday."

"You did?"

"I hoped for the best. It's all I can do."

And so he tells his poor, lonely mother of his productive efforts in Tahiti, leading to his discovery as the foremost marine photographer in the world. One of, at any rate.

"Foremost, no less."

"That's what Oybek says. He knows. He does this for a living."

"So now you might make a living too, still with the bubbles but with some *shekels* too. Did you cash the check?"

"Not yet. I don't want to deposit it here and then try to get it out."

"How do you know it's good?"

"How do you know it's not?"

"When will you listen? Will you do me a favor? Do I ask my only son for so much?"

"What do you want me to do?"

"Cash the check."

"Why?"

"So you know. So you're not such a *schmendrick* all the time, bouncing around like a. . . like a what?"

"Like a rolling stone. No moss."

"You said it."

"Okay. I'll cash it."

"Thank you."

"Don't mention it."

"And please, let me know when."

"Yes, I'll let you know."

Little Dog Laughed

Ravi's first trip to LA is not speculative. He is spared the charade of being in the neighborhood and dropping in casually, the one-act play so often required of young artists with worlds to conquer in LA, as if budding talents will emerge, given a random chance. He touches down on terra firma with rubber on the road right now. He is direct from the exotic reaches of the world with mysteries to share.

The flight is surreal, revealing the greatest mystery: He's giving up Oceania for Urbania? Or would that be Suburbania? It's like trading Tahiti for LA, except there ain't no like about it.

Los Angeles sprawls in layered excess with horrific symptoms—talk about smoke. Within the blur come seeping scabs, fresh wounds, and lesions to all horizons. Cars, billboards, lights, noise, filth, perversion, cement, garbage, chrome, glass, disease, and people in the millions upon millions rush for more of the more and more. Clogged arteries squeeze the flow to a trickle till it stops at stubborn sludge—or races madly for short stretches, people delivering themselves and their wares everywhere all the time. Barren of innocence and nature, the place buzzes and stinks, steams and festers. Breaking News is that a brand new freeway gunslinger has shed the bonds of polite company and is trying to soothe his rage by shooting commuters one lane over. Six more lanes feel crazy, wild, and free; ten more lanes make even more sense in a hundred-grand roadster, pedal to the metal on a downshift to goose the redline and really show some stuff. Oh, baby! This is me! Who the fuck are you?

With the brainpan awash in azure blue, here comes LAX and the very best hospitality Inglewood has to offer, as long as you breathe shallow, stay alert, and carry a compass. Not to worry; Oybek is sending a car, so never mind the yellow-brown cloud covering creation like a dirty blanket or the masonry cap on everything or the teeming ambition or general neurosis or specific psychosis oozing out the pores of the place with enough sweat, grit, and desperation to slump a tropical waterman.

What's that smell?

But give peace a chance; LA is not an open sore, not as different from French Poly as shit from shinola. It looks and feels different—make that sci-fi screaming insane different. Yellow-gray over a scabby crust coming into LAX is only the beginning. Then you're in, so to speak, in easy access to a vibrant urban center with many major sports teams, millions of fans, a dynamic cast of characters, trillions in net worth, and of course much, much more. LA gets a bad rap on population density, road rage, homicide, and perversion, but eccentricity is pivotal to showbiz. Personal identity is a linchpin of survival in a garish, colorful system. Any reef suffers if residents out-need the resources at hand, but it's only growing pains, and people will find more of what they need. Reality rolls in like a set of huge, breaking waves.

Oybek: what a joker, sending playful party girls to meet and greet, and not just any girls but the girls' dreams are made of, the girls next door, all grown up to full potential as hostesses with the mostesses, with the forty-eight double-Ds, dragon tattoos, six-inch heels, and the great good cheer every girl needs to practice. These three look as good as medium-budget hookers ever did. Ravi isn't into that sort of thing because he doesn't need it, never has. These days are pleasantly distracted and more than adequate along those lines. He's enjoying the matrimonial scene and realizing the comforts available with one true love. Then again, practicality is primary in La La, and the grab seems compulsory on a thing within reach. So he's willing to be amused, considering his flawed judgment of Oybek. It's best to let bygones go and let friendship develop. Best to show gratitude as the better part of discretion. Best to ensure a gilded future with appreciation. His benefactor should know that he can join in the spirit of the play, though four of these six tits are big as soccer balls and just as firm, *and I think Earlette is a guy or used to be.*

It's only harmless fun and easy too; these people are so game, energetic, eager to please, and encouraging. How could anybody help but like them? Besides, Skinny, Little Dog, and Minna won't be along for two weeks.

Besides, the work ahead is not work but fun—the program is built on fun. Ravi's first few hundred spectacular, amazing, astonishing photo picks are laid out in three products: the coffee table volume is over-produced in grandiose format, two feet by three feet for the surround sound feel of the thing—and it comes with the exclusive, just-released CD, *Sounds of the Deep Blue Sea.* Richly processed colors exude texture and pulse. The heavy-bond, plastic-coated pages are finished lithographic prints suitable for framing. What if you love two fish on the same page, back to back?

Buy two books, you cheap fuck. You wanna quibble over two bills for an entire fucking stack of museum quality pictures?

We're talking fucking art here!

Fuck.

Oybek writes the flap copy, where he calls the book, in loose translation, a reef seduction, Hollywood style. He privately predicts that this motherfucker will perform.

Executive Producer Solomon Silvergold takes exception to Oybek's performance projection if it's volume fucking sales you're talking because a fucking fish book running two hundred fucking clams is not—*not*—about to fly off the fucking shelf—not even with that shot of the flying fucking fish! How the fuck did he do that?

Anyway, who gives a fuck if it gimps off the shelf, what with distribution control and that whole supply/demand game and media bumps and internet sales to keep margins running the two hundred, two hundred fucking fifty percent they ought to fucking run? Unless we discount it sixty percent—then you'll see your fucking volume projections take the kinda fucking shape you're talking. Fuck.

The second product is your quick-reference guide in standard format with color plates and myriad data on each fish at a lower price point to reach a bigger market. "Yeah, the cheap motherfuckers. Gotta love 'um. And I'll tell you what: this motherfucker will ring the fucking bell. Twenty-nine ninety-fucking-five? Are you fucking kidding me?"

The third product is the calendar, rounding out the fucking package with twelve shots from the mix because that's how it's done these days, in packages, like we're Sony fucking Viacom or some shit, which is about the best way to goose your margins overall and pick up the chump change by the wheelbarrow on the back end with the fucking calendar. "Oh, don't get me wrong; fucking calendars—they got more calendars than a dog has fleas out there now. But this calendar is the low price ticket to the show. Get it? Now this motherfucker will perform. *And,* we make it *free* as a premium when you get three of the standards or one deluxe edition. Oh, you're gonna see the numbers jump then. You watch."

And so they watch—the staff, and they listen, enrapt—Tiffany, Blaze, Dexter, Auriel, and Edgar—as Mr. Silvergold elaborates on performance and returns. "I'm telling you it can't look any better than a package, and packaging gets no finer than such as the excellence before us, unless of course you can get to monthly billings, but we haven't got that one dicked yet. But we ought to be close. What do we got, maybe fish of the month?"

"No, sir, we didn't fall in love enough with fish of the month to call for capitalization. It's a great idea, but we just couldn't peg a medium."

"We were considering, Mr. S, a Tahitian-beauty-of-the-month calendar, mixed in with the fish, two products actually, in male or female as an option, or perhaps an upgrade, with gender mix as a standard order. We have a supplier from Brazil who guarantees the finest lift and spread in the southern hemisphere, but it feels like too many moving parts for a start-up. So we tabled the tits and torsos for now if you approve."

Well. What the fuck. The package is in production, target-marketed, focus-grouped, revised, tweaked and ready to roll. This is timing. *This* is synchronicity, with Ravi's visit putting him *in the flesh* on *The Tonight Show*—"Are you fucking kidding me? We got The Late Show? What did that cost?"—where the *goods* will be held up to the camera, *also in the flesh*, introducing a new phenom in photography and art and fish and. . .

"What? Fish?" The zany one, himself, can't believe the prompter actually says fish, as his sparkly eyes offset his Cheshire grin. He doesn't ask: *What the fuck can you do?* Doesn't need to, and he says, "I kid you not, it says photography and art and fish, right here. Come on, Cliff, swing around and show it. They don't believe me. Look! Right here! See it! Okay—hey! Ravi Rock. . . ulz. Welcome!" So proclaims the oracle of late night to the viewing world.

And so begins the miracle of birth, by which a revelation of beauty and artistic prowess reaches sixty million people in sixty-two countries! This *objet d'art* in varying incarnations is made to exist in the minds of one-tenth of one percent of the viewing audience. One-tenth of one percent of those retaining the image go out in the next three days and buy one or more components of the package. . .

Wait! What is that sound. . . that sound in the distance? Is it the tintinnabulation of the sales, sales, sales massive sales to warm the soul of art in ultimate performance? Do I hear the angels in their sweetest refrain: cha-ching cha-ching?

Oh, baby.

What appeared at first blush to be a large book, a medium book and a calendar is actually a social, cultural event—an artistic breakthrough and spiritual attainment that may well rock your world if you buy it. To call it the next big thing would belabor the obvious. Never before have so many failed to imagine so much—until now. Now they see.

Many people in the studio and in subsequent studios on the path to media significance tell Ravi, "Wow, that's really something," which is code for *smashing success, blockbuster, bell ringer, cultural impact* and yes, *the next big thing.*

•

The package tracks more profitably than a third-world dictatorship. Staggering returns soon lose meaning. Revenue becomes a number on paper. Then come peripherals—the lifelike action figures at twelve dollars each for the individual fish or a more economical fifty dollars for the reef fish community, though the community is actually in segments, with separate economies available for the wrasses, angels, damsels, puffers, eels, butterflies, and invertebrates. The Ravi action figure is only thirty dollars, with accessories that cannot be economized in a package because sometimes an artistic aesthetic requires *à la carte*, in case a young Reef Ranger—the lifetime membership club the kids love—begins with the snorkel ensemble action toys and works up to the scuba ensemble action toys—with separate strap fins for *Action Ravi*!

From there, the truly committed kid can get the rebreather ensemble action pack, with peripherals available to match any kid's imagination, like a little decompression chamber for when the Action Ravi doll gets bent, or a portable marine surgery unit with tiny instruments when Action Ravi needs an embolism removed.

Surgically?

Oh! Or the authentic Reef Ranger medevac helicopter or the dive boat or the video games, which sell like crazy, though everyone agrees that video alone won't capture the essence. . .

Performance goes from staggering to numbing, and, though taken in stride, it brings a few wobbles. Ravi resists praise from so many well-wishers who simply love a hero, even if it's the hero of the hour, because this has gone on a few hundred hours, and he's also numb! More impressive praise comes from the technicians at the core of every appearance. Even they see it! And they are not known for kissing ass!

The support crews—those tiny names at the end of every show—sense a phenomenon with more shelf life than your average media product line. These audio, video, techno pros seem less needy than the on-camera "talent" or administrative others appearing higher on the credits. They praise and thank Ravi for taking things to a new level. They tell him their magic is easier to make with his magic to build on—easy, anonymous people since nobody really reads the tiny names. They credit him for making their work happier, for helping them show their stuff.

Does a vibrant reefdog on intimate terms with Neptune really need makeup? No, he does not. But an hour of dabbing, brushing and tweaking turns the untouched, fabulously handsome *before* into the electrifying *after.*

The Ravi syndicate enjoys copious management in its many revenue centers, but even a wizened marketeer of Solly Silvergold's aggressive second nature could not foresee the scope of secondary development in the offing. That is, *The True Story of Ravi Rockulz* is either leaked or talked around or something or other, till the man who saves reefs and little fishes in the tropics with beautiful women at every turn also becomes a hero, surviving death-defying odds in shark-infested waters.

The fish guy swam in from the aggregation buoy at night.

What's an aggregation buoy?

It's this thing. Twenty-two miles. And these guys beat him up. Bad guys.

Twenty-two miles? Your dying ass. Nobody swims twenty-two miles.

They do in the English Channel.

That's different.

Why is it different?

Because it is.

What?

Did somebody say something? Oh, yes:

Soon to be a Major Motion Picture Event!

This could be big—very big. The talk is big right off the bat. Nobody has the chutzpah to call it huge before the money is in place, but then Willis is *very* interested in the part on two conditions: 1) that his girlfriend, an unknown but lithesome blonde who can easily dye to black and can work wonders with a modicum of putty to actually render Polynesian perfection, will play the younger woman and 2) Angelina will play the older woman. Oh—and he also stipulates that 3) the director's understanding of action/adventure will be subject to the sole ruling of his, Willis's, agent. So far so good. What could be more reasonable? Except that Willis never asked Angelina what she thought—and she thinks Willis is older than her father, which he isn't, but still, this puts one-up on the line, threatening to boil over with ugly innuendo, not to mention potential.

The options get renewed because of the simmering oasis just ahead and also as a defensive measure to keep the jackals from stealing what the option holders have paid good money for all rights to. More good news is that nobody balks at the option renewal acceleration clause. We're talking *de*fense!

But fallout reaches terminal velocity when the lithesome girlfriend splits for greener pastures when Brian Highlander ends his steamy liaison with Ashley Hetherington. Speculation runs rampant, but that's incidental to the Willis connection, which, speaking of a little putty, seems, in a word, pathetic. With Brian Highlander available? Get serious.

Never mind. Not one minute after the second option lapses, new options are dangled before the hottest performing agents and packagers in town. Not to worry. This bait shall make them frenzy. Just you watch.

So the man becomes the myth, the legend, with the most amazing artistic commitment since. . . well, we hate to say this because we'll get so many letters, but since Vincent Van Gogh. The difference is that Ravi Rockulz is happily married to a fantastic beauty and didn't cut his ear off. Send your comments to moltencore.com. . .

And so it flows.

An urgent meeting of market professionals, producers, directors and sage associates is called to plan strategy on the Speedos. That is, we need himself on the set in his skimpy skivvies without looking prurient or salacious—without triggering the mad lust of LA's fervent fans. Any ideas? Because leaving the Speedos under wraps, as it were, is leaving huge money on the table.

Ravi has two ideas: he can stand up from the guest seat and take off his shirt and pants to reveal the Speedos, which is a natural thing to do in French Poly, and the viewing audience will see.

The echelon stare in awe and wonder that such a simple solution may meet the criteria, avoiding the sex-mongering accusations sure to come. But it just won't work; I mean, really, a man taking his clothes off on camera? Come on—and not just any man, but *him*?

Okay! The second idea is that they cut away to actual underwater footage of Ravi in his scuba gear, holding his camera with its strobes sticking out and so on. That way the cameraman can zoom in on the wavy tummy and lumpy nether.

"Wait a minute. . . I'll be wearing a wetsuit. . ."

"Yes! That's it!" Three top tech execs cry out in unison, agreeing while adapting the idea to what happens best in LA: technical excellence. They'll stage a simulation! "We won't actually be in the ocean, bubby."

And so it comes to pass at hardly over budget, not even a million dollars, which might sound excessive as the raw cash required to put a man-size tank on a sound stage, but when broken down to drawings, engineering, materials, including one-inch tempered glass, construction, the crane, the truck, the lifts and dollies and logistical coordination between the writers' union, the construction union, the stage prop union and the stage handlers union, along with legal disclaimers and backup docs, it's a steal. Are you kidding me?

The segment runs seven minutes, cutting into a commercial break that ups the budget another hundred grand or so in lost revenue from said commercial break, but at this point, it's the commitment that's going to count. Sure the naysayers are scoffing and scorning the silly shit they're trying to pull on *The Evening Show*. They splash so much water on the set that David slips and falls on his ass. He has the wits to make it look like a setup—what a ham, what a natural, what a beauty—but it isn't a setup, and his hip may be fractured. As if that's not enough, they short-circuit the audio and go to break for seven more minutes, giving up some freebie public service announcements, after they met their PSA requirement for the ratings period last fucking week!

But jeez, Louise, did you see the frickin fuckin' dingdong on that fish guy?

Bingo! Or, as Executive Producer Sol Silvergold elaborates, "Motherfucking bingo, you doubtful, shit-eating motherfuckers!"

Mr. Silvergold sounds upset but really is happy. The tirade comes the next day before lunch when nobody can tell if Solly feels the joy or another coronary coming on. But he's always in a better mood after eating, especially on Wednesday when it's the huge fucking corned beef on rye special with one of those semi-kosher dills bigger than Jimi Hendrix's dick—bigger than it used to be anyway.

"Ha! Am I right! *Gott!* Did you ever eat anything so delicious? What is it? The mustard? The little bit fat? The bread? What? Did you ever?"

No, nobody never. After lunch Solly settles down. It's predictable, part of a pattern: "Fucking motherfuckers. They're gonna tell Sol Silvergold who or what is not going to be big? Fuck you, motherfuckers. Fucking *mamzers*." And he laughs. Solly laughs, which proves that he's happy and in a good mood and pleased, and everybody else can laugh too.

"Hey, kid," he fondly asks Ravi. "You know from mamzers?"

"Ken, ktsat. Me-ha-mamzerim, megiaa ha-balagan ha-godol." Yes, a little bit. From the bastards comes the big man.

"Hey. The kid is French. But I think he knows. Hey, kid. You from southern France, or what? Hey, Jews everywhere now. The fuck. They accuse us of running showbiz. Did you know that? Did you? Hey. Fuckinay, baby! Ha!"

So the whole wide world laughs—as it murmurs and mumbles snippets and images of fish, fish books, fish calendars and the fish guy—and what Solly said about Jimi Hendrix's dick even as everyone is thinking that it's time for Jimi to roll over for the motherfucking moray eel in the fish guy's shorts.

When lunch at Solly's is done, and it looks like another money gusher coming on, thanks to the fish guy and the best motherfucking management money can buy, Solly says, "Ha! Don't you worry, kid. You're gonna be a very rich man. Rich! Wealthy? I don't know. But rich!" Then he tosses a set of keys in a lazy arc to Ravi, who makes the snatch casual as a receiver with magic hands. "Drive this till you get settled. Don't take more than a year. Okay, five years. Ha!"

The car is right out front, presenting the next challenge in a blaring announcement that the waterman has sunk in the mire. The gleaming statement of material excess sitting at the tow-away curb is a flame red Jaguar convertible with matching interior, top down. Ravi's blush doesn't match, but not for want of trying. His embarrassment over-whelms, till Oybek whispers gruffly in his ear to direct the action: "Get in! Look happy! Wave! Smile! Dig it, motherfucker!" This last is not a cliché but a basic directive based on continuing survival with a double dollop of prosperity.

Ravi's hesitation doesn't carry from the curb to Solly's big window on the thirty-fourth floor. He waves up. Solly waves back down. It's a deal.

It's a goof that doesn't mean to be a laugh, but Ravi feels con-strained laughter aimed his way—look what happened to the fish guy. He's more or less comforted by friends who assure him that it's a toy, a nothing to have fun with and maybe be proud of because it's also a measure of success—and he's doing extremely well. It's not a reflec-tion of who he is or what he values. It's merely a mode of expressing a glorious victory over simple needs and practicality. Which works for most commuters in LA, but Ravi loves his life of simple needs and practicality. And he can't help but feel that the obtrusive red car does reflect values—wrong values, and who he is and what he wants—and it's just not so.

Here too, a reefdog adapts, wincing a bit less when he sees the red car glaring brighter than the sun. The brilliant redness blinds and annoys but it's sometimes fun, and it's a car—just a fucking car, like a beater Tercel used to be, what basic transportation came to, and that's all it is. He'd throw some tanks and gear in back if he had a reef nearby.

The turnaround perspective comes out of the blue, as it were, in a lightning bolt of insight and understanding. Celebrity by this time has become a challenge, then a burden, then a bad feeling of life forsaken in swarms of fans, with the dashing red car a homing beacon on their hero. Ravi avoids certain routes that will surely expose him to more of the same, routes through thick fan habitat—fans whose loss of personal identity has left them bereft of anything but the stars to look up to. They stop in their tracks to point a finger and utter his name. He qualifies as a sighting.

One early evening when the radio announces triple fender benders at three exits in a row on just the freeway he needs to get home in less than an hour, he takes the low road, to try for an hour and a half.

Somewhere on the fringe of West Hollywood, headed for Santa Monica, he approaches a group of young prostitutes in a known sex-zone. They yell at the likely john in the hundred grand car who could splurge on a five-bill blowjob and not even feel it—that would be the money he wouldn't feel, not the blowjob; oh, baby. A guy in a red Jag ragtop might not even feel a five-bill tip. He won't return their gaze, even as traffic slows to a crawl, and soon he's near the line-up of tawdry boys in short shorts, heavy eyeliner and other facial pastes, putties, and colors. The scene is busy, garish and colorful like a reef but not so innocent. Violent spawning and unnatural acts form their own dark order. This is depravity in its lowest form as a means to an end. Well, one of the lowest forms, around here.

A furtive boy steps off the curb to put both hands on the passenger door and say, "You're the fish guy. Ravi Rockulz." Ravi looks up casually enough and can't help a double take—is that rosacea or rouge over Kaposi's? What difference does it make, except to the young man? It could make a difference to him and surely must. The boy says, "I love you—no, I mean, I really do. I love your fish. You make me want to be a fish. I want to be you. God." And he yells to the other boys in the shrill excitement of a genuine siting, "Hey! It's the fish guy! It's Ravi!"

So the boys of the evening gather round, chattering like birds roosting at dusk, with their bangles, half t-shirts and flaunted emotions—unusual boys going stranger still when they morph in macro, leaning into the car. Up close in lingering daylight Ravi sees the soiled life. But they are not the living dead; they're up and at it, surviving another day, as people must, on dollars earned. They gather without shame, quickly slipping out of character, shedding lascivious postures to become fans in appreciation of the fish guy and what he does and where he's been and how he thinks, as if a fish guy is different from other guys, as if the fish guy knows, sees and feels what is dear to them. And this is a reef, maybe, and he's here.

An indelible imprint on Ravi Rockulz's showbiz career careens out of nowhere on a salacious, disturbed boy whose lipstick is smudged over one cheek from recent service or as suggestive merchandizing. "I got the big one, you know. It's so huge. I love that. I get off about three. I mean, unless it's really busy, you know. People don't realize how hard we work. We're like everybody else. I used to be homeless, but now I have a place and a few things, now that I suck cock, you know. Anyhoo, you know, I can buy things now, too, and I like to open my book, your book, when I get home. It makes me feel, you know, so. . . I can't really tell you what it makes me feel, but it's so good." The boy is twenty, give or take, and could have been a stunt double to Leonardo DiCaprio—same puffy face, sandy hair swept sideways, ski nose and baby blues. Unless. . . Unless he's more spot on for Johnny Depp, considering the eyeliner and method insanity in every posture, move, and word. And he cries, just as Ravi cried on cleaving emotion—cried for something unnameable but knowable, rare and of the greatest value.

The wayward boys on the driver's side touch the fish guy in appreciation of his gift or in order to say they did. One caresses his hair. One offers to pay five bills to suck off the fish guy, and he laughs nervously, sincerely. Most of the rest laugh too, waiting to see if the fish guy will. Offering thanks all around with a quick nod, Ravi peers ahead to traffic, starting to move. Even a crawl would ease him out of this bind, and so it does. So he says thanks again in gratitude to such great fans, and that's that, except for the boy who gets home late and feels good, looking at fish pics.

"Thank you, Ravi! You're so great. And I love your car. It's a flame angel, just like you. Please come and see us again. Okay?"

Ravi waves, as the flow picks up to twenty-five for another half hour, giving a waterman time to ponder the strange ways of God or Neptune or whomever, finally reaching an on-ramp beyond fender benders. It's some crazy fucked up shit all right. But those guys. . . those guys back there. Man. How can they get it so well and wind up so far from clear, blue water?

Fan appreciation is the lifeblood of the industry and can come where least expected. The tawdry boys are not polite subject matter for a talk show or even with associates, who may have spent a grand or two on that very same strip, making them what, any different than the boys? But not sharing fan appreciation does not diminish the value of the fans. The tawdry boys are victims of a tawdry world, but a glimmer shines through. Sexual innuendo notwithstanding, Ravi's little secret is that he loves those guys because of what they saw and had to say about it and mostly for their appreciation—for the time they took to feel the magic below sea level, as conveyed in the work. At least one of those guys lets himself go thousands of miles, away to a reef in his mind. That guy sees the light, and that is attitude—*his attitude connecting to my attitude.* That guy gets it, and that's a laugh, considering what else he must get.

•

The studio techs help again with street cover for anonymity, mobility, privacy and a normal life or approximation thereof. A baseball cap, shades, and a three-day growth restore the amazing reefdog to life among commuters and consumers. Newly amazed at this dreamy place, this phantasmagoria seeking realization—this LA—he feels many people staring, but it's not just at him. They stare at every anonymous pedestrian in three-day growth, baseball cap, and shades, knowing that greatness is strolling down the street casual as you please, if only they can find it.

Is that you?

In collective anonymity, everybody looks famous, maybe, kinda sorta. A few look like bit players, so familiar but hard to place. Some capture the beauty and loss of souls unbound, seeking a role and reasonable direction. Do you realize the potential here?

Among faces drawn in comedy and tragedy are huge talents awaiting discovery at street level. The dry cleaner no longer looks like Charlie Chan or speaks of number one son; he animate and crazy as chop-socky original, martinize to modern specs.

The ice cream guy has scorpion tattoos on his neck and glares in searing drama through special contact lenses of incandescent blue for this audition, in case you happen to be or know or might be able to get in touch with. . .

Waiters, waitresses, cab drivers, clerks and the whole service army wear second hats over their first, ready for the break because it will come. Until then, they're kindred spirits, backstage. "Hey. You're the fish guy. Right on, man. You're terrific."

Recognition does feel good—a certain return on effort, until he hears the recognition and turns, to see that the guy recognized looks amazingly like the fish guy but is not. *How could he be? I'm the fish guy. I wear a disguise, and for what? So some nebbish can claim the glory? Fuck.*

This too is unsettling, till later that night. Reviewing his work, as many artists do, critiquing or trying to see what a viewer might see, Ravi stops on a dazzling plate, a shot for sore eyes, a bell-ringer in brilliant red. Normally a shy fish, this flame angel presents the classic mug, front and a bit off-center. Fish are presumed cold, but this fish is hot on a point. This flame's eyebrows bunch in consternation. Behind him peeking out, his mate waits. On a whim, Ravi checks the files for an earlier shot of a flame angel in profile. He prints it and in the morning drives down to the custom car place where the art crew takes a half hour to estimate cost of four black bars on each side of the red Jaguar. Nobody questions the request because art is a private statement of values. It can get oblique in La La, but who are we to say, uh, anything? The bid is twelve thousand "to do it right." Ravi says he'll ponder the work, but on his way home he buys a four-inch brush and a gallon of black in satin finish for sixty bucks.

It seems crazy to hand-paint a car of such magnitude, and that feels good—compensatory and counterbalanced. Yes, it's a car, just a car, and now it will show the values we hold dear. For most viewers, the dearest value is industry success, which is obvious if the driver is a known face and apparent if he's in a Jag. He could be a producer or casting wizard or special effects guru on the very best crashes, explosions, catastrophes, and cyborgs.

Ravi Rockulz is a face from the talk circuit, eminently known and just as recognizable. *Hey, it's the fuckin fish guy!* Recognition is mostly annoying, so he gets the hat and shades and boom! The fish guy is a different guy, stealing the juice, and that's more annoying. So the real fish guy holds a seventeen by twenty flame angel print in one hand and a four-inch brush in the other. Four fell strokes put paint on steel slick as eel snot for perfect black bars easy as no effort at all. Clean and simple as Neptune's calligraphy, the four bars render something more than a car, what a car. It's more fun for starters, transcending value and even upping the bucks on one-off identity and a star-studded past. The other side is more difficult, with perfection so casually stumbled onto. But he goes snake-eyed and breathes deep and slow and lets the flame flow from the bristles to the car. He recalls his first difficult cruise in the red Jag and feels corrected, at home on the urban reef. He feels the idea, on the way to Oybek's office, where he shares his epiphany on entering.

Oybek's receptionist listens patiently and says the phenomenon of non-constraint is growing in leaps and bounds, and in many cases can be seen as a classic illustration of the Oybekian influence. "It's like you, painting a Jaguar with black stripes by hand. I get what you're trying to say. We've suffered so long. We keep ourselves locked up inside. Look at the surge in special effects studios. We used to have two that supplied the industry for decades. Now we have a few hundred. You can pooh-pooh explosions and wrecks as the death of drama, but they're not. They're an extension of drama. Take the golden age and Joan Crawford. She's my all-time fave. I can't tell you what it was, but she had it. . . Oh. . . Excuse me. Mr. Navbahor will see you now." The receptionist smooths a bushy brow and bats his lashes. "Now that lady threw some hand grenades. God."

"Thanks, but they're black bars, not stripes. Bars are vertical. Stripes are horizontal."

Oybekian?

Such is the show that never ends. The contract on Oybek's desk is thick with caveats, subordinations, sub-rights, exceptions, conditions and continuing permutations. Oybek squeezes all but the last page between thumb and forefinger and says, "Standard. I review same with your best interest in my mind. Good for you. Okay by me." He folds the stack back and lays it flat on his desk for signature.

Many people between Oybek's front door and the inner sanctum lingered in the hallway to praise Ravi's fabulous launch, which gives him a fabulous foundation on which to build; just you watch. So he signs off. "Now you see. We make magic. Presto. From nozzing, we get rabbit out of hat. You see."

REEFDOG

A month later the same TV talk shows want Ravi again. Other producers say they didn't take the fish guy seriously. Now they do. They want—they stipulate—that the fish guy *be* the fish guy and appear in mask, fins, and snorkel because nobody needs all that water-in-the-tank business with the knock 'em sock 'em scuba gear and the clunky camera stuff. For what? We need *him*, the fish guy. We need him to show the body of artistic pursuit. That's where we're going with this.

Oybek masterfully declines all offers, then triumphantly resists all offers, then reluctantly agrees to see what he can do. Ravi merely declines, so the talks are off. Then they're on again—okay, no mask fins and snorkel on stage, and hey, no need to be so testy. Okay?

The world wants Ravi, especially those women sitting beside him on the guest couch. But if celebrity status went toxic, sexual objectification is worse. He has used and been used, but as a human, not as fantasy gratification. He belches, farts and picks his nose to calm them down, but they rave for more.

It gets worse. One odd host is known for esoteric humor but depends mostly on puns and bad plays on good ideas, like calling reef society the same as LA without the tuna smell. Get it? Ravi does not throttle him but rises like a tiger to chum. He grabs the host by the lapels and says, "You're not funny." The host shrivels and the fish guy exits, aware of media exposure boring in. Never mind—cut to commercial like it never happened. But the lunge and grab boost the fish guy's stock, and a producer calls with a million-dollar idea for The Jerry Springer Show, where a bunch of pregnant trailer-trashers will yell that the fish guy is the father. Then he can join the brawl.

It's funny but pitiful, and besides, "We don't need his million." Absence of need is the best icing on the showbiz cake. Ravi Rockulz could scratch his ass left-handed and pump ratings, and so he does because the show has gone sour. Oybek plays it as he must, calling for a reprieve—it's time for the fish guy to visit some fish.

They head to the Bahamas for starters, to tie in with another money-maker. The fish guy cruises Nassau streets declining beautiful hookers, till one of them pulls a ThinSkinz rubber from behind her ear, so the fish guy steps back for a fresh assessment—cut to commercial on ThinSkinz. Then to *Car Lust: We Make Car Buying More Fun than You Know What!* Then the usual panoply: ab enhancers, fat pills, hemorrhoid ointment and boner pills for when *you're* in the mood and don't want to find a bathroom. They shore things up with terrific cleavage, a few camel toes and winning smiles. Ratings aren't bad. *Nothing Fishy in Nassau* won't go to sequel, but it won't bomb. He gets in a day of reef photography but not a second day—they're flying out to the Virgins. Will that be fantastic or what?

Island hopping to Martinique is a dead reef medley of brown algae and effluvia, treated and untreated. Living coral is a mile out but will move by next year to a mile and a quarter. Ravi the fish guy shoots dead reef, but what's the market for that?

Minna goes along, regretting postponement of her professional career on the one hand but loving the scenery, travel and glamour on the other. Let's face it: she's a natural. She loves telling the camera she married Ravi years ago and he's been just as hot ever since. She declines the inevitable offer that comes over the transom then, though it's been telegraphed, predicted and mildly lobbied for a while—a center spread, such as it is. It's pitched as art, only art, but the *ohana* back home wouldn't see it that way. Ravi plays open-minded but is secretly pleased with her decision. He surprises her with a triple-header to the Maldives, Truk, and Colombo, but she declines that too. But she should reconsider because the Indian Ocean will be free of hookers, producers, and tourist noise and will allow them to. . .

"I'm preggers."

"Wha?"

"You're surprised?"

•

Yet again, a story might end on happily ever after or trickle to the near future when the beautiful young family buys a place in Malibu with an incredible loan package designed for rich people who need help because they're not yet wealthy. Oybek's money guy designed the package as a stress-free exercise that's made him the talk of the neighborhood, and it's not just any neighborhood.

Stephan Otis Monihan calls the place simply fab. "It ain't Tahiti, okay? But LA does have some stimuli to jump your neurons if you give it half a chance. And this neighborhood. . . God!" Stephan Otis is tediously optimistic on every subject under the sun and calls La La the greatest opportunity goldmine anywhere because it is what it is. Ravi asks where is what it isn't. Stephan Otis chuckles, "Surely you know that apparent reality is best not confused with that yet to be actualized."

"Surely. But *it is* millions of fucked up people, if you're paying attention."

"Okay, Mister Fish. But I'll tell you something: some of those people, including yours truly, are very busy finding ourselves and getting well." Stephan Otis brushes a shoulder that has no lint and smooths his shirt. "We're smart people. We have the money thing worked out. We want more, and that's called evolution."

"Sorry, Stephan. I didn't mean to ruffle your feathers."

"I'm not used to it, but I get it. I have no feathers. And please, call me Stephan Otis. Monihan. I made the last name up. Get it? Money—moni. . . han. You'd be amazed how much money I've made for flaky people who can't remember my name. I suppose Stephan is a more popular name now, but there's only one Stephan Otis, so if you don't mind, it really helps me out. Okay?" Ravi doesn't mind, but he doesn't say it, so Stephan Otis asks again, "Okay?"

"Yeah, fuck it, whatever."

Stephan Otis calls the house quirky but harmless and definitely doable. He raises an eyebrow on double meaning. "Are you kidding me? On the beach at Malibu for seven point seven. Get out! Would you look at these views?"

Not that a year-old baby, or the one in the oven, gives a rat's patootie about the view, but they may one day, realizing that they need more out of, you know, life.

•

The kids love the yard on the bluff—not to worry; the fence keeps them and Little Dog from going over. Skinny gives them a turn one day, showing up outside the fence, near the edge, stalking something, casual as you please, till she stops. "Meow!" She's stuck or lost.

And who goes slinking to the rescue, supple as a geriatric cat? "You tell me what else? Off the cliff I should let her fall? The cat is like family. Family!" Basha Rivka could have spared Skinny's walk on the wild side by putting out cat food as instructed. Nobody suggests neglect since it wasn't willful and all's well. Natural buffering occurs on said family relations because contrary to the common wife/mother-in-law rift, Minna and Basha Rivka have achieved symbiosis, with mutual benefit and respect and appreciation to boot. Seldom is heard a discouraging word.

Harmony came easily. Basha Rivka anticipated a shiksa: upper-middle-class, cheery but snooty, socialized in a country club that doesn't allow you-know-whom, where big-boned bores stroll fairways or chat over drinks. She was wrong. The new *mishpocha* are Buddhist, without dogma, inquisitions, pogroms, or snobbery. She is intrigued, then relieved, possibly exhilarated.

Minna is merely practical, in tune with LA, where Jews and Buddhists abound. She embraces the concept of a live-in babysitter. "I love her. She maintains my sanity." Never have two women so diffused their typically adversary roles in the care and feeding of the man between them and the infant offspring.

•

Skinny suffers no trauma at the edge of the cliff. At fourteen she forgets where and who and sometimes what she is. Hunger is an instinct, free of rational thought. If not fed, she wanders in search of food. If alone, she might howl. But she still jumps up for a meow and a sniff before laying her head on the pillow to sleep all night without snoring, though a finger on her chin gets her purring.

Minna sometimes asks, "Do you mind?"

In daytime she, Skinny, sits on his desk to watch, sometimes batting a pen or swatting a fly. *Ha! What an amazing cat.*

Malibu becomes routine, with friendly neighbors and the fabulous tastes they share. Money is the denominator. When it breaks in waves on an Oscar, a Tony, or a Grammy, a lovely entertainment may commemorate our good fortune. Neighbors convene like normal people with Olympic pools, Roman columns, champagne fountains, lavish eats, servants, caterers, acreage, valet parking, Maserati, paparazzi, and glitterati.

Money is life. Expenditure reflects performance. Performance measures success. Money can pour like Niagara, flowing to the greater body of good it might do. It can accrue interest or yield dividends or appreciate in commercially zoned lots. Young folk new to the area may experience something of lesser magnitude, like a breach in a levee with serialization, foreign, paperback and DVD rights, action toys and film options. But then come endorsements, and the levee breaks to let the mighty Mississippi flood the bottoms. Ravi Rockulz ponders philanthropy.

Equipment was never easy for a humble dive leader. Plunking six grand on a housing or three on a camera and four on lenses and hundreds here and there on the extras so vital to each outing was like sending the kids to college. He couldn't do with less, so he ponied up in faith, and the future came to pass. But it seems ironic when a manufacturer offers a housing that sells for twelve grand with the 3x viewfinder, the dome port, flat port, port rings and extensions, the strobes and arms, optical interface, and backups. Why? Never mind. "Nah. I'll pass."

Oybek rejoins, "Wha? Nah?" Oybek is fluent in the kvetch common to Hollywood and may not realize that this jargon is not actually English.

Ravi shrugs. "I don't need those things. In fact, I want to get my next shots with entry level equipment."

"You won't get better shots."

"Or maybe I will. I might encourage young divers by using basic stuff. They should go deep, but not into debt." Oybek tamps a bowl of hash to support our troops, just back from the war for democracy with duffels of the stuff; it's like 1969 and a win-win with everybody getting by and feeling better. Ravi takes the pipe to do his part. "I want to take the technical aspect out of artistic excellence. I want to sculpt with a stone ax or paint with a big brush. Can you see the value in that?"

"No. No value. What if you get a hundred grand for your pocket with this twenty thousand dollar setup?" *What'f get you hunderd too-zundolla fuhpocket you wis tvintyzoozundolla cumra?*

"Why would they do that?"

"Why not? You on. You it. The fish guy. They make it back and more. Don't be simple. Okay?"

Okay. And okay for the wetsuit, BC, reg, and dive computer endorsements, and another half mil for shaping fashion trends, what they call the new look. Boxers are out. Briefs are back. The money can make the world a better place. Besides, here comes season three, with four and five on deck, each year making more, and for what? For wearing scant skivvies that outline his cock on camera is what.

Ravi ponders Congress, but first: the stock market.

He is not obsessed with more but is grateful for what he has and loves his prospects for free time, for art. Humble origins, a tough go of it, and character intertwine. Hardly big enough for the A-list inner sanctum, he makes it in anyway on charm, humility, courage, terrific stories, and a beautiful wife. He misses the old haunts and reefs, but the shallow scene in LA can also be garishly dramatic and predatory.

He and Minna have acquaintances and friends of friends in a big, vague network. They see a few regulars at parties and events and in passing. Familiarity is nice, but friendship and trust are secondary to potential—for huge deals coming together. Opportunity is brief, action fast. Life is bad or good, depending on available budgets. Spending must be free with faith in smashing success. Jimmy the tennis pro said: *Become* the hugeness then *go for it.* Jimmy shares many chestnuts and may be the platitude guru. *Potential is awesome!*

Ravi sees potential in a reefer and a couple beers and sex with the wife. She's a hottie—Minna, the fish guy's wife, aka a fine fillet o' perch. Often spotted out and about and shot at ten frames per second in hopes of a nose pick or crack adjustment, she remains poised in the pose. Cautious and private, two of Hollywood's most beautiful don't make friends so often. How can they? They gravitate to Oybek; he is such a fabulous man.

Ravi shares his Oybek foibles with a friendly couple, Stuart and Richard, at a lavishly casual cocktail party at their home, just minutes up from Ravi and Minna's. The hosts are showbiz cogs, Stuart a producer and Richard in entertainment law. Poolside buzz is that both Stuart and Richard should be nominated this year—*for the same movie!* Richard can't *be* a film credit for executing legal docs or get an Oscar unless they come up with a special category to appreciate his marvelous contribution to *art cinématique*, and they should. Why not? They've done it before—for lesser talent, no names, please. Stuart regards Richard as a colleague, professionally, artistically and domestically, and Stuart's the fucking producer!

Stuart and Richard are keen on Ravi: has he ever worked in front of a camera—underwater? He has not, and the hosts share a telltale glance. How did he meet Oybek? So Ravi tells of miscue and rescue on Oybek's epileptic recurrence, which has not happened again since, thank God or Whomever.

The two hosts wait for a moral or a punch line. Richard finally says, "People see him as threatening. I think his amazing looks got him going in the first place. What keeps him going is another story. More on that later, if you know what I mean. But he's one in a million for getting things done."

Ravi has nothing to add, no wit, insight or elaboration, so with a bumpkin smile he confirms that Oybek sure has done things for him. Less sophisticated hosts a few minutes down the freeway might say, *Duh*. But Stuart and Richard rarely dally in the colloquial, so they respond more astutely, without audio. They look disappointed or bored, and with no pithy quip coming over the net, they flee, as if to catch a call from Morty, David, or Sol. Ravi missed a shot and doesn't care, but then he does.

Richard finds him again later to ask in confidence if he, Ravi, would do a test, underwater—a screen test. Ravi is comfortable with the gay lifestyle and senses nothing, as they say, inappropriate. Why would a lawyer want a screen test? Then again, Richard is big. "Sure. Whatever."

But just as Richard suggests a time and place, Stuart calls over the crowd, "Busted!" Stuart's rant is shrill and embarrassing. He calls Richard a slut and says he knew it all along. He smashes his glass and storms out. People try to carry on as if nothing crashed, and everyone is happy to have the scene on file. Ravi commiserates with Richard that jealousy is difficult. Maybe worse than alcoholism.

"Trust me, sweetie: the hooch is worse. We'll be kissy huggy in minutes. Liquor remorse lasts for days. . ." These are the last words Richard will speak to Ravi for months. Turning suddenly to seek his colleague and partner, Richard calls across the patio foyer. "You're wrong, Stuart! It's you! You're the one and only one!"

Stuart waits deep in shadow, apparently consoled.

•

More affable by nature and fluent in girl talk, Minna eases into a klatch that keeps up with new colors, products, looks, rumors, deals, ins and outs, and who is walking into this place right now. She calls it an unspeakable yak but goes along for the entertainment value. Busy is good, and one day we'll look back and laugh. Maybe one day soon.

But she plays a lead in the big picture. Fitting in with the girls is cast to type. She's open to discovery and goes along with pop culture, with trendy new things and a few old things, like Japanese cooking.

She takes a course. It's okay but not the real McCoy. Still, she makes friends who love her background and Hawaii. She likes tennis and the terrific court complex only seven minutes away. Regular players pick up games. A woman there is taking French and says it's fabulous, and another woman is French and concurs. So Minna revisits French; it's chic, and the three often practice after tennis, talking French over a low-fat croissant and a double decaf skim macchiato grandé with organic carob sprinkles, hold the foam.

She takes a few lessons from the pro who goes eighty minutes to the hour on Minna and would like to go another hour or three, but she begs off because the girls are waiting.

That's life in a moneyed suburb, where tennis pros have been banging housewives through the ages. Not a chance here. But here too a sign comes by chance. It's nothing really. Jimmy sends a note. Jimmy's wavy blond hair with highlights in a campy pompadour recalls Troy Donahue with a dab of Tab Hunter, or he could be a ringer for the CREW catalog guy. People double-take and ask: "Did you do CREW? The catalog?" Jimmy smiles with sculpted indifference, snugging his V-neck sweater sleeves around his neck. Shades on top hold the coif in place and frame his piercing blue eyes. What a hunk, though he could also play a sensitive supporting role, with the right script. Would he play gay? Is he? Hey, why speculate? *Talk to my agent. Make an offer. Then we'll see.* Jimmy loves Minna and says as much, "your backhand, I love it." He calls her "attractive and intelligent" and shares "a strong desire" to know her better, maybe over lunch at his place, "say one to four on Thursday if that's good for you."

The note is folded in another note, her response: The admiration is mutual. He's a great teacher, and it's not his fault if she needs both hands on her backhand. Maybe someday he'll know her better if they stay friends. Lunch at his place sounds like a terrible idea because she's not attracted to him, which is also not his fault. It's because she's in love with her husband Ravi, the handsomest, smartest man she knows. His way with ocean critters is amazing, and she'll be under his spell for a long time. So please don't bother again with this.

He can't blame her for saving Jimmy's note. She likely planned to throw it away after sending her response. Besides, what woman wouldn't be flattered, even from a cardboard cut-out with a soundtrack? She has a lesson that afternoon, so Ravi suggests they meet for a sundowner. "A drink." She says sure, but why is he being so nice. He says he's always nice and picks her up after tennis to say hey to Jimmy and let him see her affection. Then it's off to a posh café for cocktails and home for a lovely screw, like it was years ago.

The following night is another dog and pony entertainment in the neighborhood that makes the sofa, a doobie, a few beers, and a three-star movie seem like the most fabulous view available. "Would you mind too much going without me?" But as he asks, Minna enters to model her new dress, an elegant number blending velvet and silk. The Lana Turner halter wraps the neck in a slim choker, and lush flounces festoon the midriff to the knees with a devilish cut to reveal a slice of firm, tan thigh on every third step and a maddening strip of thong diving between the buns. As if that isn't enough, the sparse harness grasping the bosom is inlaid with translucent pink chiffon over the nipples, with revelations that will soon be nominated for Best Selected Short Subject. Ravi watches the little documentary and blushes. He would express discomfort, but she says it wasn't her idea. A Night for Nipples is the latest bid for awareness and money on breast cancer. Ravi thinks it gratuitous, and so it is. But Minna's tips are only two in a hefty crowd of nipples peeking through the mesh. Few will remember which went under what faces without a program.

Minna is an A-list exotic known coast to coast since they got her coming off the tennis court in a sweat. Personal revelation for a social cause is a trend, and the nipple buffet includes mashed nipples, carefully swathed nipples, and a few nipples perked by chiffon chafe. Little boy nipples, so cute and naughty, fat fluffy nipples, relaxed and assured, silver-dollar pancake nipples, droopy or indented nipples; the nipple fest will be the talk of the town, hailed as important and socially significant. Could awareness get any higher?

REEFDOG

Best in show goes by consensus to everybody's favorite money girl, meaning mortgage broker, Stevie Oh Monihan. Stevie beams, so lovely on the arm of Doctor Paulo Jacinto, the fabulous surgeon from Bahia. He's the best of the very best. Actually asked to sign his work, he declined with a laugh, which didn't lessen the astounding demand for his services. He's the ultimate anywhere for augmentation, reduction, lift, spread, liposuction—and now transformation! And he's eight months out! Stevie Oh deserves the attention; she's so service-oriented, optimistic, and non-threatening to anybody's agenda. What a worthy standard bearer.

Paulo is brilliant, on the verge of a breakthrough to every transsexual's dream: hips—not plastic implants but real, luxuriant hips. Stevie Oh will be first, following some procedural refinements. Can you imagine, Stevie Oh with vivacious hips? In the meantime, Stevie Oh's nipples quell all doubt on quality or artistry. Are they augmented, implanted, or donated? But if donated, what cadaver had such splendid nipples? So plump, pert, and succulent.

Paulo is a charmer, with his glowing eyes and Latin manner, a subtle cross between Ricardo Montalban, with the distinguished good looks and Ricky Ricardo mischief—but with an eerie dash of Ramón Navarro too—oh, yes! Like in *Scaramouche*, with those mysterious dark features and deadly playful eyes! Well, Paulo isn't talking, and you can't blame him. What magician reveals his magic?

Which is all very entertaining, which is why we're here. But the greater value is in context; Minna is a classic beauty. Ravi is her man and equally classic in the clutch. Just look what a good sport, laughing along, as everyone ogles his wife's chest. Hmm. Nice.

Later, she says she loved his willingness to support her and could feel the admiration of so many for his work. He says he's happy that she's happy. "I am. I have a great time here." She rolls to him. "I'll miss it. I think it's getting time to go home."

A few nights later, in a troubling dream, struggling for air, he gives in to consequence and breathes. Mano hovers alongside, terrible and magnificent, till dawn when she rolls away, brushing Ravi with her chin whiskers in a warning or threat? Will she open wide on the next pass? No, she advances with quivering lips—

Wait! Sharks have no chin whiskers—and she makes her move! "Noohh!"

He can't tell if his yell clears the surface as he bolts. . .

The *kupuna* teach that contact is ambient and a harbinger. So he ruminates on recent days. Insight cannot be ordered up on demand. So he meditates, staring over the bluff and out to sea, as some in the neighborhood do. Thoughts fly by like birds till the sky is empty.

Nipples and a tennis pro, a solid backhand, homosexuality—*I mean the gay lifestyle*—as it relates to personal stuff, to sexual identity, change, commitment, and the extremes people pursue to find happiness, even as it mutates daily in the land of La La, where a man can become a woman for fulfillment and camera time. And camera gear and strobes and a housing for free and a cash bonus because. . .

This is the showbiz place, where every ray of light hits a performance, where stability is not on Elm Street but on a sound stage with a picket fence. It's been a good run. It's okay to have a household word for a name, once you manage the monster. TV hosts prate over rabid and Ravi, or raving and Ravi, or they call him Rocky Rockulz, testing the temper lying dormant these recent years.

Tolerance indicates personal progress. Meditation is good, even if it's popular in LA, but a man has promises to keep and miles to fly. . .

Another name caller at the airport is easily ignored, till the voice becomes Richard, who once hosted Ravi at a fabulous cocktail party at the home then shared with Stuart. Trouble is, it's Stuart's house and no longer shared, after all he, Richard, put up with, not the least of which were scenes of a jealous lush: "Hey. . . Scenes of a Jealous Lush." He makes a note on a possible script and stuffs it in a pocket. "My God, talk about tasteless. And passé and. . . oh, by the way. . ."

By the way, Richard says he's been meaning to call for the longest time, not that he has any fantasies about, you know, Ravi, but he did think Ravi was so sweet when they met, that he just wanted to be sure

Ravi knew about Oybek and his standard seventy-thirty cut, the way the caveats, addenda and subterfuge settles in the end.

Ravi did not know, but he quickly understands. He can't crunch numbers that fast but has a sense for magnitude. The money stratosphere is a mere suburb of deep space, his rightful domain. What can he do, hire a lawyer? Richard's a lawyer. "No, no, no. It's not right, and you have a case. That's what you pay us the big money for, but that's not what I'm saying. I'm just saying. . ."

Ravi comprehends, maybe. It's time to begin again.

Hey, where is Mano? In the brief moment of wondering Ravi gazes on Richard's toothy grin, feeding up, as it were. Richard hates to sell himself short, but he knows he hasn't a chance with Ravi. . . Ravi laughs. Richard doesn't. Richard says goodbye and shuffles off.

"See you, Richard?" Richard doesn't mean to be funny and doesn't want to be sad. He only wants what he can't have, which seems to be a pattern in the showbiz quarter, where some people labor for money or love yet others work for the jackpot. The jackpot rarely comes, but oh, baby, when it does. . . Meanwhile, a little forbidden fruit platter would be nice, in a hotel, so comfy cozy.

La La is on the make everywhere and all the time, and it's cool, but the jackpot and forbidden fruit tray may never come. At some point the pursuit is called stalking or failure. Which is skewed and sometimes laughable, but a friend shuffling off in a terminal can cause gratitude when least expected. Richard has granted insight to a disturbance of days—he fades to Vegas or Palm Springs or any available glimmer in the haze. Ravi calls, "Love you, Richard!" Richard won't look back but flops a hand overhead. Ravi hits his cell and watches, out of body from above, as a reefdog far from home swims against a heady current. Jostling back to the entrance, he reaches George, the broker's receptionist. "Put him on!" He waits to reach George's secretary and waits again for George, to ask how easily he might get out.

George enumerates holdings and assessments of liquidity. He assures that impressive returns are now projected at twelve points in the next six months, putting Ravi up twenty-two points on the year, which is ". . .not too shabby, my friend, and I'm glad you called because we got a. . ."

"George. I want out."

"You want out? Out of what?"

Ravi wants out of the stock market because he dreamed of a shark—not a shark, really. "I mean, it was a shark but not a. . . I know this shark, and it was a message. . ."

"Are you shitting me?"

"No, George. I'm not shitting you."

Of course George knows better, not that Ravi is shitting him but that something is amiss. He insists on time to think, to let the drugs and/or liquor wear off, so reason might stand a chance. He wants to know why. Ravi says it's because. George concedes that yesterday's news might be a concern or even an alarm, "but I'm telling you. I've studied this stuff for years and seen it many times. Many times. Sure, it's gonna whipsaw, Rav. It might get nauseating on the drop, but it'll come back up, and if you're on the sidelines, you're fucked! You must stay in! It's the only way out!" What is Ravi on? He's obviously on something because he's not all that crazy and certainly not himself. George insists but stops. "Wait!" Ravi waits for the brief moment it takes George to rustle stuff on his desk and come back to officially disclose that this call is being recorded, for the record. He will initiate the sell order, but only against his advice to stay in.

"I said sell, goddamn it!"

"It's your funeral, brother."

Timing proves propitious in a wake for the dearly incautious. Free fall begins three hours later and does not bungee back but drops with sickening speed for five days until the Feds lean on the brakes to soften the crash. Trillions vaporize. Ravi avoids loss by getting out and nets four point eight, after commission, which hardly exceeds dinner and wine with a spectacular view—and maybe a few friends, or maybe a group of friends, but what the fuck. Marginal loss is chump change compared to a total burn. George projected twelve percent by virtue of being, or twenty percent for being better. Ravi was better than that at zero percent less commission. Losing four point five would have left him rich, rich, rich if he still drove a Tercel beater and led tourist dives. But he doesn't. He keeps an eye out for Mano because he senses her near, but she remains in the murk, to his relief and chagrin.

•

And so again, a narrative weaves to a finished edge, a wisp or chafe here and there fitting nicely into the perfectly imperfect artistry of the piece. Tying loose ends on ever-loving moments, Ravi sees, knows, and feels good.

The aging mother can return home, relieved at her son's success—not with the bubble-blowing *shmegegge* but as a world-renowned marine photographer, and two exceptional grandchildren enhance the glow and leave her speechless when they promise to come for summer work on a *kibbutz*. They actually only goo goo and drool, but Minna translates. Basha Rivka embraces her, seeing her skill in mothering and cooking. Who knew?

Marine photography morphs, like life, on new angles and drama. Outings are fewer, as a body rounds the bend, with a fraction the shots per outing, showing a keener eye.

The fan base has leveled its rate of growth, but who sustains the steep curve? Still it grows on book and peripheral sales. Ravi signs autographs at LAX and is in demand with college crowds and high-brow conferences to bemoan reef death worldwide. The booking agent announces arrival at a discretionary plateau, where they may choose the most productive events.

Relaxing on an overstuffed sofa he bought for eight grand new, Ravie recalls an identical unit at *The 2nd Coming Furniture Outlet* for eight hundred, slightly used with a burn hole here or some cacka there. He scoffs at a fly-away ember and the hole it singes, not too far from some cacka, either vintage baby puke or splooge from after hours long ago when the babies were in bed. He remembers when, more or less. What would he have done with the money saved buying a used sofa? Surely the new sofa is far worse for wear than the used one was. And who needs two-hundred-dollar slacks with twenty-dollar khakis hanging in the closet?

For that matter, why does he wear boat shoes? And what might amuse a man for the balance of a sunny day? He's in a mood, verging on a funk—oh, he can sense it coming on. A little more dope would help—help him feel even more dumb and dazed. So he brews a double latte to wake up and takes ibuprofen for the headache.

He sits, as a man may do. With a devoted wife, millions on hand, two healthy children, the best little dog and cat in the world, a satisfied mother, a terrific house with views to match and rich memories, what more could there be? A scene comes up, in which he's picking wild tomatoes for dinner at the top of Pu'u Olai after snorkeling the grottos and ledges at *Oneuli* at dawn in flat water with sunbeams slanting onto the reef. He walks a road on a blustery night in French Polynesia with an older woman and rolls back, over the rail into a current. He hitchhikes down the same road with his dog and drifts the pass at Rangiroa at a hundred feet and pegs two-eighty on a rebreather. He remembers uncertainty as the basis of life as he knew it. It's faded gradually for years but with no complaints. The wife and kids, income, recognition, and fan base form a legacy. *Except that I am here, wild caught, observable in this, my captivity.*

Four volumes in five years is a fair run, with pocket guides, reference guides, posters, slogan/photo shirts and caps, toys, cards, and calendars. And it's over.

Oybek stole a few points. Who knows how much? Millions? He has enough to retire anyway. Not that working is bad. Could the day form up again? Not likely—French Polynesia still has quarantine on animals from the mainland U.S., and Ravi will not put Skinny or Little Dog through that any sooner than he'd let them lock up Leihua and Justin. But Hawaii ended its quarantine.

Minna has always believed that LA is only a matter of time. She can still get on at the hospital—on a shorter schedule with the kids.

And her family begs her to come home, and bring that haole boy went all rich and famous. Never mind. Ravi can't return to Hawaii, because he can't, or won't, because he doesn't want to. She says he can if he will. But it's built out beyond recognition. Then again, it's still quaint, compared to LA.

So Ravi flies to Maui on impulse that afternoon for a homecoming of sorts and drives casually to the south end to reckon where his soulful shack once stood. It's deluxe houses in a row that came on the market at eight to ten a few months ago, before the mortgage market went *huli* and the stock market *kapa kai*. The agent sitting an open house thinks the owner would entertain eight or even seven point six. "I bet he would," Ravi says. "I bet he would wine and dine eight. Or six. I used to live here. Before."

"Yes!" the agent laughs, recognizing an old salt who made it, "Mr. Rockulz. Yes. Offer him. . . offer him five. Oh, I'd love to take him a five. Can you imagine the look on his face?"

"I can, and I bet you would. Tell me something. This house came on the market at eight point nine. Why wasn't it eleven point thirteen, or twenty-one point zero?"

"Good question. I can find out if you want me to."

"Nah. Take him this." So Ravi feels the power of a lowball in the strike zone at 2.2 with twelve hours to accept. What the hell; that's hardly a half mil down and eight grand a month. He can make that on one lecture. Monthly might be a bitch, but bringing Minna and the kids back to neighborhood would be something.

And so it comes to pass. Minna and Ravi put their affairs in order and pack to leave the glitterati coast. Oybek arrives unannounced, though he is most surprised. "Moving? Wha?"

Farewell, if not gratitude, forms up but comes out wrong—unless it's right: "You fucked me."

Back-quoting to gain a few seconds to think and move, Oybek says, "I fuck you? No. I never fuck you."

"Seventy-thirty? I'm walking bowlegged and don't even know it."

"That! Is nothing—okay, I fuck you little bit, not too much. Hey, you are a wealthy man."

"I am not a wealthy man."

"You never have work again."

"You mean I won't need to work again."

"Yes. Is what I say."

"Yes. Is what you say. Is okay. Okay?"

Oybek shifts. "You are right. I fuck you." Oybek laughs.

"You think this is funny?"

"No. Is not funny. I laugh because we have saying swear words: *I fuck your sister. I fuck your mother* is not so good. Better, I think is I fuck you. No? Is funny. I am sorry. You are right. You know me from the time you see me. You are right all along. I am bad person."

"You're not bad person. You're greedy. Unfair. Dishonest. Yes, you are bad person. But I accept you. I accept what you've done. I can't accept you as my manager any longer. But that's okay. We're leaving."

"But we enter phase two. Phase two switcheroo. Thirty-seventy. I think you like that better."

"What other agent gets thirty percent?"

"I make you rich."

"Oybek. Is okay. Thirty-seventy. Get the documents over to my attorney. You know Richard. We change the residuals, royalties, benefits, and accruals. Yes?"

Oybek hangs his head. "Please. My friend. Come."

"Come? No. We go. We go home."

"Yes. Good. I am happy you go home. Is good for me too. But you think what I do for you. Now I want ten minutes. Not ten minutes. Thirty minutes. No more. Is too much?"

•

Twenty minutes later, they pull up to a nondescript building, ugly even in that section of town. With no signage, the building gives away nothing but dirty beige around two sliding doors. Oybek leads the way to interior shadows. "Voilà! My friend: phase two."

Ravi gazes on three thousand square feet of aquariums end-to-end and stacked on steel racks three and four tiers up around the perimeter and in from there. Most of the tanks swarm with movement, though some are conspicuously still. Puffers segregated into eight species hover, fin-to-fin, gazing out, asking why. They seem to recognize and call out: Ravi!

One row of tanks is eels—dragons, pencil eels, juvenile snowflakes, and giant morays, big and restless as young watermen, though they mourn. Oybek prattles about China and so much money you can't imagine how much, and the unbelievable premium on big fish—they *demand* giant morays in the living room, overlooking the lights of Hong Kong! "Like this big, mean motherfucker!"

Ravi takes it on the chin. Oybek dives into the new package deal, a custom print with every fish. "A fish dies. You know what I'm trying to say? All people die, sooner or later. Fish too. Okay? So, maybe it will die later or sooner—like the fish you had for lunch. Hey! You got the picture on the wall, so you don't feel so fucked so bad because you still got the picture! We can frame it for them if they want. It's another fee, and so is the freight!"

The top tier on all sides is yellow tangs.

"Look this." The second tier is flame angels. "Look. Forty-five dollars. Each one! I got idea. Custom print from original fish guy, one hundred dollars, get fish for free! You like?"

But the fish guy is mum. From a dim cubicle a Chinese man strolls to meet them. He offers no name, handshake, or business card. He recognizes Ravi by type and turns to Oybek. "Why you do this?"

Oybek shakes it off. "Don't worry, you. He will love. You wait."

Ravi walks out. He looks in Oybek's car for the keys. No. The curbstone is bolted to the asphalt, but a trash drum hefts easily on adrenaline to fly into the windshield and roll back over the hood. He can't lift it again so he kicks the door panels but knows he can't total it on a few dings. It's a fucking Bentley for Christ's sake. Ah, well, let 'em putty and paint. He tweaks the mirrors and wipers and says fuck it and heads toward home, till fatigue and a cab take over.

•

Within the week Oybek leaks his decision—via an exclusive interview in *Variety*—to leave production for now because the creative side is calling. He'll dive for reef artistry because he knows the magic down there every bit as much as the next guy and can bring it home better. After all, consider his gifted eye. "Can you imagine? I will communicate like you have never seen. I am very excited about the new magic I will make." . . . *Can imagine you like it's never seen. . .*

Oybek flies to Papeete and takes the Moorea Ferry to greet old friends. Hereata avoids the show because nobody likes to be left behind on a broken promise. He waves that off because he's back to make good. Just you wait. He'll show his stuff with amazing new equipment and talent. Then you'll see.

Moeava will not muster the boat in the afternoon, not for anybody, no matter how many crumpled hundreds fall out of his pocket. He has a trip tomorrow and two women tonight, which service includes the trash, sweeping, laundry, and general clean up. Fantasy is kept in reserve for a special occasion and sometimes holidays unless he's tired and stoned. That's when they love him, which isn't fair and may be devious and unkind but is also so much better than it was.

Oybek plucks a C-note and grabs a tank and gears up on the dock where his baggage sits. Why not? Slipping in from the end of the dock, he swims to the drop with his very first camera and housing and is amazed at how easy it is. It's a deluxe rig with "all that crap they put on there." Really, anyone can do it; it's the credentials that make the sale. He'll sort the buttons later; for now, he needs only the shutter release and power switches for the camera, the focus light, and strobes. All on, and they don't call it automatic for nothing.

Oy, fuck! No, Oy-bek. Ha! Just checking—lens cap off. Ten four, Walter Bilko, over and out. And down. Glug glug glug. Fish guy my asshole. Move over fish guy. Big fish guy is here.

Oybek's underwater photography career is as spectacular as anticipated but shorter-lived, beginning and ending in three shots. The first is murky with haunting familiarity in Mano's approach. Impromptu and implacable, she insists that she and Oybek do lunch.

Lunch is not *fois gras* but *foible au gratis* for a showbiz wizard seeking reef magic. It's hardly filling for Mano, who only takes a taste, to see. Unfortunately, she samples a leg at the knee. Oybek senses something less than smashing success but shoots from the hip like a trooper because the show goes on! He nails a predator profile in the brief moment between life and death.

Open wide is shot two.

Mano chomps precisely at femur/tibia joinery, crunching the patella, which seems superfluous at that juncture anyway. Oybek's friends and staff will attribute the cosmically clean cleave to good karma. They'll call it Oybekian and chuckle with confidence. A Cedar Sinai specialist will admit, "I couldn't have amputated this leg any better than that shark did."

Oybek will tell the doctor that the lost limb is in storage—don't worry, on ice. The doctor will advise that limbs sometimes come to him for miracle surgery as seen on TV, in a cooler, but it's not going to happen. Oybek waves him off—

"*Nyet!* You can't put it back. But I want you see for me what will be wery waluable to know. . ." That is, he wants the leg examined for tumor growth because a tumor would prove divine intervention by the Spirit of the Deep. Ramification on secondary markets will be profound. The doctor ponders Oybek's cosmic salvation, briefly, before taking a call to confirm a tee time.

Meanwhile, off the end of the dock down in French Poly, Mano has the culinary discretion to discard the appendage but comes on, out of character, for another go.

What's got into her?

Oybek's second stroke of luck is timing, one of his specialties, in this case on an offer to a higher power. He gives up the camera and housing, the strobes, cords, and all that crap they put on there.

Mano accepts.

In coming weeks Oybek will learn that veteran divers of olden times in unlimited oceans—black coral divers, spondylidae collectors, and all that lusty crowd—carried broomsticks. Sharks don't like bones, and biting a stick might discourage more bad behavior. Oybek will claim this knowledge as a survivor in the face of death. He will tell his tale on the late-night circuit, promoting his life and times and his new book, *Oybek, The Chosen One.* The amazing cover shot is close on Mano's molars and tonsils, shot three.

The housing, strobes and other crap are mangled to an amusing mess that shows up on the back cover, *photo by Oybek.* Most amazing, however, was that the digital data card remained intact, so art and art history could be made. "Is all good," he chortles. He opts for a peg leg because, "it feel like right for me." He tries an eye patch in the mirror—left eye, right eye, strap straight, strap cocked—and settles on a roguish blend of Moshe Dyan and the Hathaway shirt guy with singular intensity. A firm specializing in market response measures the peg-leg/eye-patch combo in a few focus groups willing to relate to that sort of thing. The stats seem comprehensive but inconclusive but promising but not quite yet. The most lucrative strategy will apparently be the peg leg for a year, with a revival round of interviews to release the sequel, *Oybek Is Back.* At that point the eye patch will renew interest. Plenty of time to come up with a riveting story on the loss of the eye—which should also convert to performance, given proper crafting. What's inside *Oybek, The Chosen One?* A hundred twenty amazingly candid shots show the most amazing people in the world posing with you-know-whom.

With interest fading for what's-his-name, the fish guy, Ravi's sales dwindle. Calendar sales cease. Book sales stall on a failure to renegotiate, but a small book publisher reads of the stalemate and comes forth to offer Ravi a fifty-fifty partnership on new titles with lithograph prints for pages if the reefdog is willing to keep going.

He's willing, and it feels good and looks better than ever and makes more money than a dive leader could bring home. *Oybek, The Chosen One* gets rave reviews right out of the chute, showing what a few hundred grand can do for art in America. Sales fall flat by the time *Oybek is Back*. Nobody knows fickle markets and lubrication better than Oybek; just read the book! But his bid for a round-two revival hits competition on glittering fish with a twist. Noah Greene takes the showbiz name of Rufus T. Watermelon with racist innuendo to make a splash but explains that he is black, after all, and he loves watermelon. "Now do you or do you not have a problem with that?" The jury is out on that one, with the media waiting for leadership—self-correcting between black and African American.

But then Oprah features Rufus T, asking her viewers, "You want fish pitchers? I got a fish pitcher for you." She tells them to buy the book, *Fish Pitcher from Way Back*, for a riveting, blockbusting, change-your-life, no-holds-barred account of a black man from South California making his way in the alien north country—Seattle, that is—where he gets on as a fish pitcher at the open market downtown. The sequel anticipates Rufus T as a catcher—with his hands! And these salmon run slick! At twenty pounds or better!

Ravi turns the TV off and wishes he didn't have one but knows he will as long as he can because, because. . . He recalls the olden days when a nice skull webbing would correct this unholy mockery of nature's noble beasts. Or slow it down, maybe.

Homeward Bound

The old neighborhood is gone. Next door used to be a thicket, home to songbirds and strutting mynahs. How sweetly it lingers in recall of a gossamer complex, X-spiders weaving their scrim over a house-less person or two and the occasional mongoose. But it's hardly the same—no more sunbeams in foliage; it's opaque to the south, in monolithic tribute to the will and bankroll of Stan Goodman, who made it very big in waterbeds, liberating a grateful nation from box-spring sag for a market share to bankroll twelve thousand square feet of stucco, granite, marble, glass, and steel. The front deck could be a bowling alley, and waving off the end a portly, silver-haired woman calls, "Hell-oh-oh!"

Getting to know the neighbors doesn't take long, and some of the old crowd turn up at the grocery store or the beach or out and about. Talk is warm but sparse, what with everyone aging and the old crowd thinning, mostly returning to America or gone to more practical economies or just gone.

Gene is around, getting by on coffee and nicotine. She says she's happy enough, after damn near crying on seeing Ravi and going whole sob on seeing Skinny. She takes walks along the road, now that it has a sidewalk. So she stops in, or he visits with flowers or something good to eat. It's not like it was, practical and soulful, but it's something.

REEFDOG

Crusty Geizen keeled over about a year and a half ago on the way home—opened his mouth and bulged his eyes halfway in from a second dive site on flat seas under blue skies, on a day recalled for clarity, with viz running two hundred feet like nobody could remember. Crusty tensed up and toppled, not to worry—gone before he hit the deck, coronary thrombosis.

Crusty met his match, which seems a blessing in hindsight. He'd confided to a group of doctors, game fellows up from the dive of a lifetime, ready to deepen the bonding process. He said he'd reached that point in life where a perfect day was four hours of work, maybe a dive trip like this one, nice people, yadda yadda and so on to the image of a crusty geezer getting a blowjob on a dash of curiosity as to who might be delivering, and the punch line: "I'm not doing not too bad. I got about two more weeks of yoga to stretch my neck." Uproarious laughter broke like a wave on cue.

Crusty might have looked a little queasy as he gave up center stage to a surgeon from Portland, who said Hawaii is such a wonderful place, so full of surprises. "Why, I was in Waikiki last week—and I saw this hooker. Beautiful woman. She was everything you might want in a woman, physically speaking. She's standing on the corner with this cat under her arm, and I was checking her out, thinking man, she looks good, but I got closer and saw she was holding this cat backward. I had to look twice because she had the back end up and was licking this cat's asshole. Beautiful woman, so I says to her, I says, 'What in the hell you wanna do that for?' And she says, 'Oh, that. I just blew a lawyer and I want to get the taste out of my mouth.'"

The next breaking wave took Crusty on a guffaw, what was easy for everyone to call *the way he would have wanted it*.

Maybe. Crusty was sixty-four. Ravi wants it some other way, wants to find a friend to sit with and talk about things and what to do. He knows what to do, but viz is down around twelve feet, so he isn't clear on how to do it.

Three Dreams

Calling it a mid-life crisis would over-simplify; Ravi Rockulz is materially set and does not lack in self-esteem. He's seen more adventure and romance than a convention of dentists or insurance agents, yet he feels bound as Icarus in his reach. So why is he sleeping, all the time sleeping? Because refuge occurs where it's found. A shrink might call him depressed, and sleep is a form of self-preservation, but that analysis would explain the mechanics of the process rather than the cure. He sleeps more than he should, grappling with what he can't quite bring to the surface.

The first dream seeks justice. Ravi reconciles with Oybek, a misguided, misunderstood friend who brought security and comfort to Ravi and his family. It begins on a visit, with the children jumping in childish glee at the peg-leg thump announcing Uncle Oybek. Oybek comes to make things right. Oybek usually brings something for the kids, but he forgot; he was so distracted by falling out with his friend. So he peels a twenty for each kid because a ten won't get you too far these days. Nearly toppling, he swears off the Long John Silver show he inflicted on himself. He'll go today for a modern prosthesis. The crutch bruises his ribs. It's painful but doesn't hurt as much as Ravi leaving without a word. "You would not say goodbye to your friends?" *You wooduntz a leave and no goodbye frienzyu?*

Oybek shrugs. Ravi shrugs as well and says that a house on Maui will take time to pay off, and a man needs money. "You said forty-five dollars per fish."

Oybek laughs, "That is still some very many fish, my friend."

"How many fish is it?"

"You must pay for the fish first, and many die in transport. The bastards who want to shut us down have no idea how hard it is. You average only thirty dollars each after some die—sometimes only twenty dollars. You go ahead and ship the dead fish too, but it doesn't always work. That's why I say charge money for the fish guy photo and give fish for free, no guarantee. See? If fish die, is not on us."

"Look at this. Have you heard of masked angelfish?" Ravi shows him a photo of a pale fish with subtle trim on the tail and a golden mask. "Five thousand dollars each, wholesale. Ten thousand retail. Thirty thou for a mated pair."

Oybek stares at the fish, then at Ravi. "Where you get?"

"We catch."

"You catch?"

"Look." He pulls another photo, from which the first was a detail. It's a coral head with dozens of masked angels. Some are mated pairs.

"You know this place?"

"I took this picture."

"Where is?"

Not so fast, my fine, fat friend, but the images lead to a plan: Ravi can charter a lobster boat for the trip. It's only a few days out of Honolulu. Boats are available and cheap since the Northwest Hawaiian Islands got fished out. And a lobster boat has holding tanks and seawater pumps. No more lobster up north, but plenty of masked angels. The Northwest Hawaiian Islands were unprotected when the lobsters got wiped out. That starved out the monk seals, so the Feds budgeted millions to protect the biggest marine ecosystem in the world. Not to worry—protection is mostly bureaucratic, leaving the ocean free for poaching. It's patrolled, but they can't possibly cover twelve hundred miles by whatever.

Call it an adventure. Patrol vessels are rare. Besides, flying a Korean or Taiwanese flag makes a lobster boat look foreign. They won't pursue to the west, to avoid an international incident.

The dream roils when the Chinese guy at the warehouse in Southern Cal argues that angelfish can't take the slosh and roll like lobsters, and most will die. And he sure as hell can't send out *most* of them already dead.

Oybek says a little bit dead won't matter at five or ten or fifteen grand each. You take a few more to make up for dead. Fucking fish bringing this kind of money? Fuck. And the potential for a book—and a movie!—on such heroics, bringing fish to where people can see and raise their awareness should be worth as much on the back end.

The Chinese guy cannot resist the logic of money but soon pukes over the rail and is led to the lee side, where puking is more acceptable.

The others are glum, as seas build northwest of Honolulu with Ni'ihau an intermittent speck off the stern. They want to know the target and why only one fish? Why can't they know? Why is it fixed pay with no bonus for three weeks at sea? Is it masked angels? Nobody can catch that many of a single species, so maybe bandit angles, too, and dragon morays. They only bring a grand each but sometimes aggregate, so maybe bandit angels and dragon morays are part of the plan. Like sailors through the ages, they demand to know and have their say. They're more confident at sea, less sensitive to language skills. They can ride big waves and gather gems that would go to waste otherwise. The Chinese guy handpicked these guys, rebreathers no problem. So? How much is the best team worth?

A rebreather allows dramatic depth and downtime, reducing nitrogen and reverting CO_2 to oxygen. A rebreather can accommodate tri-mix—oxygen, nitrogen, and helium—to eliminate narcosis and maximize workload. But chemistry can be hazardous, and oxygen changes at depth. Too little O_2 causes hypoxia, also known as suffocation. Too much O_2 causes hyperoxia or convulsion, which is easy on deck but causes drowning at depth in 100 percent of incidents. At seven grand each, rebreathers seem premature. Oybek says chickenshit on the front end gets chickenshit out the back, and this should be the first of many great outings for dollars at depth—and more dollars at greater depth. But rebreathers will come later for this bunch. Better to dive three, five, six times a day for now. "Get a little bit flowing cash, you."

You want the big bucks; you soak up a little more N.

At long last they suit up. The helmsman enters the waypoint on the GPS, and Ravi calls, "Oh, shit!" He's knockin' on cotton but don't worry, this won't take long. He goes below but passes the head on his way to the engine room, where he takes two turns on the stuffing box nuts, increasing the drip to a flow. Back in the head he opens the seacock along with the intake valve, filling the toilet for another flush and a few hundred flushes, or a purge—or an exorcism. He comes on deck relieved, and over they go.

Surfacing from a hundred feet, they see the vessel riding low and listing. The helmsman in a life jacket works on the life support unit that won't inflate because it's punctured.

Adrift, the divers ditch their tanks and inflate BCs manually. Their eyes burn from salt and glare, except for one, who brought sunglasses and a hat. The fuck? How did he know?

All day and night and day and night again, the tiger chases its tail, as Little Black Sambo watches the butter churn with blood. They hold hands or tie off till strength and bindings fail, and they drift apart. Sixty masked angels with a few bandits and dragons in a catch box are tethered to the lead diver and wants to sink, heavy as gold. He scans for a bottom and when a pinnacle comes into view, he opens the catch box on a downward flurry and a murmur, "*Papahānaumokuākea*." Masked and bandit angels and dragon morays writhe free of market value to blend with the blue haze and another coral home. Other oneness is brief and merciful with Mano's help and gratitude.

The dream ends on blessed suffering, on sun and salt, fear and death with bleeding, drowning, and regret—and fulfilment in one who gives life.

A scene bobs to the surface like flotsam from the hulk: At the galley settee in rolling seas, a young diver slides in beside the fish guy with a few fish prints. Ravi takes a look, as the kid says, "Not as good as yours, but. . . Do you think I can make a book?"

"Why not?"

The young diver shrugs. "They're aquarium shots."

"Aquarium shots?"

"Yeah. I let them go. See: it's the same corals in the backdrop."

So the dreamer wakes in a cold sweat and, alas. . . Justice becomes difficult. It's always been difficult, and this kid who let his fish go is imagined, not real.

But are these guys any worse than Oybek? Would you kill Oybek by mayhem?

It's 5:45. No way I'll get back to sleep with forty-five minutes to go. But I'll lay back, close my eyes, and breathe slowly. . .

•

The second dream is a sequence, beginning with a man walking into the ocean. He swims out. He descends. He's headed farther out and down, till he blows his last bubble.

That'll teach 'em to mess with the fish guy. He's out and down, not down and out because he's not broke and can make plenty more money anytime he wants to. He welcomes depth, distance, and current picking up to five knots, good thing because down and in are coming on strong. The dream fails to satisfy, given the choke and glug coming on as well. A dreamer can breathe between the water, with care and caution. Still he wakes with a half hour to go.

•

REEFDOG

Dream three drifts like a speck. It looks like a copepod or cephalopod. Some crustaceans are tiny at maturity, while giant squid grow to forty feet in two years. Both begin microscopically and feed all the time.

Ages ago, in showbiz years, the fish guy was a hit, with striking good looks, natural flair, compelling communication skills, and manners. His tall tales of primal forces felt honest and richly filled the anecdotal interviews. Ravi back-rolled into unknown seas more times than he told stories to a national viewing audience and isn't sure which is scarier. Yet his calmness attends him like a narcotic. Water moves fast and turns dark, yet he makes it enticing as a shallow reef.

The hosts felt it, more than one saying, "Gee, it's been great. Stop back anytime. Let us know what you're up to. I mean down to." Signs overhead lit up for LAUGHTER and APPLAUSE—cut to commercial and prep for the next segment, as Dave or Jay or Jon, Stephen, Jimmy, or the great one, herself, recognized the fish guy himself, right there on the sound stage, as a thing of beauty. Or they blew smoke up his ass, offering sincerely: "I mean that."

Or: "I envy you."

Or: "We're lucky to have you."

Or: "I'd like to trade with you—for a while."

Or: "*Anytime.*"

A Dream Come True

So Ravi wakes up on impulse and adrenaline equal to a challenge in daunting conditions. He flies back to LA that night, assuring Minna, the kids, and the cat that he'll be home for din by Tuesday.

He's not known in LA like he used to be and can't tell if people recognize the fish guy or have become friendlier than they were, but why would they do that?

Late-night talk shows are filmed in the daytime, and he knows where and when. At NBC Studios he's like a kid home from school. "Hey, Roland. I'm back." Roland smiles with a return greeting and checks the clipboard. "I'm not on there. I just got off the phone with Meg. Call her. It's a walk-on." So Roland makes the call, as Ravi hopes Meg still works there, as Ravi says, "Roland, man, I gotta take a whiz. Do you mind?"

Roland minds and could lose his job by letting anyone through without clearance. But who remembers a security guy on clipboard drill at middle age—by name? Nobody who's anybody, that's who—except for the fish guy. Ravi helps connect the dots between old friends on a major whiz with a nod up the hall to the men's room. The fuck? It's right there. What's a fish guy gonna do, sneak into the studio? With Meg standing by?

So Roland returns the nod, authorizing the unauthorized whiz.

It's the old duck into the head, count three, two, one and out and farther up the hall but not by much to the double swingers—doors,

286

that is—to Stage One and the brave new world of cameras, kliegs, mikes, drama, melodrama, monologue, dialogue, antics, zingers, one-ups, and the very elements of greatness, where celebrity is born or fades away—or comes back as invited for a surprise visit. The swinging doors open on old home week with pats on backs and whispered greetings. *Where you been, man? What are you up to?*

The fish guy is back in shorts and flops and a Hawaiian shirt with flying fish, and he's walking on in the middle of an interview with that hot new starlet with the cleavage to die for, but the halitosis to die from, but nobody knows that except the crews backstage who make foul jokes about its source, speculating on blowjobs instead of bulimia, what's her name. . .

"Hey! Looka this. The fish guy!" Ravi waves to the world, as the audience follows the lights with APPLAUSE. "What? You're in the neighborhood?"

"Yeah. You said stop by. Anytime."

"Yeah, uh. . . Rave. . ."

"Ravi. Rockulz. The fish guy."

It's disappointing to see a seasoned host get nervous. This has to be quick, or it'll cut to commercial and die in security.

"Okay, fish guy. Uh, you know Marci. . ."

"Hi, Marci. It's a pleasure. I'm so sorry to interrupt, but I have an urgent request for the fish."

Well, that was a lucky phrase, a clever turn to open things up so a seasoned host can move in. Twisting quizzically, he falls into step. "Okay. I'm game. What do the fish need?"

"They've been kidnapped and are being held prisoner."

Not such a good line—over the top. The host grabs the laugh for himself. "Do we need to come up with a ransom?"

"No. You need to empty your aquarium and smash it."

This could get ugly—you can't follow a laugh line with a call for violence. Changing pace with alacrity—which is how he made his mark as a younger host—the host asks: "What do I do with the fish? In my aquarium. I mean my aquarium is smashed, and I got fish

flopping all over the rug, which won't stay wet forever, I might add."
LAUGHTER.

"Smash the fish tank outside. Come on. You give the fish away.
Take them back to the pet store or give them away."

"Okay. Wait a minute. I had fish for dinner. . ."

"Not those fish. You should think about not eating those fish. But
now I mean aquarium fish." The host nods, fishing for another laugh.
"Many thousands are in warehouses near here. Many warehouses
stacked with glass tanks full of colorful fish that should be on reefs.
But they're not. And the reefs are going away. . ."

"Hey. Stick around. We gotta take a break, but we'll be right back
with the fish guy, who just dropped in." Host turns, profile left.
"Hey. Are the fishnappers in a Ford Bronco?" LAUGHTER and
APPLAUSE and. . .

Cut to commercial.

Here comes security, stopping short for the host's raised hand.
He leans near like he did a long time ago. "Hey, fish guy. You
stopped in to tell people to empty their aquariums?" Ravi nods.
"You got a new book? A movie? A toy? You had toys, yeah?
Anything?"

Ravi shakes his head. "I'm here to sell an idea."

"Yeah. That's tough. Look. Sit down here by Marci. You know
Marci?" She holds her breath to assess him sexually. "Other side.
Okay? Marci has a movie. We got a young comic in the green room
we'll bump to next week. We'll have a minute or so with you. Okay?"

"Okay."

"Okay?" The host asks the producer, who throws his hands in the
air and walks away. The security guys step back.

And three, two, one. . .

"Hey! Marci Marceau opens Tuesday at the Blue Tooth. And the
new movie is *The Deadbeat Goddess*. It looks fantastic, and so do you."
She writhes to advantage, to profiles left, then right. "Give it up for
Marci Marceau!"

APPLAUSE!

Marci exploits the short shrift with a slow rise, profile left easing to frontal with a leer, some sizzle, and a slink. The host gazes with the rest of the late-night world at her luscious ass in retreat. . .

Cut to Camera Two and reset to personal confidence. "Okay, we got broken glass out in the yard. We got nothing for dinner because we had to hurry up and get the fish off the rug and back to the pet shop. . ."

"Not necessarily back. Many were bought on-line. Just find them a home. Don't worry about the money. Smash the tanks."

"You know, I gotta say, I never saw this side of you. You're Mr. Azure Blue. Mr. Cool, Calm, and Deep. You got yourself worked up here. What happened?"

What happened? A man found himself on a reef, where he made close, personal friends and got lucky with a camera and a few contacts and made it, not huge but big, maybe even very big for a while there. . . Then he stumbled onto what he already knew but couldn't finger, till it went toe-to-toe. The old neighborhood is dying because the garish innocents are being sold for money. "I woke up."

The host shares his famous clownish incredulity. LAUGHTER. "Fish guy. Work with me here. You woke up, what, from a nap?" Mild laughter.

"Yes. A long nap. A deep sleep. Now we wake up. You know a dream can feel like underwater. Have you tried running through a dream? You can't do it. So you slow down. You drift through a dream. I dream of a reef with thousands of fish—have you ever seen a reef in abundance? Have you ever seen a reef?" Mild laughter.

"This is the fish guy I know. So why the smashed glass?"

"The glass is our confinement. Look—why would a man want a job as a prison guard? He gets to go home every night, but he's tired. He spends his days in jail, like another prisoner."

"He probably showers at home." LAUGHTER.

"Yes. I'm sure. But I'm making a point. If you have an aquarium, you put yourself inside it. You die there like the fish do, first in spirit. You shut yourself off. . ."

"That's interesting—life in a fish bowl. Why does that sound familiar?" LAUGHTER. "Hey, it's always great to see the fish guy again. We gotta run. See you tomorrow when it'll be Anna Indiana and Bones Morrow. . ."

"I'm not done."

"Come back. Can you come back?"

"Yes, but. . ."

And so it would end—the dreams, stories, and endings, wishes, free will, and consequence. So the average home aquarist, a thirty to fifty-something hobbyist focused on personal amusement, would remain oblivious to reef decimation. Ravi must think and act rather than react. Rising slowly as his slowest bubbles, out of the small talk and into the credits, he steps up to the little red light on Camera One and calls out, "Mr. Gorbachev! Tear down that aquarium!" LAUGHTER! APPLAUSE! Pull back. Finish credits. Sustained APPLAUSE! The fish guy stands firm, eye-to-eye with the late-night crowd.

He goes home to Hawaii in a wake of goodwill, apology, and friendship forever with the TV crowd. He pledges to return with more wonderful stuff and bids farewell to the last fan waving at LAX because the Wheel of Life spins inexorably, with its changes, rewards, and disappointments, but fans are forever.

Any ripple on the late-night pond will reach the far banks on a single turn of Earth. Thirty million people evolve by virtue of thought and statistically measurable behavior, however small or brief.

Just so, a lonely boy in Utah wonders what life could hold with no aquarium? But he lost six hundred dollars in fish to an imported disease, and now the on-line seller wants to sell him a backup system for quarantine, to safeguard his current reef wildlife against new reef wildlife coming from sick oceans. But he has no current reef wildlife because they all died. But two aquarium systems should be twice the fun as one. But near midnight the boy empties and disconnects his tank. He leaves it in the yard to sleep on the idea. But after a snack, before bed, he heads back out to smash it so he can't change his mind in the morning, so he can get a fresh start tomorrow on his new hobby, photography, which should cost less, not more. He fantasizes giant zoom and mysteries revealed.

A forty-something woman in a wheelchair in Fresno would prefer selling her tank or giving it to charity rather than smashing it. The fish guy wants it all to stop, but what a waste. What a nut, like one of those crackpots in the park, preaching the end. . . Giving it away could lead to somebody else setting it up, so she cuts the silicone seams in each corner, so it can still be a terrarium, but a little seed has sprouted. So she puts it the garage and fills it with garden utensils. Glass cracks, but she doesn't care.

A seasoned aquarist in Newark thinks it makes no sense, but by morning he's still thinking, and so on into the evening news, where thoughts would melt into the next news cycle, though tonight they accelerate because. . .

Turner Hultquist was only fourteen when Sumner Redstone hung onto a burning hotel balcony waiting to be rescued. Sumner Redstone got saved and went on to acquire billions and become an idol to Turner Hultquist. On Redstone's lead, Hultquist developed a distribution company and became wealthy.

Six hundred million dollars are nothing to sneeze at, but Sumner Redstone did just that, adding 8-Arms Distribution to his list of majority holdings, under CBS, Viacom, MTV, Black Entertainment Television (That's funny; he doesn't look black.), Paramount, and DreamWorks. Nominal reorganization following the takeover left Turner Hultquist out in the anonymous cold with nothing but money. That is, Redstone fired him because a new broom sweeps clean. Get out. So Hultquist got discarded blithely as debris—out with nary a nod or a word.

Call it a follow-up for balance: interviewed at home in front of his thirty foot, floor-to-ceiling aquarium with thousands of fish, including adult eels and brood tangs, Redstone brags: "I got more fish here than they do over there in Hawaii." That is, the man who swept Turner Hultquist out with the trash takes pride in his aquarium, demonstrating his dominance of land and oceans.

Turner Hultquist responds with an unfriendly takeover in kind. His camera crew arrives at his home posthaste—arrives as a local pet shop delivers a three-hundred-gallon tank. Hultquist can't decide whether to swing away with his Louisville slugger right in the living room for drama. Or he could set the tank on sawhorses in the yard and fill it for the big splash of three hundred gallons and a shitload of glass—wait a minute. Get another tank. "We'll smash it dry, with glass flying all over the fucking place. We'll smash the dry tank with the slugger and the full tank with a blasting cap—make it two blasting caps. Then we segue artfully, you know, stitch the two for a special fucking effect with Redstone on a short loop repetition of *more fish than they do over there in Hawaii more fish than they do over there in Hawaii more fish than they do over there in Hawaii. . ."*

The crew concurs on drama, art, and nuance—okay, no nuance, but with so much glass and water flying into space on double slo-mo, the point should come across. If it doesn't, they can get a third tank and just blow it the fuck up. "And we won't need blasting caps. My kid sells fireworks on the side. He's like, you know, working his way through junior high. He's got those M-80s. Cherry bombs. He says it'll be cake with cigarette fuses. There's the push—where the hell we ever gonna find some fucking smokes? Wait. The kid says he can get some. And he'll work for scale. Little prick."

A producer calls, "Grip! We'll need some goggles and body cover for Mr. Hultquist." Because it only stands to reason that Mr. H will swing for the bleachers.

So Turner Hultquist makes the news with backstory and peripheral interviews. To aquarium or not to aquarium? That is the question. Turner Hultquist says it's the fish who make the point and the fish guy who speaks on their behalf.

The fish guy calls from Hawaii to the young diver with the aquarium shots in LA. Wait a minute—you can't call a guy in from a dream! Relax, numb nuts; you know this guy. He's an Oybek recruit who *was* on his way up the evil path but get this: no longer Oybekian! He's clean! *Come to Neptune!* Yes, the showbiz card sailing his way across the poker table of life is an ace! He's back from the dark side and in the studio in mere fucking minutes, speaking out, denouncing evil and embracing reform: "Mr. Gorbachev. . .!"

By day three a billboard is up on La Cienega Boulevard not too far from the hub of your better LA traffic. Bigger than life, Turner Hultquist is smashing bejeezus out of a huge fucking aquarium, the water and glass exploding with such viral virtual veracity as to generate a traffic hazard in your face, with a message as concise and potent as a smart bomb aimed at your heart: Mr. Gorbachev. . .!

It's all the talk in a twelve-block radius, with growing speculation on whose body Hultquist's head got morphed onto—he's so pumped! *Can* the glass/water explosion combo actually carry a plotline or at least nominally connect scenes through a hundred and ten pages of screenplay? Juiciest of all: Guess what studio is actually test-marketing the concept this minute? The radius goes eighteen miles on four hundred more billboards in a blink and then, of course, another twelve-thousand-mile radius on global news pick-ups—take over this, Sumner! You reef-killing fucker!

All the rage erupting in La La motivates tankists in thirty-nine states to chew on the idea like it's broken glass, spitting it out till next week when Ravi and Minna Rockulz and their two children Leihua and Justin and Skinny the cat and Little Dog pack up for a move to a new home that's not so crowded.

The phone rings.

Hawaii State Senator Kevin Kaneshiro is on the line, asking if Mr. Rockulz will support a bill to limit aquarium extraction from Hawaii reefs. "We've been embarrassed in the eyes of the world."

"No. I will not support regulation. I will support a ban. You want to fuck around? Or you want healthy reefs?"

"Please. Mr. Rockulz. Let me do my job. Okay?"

•

Alas and again, The End.

What About the Kids and Another Move so Soon?

For starters, they're not moving to a brand new place. It'll be old home week for Little Dog, with familiar scents and old haunts. Skinny had a couple months there and did fine. She'll do better on a slower regimen, now that she's pushing sixteen.

Not only that, she got the Waikiki hooker treatment leaving LA, not exactly an anal reaming, but every groupie in LA sure as hell wanted to kiss her tuchas. Okay, not every groupie—that could chap a cat's ass—but everyone in wishing distance.

Packing up one more time is a challenge. It's more than a couple duffels and some snacks. Now it's boxes, crates, and kid stuff. Then again, most of it is still packed. The reasons for not fully moving into and absorbing the new home are many. The Hawaii place and the old place in upper LA are the same marble, granite, glass, and steel, and so is the context. LA sounds like traffic. Hawaii sounds like surf. Surf sounds like traffic. And shallow friendliness in LA was easier than growing pains in Hawaii.

Minna's family tried to connect as *ohana* should, talking nicely to the kids, teaching them *da kine*, playing with the dog and admiring the cat. It went well enough, which wasn't enough, leaving a guy recently from LA to ask his wife, "Okay. Now what?" It's a tough question for a modern woman who loves culture, pace, and stimulation, a woman willing to adapt to the needs of her family, a woman recently burdened by a major move, lock, stock, and barrel—a woman left with no better answer than a question of her own.

"You think Tahiti would be better?"

"Yes. It's French."

"Why didn't you go to France in the first place?"

He didn't go to France because it's not tropical. "And because. I wouldn't have met you."

With minimal loss on a quick resale because he bought it right, the beachfront monolith goes quick. It doesn't feel like home. For hardly over a million they get a much smaller place on the island of their convergence, a high-ceilinged *fare* of native stock, lashed in primitive beauty, with two *boudoirs*, two *salles de bains et un bureau pour* Ravi. Calling it *pas mal* feels French and safe.

Ravi watches neighbors cooling in the shallows. He picks up trash, but they leave more, so he tells them to stop—to love their sea as if they would. . . swim in it. They laugh and seem to get it.

A month or so in, on a shallow bluff next door, he sees elderly Tahitians greeting men who carry clipboards and blueprints. He walks over as the elders invite the men to a feast there, later, for *ia orana*. The men offer opportunity in money, jobs, and security. The elders offer regrets: No, you cannot build here.

Ravi wants to offer money for legal defense or any expense but on second thought introduces himself with a pledge of support.

He stops shaving. He sets buoys to block the reef from anchoring boats and gets no complaints. He watches the coral recover as his babies turn into children, as his dog trades fear of separation for the confidence of a stable home. The cat sleeps more, plays less, and watches her man.

Old friends come again for company and comfort into next phases. Monique and Cosima are an item but live separately, to better keep the peace. Moeava works his boat and takes counsel on occasion from both women, or sometimes with Monique alone when she's feeling uncertain, experimental, nostalgic, or lonely. Who can tell?

Hereata becomes *tutu*, or auntie, to share her love and balance her solitude. She cares for the children as she cared for her own. She does not pine for her *chevalier* to arrive but seems happy. Minna is grateful again for a babysitter and doesn't worry if Ravi sees the sitter home.

Ravi sees more and reacts less; no vehicle proclaims *Born & Raised*, and nobody asks, *how long have you been here?* With no development or social resentment to taint the natural beauty, he wonders: now what? Now comes the more perfect shot, for starters. Minna shows him what else for finishers, with natural aptitude for intensive care. She works four shifts a week in Papeete, and they cap most weeks with a lively distraction, an outing to Taverua reef or the *motus*—or to the Tuamotus or Papeete for shopping and late lunch, where Ravi will go whole frog on *pomme frites, une petite salade, et une bouteille du vin blanc.* He'll savor the flavors after confirming no sardines or anchovies in the salad, to spare the ocean food chain any further affront. He'll smother the fries in ketchup and watch the kids scream among the vendor stalls, their frites and sammies half-eaten. He'll wonder who they'll become, and when.

He'll catch his wife watching him, and he'll wonder why and how and what if. She'll rest her fingers on his arm and whisper playfully, "This is what became of us."

He'll lie on a bench on the ferry ride home and dream of milestones: surely he'll dive at fifty-five and sixty and should still be fit at seventy, barring illness or weight gain. Neither seems likely.

Eighty?

He'll ponder deep blue, sailfish, and far fewer fried foods in his vegetarian diet.

And so a story ends again on a satisfied note, with a man dreaming of who his children might grow up to be. He sees Moeava at the helm, following bubbles and birds in a frenzy over sailfish working a bait ball from below. Awaiting capture in the foray are several compositions of alertness and curiosity. A bill flashes in the electric moment, sail arched, lateral line shimmering, body aglow in a rainbow of emotion to match the electrons and sunbeams going eye-to-eye with the lens.

He'll rise on a discordant note and take two aspirin with bubbly soda. He'll watch and wait and consider a more prudent path.

END